I0582126

The Cursed Sight

The Cursed Sight

Lenora, the Cursed (Book One)
Jennifer Roachford

Curly Tales Publishing

The Cursed Sight

Copyright © 2025 by Jennifer Roachford

Lenora, the Cursed: Book One published by Curly Tales Publishing

All rights reserved. No part of this publication may be reproduced, stored or transmitted in any form or by any means, electronic, mechanical, photocopying, recording, scanning, or otherwise without written permission from the publisher. It is illegal to copy this book, post it to a website, or distribute it by any other means without permission.

This novel is entirely a work of fiction. The names, characters and incidents portrayed in it are the work of the author's imagination. Any resemblance to actual persons, living or dead, events or localities is entirely coincidental.

E-Book ISBN-13: 978-1-957986-11-1

Paperback ISBN-13: 978-1-957986-12-8

Hardcover ISBN: 978-1-957986-09-8

Map by D.L. Howard

Editing by Angela Knotts Morse

Cover Design by Carol Marques Cover Designs

To the ones barely holding it together
The ones who yearn for more
And the ones who finally found
What they've been searching for

One

Lenora sat on the arm of her black settee, holding a pad of paper on her lap. Her head bent over the sheet, and a strand of her brown curls, a few gold highlights catching the light from the nearby open patio doors, came loose from her low bun.

The bundle of nerves deep inside her stomach twisted. Today was the day. The Council of Ten—composed of Norraine's most respected lords, ladies, and soldiers—held her future in their collective hands. They would decide by vote if she would be the first ambassador to travel across the Sea of Norraine. The council had been in session all morning, and they hadn't taken a break for lunch. This was either fantastic or terrible news for her.

She tucked the stray curl behind her ear. When she pulled her hand back, she grimaced at the leather glove that clung to her wrist. A matching glove covered her other hand, completely hiding her brown skin. While the protection charm around her neck would stop her visions, she wore the gloves as an extra precaution.

Lenora could never touch anyone—not with the bare skin on her hands.

A shudder passed through her, causing bumps to form along her arm. She remembered the last time she touched someone. Her stomach

1

clenched at the memory, but she pushed away the swell of emotion before it overpowered her.

With a huff, she tossed the notepad with her speech onto the cushion beside her, then her body followed as she plopped down sideways onto her settee. She had read it at least a dozen times since the day she presented her case to the council, almost two weeks ago now. She had taken the time to write a masterful assertation on why she would be the perfect choice as Norraine's first ambassador, and she even had her old governess, Miss Tabitha, look it over before she stood in front of the council.

Miss Tabitha took her red pen to the speech like it had cursed her, but in the end, Lenora presented a brilliant address thanks to Miss Tabitha's help.

Lenora eyed her room from her sideways position. She had one of the largest suites in Highmore Castle, and no one dared bother her whenever she was inside the safety of her bedchamber. It used to be her mother's, and once Lenora was born, her parents redecorated it to resemble a nursery.

After her tenth birthday, the king and queen let her add her own designs and furniture, ones that suited her tastes. Lenora had selected black furniture, dark wallpaper, and thick, gloomy curtains. While her mother had made a face at the time—the queen usually stuck to bright, vibrant colors—she didn't say a word. Ever since Lenora's incident, Queen Elice held her tongue on such matters.

It had made Lenora want to yell, throw things, force *some* type of reaction from her mother. But she didn't. She held her words until her voice became quieter, her presence became muted.

Lenora closed her eyes. Why couldn't she have been born with her brother James's powers? He was an incredible earth mage, one of the strongest in the kingdom, and he was only two years younger than her nineteen. He trained with their mother at dawn, then after lunch practiced with the earth mage soldiers in the barracks even though he wasn't of age. Lenora knew that once he turned eighteen, he would head to Fort Aramu, where all the recruits trained.

With their father's work ethic ingrained into his soul, he was bound to become one of the greatest soldiers in Norrainian history. The boy took after James the elder in more ways than just his name. The Fates had already written his name in the history books.

Her younger sister Patricia was a capable water mage, though at fourteen, the only thing she cared about was disappearing into the family's secret garden with her best friend, Stephanie, swapping gossip and eating sweets. But once she got her head on straight, she would be a force as strong as the current in the Sea of Norraine.

And then there was Lenora—afraid to remove her gloves because of the fear that she'd have another "incident", too scared to get close to anyone lest she touch them, and too preoccupied with thoughts of self-worth and self-pity.

Another sigh escaped her lips. She knew she was too hard on herself, yet her thoughts always flitted back to the accident. It happened nine years ago, but the memory never faded. It stayed fresh in her mind, as though it had happened only yesterday.

A play date with her best friend, Samantha. A dip in the pond at her family's estate in Talin. No charm. No gloves. Only visions of death and a scream.

No. A screech, Lenora thought.

She shivered as she recalled the blood-curdling shriek from her friend's mouth. Forcing away the memory, she rolled onto her back and grabbed her notepad again, resigned to read her deepest desires once more.

"I come before the Council of Ten," she read aloud, "not as Crown Princess Lenora Moore-Taylor, but as Lenora, citizen of Norraine. In this capacity, I present my name as a candidate for ambassador to New-ton. There are many challenges we face in our kingdom..."

She had listed what she thought were difficulties the citizens faced, and how, by sending her to Newton, she could learn from a more established kingdom. Then she had rattled off possible ways in which she could improve the people's daily lives with the information she garnered. Newton had such a rich history, and the people were thriving. Surely Norraine could too if they sent the right person willing to gather as much knowledge as possible.

Norraine had spent decades in a civil war, with a dense line drawn between mages and non-mages. Her mother finally ended it twenty years ago, yet there was much work to do in order to heal the old wounds that still seeped discord and hatred between the two groups. Lenora had to help Elice staunch the bleeding. Her idea was to travel to a kingdom where mages and non-mages got along.

The real work would prove difficult, but she was willing—no, *begging*—to be part of something great to prove her legacy. She spent the last nine years living in fear of herself, of her own two hands. She wanted to be brave for once, in a way that didn't require her to remove her gloves or her charm.

The necklace lay sideways, and she picked it up to inspect it. Her mother had given her this clear gem the minute she was born, based on the superstitions of their Newton heritage.

Apparently, her maternal line was cursed. It had no rhyme or reason and affected people seemingly at random. Her mother's mom was born in Newton and passed this curse down to Lenora, but how and why it began remained a mystery.

She supposed a more intrinsic reason for returning to her ancestral home would be to help her find the answers to her most desperate questions. Her most pressing being, why did the curse skip so many generations to land on her? There hadn't been anyone cursed with this affliction for generations. She didn't think she'd done anything to deserve this. All she'd done was been born. Now, due to her cursed powers, she couldn't touch anyone without activating a vision.

A vision only of death.

A knock on the door drew Lenora from her thoughts. Though she had a lady's maid, they avoided each other—Lenora, because she was afraid to touch her, Morgan, because she was afraid to *be* touched. So Lenora pushed herself up from the tiny sofa to open the door.

On the other side of the frame, a servant bowed. "Your Highness. The Council of Ten requests your presence."

She sucked in a sharp breath. With a quick "Thank you," she walked past him and bounded for the council room, taking measured steps even though all she wanted to do was run.

The council must have reached a decision. Her heart thundered in her chest. She couldn't get there fast enough.

When she knocked on the council room's double doors, they swung open immediately. Stepping through the entryway, she took in the council members, who had all stood upon her entrance.

General Victoria Lee was the first person she saw, her smiling face encouraging Lenora forward. She had trained with Vic ever since she was a child, and thanks to the general's fierce attitude and unbelievable strength, Lenora had become quite skilled with the short sword, her preferred weapon.

Next to Vic stood her husband, Andre Lee. He winked, and Lenora forced down the smile that threatened to find its way out. Andre was like an uncle to her. Her father, her aunt Alice, and Andre had been best friends since they were babies.

Her eyes glided down the rectangular table until they landed on her father in his green military uniform. James Taylor wore a stoic expression, his frown wrinkling his brown skin. She was used to this—he always put on his tough-soldier face when in front of the council, yet he had the warmest smile and softest hugs when in private with the family.

Finally, her eyes landed on the woman in a soft blue gown seated next to her father. Queen Elice Moore-Taylor sat straight on her throne-like chair on the opposite side of the room. While her chair matched the king's, it was placed at the head of the table. Though they presented a dual front, everyone knew who was really in charge.

Her mother's dark curls had gray strands sprinkled throughout, some peeking beneath her six-tined crown, and they flowed loosely all the way down to her hips. After all these years, Elice refused to cut it any shorter than that. She often spoke of her days living in the broken-down cottage in the middle of the Jani Forest and how she never wore her hair short out of habit.

Lenora wore her own light-colored curls to her shoulder, though she often tied them behind her head with a band, hiding as much of the contrasting shades as possible.

Queen Elice beckoned her forward, and Lenora stepped to the middle of the rectangular table. Someone had pulled an extra chair for her, and once she sat, the entire room sat with her.

"We have summoned you today," her mother began, "because the Council of Ten has voted on your proposal to become Norraine's first ambassador to Newton."

Lenora held her breath. This was it. Her fate had already been judged, voted on, and decided.

Elice paused, meeting Lenora's eyes. "The council is officially split: five to five."

All the air in her lungs froze. Lenora couldn't breathe.

No. This can't be happening. If the council is split, then that means...

"I must now cast the deciding vote, as the official tiebreaker." Elice looked away, and Lenora braced for what would happen.

Her mother had opposed this proposition since Lenora first brought it to her attention several months ago. Elice would never let her daughter go to Newton as the ambassador—she had even suggested they could go on "vacation" since Lenora was so inclined to go.

That wasn't good enough. She needed this opportunity to show she could be powerful without being in her mother's shadow. By Lenora's age, Elice was skilled in three elements—air, earth, and water—and was fighting against the Fire Lords, the rebels who threatened the kingdom for decades. Elice had mastered dream walking and could even pause time, traveling across great distances within her mind to speak with people's spirits. By nineteen, Elice had defeated the Fire Lords and imprisoned Orser, the rebel group's leader, in the Tomb of Souls.

One day, Lenora would be queen of Norraine, and all she had to show for it was great sword skills, thick gloves, and loneliness.

She clenched her eyes shut. All her hard work drafting the official proposal, creating a mock timeline, and planning her proposed day-to-day schedule was for naught. Her mother would never...

"I vote in favor of your proposal."

Lenora's eyes snapped open as her mind worked to catch up with her ears. "You ... what?"

Elice cracked a smile, and all around, the Council of Ten chuckled.

Lenora took in their laughter with wide eyes. "I can ... go?"

When Elice nodded, Lenora wanted to jump from her seat and run to her mother's lap like she used to do as a child.

Yet with the council's eyes on her, all she did was nod and give her thanks. She needed a majority vote, and she got it.

All thanks to her mother, the last person she thought would allow her to go.

Two

The hem of Lenora's dress swayed behind her as if she commanded the wind. Usually, she spent her mornings in training with Auntie Vic. However, with her impending trip across the sea, her entire schedule had been rearranged. In under two weeks, she would travel to Newton as the first ambassador in almost a hundred years. She'd be away from home for the first time in her life, and she'd be gone for four years.

Lenora had spent all afternoon packing, but she forced herself out of her room in search of her best and only friend, Lawrence Lowe. She had yet to tell him in person about the good news. She suspected he would have heard all about it by now, since gossip at Highmore Castle spread like fire magic among a dry thicket.

The lunchtime hour had just ended, so she bypassed the dining hall in favor of the training field. Even though spring brought more sunlight, a fresh breeze welcomed her as soon as she stepped outside. She walked past the open courtyard with a large water fountain and moved toward the outskirts of the grounds where the barracks were located. Soldiers in their green pants with matching short-sleeved shirts and hats took up most of the field between the four metal buildings.

However, her mother's specialty unit—her Army of Mages—had their own section near the outer wall. Uniforms in yellow, green, blue, purple, white, and some red spread out on the other side of the grounds, practicing their own forms of magic.

She felt the gusts of wind from the nearby air mages in yellow, heard the roots being upended by those in green. Water tunnels shot forward from the hands of mages dressed in blue. Seers—like her, though better able to control their powers—in purple practiced deep meditation techniques with the healers in pure white. Finally, a small portion of red uniforms were scattered about. The fire mages were welcomed to the unit by Queen Elice herself, but after the long, arduous war, only a few fire mages remained in Norraine. At least above ground. Some had disappeared at the end of the war, never seen or heard from again.

Lenora stopped near the edge of the field, her eyes surveying the unit. She knew exactly where to find Lawrence.

A water mage in a bright blue uniform shirt and black pants sparred against a non-mage soldier in all green. Lenora loved these fights. The rules were simple—a mage could use their powers to subdue their practice opponent, and the non-mage could use their weapon of choice. Only a highly skilled non-mage soldier entered these types of spars, and only if they thought they stood a chance of winning.

Lenora spotted her best friend as he lifted his twin short swords and spun until he faced her direction. His eyes remained locked on his opponent, Corey, an expert water mage.

Lawrence wielded his blades like they were part of him. He swiped and jabbed, avoiding the spouts of water Corey hurtled his way. They each took hits—one slice from Lawrence's blade to Corey's shoulder, a shot of Corey's water to Lawrence's gut.

Lawrence's quick feet brought him close enough to swipe at Corey's stomach, but at the last moment, the mage jumped back. Lawrence employed close combat, even as Corey directed a water funnel into his face when he took a step forward.

Spinning on his heel, Lawrence feigned left, then ducked right, directly into Corey. He tackled the mage to the ground, pinning his forearm against Corey's chest. Beads of water slid down Lawrence's light brown skin and dripped onto Corey's shocked face. The sharp tip of Lawrence's swords pointed at Corey's neck, and the metal hilt of the other pressed into his side.

"Fates," Corey muttered, then blew out a breath.

Grinning, Lawrence removed his blades and lowered them to the twin sheaths at his hips, one on either side. Corey lifted a hand, and Lawrence pulled him up.

"Best two out of three?" Lawrence asked, his head tilted to the side.

Lenora stepped closer, catching their attention.

"Your Highness," they said in unison, bowing as she came to a stop before them.

"I hope I'm not interrupting," Lenora said, her gaze locked on Lawrence. They spoke without words now, and each could tell what the other was thinking without having to say it. Her eyes told him *I need to speak with you.*

He nodded in understanding, then tapped Corey on the chest. "I'll see you later."

The mage chuckled. "You owe me a rematch, Lowe."

When he walked away, Lawrence shook his ear-length brown curls, splaying water around.

Lenora covered her face to avoid getting wet. "Are you done?"

"My apologies, Princess," Lawrence said, though his eyes glistened with mischief.

Her lips thinned, knowing he was toying with her, but she didn't want to give *him* the satisfaction of knowing she knew. "I was hoping we could talk."

"But we are." He tilted his head, still pretending to be coy.

She crossed her arms. "Alone."

Lawrence raised his hands. "All right, I'm sorry. I haven't seen you since breakfast and I've missed bothering you. Let me get one more joke out and I'll be done. I promise."

"Oh, those were jokes?"

This time, it was Lawrence who looked vexed. "You love my jokes."

"Come on." She sighed, then turned around, knowing she wouldn't get to her point if they continued this way. After five years, she knew Lawrence better than she knew herself.

Walking away, she headed toward the metal barracks, and his boots stomped behind her. Four large buildings formed a rectangle, with a gathering space in the middle. At the end of the day, all the soldiers would gather in this quad, sitting beside a fire or huddled in groups. Her mother had told her stories about how she used to sneak off and watch them, back before mages could freely join the army. Back when Lenora's grandfather had banned magic use. Back when Elice, who was missing for almost eighteen years, finally returned to the castle.

Lenora came to a stop in a secluded corner beside the largest building. She'd heard her mother's story all her life—how the seer Lenora was named after lied and tricked an entire kingdom into thinking Elice's powers were bad, all so she could use Elice for her own agenda. Lenore, her mother's guardian for almost eighteen years, manipulated the king's and queen's fear of mages, then kidnapped Elice and hid her in the Jani Forest. When Elice finally escaped, she learned the truth about her family and Lenore.

Lenora closed her eyes, still facing the cold gray exterior wall. *Lenora.* She always thought her name was a horrible joke. To be named after such a conniving, wretched woman made Lenora almost sick to her stomach. And the fact that they were both seers? She didn't understand why her mother would do something so cruel.

She didn't care if Lenore turned out to be good in the end. So what if Lenore's sole purpose in life was to make sure Elice was as strong as possible, strong enough to defeat the evil fire mage Orser? Lenora didn't care that Lenore had worked with the goddess of fate herself. None of it excused Lenore for taking advantage of her mother and grandparents.

A cough jolted her out of her thoughts. With a spin, she turned to face her only friend.

"I heard the news," Lawrence said, a smile on his face.

A wave of emotions passed over her. Suddenly, everything felt too real. She was really leaving. In less than two weeks, she'd take on a new role—one that would bring her closer to the root of her power, to finding herself, to helping her people thrive. She felt herself frowning, causing his smile to fall, too.

"Hey," he said, "what's wrong? I thought you'd be happy."

"I am." She nodded, her head bobbing up and down vigorously. "I am. It's just ... I don't want to make a mistake. So many people are counting on me. When I'm there, I'll represent all of Norraine. And I... I can't fail."

Lenora buried her face in her leather gloves, hiding the worry and shame she felt. No matter how many times her family told her they loved her—and she knew they did—she could never shake the feeling of not being *good enough*. She wasn't strong like her brother James or as sweet as her sister Patty. She definitely couldn't measure up to her mother's legacy or her father's sword skills. How could she be queen when she couldn't even touch those closest to her? How could the people of Norraine trust her when she couldn't even trust herself?

The tips of Lawrence's boots came into view through the cracks between her fingers. She allowed herself a few calming breaths before she looked up at him. Her tears stayed where they were, behind her wall of shame. In the years since the accident, she'd added layer upon layer of self-reproach, building up a barrier until she learned to stop the tears on command. Now, they never came. Crying was a rare event, and her subdued emotions became a comfort for her.

It was better to show less emotion, show less care, than gain someone's sympathy. With sympathy came touching, and Lenora learned at an early age that touching was bad.

And she would never touch anyone ever again.

"It'll be all right," Lawrence whispered. "You're going to be a great ambassador, Lenny. And if the council approved all of your measures, I'll be by your side the entire time."

"They did," she said. "I get to select my personal guard. You'll be one of them." She reached a fist forward, and he bumped his fist against her glove. It'd been their own version of a handshake, one they'd sort of just fallen into. It was the only form of physical contact she'd give another, since she couldn't actually touch anyone with her bare skin.

It was as close as she ever got to touching him or anyone else in nine years.

Traveling cases filled Lenora's room that evening, from the bed to the settee to every available bit of floor space. Though she had only found out about the council's decision a few hours ago, she had the servants bring out her suitcases so she could begin packing. With her proposed plan fully revised and accepted, she would leave Norraine in less than two weeks. She had to pack now if she wanted to bring everything she needed—and wanted—for her four-year tour.

A sweet, satisfied sigh escaped her lips as she surveyed the organized mess. When she heard a knock on the door, she floated toward it as if she were an air mage being carried by a willful gust only she could control.

Her mother stood on the other side, doing her best to maintain a regal smile, but the corner of the queen's mouth turned up into a smirk at the state of Lenora's room. "You're already packing?"

Lenora nodded eagerly as she welcomed Elice into her suite. Kicking aside an empty suitcase, she made her way to her settee. "I'm too excited, Mother. This is going to be an amazing experience. I can't wait to meet our Newtonian family and represent ours and all of Norraine."

Elice sat beside Lenora. "This is a momentous occasion, Lenny. You must remain poised and alert at all times. Norraine has never before sent a royal envoy to Newton. And for four years..."

Sitting tall, Lenora squeezed her hand into a fist. "Which begs the question... Why did you vote in my favor? This whole time I've been lobbying my case, you made it seem like you didn't want me to go. You *told* me you didn't want me to. What changed your mind?"

"Oh, sweetheart," Elice began. "As your mother, I didn't want you to. But as your queen... I have to let you. It makes sense, after all the hard work we've done to reestablish trade with Newton and the failures we've had in our negotiations with other lands. Newton has been more receptive, but kingdoms like Alegría still remain closed to us. By sending you, we have an envoy who will put Norraine first. You care so much about our kingdom. I trust you will make the right decisions when it comes to new policies and trade programs. Besides, the plan you put forth is a great one."

Lenora bit back a smile. She had done some research thanks to one of Miss Tabitha's projects before graduating last year. After reviewing past and current trade systems, she had found a few issues. The only ports in and out of Norraine were in the Swamplands, which flooded in the spring and fall, and the Fishing Villages, whose docks were in desperate need of repair.

By opening alternative routes along the west coast near Fort Anchor and restoring the Fishing Villages' docks in accordance with Newtonian standards, they could circumvent the risk of losing valuable shipments. She also found that Newton benefited more from their spice exports while only importing a few goods, like wheat. But Norraine had a huge fish market Lenora suggested they tap into.

Elice angled sideways so she could look directly at her daughter. "Also... Well, I know how important it is for you on a personal level to visit Newton. You can learn so much about your powers—far more than you can learn here."

Turning her head away, Lenora hid her desperate expression from her mother's knowing gaze. "I only hope I'll find some help. There must be books, or even someone from the Newton line who knows more."

"There's only one way to find out, which is why I decided to let you go. And I wrote a letter to King Jerome to let him know you're coming."

Lenora nodded. Her grandmother Julice had written to her brother years ago to ask for any and all information that could help her grand-daughter's plight. King Jerome wrote back, saying he knew nothing, but perhaps he could help her if she were actually there. Maybe he could provide her with access to his library or allow her to speak with other seers in Newton. Surely someone could point her in the right direction.

"Lenny." Elice's tone turned serious, and Lenora's gaze snapped back at her. "You must be extra cautious. The people of Newton call it the cursed sight for a reason. The people of Norraine fear your powers, but I suspect it is nothing compared to what the Newtonians feel. You must wear your charm at all times and never remove your gloves."

"I promise," Lenora said. "I won't take off my necklace or my gloves."

She didn't need her mother's warning, though. The memory of her last vision always stayed in the front of her mind.

Three

Briny air clung to Lenora's nostrils with every inhalation. With it came fond memories of camping with the Nomads along the southern coast. Her heartstrings tugged as she remembered the first time she caught a fish with Sophia Cooper, her mother's best friend and a master healer. Lenora was seven, and the healer took Lenora on her family's private boat for the day while Elice and James stayed behind at camp. Lenora had been so excited to be off on a journey by herself, without her parents or younger siblings.

That was before Samantha. Before the vision. Before... Well, just *before.*

Now, after spending the last two weeks planning and packing, she would enter a new stage of her life. She hoped it would be one without the heavy weight of *before.*

Sucking in a deep sigh, Lenora stared at her family. They stood a few feet away beside the tiny dock as soldiers and servants loaded rowboats bound for the ship sitting in the Sea of Norraine. Since the kingdom didn't have a full-sized dock, sailors had to drop anchor offshore and transport supplies via smaller boats.

The smiles her mother and father wore reminded her of how important this day was. She was ready to leave her past behind. In Norraine, she lived under her mother's infamous shadow, her father's pride, her brother's skill, and her sister's charm.

But in Newton, she could form herself anew. She thrummed with anticipation. Excitement coursed down her spine, threatening to spill into every part of her.

Sophia walked down the beach and patted Elice on the arm as she passed. Lenora had always admired the two ladies' friendship. They were more like sisters, gossiping and giggling like children whenever they were together. Knowing her mother's lonely upbringing, she was happy her mother had found such close friends in her lifetime. She hoped to one day have her own strong connections.

Sophia came up to Lenora next and bumped their shoulders together. "You look contemplative."

Lenora held back the snort that begged to escape. "Don't I always?"

Laughing, Sophia turned her gaze to the rising sun and lifted a hand to block the rays. "Not a cloud in sight. That's a good sign."

"I suppose." Lenora squinted, looking up at the sun as well. She wasn't a sailor, but if clear skies meant good omens, she'd take it.

"Can I give you some advice, young one?"

Lenora met the healer's gaze. "I'll take all the advice you can give."

Sophia smiled and placed a hand on Lenora's shoulder, not afraid of being so close. With anyone else, Lenora might have jumped out of reach, but Sophia always had a way of calming Lenora's frayed nerves. "This trip is not just about Norraine. It is also about Lenora. I know how you are, Your Highness. When you get there, you'll make it all about the people. You'll forget to be *Lenora* and remain the *princess*."

Lenora looked at the sea, the rippling water moving in time with her heartbeat. "I'm the crown princess. My job, my sole purpose, is to put the kingdom first. To put the people first. I'm afraid I'm not Lenora without Norraine."

"Is that really what you think?"

Lenora held her bottom lip between her teeth, cautiously meeting the healer's gaze.

Sofia huffed and tucked a stray gray hair behind her ear. "By the Fates, you're so much like your mother without even realizing it."

Lenora's eyes widened. "I'm nothing like my mother." She'd never been told that, so why was Sophia saying it now?

"Do you think it's bad to be like Queen Elice?"

"That's not what I mean." Lenora sucked in a breath and tried again. "I mean, I'm not good enough to be like her."

Sophia's eyes narrowed. "I once knew a girl, almost the same age you are now, who thought she wasn't good enough, either. She had so much strength, yet when she looked in the mirror, the only thing she saw was fear. At the time, the kingdom feared people like her, so she believed all the bad things they said about her. For a while. Do you know what she did to change the way she thought about herself?"

Lenora looked away. "She became queen."

"No."

Lenora raised her gaze. "I thought this was about my mother?"

Sophia smiled. "It is." Instead of waiting for Lenora to reply, she answered the question herself. "She became *Elice*. She didn't have to be anyone but herself. And then she realized she was better than *good enough*. She was perfect just the way she was."

Swallowing down the tightness in her throat, Lenora grasped at the healer's words. Though she didn't know how to use them, she tucked them away, holding Sophia's parting wisdom close.

"You have to find yourself, Lenora," Sophia continued. "And then you'll realize life is not about the dresses or the politics—or even the gloves."

Tears welled in Lenora's eyes, but she pulled them back before a single drop fell. When she looked at Sophia again, she offered the woman a tiny, watery smile. "I'm going to miss your advice, Sophia."

The healer grinned. "All it takes is you leaving to finally listen to me, huh?"

A high-pitched voice caught their attention. Patricia ran across the dock, her thick curls swaying in the breeze. "Sister," she yelled, coming to a stop in front of Lenora. "Father said that the captain said it's time to go."

All at once, the air flowing into Lenora's lungs stopped somewhere in her throat. "Thanks, Patty," she squeaked out, then forced a smile.

Sophia chuckled before she turned toward the beach, surveying the row boats loading up with supplies for the voyage.

Patricia grabbed Lenora's black dress, bunching up the fabric near her hip, and pulled her toward their parents and brother. "I'm going to miss you, Lenny! But I know you'll bring back some amazing stories, and maybe some cool presents. Don't forget to write to me, either. I know I bother you sometimes, but we're still sisters. Right?"

Lenora matched her little sister's quick pace. "Of course, Patty. I'll write to you every day."

Patricia snickered. "Not *every* day, silly. You'll be far too busy for that. You're an ambassador now! You'll barely have time to do anything other than sit in on boring old meetings. Just write to me when you can."

As they came to a stop before the plank that led to the boat that would ferry her to the ship, Lenora couldn't help but shake her head at her sister. "I promise I will."

They shared soft smiles before their brother stepped forward and squeezed them into a hug. Lenora held still, keeping her arms pressed to her sides. Her brother liked to catch her off guard every now and then, simply to annoy her.

"This will be the last time in four years the three of us will be together," he shouted, way too loud for Lenora's ears.

"Get off, James," Patricia yelled back, pushing at her brother's muscular chest. She barely made him budge, and he just squeezed harder.

"I'm sure I'll be able to visit," Lenora said, though her words were muffled against James's shoulder.

A whistle rang across the water from the ship, and James finally relented as the captain began shouting orders at the crew, which could be heard from where she stood dozens of feet away. Lenora eyed her siblings, committing their faces to memory. James's sharp chin and deep brown eyes. Patricia's goofy grin and soft curls. The next time she saw them, how much would they have changed? Would they look older, taller? Would James have more muscles in his already fit physique? Would Pat have grown out of her silly stage and become a refined young woman?

"Go have fun on your adventure, Lenny," James whispered. The quietness in his voice made her choke back tears, only now realizing her eyes were watering. She blinked them back, holding tight to her emotion.

Behind her, she felt her parents' overbearing presence. She always knew when they were near. Turning, she took in her mother's tear-stained cheeks and her father's trembling smile.

Her father stepped forward first and pulled her into a hug. Lenora buried her face against his chest, wrapping her gloved hands around his waist. When the king finally pulled back, he kissed the top of her head. "Be safe, Lenora. Always be on your guard. Make sure you know where your sword is at all times."

Lenora rolled her eyes at him. "This is a peaceful time, Father. I'm going as a guest and representative, not a soldier."

He tucked a golden strand of stray curls behind her ear. "You're always a soldier. Remember your training."

"Don't scare her, James," her mother said, stepping into Lenora's line of sight. "You're right, Lenny. This is a peace mission. King Jerome is welcoming you with open arms." Then she gave her husband a pointed look, to which he just shrugged his shoulders.

Another whistle, and this time, Lawrence ran down the plank from a nearby rowboat. "Your Majesties, Your Highnesses," he said, bowing. "The captain says it's time. He doesn't want to lose this fair weather."

Lenora threw herself into her mother's arms, tucking her hands against her stomach.

Elice latched on tight. "I love you," the queen whispered. "Please be safe. Write to us as soon as you get settled."

Lenora could only nod. Her throat constricted as she pulled out of her mother's embrace. With a quick wave to her family, she followed Lawrence up the wooden plank. When she sat in the boat, she turned back one last time.

Her father held on to her mother, both with tears streaming down their faces. Her brother waved his arms high into the sky, and Patricia covered her mouth with her hands as if holding back her own sobs.

With her chin raised, Lenora waved once more before turning toward the ship in the distance as her guards rowed away from the dock.

The rocking of the waves lulled Lenora into a sense of comfort. She loved being on small boats, but this was the first time she ever rode on a vessel this large. Though the captain reserved a private room for her, she declined, preferring to find a spot near the bow. She leaned against the railing, her hands grasping the firm wood. Only half a day had passed since they all loaded onto the ship, and she had already settled into the constant sway of the sea.

Behind her, the ship's crew moved about, following the captain's and his first mate's orders. Like a well-practiced crew, the sailors adjusted the sails to catch the wind each time it shifted, cleaned the deck, kept watch on the tides and the weather, and other things she didn't know the purpose of.

Her five hand-selected guards kept close, and that allowed her to relax enough to watch as Norraine drifted farther away until all she could see was water.

Lawrence stopped by her spot on the deck, a large grin on his tanned skin. "Can you believe it yet? We're more than halfway there now. The crew says we should dock a little after noon."

She rested her elbows on the rail, the thick beam grounding her excitement. "That's only a couple of hours from now."

He nodded, mimicking her position on the rail. They stood that way, content in their silence, until members of her guard huddled closer. Soon, all five guards leaned against the wooden beam, all watching with anticipation as the ship inched closer to its destination. The sense of connection she shared with her Norrainian soldiers reminded her just how small her tiny island was. Besides sailors and messengers, no one had traveled across the Sea of Norraine in decades, and Lenora and her guards were the first in generations.

The Last Mage War truly took more from her people than it gave. She hoped to add something better when she returned.

A sharp bell echoed from above, and Lenora looked up to see the sailor in the crow's nest pointing south, his telescope held to his eye. "Land!" he bellowed, which started a frenzy on the ship as the crew shifted sails and readied the anchor.

Lenora's heart raced as she jumped to the tips of her toes. Her own soldiers did the same, their eyes trained on the horizon. Everyone stared wide-eyed, hoping to catch the first glimpse of Newton in the distance.

Time seemed to slow as Lenora waited with bated breath. Just as she closed her eyes against the anticipation building within her, she heard the first enthusiastic squeal.

"I see it!" Marianne, one of her guards, yelled.

Lenora popped her eyes open. There it was, a strip of land just at the tip of the horizon. Tapping a rhythm against the wooden rail, Lenora struggled to keep her excitement inside. She wanted to jump up and down, screeching and talking loudly with her guards.

Instead, she pushed it deep, burying it with everything else. Maybe when she was alone in Stonehold Castle, the residence of King Jerome, she could let out a yell into her pillow. For now, she drummed her fingers and bit the inside of her cheek.

She wouldn't allow herself anything else. The pressure, the expectation—she had so much to live up to. When she looked in the mirror, she found herself lacking. She was a weak mage with only one terrible trick, an above-average soldier and swords person, with golden strands in her hair that made her even more of an outlier. In order to accept herself—and her role as the future queen of Norraine—she would need to become something better.

And there in the distance was her first chance.

Four

As the ship approached the docks of Port Arcadia and dropped anchor, Lenora took in as much as she could see. The only ports back home were the small docks at the Fishing Villages, but they were built for smaller ships. Even the piers in Nomad territory were tiny and required the use of rowboats to ferry people and items to the ships just beyond the harbor.

Lenora couldn't believe the stark contrast with Newton's port. Dozens of tall buildings stood in the background, making up the town. It stretched from east to west, and as they drew closer, she realized she couldn't see where the town ended on either side.

Six docks stuck out above the water. Two slots already harbored ships, so the captain ordered the sailor at the helm to guide them to the right.

Lenora understood the reason right away. The dock had a number "one" painted in vibrant yellow. A crowd surrounded it, and she could hear the cheers from her spot on the ship. A ghost of a smile touched her lips. The Newtonians were just as thrilled about her arrival as she was.

A section in the middle of the crowd stood out to her. Several guards in dark gray uniform formed a circle around someone in the center. As the ship drew closer, she could make out more details—a silver crown atop the man's head, a long green robe, his head held high above his rigid form.

King Jerome.

The ship inched to a stop right beside the platform, and the sailors set about lowering the gangplank. Lenora rolled her shoulders as her guards gathered behind her. She hardened her face, lifted her chin, and set her feet to march to a steady beat as she walked down the board.

I have to make them proud. My parents, my brother and sister, everyone in Norraine—they're all counting on me to represent them well. I cannot fail.

She focused on the man before her. King Jerome wore a gentle smile on his wrinkled face. His sandy brown skin looked worn and tired, but his eyes glowed as he stepped forward to greet her. Though his hair had gone completely gray, he walked with an ease that most sixty-five-year-old men didn't have. The ground seemed to bend and move with him, catching his every footfall.

As soon as Lenora took her first step on Newton's land, she drew in a deep breath to steady her roiling emotions. Jerome stopped directly before her, and they both bowed to each other.

Lenora placed a hand over her chest, using her people's customary sign of respect. "King Jerome," she began, her head lowered as she kept her eyes on his. "Thank you for receiving me. It is an honor to serve as Norraine's ambassador to your esteemed kingdom."

Yes! I nailed it!

She contained her grin, even as her insides beamed with pride. Her voice echoed across the plaza, and she was sure everyone heard her strong tone. The beginning of her ambassadorship was off to a great start.

Jerome lifted his head and held out his hand. Shocked by his kind gesture, Lenora followed suit and placed her gloved hand in his. His wrinkled skin reminded her of her grandmother's. Julice was five years younger than her brother, yet she had the same age-spotted hands that warmed Lenora to her soul.

"The pleasure is all mine, Princess Lenora," he said, his words careful and slow. Lenora noted his thick voice and slight accent, much heavier than anything she'd ever heard before. "We welcome you as a daughter of Newton." He spread out one of his arms, and the crowd cheered. He leaned in closer to speak above the noise. "This is your maternal ancestral home. Though you represent Norraine, you are still a child of Newton. I hope you will always feel welcome here."

When he stepped back, he gave her a firm nod, and she nodded along with him.

Though his words made sense—her grandmother was technically still a princess of Newton—she didn't feel a link to this place yet.

Maybe one day she would.

King Jerome led the way through the parted crowd, and a mix of his soldiers and her guards formed a barrier around the two royals. Through the gaps between guards, Lenora took in the smiling faces of the Newtonian people. Men, women, and children hollered and waved, shouting their greetings and welcomes as she passed.

At the end of the path sat two silver carriages with four horses harnessed to the front of each. A few horses, likely meant for the Newtonian soldiers, stood off to the side, and benches on the front and back of her coach had enough room for her guards. The carriages bore a flag with the Newton insignia—a silver stone tower on a vibrant green background—on either side of the wagon. Four thick wheels made of solid iron lifted the vehicles three feet into the air, and a coachman lowered a two-step ladder for her to climb.

"The castle is a few hours from here," King Jerome said. He pointed to the bench seat inside, where a basket and a pitcher of water with a lid took up one half of the space. "Please help yourself."

"Thank you, King Jerome."

Her guards loaded her luggage on the metal racks beneath the benches, then climbed onto the exterior seats of the carriage, some sitting beside the coachman and others claiming onto the back. Lenora caught Lawrence's eye as he took a spot up front, and he gave her a wink, the hint of a smile touching his lips.

She waited for the king's nod before she stepped into the carriage.

Dark green velvet filled her vision. From the inner walls to the plush seat to the carpet lining the floor, the warm, earthy color was inescapable. Lenora bit back the overwhelming urge to grimace and sat on the cushioned bench.

With the emerald curtains drawn open, Lenora sat back and watched the town fly by as the coach took off. The smooth stone path under the wheels made the trip comfortable, with minimal jostling and bumping. Already she noticed information she could take back home with her—the Newtonians' slight accent of the same language spoken in Norraine, the smooth roads, the large dock with enough room for multiple boats. What she could learn in four years had her thrumming in anticipation.

After the view of the bright town rolled into darkness, Lenora pushed herself against the window. She'd studied the map before she came—before she even drafted her proposal for the council. This was the Dark Forest, the land between the northern port towns and the central mountain region. The path led them through the heart of the forest, where sunlight scarcely traveled between the canopy above. Dappled rays highlighted the surroundings, and Lenora took in as much as her eyes could see.

In the distance, a howl alerted her senses. Then, as if responding to a call, two more wolves belted out. A shiver ran up and down her spine, causing the hairs on her arms to rise. Wolves were not native to Norraine, so she'd never heard their howls before, though the sound reminded her of the noises pet dogs usually made. It both invigorated and frightened her. With so many soldiers and an incredibly powerful earth mage close by, she knew not to worry. King Jerome must have traveled this path numerous times. His earth powers were legendary, even in Norraine. Surely he could handle a wolf—*anything*—if the creatures were the vicious type.

Once the howls died down, Lenora grabbed the basket and rummaged through it. She found a glorious amount of fresh fruit, crackers with herbs baked right in, and dried meats sliced thin. The spices on the meat made her tongue burn, but in the most delicious way. She added this to the list of things she'd bring back home at the end of her mission.

With her stomach satisfied, she settled into her seat and watched as the Dark Forest gave way to a beautiful field. The trees thinned, and the sun once again shone. Flowers grew in abundance, and farmlands littered the space all around her. Just before she drifted into a nap, her eyes struggling to remain open, she spotted the first peak of Ravis, the mountainous region that made up the central part of Newton. She sat forward, ready to feast her eyes on the castle that would be her new home for the next four years.

Great cliffs jutted out as the carriage rolled along. She almost missed the buildings and houses, but she blinked right as a mother and child stepped through what looked like pure rock. A wooden door closed behind the woman just as the carriage drove out of sight. Lenora peeled her eyes open so she wouldn't miss anything else.

That was when she realized exactly what she was looking at. The rocks were beautifully arranged stones built directly into the mountains to form houses. The sun had passed its zenith mere hours ago, so the people lingered about and enjoyed the last few moments of this lovely spring day. She noted the size and magnitude of the structures these people called their homes. Some were as small as a hill, and others were so close together she assumed they were one building.

Lenora's mind raced. She couldn't wait to wander around the kingdom, to find out how these people lived and how they built these intricate homes. Mages made up about seventy percent of Newton's population, compared to only twenty-five percent in Norraine. With earth mages being the majority of Newtonians with magic, she guessed they constructed most of the structures.

She would have to ask King Jerome about the workings of magekind here in Newton.

As well as that *other thing*.

Finally, after her eyes strained from holding them open for so long, Stonehold Castle loomed before her. Since it was surrounded by an enormous stone and iron fortress, she could only see the tops of the towers that reached high into the sky. Six tall, circular turrets rose above the mountainside. Guards stationed on top of each one looked down on the carriages as they approached, and the metal gates creaked as they inched open.

Once the carriages moved past the barrier, she saw the castle in all its glory. The entire structure clung to the gigantic mountain. Two battlements connected to the rock wall on one side and large towers on the other. These two main towers connected to the other four, forming a hexagonal walkway patrolled by more guards. The soldiers disappeared into the mountain as they walked through the entrances, making Lenora eager to see the inside of the castle. Though she had explored a bit of the Emori Mountains and its tunnels and cave systems back home, she couldn't imagine what a castle built directly into a mountain looked like.

The carriage came to a halt, and the door opened. Lawrence's grinning face met her, and she graced him with a rare twitch of her lips.

"Your Highness," he whispered, his voice shaking with enthusiasm.

"Lawrence," Lenora said, taking his extended hand and climbing down the steps.

The air had a slight mineral scent. She breathed it in, basking in the new environment. Her lips quivered as she held in her emotions.

I'm actually here. My dream to explore the world, meet new people, and find a way to better my kingdom is finally coming true. And I'm one step closer to learning how to control my powers.

Her head spun with the anticipation of what lay before her. Only her family and Lawrence knew about her deepest desires. She'd longed for change, for something more to happen to her. For reasons beyond her understanding, the Fates had cursed her with this power. In Newton, maybe she could finally do something to end her plight—something other than hide her hands and never remove her necklace.

King Jerome stepped down from his carriage and spun toward her, smiling and opening his arms. "Welcome to Stonehold!"

A tiny smile tugged on Lenora's lips at her great-uncle's energy. She never knew either of her grandfathers—her maternal grandfather, King Edgar, died a couple of years before she was born, and her paternal grandfather died when her father was only a year old. Watching this kindly old man warmed her heart, making her wish she'd been able to meet the men she never had a chance to know.

Behind Jerome, two arched metal doors swung outward, held open by two soldiers. A group waltzed past the opening. In front walked an elegant, light-brown skinned woman in a blue floor-length gown with silver curls hanging down her shoulders and swaying behind her back with each step.

A brawny middle-aged man with a grim expression and hard eyes strode directly behind the woman, though his pace outmatched hers, and he soon overtook her for the lead.

Two others, a man and a woman, walked side by side, bringing up the rear. The man's eyes shifted in all directions, never once settling on anything or anyone for too long. The woman's expression was strong and focused, and she wore a gentle smile as she held Lenora's gaze.

"Ah, my family," Jerome called, extending his hand toward the woman with gray hair, who grasped it as soon as she was close enough. "Allow us to make introductions. Lenora Moore-Taylor, Crown Princess of Norraine, please meet Queen Katrina, my lovely wife, Prince Remy, my oldest and heir to the Newton throne, Prince Tyree, and Princess Matilda." He waved at each person, indicating their names as he spoke.

Lenora bowed, both hands over her heart. A snicker brought her eyes up. Prince Remy had his head bent low as well, just like the rest of the family, but his eyes were trained on Lenora's hands as she formed her people's customary sign of respect. A slight grimace lurked behind his twisted smile, and a heavy weight made her stomach sink.

Princess Matilda must have caught the sound and look on her brother's face. She cleared her throat and stepped forward with her hands extended toward Lenora. "Welcome, Princess Lenora. It's so good to have another daughter of Newton in the castle."

Lenora fought the urge to snap her hands back as Matilda grasped her gloves, giving them a light squeeze.

"Don't be so daft, Tilly," came a gruff, low voice. Lenora followed it to Remy's face, to his dark eyes directed at her. "She's no daughter of Newton."

Prince Tyree shifted uncomfortably, taking a step backward as Matilda turned to face her oldest brother. "Watch your words, brother," Matilda said, her voice quiet but firm. "We must be kind to our guest."

"I'll not take advice from you." Remy stepped past Tyree, who squirmed under the mounting pressure of his siblings' stare-off.

"As if you ever take advice from anyone." Matilda narrowed her eyes, and her hands bunched into tight fists at her side.

Pebbles shook beneath Remy's feet as he clenched his hands as well.

"Why should I? Soon, I'll be king. Then you'll all be sorry."

Lenora's eyes widened, wondering what kind of sibling rivalry she'd walked into. She couldn't fathom talking to her siblings or them speaking to her like this.

King Jerome barged in between his three adult children, even though Tyree seemed afraid of all the conflict. The king's arms rose, and pillars of rock reached up from the earth in front of all the siblings. Strong arms reached around Lenora's waist, pulling her away from the jagged rocks. Looking over her shoulder, she saw Lawrence's face, but his eyes were focused on the feuding family before them.

"Enough!" Jerome bellowed, and even the ground beneath Lenora's feet echoed with the sound. Once the shaking stopped, the king drew in a deep breath and leveled his eyes at his children. "How dare you make a mockery of our great kingdom by insulting our guest?" He narrowed his eyes at Remy, who scowled at his father. "Princess Lenora is an ambassador looking to strengthen our ties with Norraine, yet you offend her and humiliate our family by acting like children."

Remy pushed at the pillar with his powers, collapsing it to rubble at his feet. "I'm not the one making a fool out of our kingdom, *Father*. You've sat on the throne for so long you don't even know what's best for our people anymore. And this"—he pointed at Lenora—"is not what they need. Newton is the strongest kingdom in the world. We don't need to make friends with weak nations that can't even get their lives together long enough to stop their own infighting. Look at them—they send a child to do their work for them. And you disgrace our kingdom by allowing her to stay for four years. She can't even stand on her own feet, just like her sad excuse of a kingdom."

At this, he gave Lenora a pointed stare, then shifted his gaze to Lawrence, who still held her close. Jolted by the insult, Lenora stood upright, pushing away from Lawrence. It was too late to fix her moment of weakness, however. Everyone had seen it.

With another glower in Lenora's direction, Remy stalked off toward the castle doors. "Come, Tyree," he shouted without looking back. Startled into action, Tyree snapped his head in the direction of Remy's voice and hurried after him.

Jerome shook his head. "Well, that was a bit misguided." He turned his attention to Matilda, but she took a step out of his reach.

Her lips turned downward, and she looked on the verge of tears. "Misguided? Is there no wonder how they became this way?" Without another word, she took off toward the open field behind the towers.

Silence followed Matilda's exit. Only then did Lenora realize how every single soldier—the Newtonians and her own guards—had moved closer, ready to step in. She caught Lawrence's gaze, and anger seemed to radiate off of him as his lips curled up into a snarl.

King Jerome's voice brought Lenora's eyes back to him. "Please forgive this ... spectacle. I promise, my son doesn't speak for me."

He seems to have a lot to say, regardless. Lenora pursed her lips. Never before had she felt so uncomfortable—and that was saying something. With the way her powers worked, she practically *lived* in discomfort.

The king lowered his head, offering her a silent apology. "Let's not dwell on my son's antics any longer. Dinner will be served promptly at eight. It's not yet five, so that should give you some time to get ready after your long journey across the sea. Come. Let's get you settled."

Jerome spun toward the nearest servant and ordered them to escort her to her suite. Queen Katrina lingered a moment, her lips in a thin line. Then she turned and walked behind her husband, though her head angled over her shoulder occasionally to stare at Lenora.

Lawrence leaned in close to Lenora's ear, and his breath tickled the nape of her neck as he spoke. "What in the Fates' names is going on here?"

All Lenora could do was shake her head before following along after

33

King Jerome.

She had no idea what had just happened, but she had a feeling she would soon find out.

Five

Lenora's five guards followed her all the way to the double doors. She paused at the threshold, looking back at her travel-weary sentries.

Jerome must have sensed her hesitation. He stopped in the middle of the foyer and whirled around. "Is something the matter, princess?"

"My guards," she began, nodding at the group behind her. "I'm sure they'd like to rest as well."

They had made the same journey she did. If she was tired, they would be too. However, in the back of her mind, she couldn't quite shake the feeling that she should keep them close. If only her power of sight worked like a normal seer, then she could allow herself to follow this prickle of intuition. She wondered if it would incite a vision, were she like the others. Most seers, however, could not force a vision. Not for the first time, Lenora wished she had been born with a different, stronger power. One that actually felt useful.

Jerome clapped his hands together, and the sound resonated in the front hall. "Of course. Please allow my soldiers to lead yours to the service quarters. Accommodations have already been arranged."

Lenora nodded, then turned to dismiss her soldiers. Lawrence hung back long enough to catch her eye. After knowing him for so long, she could understand his expression better than words. His eyes asked, *"Will you be all right?"*

She gave a quick nod.

After a nod of his own, Lawrence walked outside with the rest of the soldiers toward one of the looming towers. Now alone with her mother's uncle and his wife, Lenora pushed away the awkward feeling that rose inside her. So far, the man seemed warm with her, yet his grown children acted so distant and cold toward him. His oldest even had the nerve to humiliate him in front of the entire family, his soldiers, and their royal visitor.

Lenora thought back to Matilda's parting words. How did the heir and second son become this way? Clearly there was something going on in Stonehold Castle, and Lenora had stepped right into it.

She decided to write home as soon as she could. Knowing her parents, they'd want to take every precaution necessary. Taking a step past the threshold, she finally took in the castle's interior. Although the outside looked hard and rigid, the inside flowed like the soft canopy of the forest. A blend of dark browns and various shades of green welcomed her. Wooden beams made her eyes trail up the high vaulted ceilings. Lush velvet carpets the color of moss, rich walnut furniture, and silky emerald curtains warmed the space.

Following behind the king and queen, she stepped from the foyer and into an open room that looked similar in size to the ballroom at Highmore Castle back home.

King Jerome slowed his steps, smiling as he took in Lenora's wide eyes. "I do hope you enjoy your time here in Newton and in Stonehold." He sighed, looking around at his home. Then he narrowed his eyes, lowering his voice. "By the way, Queen Elice's letters told me of your ... powers, of which I sympathize. Our line has the misfortune of passing down this ... trait. There isn't much literature on the subject, but you're welcome to any of the books in the library during your stay. If there's something to be said about … well, about *it*, then it should be in there somewhere."

Lenora gulped down the anxiety rising in her chest. She nodded and mumbled a quiet, "Thank you."

Queen Katrina passed a glance at them, and Jerome took that as his cue to lead the way again. Up the grand staircase in the center of the room, he pointed out a few pieces of antique furniture that had been in the family for centuries. Paintings of past kings, queens, and other important family members from minor branches lined the halls. Near the middle of the hallway, Jerome stalled, looking up at the face of one of his ancestors.

One of my *ancestors*. Lenora stepped closer, wanting to study the face of someone from her past.

He tapped the corner of the frame on an inscription in fancy lettering. "Queen Lizette. She was the first queen to rule without a king."

Lenora read the year. 541. She recalled the current year based on Newton's calendar, which had almost a thousand-year difference to Norraine's. Since it was Year 1047 in Newton—and only Year 347 in Norraine—that would make this painting over five hundred years old.

As if reading her mind, Katrina gave a slow nod. "She lived over five hundred years ago. Unfortunately, she was forced to renounce her title after a short four-year reign."

Leaning closer, Lenora surveyed Queen Lizette's features. She had pronounced eyes, a sharp chin, dark curls, tawny-colored skin, and a slight smirk on her thin lips. "What did she do?"

Jerome stepped away from the painting, his voice dropping an octave. "Her family claimed she was insane. Once she was dethroned, she was hanged, and most details of her reign were struck from record."

With a shake of his head, he continued down the hall.

Lenora pursed her lips as she spared one last glance at her maternal ancestor before walking behind Queen Katrina. At the end of the hall, a lone sentry stood watch in front of a wooden door with metal framing.

The guard bowed his head, stepped to the side, and pulled the door open.

"This wing holds the guest suites," Jerome announced. "We currently have over twenty guests and their families from around the kingdom in residence. From lords and ladies to diplomats and high-ranking officials, Stonehold serves as a year-round civil retreat. We will hold a reception in your honor next week, so you'll have a chance to meet everyone of importance."

Katrina smiled. "And trust me when I say the Newtons are notorious for hosting fabulous balls."

As they walked past closed doors, Lenora imagined the type of people she'd be introduced to. Back home, she was used to the same guests who attended every function. Most were Norrainian lords and ladies, but there were also several highly distinguished military members. That was how she met Lawrence. His parents served under her mother and had moved up the ranks. She didn't know what they did before they joined Norraine's army, but they soon became two of Queen Elice's most trusted captains. Both were skilled warriors and trained Lawrence to be just as strong.

Jerome came to a door at the end of the wing and brandished a key. He unlocked the door and pushed it open to reveal a vast suite with an open sitting area and several doors. After giving Lenora the key, he motioned for her to step inside first before he and Katrina followed.

"There's a bedroom, bathroom, patio, and walk-in closet," he said, pointing out each door. "The staff will be in shortly to deliver your luggage and help you prepare for dinner."

Katrina extended her hand and gave Lenora's gloved fingers a soft squeeze. "We will let you get comfortable, princess. Please ring the bell"—she nodded toward a pull string by the patio—"should you need anything, and a maid will come right away."

After a few more thank-yous and goodbyes, Lenora was left alone for the first time all day. She'd been up since before dawn, took a half-day ride on a ship, and rode another few hours in a carriage. Her full-day training routine with General Vic seemed easier than the traveling she'd done today.

Lenora examined the room—from the beige lounges in the sitting room, the canopied four-poster bed in the bedroom, the accommodations in the bathroom, and finally the patio. The guest wing had a view of a grassy field in the distance, far outside of the castle's stone perimeter, and to her left was one of the six circular towers.

The barrier encircled the entire palace, but she could see several gardens and a large, picturesque grove of trees within the boundary. The image brought back memories of her family's estate in Talin, where her father grew up and where she and her siblings shared many vacations with her parents. Something pulled tight in her heart, and she allowed herself a gentle smile.

Only now did the feeling of separation sink in. She knew she wouldn't see her family for months, maybe even years. The only thing she could do to overcome the longing of her family's proximity would be to write to them. To get out on paper exactly what she was doing and seeing and feeling without them.

She left the patio and entered the sitting area, only to realize there was no desk with writing supplies. Her belongings had yet to arrive, and she felt the sudden urge to write a letter to Patty. But how could she without paper and a pencil? She could ring the bell Katrina had pointed out, but the need to move *right now* overwhelmed her, no matter how tired she felt.

Though she'd spent most of her time alone, she reminded herself that she was on a grand adventure. Now was not the time to fall back into her old habits and hide out in her suite all day.

Lenora tapped her chin with her finger, her lips pursed in thought. If

Stonehold was anything like Highmore, there would be one place where she could always find paper and a writing utensil.

The library.

Opening her door, she peeked down the empty hallway. There was no one around, but she at least remembered how to get back to the beginning of the hall. From there, she could ask the guard how to get to the library. Besides, taking a walk around the castle sounded like the perfect way to pass the time until dinner. She didn't want to sit in her room doing nothing for two hours before she had to get ready. All she would do was change her dress—from one black gown to another—and adjust her curls into the same slicked-back bun.

When she came to the guarded door, she raised a hand but held it aloft. Should she knock? Or would it be all right if she opened it herself? She decided to rap on the door, and not even a second later, the guard pulled it open.

"Good evening," she said once she properly exited the wing, and the door was shut once again. "Can you direct me to the library?"

"Of course, Your Highness," he said. "I can guide you, if you wish."

Lenora nodded. "Thank you. I would greatly appreciate it."

After he bowed, they walked down the hall, the guard walking just slightly ahead of her. She walked a slow pace, taking her time looking over the portraits once again. Her eyes strayed to Queen Lizette, and this time Lenora stayed for several breaths with the guard by her side. She wondered if the queen was truly mad or if there was another reason for her forced abdication. She made a mental note to search the library when she had some free time. Surely not all mentions of her had been erased from history, considering she still had a portrait in the Hall of Kings and Queens.

As she walked past the rest of the portraits, she thought about her own research. King Jerome said she had free use of the library to investigate her own condition. However, he never confirmed whether there was actually anything on the matter, only that she could look.

She didn't want to give up hope, but there wasn't a positive outlook, since he couldn't outright tell her there was a book about the cursed sight she inherited through her Newton ancestry.

Passing through the main corridor, they entered the next hallway and found four sets of double doors. The guard led her to one that stood taller than all the others. Once he pushed them open, she understood why.

The royal library was massive. Her eyes strayed up, counting each floor as she went. It stood five stories tall, just as high as the towers. She stepped fully into the space and spun in a circle. Then it dawned on her. The library was *in* one of the towers, its circular form made clear as she stood in the middle of the mosaic-tiled floor.

The guard chuckled as Lenora remained fixated on the high ceiling. "Shall I take my leave, Your Highness?"

"Yes," she replied, her voice breathless. "You may go. I think I'll be here for a while."

He bowed, but she barely saw him out of her periphery. In the background, she heard the doors shut, leaving her to gawk in solitude at the exquisite space.

Stairs in the back of the room spiraled up to each floor, and a walkway with high rails ran in a circle around every level. She could easily get lost between all the shelves. She let out a dry chuckle. Her parents were huge book lovers. Her mother would purposely get lost in here and beg to never be found.

Lenora's chest constricted again, and she set out to find a desk. Not only did she need to write to Patty, she would also write to her mother. The queen would love to know about this library, and maybe she would promise to come visit soon. Perhaps the whole family would come.

Lenora smiled—then crinkled her eyebrows because she was *not* used to smiling.

She made it to the second level, where a desk and some writing supplies sat, when the door creaked opened. Peering over the rail, her heart made another leap.

"Lawrence," she said, recognizing him in his uniform even from this distance.

He looked up, smiling once he saw her. He bounded up the stairs two at a time and made it to her side within a minute. "I found you."

She allowed herself to relax in his presence. "How did you know I was here?"

"I could track you anywhere." A smirk graced his lips as he drew closer.

"Don't lie. The guard from the guest wing told you, didn't he?"

He chuckled low, shaking his head. "You'd never believe me if I told you the truth."

They stood by the desk, her letters forgotten, when the door opened again.

Lenora moved to look over the rail, but Lawrence growled, his arm shooting out to block her. She almost laughed at the sound, until a sharp, angry voice traveled up to her ears.

"Close the gods' damned door, Ty."

Six

R emy. Lenora recognized his rough voice immediately.

"Sorry, Rem," came Tyree's hesitant muttering, followed by the sound of the library door shutting.

Lawrence dragged his arm away from Lenora and placed a finger to his lips. His eyes narrowed, and his nose twitched as if he smelled something foul. Quietly, he motioned for her to step back toward the open window.

"Is everyone ready?" Lenora heard Remy ask.

"Uh, I think so." She could practically hear Tyree scratch his head.

The sound of a fist meeting flesh met her ears, and she froze. Tyree let out a squeal, and after a bit of what sounded like shuffling, she heard something collide with the wall and several books crash to the floor.

"What do you mean 'you think so'?" Remy's voice was cold and harsh. "Do you realize what's happening tonight? If just one thing goes wrong, the whole plan is ruined. Do you know what happens to people who conspire to kill a king? I'll spell it out for you—they're *hanged*. We're committing treason, you imbecile. So I'll ask you again. Are the soldiers ready?"

Lenora froze beside the window, and Lawrence's body had gone rigid. She couldn't believe what she was hearing. Treason? Remy and Tyree talking about killing a king? A shudder ran down her body, and the movement brought Lawrence's attention back to her. His eyes hardened, his fingers tightened into a fist, and his breathing quickened. He looked as if he were preparing for an attack.

She and Lawrence were partially obstructed from view beside the window. However, if Remy or Tyree walked to the other side of the lower level, they'd be spotted right away.

Lawrence used a finger to push her flush against the wall and looked out over the open window. Lenora followed his line of sight. They were only two stories up, and the stone walls of the tower, though smooth and immaculately laid, had several natural foot- and handholds. She met Lawrence's eyes—they were both thinking the same thing.

She'd trekked the Emori Mountains with her family before, scaling and climbing over its various ranges. Her confidence was high, and she also trusted Lawrence's ability to descend this tower.

What she didn't know was what awaited her at the bottom. Night had set in, blanketing the grounds in darkness. Only a few lampposts dotted the field. Judging by the way Remy and Tyree were speaking, the Newtonian soldiers were also in on this coup.

If Remy or Tyree saw them escaping, would they alert the soldiers? What would happen to them if someone passed underneath this tower as she and Lawrence were climbing down?

Remy's hushed, angry tone carried up to her. "I'm going to the king's suite now. Both of them should be inside, readying for dinner. I just need you to secure Matilda. Quickly. Make sure it's quiet. I don't want word of an attack reaching the maids' ears before I've had a chance to deal with our parents."

"But what about the visiting princess?" Tyree asked.

Lenora's eyes widened as she listened with bated breath.

"Take care of her first before you handle Matilda."

"And her guards?" Tyree's voice wobbled, taking on a high-er-than-normal pitch.

"They're all in the service quarters. Once I take care of our parents, I'll give the order to dispose of them."

"But what about her family? Surely they'll come—"

"Ty! Enough! The Norrainian princess is a liability. Just get rid of her. We have a chance to seize power. At the rate father's going, he's going to outlive us both. I'll never see the throne, and if I do, I'll be too old to enjoy it. To make something of it. You and I are on the cusp of total control. Isn't that what we talked about? You by my side as I claim what is rightfully mine?"

Lenora blew out a slow, steady breath. She couldn't believe Remy wanted to kill his parents just so he could become king sooner. He was already forty-three years old and wasn't getting any younger, so she could understand him being restless. Lenora herself knew her mother would live to an old age, Fates willing. It seemed highly likely that Lenora wouldn't see the throne until she was old and gray herself.

But that was what she wanted. She wanted her mother to live a long and beautiful life. She never wanted to think of her mother's passing, which was why she never wanted to touch Elice with her bare hands.

Remy, on the other hand, outright planned his father's death. What kind of child did that? To think of killing someone, let alone your own flesh and blood, was abhorrent to Lenora. An angry heat spread through her, utter shame at being related to these two men.

Daughter of Newton. Is this who I really am?

Lawrence gripped her gloved hand, and she understood the meaning behind the gesture. *Hurry! We have to leave.*

Steeling herself, she faced the window and quietly climbed onto the ledge, then she eyed the first stone. She could slip the toe of her boot into the space right above it. Just below that crack, she spotted another, then another, until darkness obscured the rest of the wall. With the first part of her path mapped out, she turned and lowered her foot into the first nook, gripping the edge. Thanks to her gloves, she didn't feel the cold bite of the stones.

Lawrence took a deep breath before joining her descent, but she kept her eyes focused on each crack before she lowered her body. Through the open window, she could still hear Remy's angry voice and Tyree's worried responses before the sound of their footsteps echoed on the tiled floors. Then everything fell silent, as if the night itself knew what would happen that day.

Before she knew it, she made it to the first-floor window. Several thoughts swam through her mind, but she needed to make a quick decision.

Do I maneuver around the window? Jump down?

There was no time for hesitation. She pushed against the wall, then bent her knees as she fell. Landing smoothly was not the issue—it was the sound. She softened the drop of her body by tucking and rolling, dirtying her black-laced dress as she met the ground. She had made the right decision, though, because the landing made little noise.

A moment later, Lawrence did the same, jumping from the tower and rolling across the dirt. Lenora brushed herself off as she stood, and Lawrence quickly rushed to her side, pushing on her shoulder until her back pressed against the wall.

"I need to get you out of here," he said, his voice rushed but quiet.

She nodded, then immediately shook her head. "I need to warn King Jerome. And we need to get my guards."

He gave a quick shake of his head. "There's no time. You must leave."

Lenora's head rushed at the thought of leaving without helping at all. "I need a plan."

"I'll steal us a couple of horses. We need to get back to the docks at Port

Arcadia. Then we'll secure passage back to Norraine."

"It'll take us hours to get back to Port Arcadia."

"We'll have to ride all night. We'll stop if we need to, but I fear we may have to keep going if we want to put some distance between us and Stonehold."

Lenora pursed her lips. Lawrence was right, of course, but the thought of leaving her soldiers here during this coup didn't sit right with her. "We'll fare better if we have my other guards. They'll be extra protection. Plus, I don't want to leave anyone behind. You heard what Prince Remy said. He plans to kill them, too."

Lawrence ran a hand through his brown curls. "They're all the way on the other side of the castle in the army's wing. Besides, every one of them would lay down their life to protect you. This head start means the difference between getting out or getting caught. I swore an oath to your parents, to our queen and king, to do whatever it takes to protect you. Even if it means throwing you over my shoulder and getting you out of Newton."

She lifted her chin, narrowing her eyes at her only friend. "I'm not leaving them, Lawrence."

He groaned, tugging at the ends of his curls. "Fine. Meet me at the stables. I'll get as many guards out as I can. But stay hidden. Don't let anyone see you."

With a single nod, Lenora took off, her side flush against the wall, running toward the back of the grounds where she saw the carriages roll off to. She didn't know exactly where she was headed, but as long as she stuck to the shadows, looked around every corner, and kept her ears wide open, she'd be fine.

She rounded the library tower where the wall of the castle dipped inward, leaving an open field of grass. The next wall connected to the tower a few feet away, but that went in the opposite direction from where she assumed the stables were. Only a few lanterns lit the exterior wall, and if she followed it, she'd be right underneath the glowing light. Anyone could spot her.

She squinted into the distance, hoping to find another option, but the crunch of a footstep made her whirl around.

"Well, what do we have here?"

Her heart raced at the sound of Remy's deep voice. Forcing her emotions from her expression, she faced her distant cousin. "Prince Remy," she said, her breathless tone betraying the hard set of her face. "I'm just out for a stroll." Internally, she cringed at herself. *Never supply information*, she chided, echoing her mother's advice. *Always answer an unwanted question with another question*. "Are you heading to dinner?"

Remy stood in the tower's shadow, his figure angled away from the nearby lamppost. With a chuckle, he sauntered into the light, exposing the wicked smirk on his face. "I was just on my way to the dining room when I thought I heard a strange noise outside. Thought I should investigate. It's a good thing, too. Wouldn't want my young cousin outside alone at night."

Every nerve in her body rang with alarm. She'd heard his words loud and clear—he planned to kill his father, mother, and younger sister. She was a liability, and he wouldn't let her leave to warn anyone before he had the chance to seize power.

There had to be some way she could escape. Inside the skirt of her dress, her prized dagger, gifted to her by her father, rested in its hilt around her lower thigh. Her father had always taught her to keep it close. If she needed to, she'd wield it against Remy.

But what about her guards? Could she buy Lawrence enough time to get them out? That was what a good leader did, right? Sacrifice themselves for the good of the ones they cared about?

If it meant they had a chance to escape, she'd do whatever it took to distract Remy.

"I'm actually heading back to my room now," she said, moving to the side to walk up the lit path.

Remy blocked her stride in one quick motion. "Allow me," he began, showing his teeth in a wide grin. "I wouldn't want anything unseemly to happen to you on your way back." He waved his arm expectantly.

Lenora forced a smile as she nodded, then stepped beside him. He led her across the too-silent grounds. She looked around for help, yet not a single person wandered around, and the eerie glow from the lampposts every few feet added to the rising tension in her body.

The prince remained quiet. She chanced a look at his face and jerked back when she caught his eyes on her.

"You seem tense," he whispered. The tone made her shiver. Everything was too calm for what she knew was going to happen tonight.

"Just contemplative." She used the word constantly thrown around to describe her. "I get that a lot."

He faced forward as he opened the castle's wide double doors. She quickly noted the absence of the soldiers and servants that were lingering about mere hours ago. Where had everyone gone? Did the coup already start? Where were the maids and other household staff? She thought maybe the soldiers rounded them up, too, along with everyone else not directly involved in the plot.

Remy guided her toward the staircase. "You know," he said, his voice still low, "I was alone in the library just now. Perhaps my mind was playing tricks on me, but I could have sworn to the goddess that I heard something—or someone—in there with me."

Lenora begged the tightness in her chest to relax as sweat grew on her brow and on her palms, making her gloves stick to her hands. She repeated his words in her head. He was trying to goad her, to make her slip up. She couldn't say she was in the library or point out that he wasn't alone. All she could say was, "Oh?"

He chuckled again, and the sound echoed off the portraits in the hallway. "Yes, but I suppose you wouldn't know anything about that, would you?"

She forced her head to shake. Her eyes met the cold ones of Queen Lizette as she passed. The ancestor both she and Remy shared, who was possibly insane. Perhaps the story was incorrect, and she was wrongly hanged. What if she was a victim, just like King Jerome? How would Remy rewrite his father's legacy? Would he say Jerome was a kind, just king, or an old fool?

They made it to the guest wing, and Lenora realized the guard was gone. Were the guests beyond the door slaughtered in their rooms? Was she next?

As discreetly as she could, she slid her hand to her thigh, feeling the outline of her dagger. While she would prefer to fight an earth mage like Remy with a long sword to maintain a distance from their attacks, she would have to make this work. Besides, it was all she had on her, since this was supposed to be a time of peace.

Thank the Fates her father taught her to always be prepared.

As they approached her door, a lone figure stood beside it. Remy grabbed her arm, making her realize she had stopped walking on her own.

"Greetings, brother," Remy shouted, and both Lenora and Tyree jumped at the sound.

Tyree raised a hand. Lenora eyed his trembling arm and the way his eyes stared pointedly at the floor. She thought back to his behavior when they first met. He was nervous. Was it because Lenora had shown up on the day of their attempted coup? How could he face his father, mother, or sister knowing what he knew? His shifty stance and eye contact explained so much now.

The coward. Lenora narrowed her eyes as they came to a stop and Remy released her arm.

"Guess who I ran into on the way to dinner?" Remy pointed, but Tyree wasn't even looking to catch the motion. "And you wouldn't believe where she was. Outside the library tower."

"Huh. Weird." Tyree's voice sounded monotonous, devoid of emotion.

"Directly below the open window, might I add."

"You don't say."

Lenora stared at the two as they spoke like she wasn't even there. Her body screamed at her to move, to run, but she knew she wouldn't get far. Though he seemed hesitant, Tyree was an air mage, and she was sure he would suck all the air in the hall and funnel it at her if she tried to escape.

Remy spared her a glance before he squared himself before his brother. "I suppose I saved you some time, Ty. Now you don't have to go looking for her since I brought her straight to you. You're welcome."

Tyree finally looked up, meeting Remy's eyes. "Thanks."

With a tip of his head, Remy turned down the hall and walked away, calling over his shoulder, "You know what to do."

Lenora felt for the key Jerome had given her, only to realize she had left it inside. Her door was unlocked. She could run inside and barricade herself in there.

Before Lenora could blink, Tyree waved a hand, throwing open the door with his air magic, then blew her into the room.

Seven

The blast caught Lenora off guard, but she spun with the force, lifting the hem of her dress and snatching the dagger from her hidden sheath. When she faced Tyree, she raised of both her arms in a defensive position by her face, the blade in her right hand. She'd had years of training with air mages—her mother was her first opponent, and even though Queen Elice was blessed by the Fates with three powers, Lenora learned over the years that her mother preferred air magic.

A deep breath, in and then out, was all she needed to fall into rhythm. Air mages favored long-range attacks. She glanced at her surroundings, noting every piece of furniture and how cramped the space was for that kind of combat.

Lenora's strength lay in close-range fighting with a short sword, her weapon of choice. However, that was still packed away somewhere in one of her bags. She didn't know if the servants had even brought them in yet. For all she knew, the maids were dead or locked away somewhere while the insurrection transpired.

So her dagger would have to do.

Tyree threw himself into the room headfirst.

Mistake number one.

Lenora sliced through the air, aiming directly at his face. His eyes bulged, staring at the weapon as if he'd never seen one before. He likely wasn't expecting her to fight back, or at least not like this.

With a swiftness she didn't think him capable of, he leaned away from her attack, then brought his arms forward. A swirling wind followed his motion, hitting Lenora's stomach and forcing her backward.

She turned away and out of the stream, and he switched directions to continue pelting her with air.

"Just give up, cousin," Tyree shouted over the sound of the rushing wind. "The sooner you accept your fate, the easier it will be for you. I promise to make it quick."

Lenora almost smiled.

Ducking, she dropped to the floor, her glove landing on her palm as she crouched. With her back leg, she pushed herself and launched at Tyree. The motion caught him unaware again, clearly not used to her style of fighting. Mistake number two.

Pour your all into every step, every punch, every slice of your sword.

Her father's words echoed in her head. King James was a non-mage skilled at fighting mages. He went to war against the Fire Lords—fire mages bent on destroying Norraine—and all he was armed with was a shield and a sword.

And he taught her everything he knew.

Her dagger led the way as she charged at Tyree's torso. He twisted, and the blade ripped through the side of his shirt. He staggered back as a thin spray of blood shot out from the opening.

"Gods," he yelled, clutching his side.

Lenora landed in a squat, surveying her winded cousin. He didn't seem to be used to combat.

Weak.

But if he was so weak, why did Remy leave him to fight her alone? Why did he trust Tyree to finish the job?

Lenora glared at the man before her. They thought she was weak too, possibly weaker than Tyree.

I'll show you who's weak.

She didn't give Tyree enough time to catch his breath before she struck at him again. He ducked, dodged, and tried to shoot her down with his air magic, but she was too close for his attacks to have lasting effects. Her speed forced him to drop his hands every two seconds.

With the couch behind him, she feigned a slice with her dagger while aiming a punch at his gut. To her surprise, he caught her fist.

A smile spread across his face as he looked from her glove to her face. She tugged her hand to free it from his grasp, but he held firm. Rotating her body, she finally escaped his grip, losing her glove with the force of her movement.

Alarm threatened to set in as her eyes fell to her gloveless left hand. Vaguely, she knew that her hold on her dagger had loosened, and Tyree reached for it. Lenora realized too late, and she gave a last-minute yank on her blade at the same moment that he pulled on her hand. The blade dislodged, falling to the floor with a clank.

Lenora's eyes widened as her other glove came off with it.

Her breathing came in short, panicked puffs. She was never, *ever* supposed to take them off.

"No," she mumbled, the sound barely escaping her open mouth. She didn't have time to look for her gloves before she felt a cold hand wrap around her throat.

Tyree pushed her across the room and against the wall, his fingers squeezing her neck. "I'm truly sorry about this, cousin." He gulped, his eyes focused on hers. For the first time, she realized she had never held eye contact with him before now. His eyes were a light brown, and the single wall sconce beside her made them glisten.

At least he has the decency to look me in the eye.

He brought his other hand up to her face, right in front of her nose. "This'll be quick."

Then he pummeled her face with air. He threw a heavy, forceful gust directly into her face. She held her breath for as long as she could until the pressure from the air and the pain on her neck from his viselike grip became too much.

Just when she thought she couldn't handle it anymore, his power stopped. He pulled his hand back and wheezed in a deep breath, then shoved it forward again.

He has a weak stamina. So much for a quick end.

Lenora used this opportunity to bring her knee up into his groin.

With a groan, he yanked his hand away from her neck, ripping her necklace. It fell to the ground with her as she collapsed to her knees. The chain had snapped at the clasp and landed beside her before it rolled a few feet away.

Lenora couldn't focus on where it ended up. Not when her dagger stared right at her. She scrambled for it, her fingers mere inches away. Just as she grazed the metal hilt, Tyree's hand grabbed the bottom of her boot.

Lenora kicked out, forcing her legs to push against him to give her the extra inch. Tyree's thin frame landed on hers, slamming her to the floor.

They both let out an *oof* with the force of the collision.

And the dagger slid out of reach.

Rolling, she threw herself over Tyree, but he held on to her wrists, preventing her from grasping the dagger. She strained against his hold, the fabric of her sleeve tearing as she struggled to grab the hilt. She was *so close*. Yet it was not close enough. There was only one thing she could do now.

She closed her eyes against the tears that promised to fall.

But she had no other choice. She only had one trick up her sleeve, and it happened to be the only one she promised herself never to use.

Lenora looked down at Tyree. If she didn't do this, she would die. Tyree would kill her, or Remy would if he didn't.

Fighting against his grip on her wrist, she brought her hands toward his face. He stared at her with a crinkle on his brow, watching as her fingers splayed out.

Before she could second-guess herself, she dropped both hands on his cheeks, framing his face.

The force of the vision hit her harder than she anticipated. It had been nine years since she'd last had a vision, and she braced herself, but she didn't remember how strong they were until this one sucked her in.

She heard Tyree's gasp as the vision overtook them both, bringing them into the future.

Into *his* future.

The edges of Lenora's sight blurred, and the world around her morphed into another scene. An empty stone throne sat in the background, its jagged edges too sharp to touch. The open room was decorated with green drapes, brown furniture, and tall gray walls, with a pennant behind the throne bearing the royal Newton symbol. An open window showed the night sky, and a thick branch protruded from it, snaking around the throne room.

Floating above the ground like she would in a dream, Lenora followed the branch to where it ended behind Tyree. He wore the same clothes he had on now, and he stood in the center of the chamber. This wasn't the Tyree from her present, and this Tyree couldn't see her.

His mouth hung open, belting out a silent scream. His face contorted in pain, and a single tear leaked from his eye. Lenora looked for a sign of injury, stopping when her eyes landed on his cause of death.

The tip of the branch protruded from his chest. The sharp, pointed end faced her, dripping his fresh blood onto the gray marble floor. She covered her mouth to hold in her scream, even though in the back of her mind she knew no one could hear her.

As if drawn backward into the present, the vision obscured. Just before she left the future, she saw Remy, looking exactly the same as when she'd last seen him. He stood behind Tyree, his hand pointed at his brother's back as he withdrew the pointed branch with his magic, causing Tyree's lifeless body to topple face-forward into his own blood.

Lenora choked on her inhalation, removing her hands from Tyree's face to cover her mouth in the present. She rolled off of him, landing on her back. Awareness hovered near the surface of her mind, and she flipped herself over again. She crawled to her dagger, lifted it, then pushed herself to her feet.

Spinning, she expected to come face to face with an angry Tyree.

What she saw instead nearly broke her.

Tyree knelt on the floor, his head buried in his hands as a sob racked his body. He rocked back and forth, muttering unintelligible words.

Hesitantly, she raised her dagger and took a half-step forward. Tyree remained where he was, as if unaware she now held a dagger above his head.

With the dagger in both hands, the sharp end pointing down at the crown of his head, she could end his life.

I could escape. Find my guards and ride all night to Port Arcadia. Then I'll find a captain willing to take us back to Norraine and forget this night ever happened.

With her teeth clenched, she plunged.

Her dagger swung down, down, down, until she pulled back at the last minute.

Groaning, she threw the blade to the floor and crumpled to her knees beside Tyree. Her arms shook as they wrapped around her legs, hugging them close to her body as she tried to calm her racing heart.

I can't do it. I can't.

Tyree looked up then, his eyes red. He shook his head, still muttering. "Cursed... By the Goddess... You're cursed."

Lenora nodded, her bottom lip trembling. "Yes, I am."

She thought she could come to Newton for answers, for help with her powers. Turned out, she found herself in danger, with no obvious way out.

Tyree looked over his shoulder and grabbed the broken chain of her necklace, then held it out. "I-I know what this is. It's a protection charm. You wore this and your gloves to stop ... the visions."

Lenora grabbed the white gold chain, eyeing the clear stone dangling at the bottom. "This was gifted to me the day I was born. My mother said it was special."

"It wards off the cursed sight." His eyes bulged, and he looked around as if seeing the space for the first time. "Remy."

She sucked in a breath, remembering the vision. "I'm so sorry... I didn't mean... I had to—"

Tyree picked up the dagger and stood. He flipped the blade around, then offered the hilt to her. "We need to get you out of here. Now, before he finds out you're still alive."

Lenora jumped to her feet. "What?"

"He's going to kill me anyway, so I might as well do something good as my last deed in this world. It's too late for my parents, and maybe even Matilda, but not for you." He grabbed her forearm and pulled her toward the door he had broken with his wind, peeking his head past the threshold. "I'll get you a horse. You know how to ride, right?"

She nodded frantically. Then she thought of Lawrence. He might be waiting for her, hopefully with the rest of her guards. Her resolve renewed within her. "How will we escape?"

Tyree frowned, his eyes looking guiltily back at her. "Remy's a little busy at the moment. And the soldiers are ... occupied."

"Then lead the way." She knew now why the palace was empty. All the soldiers were busy helping Remy stage this rebellion against the king.

They wandered through the hallways, and her mind went to King Jerome. Would he have a chance to escape Remy's murderous plot? Would Jerome be powerful enough to fend Remy off? And what about Queen Katrina and Princess Matilda? He'd said it was too late for them, but surely they couldn't already be dead.

As they stepped outside, the fresh spring air greeted her, a sharp contrast to the sense of death inside. He led her around the castle until the stables loomed ahead of her, and she rushed ahead of Tyree toward the door. The only sounds from inside were soft neighing and a few horseshoes rubbing against the dirt.

Slowly, she inched the lower half of the door open, hoping to find Lawrence or one of her other guards. She gave it a moment, then two, but there was no sign of anyone. She walked to the first stall and looked inside, but she only saw a horse.

"Psst," Tyree whispered, already pulling a horse from its stall.

"I'm coming," she said. She waited, hoping the sound of her voice would draw Lawrence out from his hiding spot.

"You must hurry, Lenora." He threw a saddle over its back and began strapping the belts.

She ran to his side and helped him ready the horse. A bag with a canteen full of water hung around a post, so she grabbed it and hooked it across her chest.

"What were you looking for?" Tyree asked once he finished with the straps.

"My guard. He was supposed to meet me here." She looked around at the stables again.

"Remy had all your guards rounded up. I doubt he could have escaped."

She frowned, her heart plunging to her feet. "If you see any of them, will you please let them know..." She stopped, her words dying in her throat. It was unlikely Tyree would survive the night, let alone find any of her guards.

As if reading her mind, he placed a hand on her shoulder. "Don't worry about me. This is my fate, not yours. Now, listen to me. The front entrance is locked down, but there's a gate east of the outer field. Remy didn't bother worrying about that one since it leads to Mount Ravis and the Great Gorge. No one goes in or out of that gate. You want to head north to Port Arcadia once you make it past the wall."

She nodded, tucking her necklace into the bag.

"I wish I had a compass." He looked around, his eyes roaming the stables.

"I can navigate without a compass." She grew up with James Taylor as her father. Of course he taught her how to find true north by stranding her in the middle of the Lowlands without a compass. In the middle of summer. With one canteen of water between the two of them. When she was only twelve.

Always know how to find your way home should you ever get lost. And never, ever give up, even when you lose all hope.

"When you get to the Dark Forest," Tyree continued, "don't stop. Under any circumstances. There are beasts that will hunt you down, not just the wolves."

Lenora froze. "Wolves?"

"Yes. The king employs them to hunt. And they make the forest their home. Best to ride straight through and rest once you pass the forest's edge."

A lump formed in her throat, but she swallowed it down. She never realized people could train wolves to hunt *for* them.

Tyree looked at her. His eyes stilled, his body relaxed, and his chest rose and fell in time with a deep breath. "Be on your way, then."

She placed her foot in the stirrup and threw her leg over the saddle. Tyree passed her the reins, then patted the horse.

"Thank you," she said, glancing down at him.

He shook his head. "I don't deserve your thanks. But you deserve an apology. I'm sorry, Lenora. I wish... Well, it doesn't matter what I want anymore, now, does it?"

Then he smacked the horse's bottom, sending it trotting through the stables.

Lenora didn't look back as the horse rushed through the door. If she turned her head, she might go back. Might return to her doom, where Remy would surely attack her himself.

Her heavy heart weighed her down into the saddle. Her guards were back there, hopefully still alive. Hopefully Remy wouldn't kill them. He might take them as prisoners, though. She hated to leave them behind to such a fate. Remy seemed the type to relish torture.

She leaned forward in the saddle, fighting the urge to return. Instead, she gripped the reins tightly and spurred the horse to gallop through the field.

Eight

The only sounds in the darkness came from her heavy breathing and the horse's trots as it galloped through the rocky hillside at the western edge of Mount Ravis. Lenora stopped the horse once beside a creek, allowing it to drink. She filled the canteen and gulped it down, then she refilled it before she urged the horse to take off again.

It complied, reigniting her dwindling hope. Despair had set in the longer she rode and the closer she got to the Dark Forest. What in the Fates' names did Tyree mean when warning her about the wolves? Surely she had misunderstood him. It was unlikely that animals, especially those as wild as wolves, could follow explicit instructions. They hunted whenever they wanted, not because a human—mage or otherwise—told them to. That was what she knew about other animals, so the same could be said about Newton's wolves, right?

A few feet ahead was the tree line—the beginning of the Dark Forest. A full moon hovered overhead, and she glanced up at it, soaking in its light before she entered the darkness. She pulled back on the reins, slowing the horse to a careful walk, too spooked herself to enter the shadows cast by the enormous canopy above. When they entered the forest and nothing seemed amiss, she nudged the horse into a trot.

This is just like the Jani Forest back home. I've explored countless trails and creeks all throughout the Jani, and nothing bad has ever happened there. Well, at least not to me.

She grimaced, blocking out the horror stories she'd heard all her life. About how Orser, the rebel fire mage who started the Last Mage War, killed his parents in the Jani because they'd tried to kill him first. How Lenore kidnapped Elice and kept her hidden in a cottage in the middle of the forest. How her mother killed Lenore in that same forest, and how the entrance to the Tomb of Souls—the Fates' forsaken place where lost souls go after death—is purportedly located in that exact spot. Not to mention the Blood Flower—the plant so mysterious and powerful it brought Orser back from the dead.

Lenora fought the shiver that ran down her arms, blaming it on the cold. It must have been the middle of the night, after all, and all she wore was the same black dress with delicate lace she donned when she got dressed in Norraine yesterday morning.

Has it not even been a day since I left home?

Tears willed themselves to fall from her eyes, completely unbidden. She wiped her eyelids, silencing the emotions that welled up. Now was not the time for that.

But that didn't stop her mind from wandering with despair. She worried about Lawrence and her other guards. She even thought about Jerome, Katrina, and Matilda. That poor family. What were her guards and the royal family doing right now? Were they even alive? Then she thought about Tyree and her vision. Had that come to pass yet? Were Tyree, the rest of his family, and her own guards dead, all murdered by Remy?

The horse shook its head, its silky mane shuffling. Lenora looked down at her trembling hands, which were causing the reins to bump against its neck.

A shuddering breath later, she steadied herself enough to resume a normal hold, but her thoughts strayed back to Tyree.

That was the first time she'd used her powers in nine years. The last time...

The last time, she was only ten years old. It had nearly ruined her, but it did destroy a precious friendship.

Samantha.

Lenora forced the name out of her mind. She didn't have time to dive into her memories. Besides, it was too late for Samantha. Her vision had already confirmed that for both of them.

After what seemed like an hour of riding, Lenora slowed her horse to a walk again, though a brisk one. Tyree's words about not stopping in the forest stayed in the forefront of her mind, despite her growling stomach.

Before she had the chance to return the horse to a trot, she heard a howl in the distance. The sound sent a chill down her spine.

"Fates," she whispered, then used the heel of her boots to encourage the horse to gain speed. It responded immediately, using its powerful legs to rush through the trees until it reached a gallop.

The howl sounded far, maybe a few miles, but she didn't know these creatures well enough to guess how quickly it could move.

She had to make sure it couldn't catch her.

Another howl resounded through the forest, followed by two more. A pack of wolves was after her. That sent a jolt through her, and she used that to urge the horse forward. "Come on," she shouted, guiding the horse around thick tree trunks.

With a quick calculation, she estimated she'd been traveling through the forest for about two hours. That was roughly halfway. Could she out-gallop a wolf pack for two full hours?

A few minutes later, she received her answer. A wolf appeared in her periphery, running alongside her. She felt the horse pull away, and she allowed it to steer them around several trees to avoid the wolf.

That thing came out of nowhere.

It had managed to sneak up on her, and she cursed herself for not being aware of its presence. She scanned the forest, finding three more running beside the first, encircling her and the horse.

Her throat instantly dried up. They meant to trap her.

Grasping the reins, she yanked left and then right, guiding the horse in a zigzag. The wolves stayed on pace, communicating with each other through yelps and barks.

Then they pulled back. Wide eyed, she looked over her shoulder to see all four disappear from view.

Something's not right.

As soon as she had that thought, something solid collided with her, knocking her off the horse.

Lenora landed on her side, her head hitting the hard ground, but she only lost focus for a moment before she turned into the motion, rolling onto her hands and knees. Her fingers splayed into the dirt, and the damp forest floor seeped through her dress. The horse reared onto its back legs, whinnying loudly, before it shot off deeper into the forest.

A sharp ache exploded on her ankle, and she turned to see a huge brown maw wrapped around it. The wolf bit down, sending blasts of pain up her leg. She screamed out, the sound ringing in the expansive forest.

The wolf yanked, and she swore her foot would come off with it. Instead, it dragged her backward as the other four wolves returned.

They bit down on her limbs, tugging her in the same direction, like a coordinated unit. One even took a bite of her brown and gold hair, pulling it free from its raggedy bun. The yell she gave turned into a grunt when she kicked out, hitting the jaw of the large wolf at her ankle. She thrashed around, smacking and kicking whatever she could.

As if unwilling to be struck, the wolves took a step away from her flailing. She sensed their confusion, which only added to hers, but she used that to her advantage.

Lenora grabbed her dagger from its sheath, brandishing it and waving it wildly. "Get back!" She knew they couldn't understand her, but she yelled it again just to make herself feel better. "Get back, or I'll slice you open."

The biggest of the wolves yelped, its jaw likely already bruised from her boot. Lenora rose to her feet, backing out of the circle. Somehow, the big wolf—perhaps the leader—narrowed its slanted eyes at her, then snapped its jaws.

When the rest copied the wolf leader's movements, Lenora took off.

The wolves ran right after her.

She hobbled left and right, weaving around the trees on her injured ankle. Blood continued to ooze from the wound, but she pushed on, ignoring the pain and the horrible wobble in her step.

Then, when she thought she couldn't run any longer, when the pain had grown too strong, the wolves let out a howl in unison. She threw a glance behind her, only to find all five had stopped in a line beside a tree. The leader paced back and forth behind it, its narrowed eyes fastened on her.

Thanking the Fates for whatever halted their pursuit, she plowed on, wanting to put as much distance between her and the hunting wolves as she could.

Soon, Lenora's run turned into a hobbled jog, and then into a limping walk, until she couldn't focus on anything but the pain in her ankle and the scrapes and cuts on her arms and legs from the wolves' attack. Even her scalp throbbed where a wolf had pulled on her hair.

She leaned against a sturdy tree and closed her eyes, telling herself it could only be for a minute before she had to press on. Then she forced herself to move. She took one shuffled step and cried out—from both the throbbing ache and the sight before her.

In the distance, right in the middle of the forest, stood a tiny cottage with one small window and an old wooden door.

It seemed straight out of a story, one she was quite familiar with—like her mother was here telling Lenora about her life growing up in the old cottage in the Jani Forest. When Lenora was a child, Elice would run a comb through Lenora's curls, her sweet voice soothing as she recounted her life's story.

But this wasn't her mother's story. This was no children's tale. A pack of wolves hunted her through the night, and a mysterious cottage precisely in the middle of the deep, dark forest loomed right before her eyes.

This *definitely* was not a tale she'd heard before.

A distant howl lit a fire in her belly, reminding her she had no other choice but to seek shelter.

She hobbled toward the house, noting the late hour. However, this was an emergency, and her life literally depended on waking up whoever lived inside, no matter how upset they'd be at the intrusion.

If they even answer.

She banged on the door once, and it creaked open as soon as her fist connected with the wood.

Ignoring her base instinct to run away from this strange house with a too-willing unlocked door, she pushed it open an inch and peeked her head in. "Hello," she called, hoping to alert the owner of her presence. "Is anyone home? I... I need help."

The word "help" sounded awful to her ears. She wasn't used to asking for assistance. She wanted to do things her way without anyone's help. It was how she thought she could prove herself, to show how she deserved to be the crown princess.

Now, she had blood trailing down her leg and puddling inside her ankle-high boot, claw marks on her arms, bruises all over her body, and she hadn't eaten in hours. She was stubborn, yes, but not stupid. Right now, she needed help.

When silence persisted in the dark cabin, she raised her voice. "Hello? Is anyone here? Please, I just need a bandage or a towel, and then I'll be on my way."

More silence.

A weighty breath escaped her, and she leaned against the door frame. There was no one here, which was a blessing directly from the Fates.

Lenora allowed herself a moment to breathe before she took in her surroundings. The small cottage only had one large room. Directly in front of her, a table with a solitary unlit candle stood lopsided on its mismatched legs, a single chair tucked underneath it. To the left, a ruddy sofa with only enough room for two leaned against the wall. On the right, a short counter, a cabinet, a sink, and a stove that had seen better—and cleaner—days took up the other wall, and a single cot lay in the corner with a worn blanket haphazardly thrown across it.

If someone lived here, they likely lived alone.

Who knew when they would be back, if they even still lived here, so Lenora set to work. Lighting the candle with the match beside it, she took another quick look around. Then, hopping on one foot, she entered the kitchen space.

Setting her dagger on the counter by the sink, she rummaged through the tiny kitchen, opening the overhead cabinets until she found a discarded white towel. It had holes and stains all over it, but she couldn't be too particular about what the Fates had gifted her—and they hadn't given her much.

Now that she could take in a full breath, pain radiated throughout her entire body, and exhaustion threatened to overtake her. She needed to clean herself up, catch a bit of rest, and then find her way north to Port Arcadia.

Lenora turned on the faucet, and brown water spilled from the spigot, hitting the bottom of the sink with a loud *clunk*. She gagged, her empty stomach protesting the sight and rotting smell.

Oh, Fates, what did I do to deserve this?

Settling for the murky water, she let it run for several seconds until it looked less chunky before she ran the towel under it.

At least it's cold.

Turning off the faucet, she closed her eyes, reminding herself that she needed to wipe away the blood from her arms and legs, otherwise she'd continue to mark her trail for the wolves. She didn't want to make their job easier for them. Even if it would likely be painful to touch the bite marks on her ankle and limbs.

Lenora bent over to remove her shoe when a roar made her halt. Still in her squat, she straightened her back, nearly dropping the filthy towel.

That didn't sound like a wolf.

Gulping, she took in one, two, three breaths, but the sound didn't repeat. Thinking she must be imagining things, she reached for the laces on her boot.

The cabin's door splintered open, sending pieces of wood in all directions. In the doorway stood an eight-foot-tall brown bear, its muzzle wide open as it let out a deafening roar.

Nine

Her ears rang with the sound of the beast's bellow. The towel slipped from her hands as she stared wide-eyed at the bear, its bronze fur directly in her line of sight. It stood on both hind legs with its massive paws high in the air, blocking the entryway where the broken door halfway hung off its rusty hinges. Sharp claws extended from each digit as it flung them around before the bear dropped onto all fours.

Then it charged.

Lenora fell back into the corner of the kitchen space, her hip bumping into the counter. A glint of silver caught her eye, and she reached for whatever she could to use as a weapon against this enormous animal.

She had never loved her dagger so much before. It lay right on the counter where she left it while she had searched for the towel. Grabbing the weapon, she turned in time for the beast to stop inches away from where she held the blade up toward its jaw.

Her arm trembled as it stared her down. Something shimmered in its eyes, almost like recognition. It was similar to the way the wolf had looked at her when she spoke to it.

Gulping, she sent a prayer to the Fates before she tried her hand at reasoning with this animal. "Listen ... bear. I won't hesitate to slice your face in half."

Reason. Sure.

The bear lowered its head until it was level with hers, its eyes meeting her gaze and holding it for several seconds. Then it let out a roar, screeching directly in her face.

Saliva smacked against her cheeks as it continued to growl, but she refused to lower her weapon.

When it stopped screaming, it huffed, blowing out a stream of hot breath on her wet face. On its inhale, the bear's eyes shot open, and it backed away.

Shaking its head, it pawed at its nose. As it maintained her eye contact, it stepped closer again and took another sniff. Lenora's mind reeled at its behavior. Never before had she seen an animal behave in such a way. Why was it sniffing her like this? Sure, she'd been running for her life for hours, but she didn't think she smelled *that* horrible.

The bear drew itself up to its full height. Lenora raised her dagger to follow its movement in case it attacked.

Slowly, the fur on its body disappeared, except for the top of its head, where it transformed into thick brown dreadlocks tipped in gold. Its maw, with thick, sharp canines, shrunk, and its muzzle became a strong jaw.

A human jaw.

No, a man's jaw.

Lenora shrieked as she stared up into the human eyes before her, the honey orbs glistening as the man looked right at her. He lifted his hands, and Lenora raised her dagger, ready to block his blow and then stab, but he grabbed both of her wrists, holding her steady.

She didn't feel faint until that moment when the blood loss finally made her woozy. However, she was *not* going to faint in front of this ... whatever he was.

She spun on her weak legs out of his hold, landing beside him, then pressed her dagger against his neck. "What are you?" She held the blade against his skin, yet he didn't back away.

He growled, showing his very human teeth, but the slight widening of his eyes let her know he was surprised by her speed. "What are you doing in my house?" His deep voice rumbled, echoing in her ears. There was a slight accent, something she couldn't place. It differed from the Newtonians' speech patterns, with a heavier tone on each syllable.

Lenora's eyes traveled to her blade, then down to his chest. Only then did she realize he was shirtless. She snapped her eyes up, then pushed harder against his neck. He towered over her, so she had to stretch her arm high to keep the pressure where she wanted it against his artery. One wrong move and she would swipe.

"Answer my question first. What are you?" She swallowed her fear. Did she really want to know what kind of creature he was? First, he was a bear, and now he was a shirtless human. She didn't want to know what kind of creature could transform from bear to man since her mind still reeled from the events of the day, but she held steadfast to her question.

He turned toward her, causing the blade to nick his skin. Lenora stepped back, and he advanced another foot until they both stood in the middle of the room, close to the raggedy table.

"Stop!" she yelled, pulling one bare hand behind her back to avoid touching him and causing another vision. She couldn't handle another one on top of all she'd experienced today.

"You're not going to hurt me," he said, a small quirk on his lips. Then he bent his head closer, and Lenora froze as he sniffed her again. "You're the one they're looking for."

Her dagger wobbled, and she sucked in a choked breath. He probably worked with the wolves, for the king—who was most likely now Remy. Now that this ... bear-person had her, he would take her back to Stonehold. But she wouldn't go down without a fight.

She swung her fatigued arm, stabbing toward his neck. He backed away before the sharp tip made contact, and he raised his hands in defense.

"¡*Espera!*" he hollered, but Lenora swiped at his bare chest. "Hold on!"

Ignoring his words, she continued to swing her blade until his back hit the wall beside the cabinet. She grabbed the tip of the hilt between two fingers and squared her shoulders. Aiming just above his head, she threw the dagger. She could tell by his agility he would either duck or dodge the toss. While she had never purposefully missed before, she only wanted to distract him long enough so she could run for the door. Forget the towel, forget the blood. She'd take her chances running from this creature just like she did the wolves.

She spun, then took one step on her injured ankle, and the mind-numbing pain hit her. Her leg buckled as she screamed, and her body toppled over. Strong arms wrapped around her middle, holding her up.

"I got you," the bear-man whispered.

A whimper left her lips as she dropped her head, defeat sinking in. Her brown hair, tugged loose during the wolf attack, fell forward, and she glimpsed the golden highlights even in the dim room. People used to make fun of her for her unusual hair, especially in combination with her powers. They called her odd, strange, and—she cringed—cursed. It wasn't her fault she was born with a head of mostly auburn hair, with golden streaks peeking through. She never asked for her powers. That didn't stop the taunts, though.

Pain radiated through her leg, and she lifted her foot to ease the pressure. She wouldn't make it to Port Arcadia like this. She couldn't even make it out of the cottage. Her body ached because of the other cuts from the wolves' claws and teeth, her head throbbed from hitting the ground and the wolf pulling on her hair, and her bleeding ankle was out of use.

"Are you going to turn me in?" she asked, looking over her shoulder to meet the caramel eyes of her attacker.

His gaze softened, and the corners of his lips turned down as he shook his head. "Is that why you attacked me? You thought I would hand you over to the wolves?"

She swallowed, studying his face for any hint of malice. His thick eyebrows crinkled, and his sharp chin jutted out as he waited for her response. Though only a single candle lit the room, she noticed the way his light brown eyes roamed her face. They lingered on her hair, and she straightened out of his hold, years of insecurity rearing its head.

Lenora faced him, standing on her one good leg while the other rested on the tip of her muddy boot. "You don't work for them?"

He blew out a huff, distaste clearly showing on his face. "Nah. The wolves and I don't get along."

"What..." She paused, wondering if he'd answer her question this time. "What are you?"

He tilted his head to the side. "Why are the wolves after you?"

She pursed her lips. "I overheard something I wasn't supposed to."

He regarded her for a moment, then he turned to the sink and retrieved a metal box from beneath it. From inside, he pulled out a tin and a fresh rag. "For your injuries," he said as he handed them to her.

Lenora avoided touching him while she grabbed it, then opened the can. The scent of fresh herbs hit her nose as she dipped her finger in the medicinal ointment. She applied the cream to the visible cuts on her arms, then eyed the bite on her ankle.

The man simply watched as she bent down and applied the dressing, then wrapped it tightly with the folded rag. She tied off the end with a soft sigh, already feeling the ointment working its magic. "Was this made by a healer?" she asked.

He nodded, crossing his muscled arms over his broad chest. Lenora finally risked a look at his body, relieved to see him wearing a thin pair of short trousers. She didn't know what type of magic he had, but it seemed to be some kind of power that allowed him to not only transform into a beast, but to also change back into a human with pants.

"What happened at the castle?" he asked.

"How do you know something happened?" Lenora avoided his astute gaze by securing the lid back on the tin and placing it on the wobbly table.

"There's something weird going on with the wolves, and whenever wolves are involved, Stonehold is involved. I sensed ... something, so I went outside to investigate. Do you work there? Are you a lady's maid?"

Lenora shook her head. She didn't know if she could share any of the events with this stranger. However, if Remy had been successful, the entire kingdom would soon know what happened. At the very least, they'd know Remy deposed Jerome for the crown. Could she trust this man—if he even *was* a man?

She stared at him for a few moments, and he held her gaze. A force pulled taut within her chest, yanking something forward from deep inside her. Her lips trembled, and her eyes watered from the emotions and the pain she'd hidden all day.

"My name is Lenora Moore-Taylor, princess of Norraine," she began, stepping forward and lifting her head high. "Prince Remy wants to kill me because I heard him planning to murder his father, King Jerome. The king ... he's my mother's uncle, and he welcomed me to Newton as Norraine's first ambassador. But now... Now, he's probably dead, and I don't know what happened to the rest of the family or to my guards because I fled. Like a coward, I fled. I abandoned my soldiers and my ... my best friend."

Lenora looked down at her clenched fists, bringing them toward her face. She opened her hands, spreading her fingers to stare at her bare skin. "But I can make this right. Correct my mistake and fix all the wrongs that happened here. I need to get to Port Arcadia and then on a ship to Norraine. I'll tell my mother, Queen Elice, what happened, and we'll return for my guards. If they're still alive. If they're dead, then I'll avenge them by making sure Remy pays for what he did."

By the end, her breath came in ragged puffs as anger radiated out of her. If she were a fire mage, she was sure she'd be burning from the rage she felt deep within. The truth of every word she spoke lit a fire in her bones. Remy would suffer—she'd make sure of it.

Finally, she looked away from her cursed hands and into the man's eyes. A soft gasp escaped her mouth as her lips parted. His eyes burned just like hers—with anger and outrage. His jaw was set tight like stone. From the way his chest swelled up and down, Lenora realized his breathing was in tune with hers.

"I'll take you to Port Arcadia," he promised, stepping close.

"You..." she trailed off, then shook her head. "You don't have to. Just tell me where to go from here and I'll be on my way."

"There are wolf guards all throughout the forest. You'll never make it on your own. But the wolves... They won't come near me. If I take you, I'll make sure you get back home safely."

She stared at him for way too long, her eyes never straying from his face. When she remembered her voice, she uttered, "Why?"

He looked taken aback, stepping away and clearing his head with a shake. "I have my own reasons. Besides, I have business in town tomorrow. It's not out of my way."

Lenora nodded, accepting his offer of help. That was why she entered this cottage to begin with, even if it came in a different form than what she was expecting. "All right. Thank you... Wait, what's your name?"

The bear-man swallowed thickly. "Call me Xander, *princesa*."

Ten

Morning light filtered through Lenora's closed eyelids as chirping birds drew her out of her slumber. She sat up with a jolt, remembering where she was. She was inside a stranger's cabin, sleeping on his bed while he slept on the lumpy couch that was much too small for his frame.

The hard cot reminded her of her family's camping trips in Nomad territory. They had slept in tents along the beach, as was Nomadic custom, and she complained the entire time. Granted, she was a spoiled brat when she was seven, still too young to understand the way different customs worked. If she had known then what she knew now, she would have relished the chance to sleep along the warm shoreline with her family and friends close by.

Now, she ached all over, and the rag around her ankle was stained red with blood. Her stomach growled, alerting her of its emptiness. She ran a hand through her curls, snagging on the thick knots. It was a rare occurrence for her hair to hang loose. If she were bolder, she'd smell herself, but she didn't need to—she knew she reeked of old sweat and mud.

A shuffle from across the room brought her eyes to Xander. He held a bag in one hand, his other grabbing things from the shelf above the stove to throw inside. Lenora stared at the muscles on his tanned back as he reached for the top shelf. He still hadn't put a shirt on, and she couldn't tell whether she liked that fact or not.

Xander's shoulders froze, and he slowly flattened his feet on the floor before he turned to meet her eyes.

A blush rose on her cheeks. What little daylight that spilled from the one window illuminated his face, his honeyed eyes glowed, and his bright smile highlighted his sharp cheekbones. Obviously, by the humorous glint in his eyes, he knew she had been staring.

"Good morning," he said, his tone too bright under the circumstances. He jutted his chin toward the table, and Lenora followed the line, all too eager to look away from his face. "There's a bit of porridge, since you're so hungry."

"How did—"

"Your stomach's been growling all night." He returned to his packing but kept his body angled toward her. "I'm surprised I didn't wake you with all the noise I made while cooking. But I supposed with all you've been through, your body needed its rest."

Lenora lifted herself off the bed and hobbled to the chair. It tilted when she sat, but she ignored it as she tucked into the soft, warm grains, the taste of sweet honey waking her taste buds.

Xander appeared beside her, chuckling as he watched her devour the food. "You really were hungry."

"This is so good," she said over her spoon, ignoring all of Miss Tabitha's princess etiquette lessons.

"It's just porridge." He placed the bag on the table and crossed his arms.

"I've never had it before." She licked the spoon, then placed it inside the empty ceramic bowl.

"You guys don't eat porridge in Norraine?"

She shook her head, then stood with the bowl. "We usually have sweet pastries, eggs, and smoked meats for breakfast."

He followed her as she hobbled to the sink and turned on the faucet. Brown water continued to pour out, so she waited until it cleared a bit before she washed it.

"You're a princess," he began, his tone dumbfounded, "and you wash your own bowl."

Lenora looked over her shoulder at him. "I blame my parents. They have different ideas about what it means to be a normal princess."

His smile warmed the ache in her heart at the mention of her parents. "Let me do it for you." He reached for the bowl, and Lenora, caught off guard, let it slip from her fingers. His hands had gotten too close. *Way* too close.

The shattering of the ceramic against the metal sink echoed in the small house. Lenora hurried to shut off the faucet to pick up the broken pieces. "I'm so, so sorry, Xander."

"*Está bien*. It's okay." He reached again, aiming for the shards to help clean the mess, but Lenora jumped back before he accidentally touched her.

Before *she* accidentally touched him.

She drew in a shaky breath, clutching the fragments of the bowl against her chest. His mouth hung open for a few seconds before he snapped it shut. He threw the broken pieces in his hands onto the counter, then took a step away.

"We should..." He stopped himself, wiping his hands across his pants. "We should get going. The wolves usually report to Stonehold at dawn, but there might be a few still roaming around the Dark Forest. We better get a head start before they start tracking again."

All she could do was nod, tossing her shards on the counter as well.

He grabbed a gray shirt from the couch and slipped it over his head.

Then he threw the bag over his shoulder and walked to the door, holding it open for her. She hobbled through the door silently, her eyes taking in the forest in the daylight—well, what little daylight reached below the canopy.

As they walked, she felt his stare, so she met his questioning gaze. A question of her own burned in the forefront of her mind, and she had a feeling he'd be able to answer it. "Last night, while I was running from the wolves, something strange happened. They stopped following me. They could have overtaken me, injured as I was, but they just stopped."

"You probably entered my barrier," he said. "I marked my territory so the wolves don't get too close to my house. It also wards off other creatures. Animals don't like entering another's territory, especially if it's bear land."

"So, you really are a bear?" She carefully maneuvered around a fallen log, but she caught his smirk from her periphery.

"Why are you afraid of touch?"

She narrowed her eyes at him. "Are you always going to answer that question with another question?"

"That depends." He jumped over a downed tree, landing in a squat, his dreads swinging with the motion.

She hopped over the same tree, perching on her good foot right next to him. His lips turned into a sideways smile, and he nodded approvingly at her.

"Besides," she said after gaining her breath. "I'm not afraid of touch."

Xander turned, drawing closer to her. She took one step back, her ankle protesting the pressure, and he followed until she brushed against the trunk of a tree. He lifted a hand toward her face, and Lenora stared at it, her eyes wide. When his fingers hovered over her cheek, she sucked in a breath. Then he pressed the tips of his fingers against her skin. Lenora closed her eyes against the sensation.

It had been years since someone outside her family touched her this way. Not even Lawrence was brave enough to place his hands on her exposed skin. She let out a trembling breath, shocked at the warmth of his fingers on her cheek.

The thing about her powers that no one seemed capable of understanding was that anyone could touch her. It was *her* touching everyone else that was the problem.

She forced her eyes open. His were focused on her lips, but they jolted up to hold her eye contact.

He pressed his thick lips into a line, then pulled away. "I guess I misread you, *princesa*."

He walked away, and she compelled her wobbly legs to trail after him.

Their trek was slow, considering Lenora's limp made it difficult for her to walk fast. Around midday, they stopped for a break to fill their stomachs with the water and bread Xander had packed for them.

That was when they heard the first howl.

Lenora sat straight on the log they were using to rest. She turned her head toward the sound, her heart thundering as she waited for the wolf to show. A brisk spring breeze flew by, grabbing her curls and brushing them past her face. Brown leaves, the remnants of a cold winter, rolled across the forest floor, and the branches above her head rattled their fresh, green growth. No other howl followed the first, but she kept her ears open regardless.

"*No te preocupes*," Xander muttered around his loaf. "Don't worry. Like I said, they won't come anywhere close to me. Even if they smell you."

She still didn't relax, no matter how comforting his words were. "I'm sorry, but the last time I heard a wolf's howl, my leg was almost bitten off. I'm just a little on edge."

He looked down at her foot and the bloody towel just above the ankle of her boot. "When we get to Port Arcadia, we'll get you some supplies to properly take care of that."

That reminded her of the pain, but she shoved it down. No daughter of Elice or James would ever let pain stop them from completing a mission.

"Thank you," she mumbled, staring at her hands. In the last nine years, this was the first time she'd seen them in nature's light. It amazed her how soft the skin looked. She was sure the gloves would have worn her skin raw, but whenever she risked taking her gloves off, they still looked pristine. Even now, after all the dirt and blood, she kind of liked the way they looked.

They would still bring others harm, though.

Xander eyed her hands, so she tucked them in her lap. He stared at where her fingers hid within the folds of her skirts, his keen eyes showing just how much curiosity he had. He met her gaze with a smile. "No need to thank me."

"Why does the king use these wolves to hunt, anyway?" she plowed on, happy to distract him. "How does he control them? And does the power to control them shift when a new king or queen takes the throne?"

Xander sighed, opening the lid of his canteen and taking a swig before answering. "He uses them because they're great trackers. Excellent sense of smell, you know. And King Jerome doesn't really control them. They're all volunteers—soldiers, if you will. And ... well, just like any soldier, they follow the orders of whoever's in charge. If Prince Remy really killed King Jerome, then they'll do whatever he says."

"Like hunt me down." Lenora ripped off a piece of bread and popped it into her mouth.

"Unfortunately, yes. Wolves are incredibly loyal. If they accept Prince Remy as their king, then they won't stop until they find you. Or until he orders them off."

"Then why won't they come after me if you're near? If they want me so bad, why don't they just ambush us here and now?"

Xander chuckled to himself and took another sip. "Norrainians don't know much about other lands, do they?"

Lenora glared at him, making him laugh harder.

He held up his hands when she huffed. "Okay, I'm sorry. It's funny to me, that's all. There's a big history here—between wolves and bears—that you don't know."

Lenora crossed her arms. "That was the whole point of my mission. Norraine has been cut off from the rest of the world for so long. All the stories of other kingdoms have been long forgotten. I was supposed to be an ambassador, to come to Newton to learn about our ancestors and hopefully bring back something more than rare spices and trade deals. I wanted to make big changes. I wanted to give my people a better kingdom, a better world than what they've known. We've been so bogged down with civil wars and hatred. I just wanted to... I don't know, give them something more. I wanted to *be* something more. And now..."

She trailed off, her sight blurred from the tears welling in her eyes. Xander's warm hand rested under her chin, pulling her head until she stared at him through her watery vision.

"When you get back to Norraine," he said, "I know you'll make all those changes and more." The tone in his words, the way he held her gaze, made her realize he meant what he said. He truly believed she could do it.

The doubt she'd buried herself under since she was a child slowly chipped away, some of her self-loathing falling to the forest floor.

Another howl sounded in the distance, and that brought her out of her stupor.

She shook her head, clearing it from all the hope that had managed to slide under her thick, hardened skin. "Let's go before the wolves decide to forget whatever makes them afraid of you."

Eleven

The thick trees of the Dark Forest thinned, becoming sparse as they entered the outskirts of Port Arcadia. Lenora's ankle had swelled, sending tendrils of pain all the way up her leg. Xander had side-eyed her with furrowed brows every few minutes, asking if she wanted to take a break. Every time, she shook her head, saying she was all right.

As the sun set behind the town's buildings in the distance, she was about ready to collapse to the ground. Xander led them down a side path at the edge of town, his feet still light and his eyes on a continuous prowl of their surroundings.

He stopped at the corner of a three-story building and leaned his head around the edge while Lenora pressed her back against the wall. When he looked back at her, he gave a single nod, and she hopped along behind him as he entered the alley.

The dark brown buildings made it difficult to see much at night. A handful of lampposts lit the side street as they walked to the entrance of an inn a few doors down.

Xander pushed the door open and stepped in first. The light and scents of baked bread and hearty spices lit her senses. He looked over his shoulder with a grin, beckoning with his head for her to enter.

She walked right in, not waiting a single second longer. She didn't care that she smelled something fierce or looked downright hideous. Inside, there was food, shelter, and a place to sit. Let the wolves find her, as long as they waited until *after* she ate and took a bath.

The main entry was a narrow space with a bench and a coat rack, already packed with several jackets and hats. Just beyond, Lenora caught sight of a few tables and chairs, some of them occupied by laughing men and women who held frothing mugs or forks full of food.

Lenora's stomach rumbled. Xander made a noise, something between a whine and a grunt, as he eyed the diners before he turned in the opposite direction of the tables.

She watched as he walked right up to the empty bar and greeted the large man behind it with the biggest grin she'd ever seen on his face. Taking careful footsteps so she didn't display her horrible limp, she listened to their conversation.

"Well, well, well, look who decided to show up," the man said, clasping Xander's arm near the elbow. Xander copied the motion, grasping the older man's inner arm. The two held on tight and gave a single shake. "Come look at this, María. It must be someone's birthday."

A plump woman in an apron appeared from behind a swinging door, holding a wooden spatula. When she saw Xander, she let out a gasp, covering her mouth and sending food flying from the utensil across the bar. "*Diosa!*" she shrieked, then ran around the bar to envelop Xander in a hug. "My goodness! What are you doing here? It's not my birthday."

"Or mine," the man said with a laugh.

Xander looked behind, smiling shyly at Lenora. She walked the rest of the way until she stood beside him. The man's and woman's expressions went from pleasant curiosity to full on surprise.

"You brought a girl!" María screeched, and Xander snapped his eyes toward her.

"No, it's not like that," he hurried to say, waving his hands. He dug his hand into his pocket, then dropped a few silver coins onto the bar, the clink quiet over the din of conversation in the room behind them. "Listen," he whispered, "we need two rooms. And some food. Quickly and quietly."

The man nodded, but he reached over the bar and slid the coins back to Xander. "You got it. But you know your coin's no good here."

"Pedro," Xander began, but was immediately cut off.

"I don't want to hear it," Pedro interrupted. Then he waved toward the two chairs in front of him. "María will bring each of you a plate. Have a seat. You two look like you need it." He made a pointed glance at Lenora's arms, where her healing cuts were visible through the rips in her lace sleeves.

María smiled at them. "You know you're always on the house. You and your guests." Then she disappeared with Pedro behind the door.

Xander plopped onto the closest stool with a groan, resting his elbows on the table and his head in his hands. Lenora took the seat next to him. As soon as she lifted her sore foot, a groan left her mouth. It felt so good to finally take the pressure off her leg.

Lowering his hands, Xander met her eyes. "Sorry about them."

"Don't be," she said, hiding her smile. She blinked, realizing she hadn't smiled at a stranger like this in years. Having to let down her guard, worrying about so much more than her powers, distracted her from her past. In that moment, however, her emotional wounds rose to the surface again, and she looked away from Xander's face.

María and Pedro returned, each carrying a plate of food. Xander thanked them and began eating. Lenora offered her own thanks before she took in the healthy portions in front of her. She couldn't identify anything on her plate, though, so she looked up at them. "May I ask what this is?"

María and Pedro shared a glance. Pedro grumbled something in another language, likely the same one Xander had been letting slip now and then.

Xander responded under his breath, his focus on the food.

Clearing her throat, María gave an uncomfortable smile as she pointed out various items on Lenora's plate. "We call this gallo pinto, but it's just rice and beans. This is mole de pollo, a chicken dish with a rich sauce. And these are tortillas. You can use them to pick up pieces of food or eat them by themselves."

Lenora considered that for a moment. "Kind of like bread?" She looked at Xander for confirmation. He angled his body toward her, then ripped off a piece of his tortilla. He cupped it, scooped up a bit of the sauce, and threw it in his mouth.

Lenora looked on with wide eyes, her stomach rumbling. She hurriedly ripped off her own piece, picked up some sauce, and shoveled it into her mouth too. The sweet and savory flavor erupted on her tongue. She moaned, covering her mouth with her hand. Pedro chuckled, and María nodded approvingly.

"Let me know if you'd like more," Maria said, then she winked at Xander and returned to the kitchen.

Pedro grabbed a towel from behind the bar and began wiping down the counter, speaking to Xander in the language Lenora didn't know. "*¿Cuanto sabe ella de nosotros?*"

"*Nada,*" Xander responded, his voice deadpan.

"*¿Qué estás haciendo, Xander?*"

"*Solo estoy comiendo.*" Xander stuffed a large piece of chicken into his mouth, though his narrowed eyes bore down on Pedro.

Lenora chewed slowly, eyeing both men as they stared each other down and wondering who would back down first. To her surprise, Pedro lowered his head, muttering, "Of course."

Xander's hand flew to Lenora's shoulder, his grip hard. She almost dropped the bit of tortilla from the sudden movement. Turning, she saw him draw in a deep breath through his nose, sniffing the air as if he were trying to gather information from it.

His eyes narrowed as he met her gaze. "Wolves," he whispered, then he used his other hand to usher her by the waist off the stool.

Lenora allowed him to guide her toward the swinging door into the kitchen. María looked over from the stove, but Xander pressed a finger to his lips. The woman frowned, then ran through the door to the bar.

Xander's grip remained on Lenora's waist as he pushed her into a nook against the wall near a supply cabinet. He squeezed in right after her, using his body to shield her from view.

Her heart pounded, and blood rushed to her ears. She could feel his beating since her chest was pressed against him.

She heard the faint *ding* of the bell above the front door. Soon, the pounding of boots resounded through the entire inn, along with the hushing of several patrons quieting each other. The growing silence became deafening, and Lenora wished they would all talk again so she didn't focus on her racing heartbeat.

"What's going on here?" she heard Pedro shout, even though the entire inn had quieted.

A single pair of footsteps broke the silence until they came to a brisk stop. Then the sound of an arrogant voice reached her ears. "Are you the owner?"

"Yes, along with my wife. Now what business do you have bringing a dozen soldiers into our establishment?"

Lenora felt Xander's chest rise. They must have both realized the same thing at the same time. Twelve soldiers. They couldn't escape from twelve of them. Not with her leg like this.

"Search the place," came the soldier's prideful voice. Lenora filed it away in her memory. She wanted to recognize his voice if she ever escaped and saw him again.

A dozen sets of boots stomped on the wooden floor, and Lenora willed herself to remain still. Xander's body pressing against her helped. He stood as strong as a statue, giving her the inspiration she needed. She didn't know for certain, but she guessed these people could transform like Xander, and they were the wolves he scented while they were eating. They could probably transform from human to wolf, just like Xander could from human to bear.

If that were true, then their sense of hearing and smell would be strong. Which meant she couldn't move, couldn't make a sound, otherwise they'd know she was there.

She and Xander stood that way, inside the tiny alcove in the kitchen, for several long minutes.

"Come, now," María said after a while, her tone rising. "If you tell us what you're looking for, we could help you."

"She's not here, Captain Acosta," came another voice, one Lenora hadn't heard yet.

The captain growled. "I can still smell her. You, owner, get me the guest book." After some shuffling, Lenora heard the sound of a book slamming closed. "You're sure this is everyone who's checked into this inn? Have you seen a girl with brown and gold hair, wearing a black dress? Possibly with a leg injury?"

Lenora's hands flew to Xander's chest, grasping his gray shirt. He also tensed, his grip tightening on her waist. Their breaths mingled as she stared up into his eyes, feeling his apprehension rise. She realized how close they were—she could see the tiny specks of dark brown inside his golden eyes and feel the crispiness of his raggedy shirt. Slowly, she pried her fingers from his clothing, carefully tucking them against her chest. His hold, however, remained steady on her, keeping her in place.

"No, sir, we haven't," Pedro answered, his words strong.

The captain growled again, cursing.

"She could be hiding somewhere else in town," the other soldier said, though he sounded unsure.

"Let's continue our search," the captain said, the smugness returning to his tone. "The entire port's locked down, so there's nowhere else for her to go. We'll find her eventually."

Boots scrambled around for a minute, and then the front door slammed shut. Lenora breathed in deeply, but she refused to move an inch. Xander, still holding onto her, stayed where he was—between her and the kitchen door.

After another minute, the patrons returned to their conversation, though much of the joy was missing from their voices. The door behind Xander creaked, and he looked over his shoulder before he exhaled in relief.

He backed out of the alcove, and Lenora caught María's and Pedro's upset faces.

"What's going on, Xander?" María whispered, though her tone was harsh. "Why are you hiding from the palace guards?"

Xander looked back at Lenora, who gave him a nod. The entire time she listened to the soldiers running up and down the inn, ordering María and Pedro around, she worried they would be angry at her for bringing this upon them.

Lenora stepped forward, meeting their eyes. "They're looking for me." She quickly explained who she was and what she knew, including stumbling into Xander's house and how he was helping her find a ship back home. Now that she spoke it aloud, she realized how she had involved three innocent people in her mess. She opened her mouth to apologize when María cut her off.

"You heard what the soldier said. The port is closed—locked down. The only way you can get back to Norraine is through another kingdom."

Xander, who had been running his hand through his dreads, stiffened. "Like Alegría." He looked at Pedro, then his gaze flitted to María, and the three of them seemed to have a silent conversation.

María finally broke their eye contact and turned a sorrowful expression toward Lenora. "I'm sorry, Your Highness, but the path into Alegría is ... treacherous. First, you have to go through the Dark Forest, where the wolf guards regularly hunt. Then you have to travel through *El Abismo*, the Great Gorge. The canyon is littered with all manner of creatures. Most of them crave blood. I'm sorry, but you wouldn't survive the journey."

"That's why I'm taking her."

Lenora, who had hung her head, snapped her attention to Xander. He stood with his head held high, brimming with confidence. Her mouth fell open as she stared in awe at his composure when all she wanted to do was lie down in defeat.

Pedro shook his head. "You can't go."

"You *shouldn't* go," María retorted.

"It wasn't a question." Xander looked down at them, though he was just as tall as Pedro, and María was not much shorter. "I'm the only one who can make sure she gets there safely. I've made the journey before, and I can do it again. That's the end of this discussion."

Lenora noted their lowered eyes and how they closed their lips tightly together.

She knew that expression. She saw it every day. The question was, why did these elders stare at Xander as if he were in charge?

Twelve

Xander led the way upstairs to the third floor. At the last door in the hall, he brandished the key Pedro gave him and opened it. Stepping aside, he motioned for her to enter first.

Lenora walked inside, surveying the cozy space. An unlit fireplace and a square table took up the left side of the room, and a small bed lay in the middle of them. On the right, an open door revealed a small bathroom with a bathtub, sink, and toilet. She sighed, eager to hop right into the tub.

Xander hovered at the door, one foot on either side of the threshold. "While you rest, I'll go find some supplies for our journey."

"Xander," she began, taking four strides until she stood before him. "You don't have to do this. I'm a complete stranger, and this path is dangerous. I can't ask you to risk your life for me. My guards... They're probably already dead. If something happens to you, I wouldn't forgive myself."

He smiled, a soft, gentle curve of his lips. "*Eres increíble*," he whispered, bringing his hand to her chin.

Lenora closed her eyes for a moment, melting at his tone. "I have no idea what you're saying."

Xander chuckled, then stuffed his hands back into his pockets.

"You're incredible. You're going through something so horrible, yet you stop to think about others before yourself."

She frowned, folding her arms across her middle. "If I had thought about my guards—"

"Don't do that," he interrupted, shaking his head. "They did what they were supposed to do. They protected you so you could escape. So you could get home and return with your own army. Like you said, Prince Remy will pay for this. He'll pay for underestimating you."

Her chest swelled with pride—pride she hadn't felt in ages. Someone believed in her, someone she didn't know. But if Xander really knew her, would he be saying those kind words? If he knew the danger lurking behind one touch of her hands, would he look at her with those gentle hazel eyes of his?

He took a half-step closer, and she held her breath at his closeness. Then he paused, his mouth parted as if he meant to say more, but he shook his head. He reached into his bag and retrieved the tin can with the healing ointment, passing it to her with a wary eye on her hands. "I'll be back soon, *princesa*. Hopefully with a change of clothes for both of us. Try to rest. We'll leave at dawn."

He hesitated by the door, looking over at her with pursed lips. Then he left, closing the door behind him.

Lenora waited, staring at the closed door for several heartbeats. She'd never felt this rush, this sense of weightlessness, before. Her traitorous heart went back to Lawrence, clenching as she thought about him sacrificing himself for her. If they had stayed in Norraine, he'd still be alive. All of her guards would. How much different would her life be if she never became the ambassador? If her mother had simply voted against Lenora's wishes? She would have remained in her comfortable castle, hiding behind thick gloves and her charm necklace, stuck inside the shell of the person she could have been.

And I wouldn't have met Xander.

She groaned, forgoing the bath in favor of sleep. Stumbling her way to the bed, she threw herself on top of it. Finally, her thoughts slowed, and she fell into a fitful sleep.

When she awoke, she lurched forward, sitting upright. The sudden jolt made her aching body throb, and she cursed her anxious mind.

Sighing, she pushed herself up and walked on aching legs to the window, pulling back the curtain to look down into the empty alley. Only the full moon in the night sky lit up the street, since the few lampposts lining the alley had tiny candles that didn't spread their light wide enough.

A clock on the wall beside her showed it was well past midnight. Xander still hadn't returned, so she walked into the bathroom, resorting to cleaning herself up with the supplies provided by the inn rather than taking an actual bath. With a fresh, soaked towel, she wiped at her injuries and applied more of Xander's salve, then covered the open wound on her ankle with torn strips of clean cloth.

She wet her hair in the sink, then ran her fingers through her tangled curls, ignoring the dirt and grime. After a few minutes of detangling, she applied a bit of hair oil from one of the bottles lining the sink and twisted it in a bun at the nape of her neck. Since the guards had used her hair as an identifier, she'd have to conceal it as much as possible.

Then she returned to the bed, perching on the corner and staring at the door.

Waiting.

After a half hour, she stood and paced the floor—noticing with a grimace how that was her mother's signature move whenever she was worried.

She forced her swollen feet to still, but her hands wrung around each other.

JENNIFER ROACHFORD

How many hours had it been since Xander left for supplies? Two, maybe three?

She hopped on one foot to the window, hoping to catch a glimpse of him walking into the inn. Resting her head against the cool glass, she shut her eyes. She was a princess, not some love-sick sap, waiting for a stranger to rescue her.

She could save herself.

Her father had taught her well, and she had her mother's blood running through her veins. She would survive the Dark Forest and the Great Gorge on her own.

Besides, she didn't want anything bad to happen to Xander. He brought her to Port Arcadia like he said he would—she wouldn't further subject him to her messy situation. If she left him behind, he'd be safe.

Lenora hobbled to the door, easing it open and then closing it as quietly as she could. Through the hall, she walked with soft feet as she came up with a plan. She would likely have to steal some supplies, but when she returned with her mother, she would come back and compensate—no, overcompensate the people she stole from. One of those items would have to be a compass so she could navigate the forest and the dreaded canyon. Then she would find a port along Alegría's west coast. Surely they had a harbor and ships.

She combed through her memory, but she came up short. She knew very little about Alegría. All she remembered was an old trade deal and how her mother had reworked it several years ago, but other than a few casual mentions, Norraine's history books had next to zero knowledge of the kingdom. This was how closed off her people were from the rest of the world. And why she needed to change it.

When she made it to the bottom level, she surveyed the inn. Not a single guest lingered around the dining hall or the foyer. She hurried to the front door, but the sound of another door opening and voices erupting from the kitchen made her pause.

Xander.

He had probably just returned with the promised supplies, and here she was, sneaking away like a thief in the night.

But it's for the best. He doesn't need to be involved in this.

She reached for the handle when she heard an angry shout.

"Are you crazy?"

That was María.

Xander shushed her, and Lenora found herself drifting closer to the kitchen.

"You're going to get yourself killed," María continued, but only a little quieter.

"I've already decided, María," Xander whispered.

"Why are you willing to risk your life going back home?" Pedro asked, his voice barely audible. "You know they'll kill you on sight."

"I have my reasons." Lenora squinted at Xander's voice. He used that phrase with her when she had asked him why he was helping her.

"Do those reasons involve fulfilling a death wish?" Lenora pictured María saying that with her hands on her hips. She crept closer to the bar, then walked around it on the tips of her boots as María continued. "Word is spreading around town that the entire Newton family was massacred, and that Prince Remy is the only one to have survived because *he* was the one who killed them. People know what happened now, and everyone knows the castle is looking for the missing princess from Norraine. There's even a reward for information."

"Are you sure you want to do this, Your Highness?" Pedro's question made Lenora frown.

Your Highness?

She pressed her ear against the door, waiting for Xander's answer with bated breath.

The door swung away from her face, and Lenora almost fell forward. She stared up at Xander's face, his expression as hard as stone. Behind him, María and Pedro stared with comically wide eyes.

Lenora backed away, and Xander followed. He gave away nothing with his eyes or the tight set of his lips. She couldn't read him, but she could definitely feel the change in his aura.

"Why did you leave the room?" he asked, holding two bags at his sides.

Lenora had never experienced someone demanding anything from her. This simple question made her feel compelled to answer, and she was not one to obey *anyone*. "I didn't know I was a prisoner."

He worked his jaw and took a step back. "You're not. I'm sorry." He rubbed a hand down his face, and she saw the exhaustion for a moment before he put a mask on his features. She narrowed her eyes. Did he always wear a facade? Was she just now noticing? Her heart pounded as she reminded herself she knew absolutely nothing about this man.

María and Pedro muttered their excuses, then slipped from the room, and Lenora eyed them all the way through the hall until they ascended the stairs.

As soon as they disappeared, she rounded on Xander. "You lied to me." There was no point in pretending she didn't hear their conversation.

He pressed a finger to his lips, then waved for her to follow him. Reluctantly, she obeyed and walked quietly behind him up to her room.

Xander allowed her entry first, then closed the door behind them and set the bags on the floor. "Okay—"

"Who are you?" Lenora interrupted, her tone an angry whisper. She huffed, throwing her hands in the air and letting them slam into her sides. "Forget '*what* are you?' *Who* are you, Xander? Tell me the truth." She stood in the middle of the room, her chest rising and falling with her anger and confusion.

He remained by the door, as if refusing to get too close. "I wasn't supposed to tell anyone."

She crossed her arms. "I've been honest with you since we met. I guess my mistake was trusting a stranger."

Xander leaned against the door and closed his eyes. "I'm supposed to be dead, Lenora."

She dropped her arms, and her mouth fell agape. "What?"

He pushed himself up and met her in the middle of the room. "No one is supposed to know I'm alive. If anyone finds out, I'll be killed."

Lenora took a step back. "Xander, this is... You're scaring me."

"I know, *princesa*, I know." He sighed, then rolled his eyes toward the ceiling. "Goddess, help me."

She continued backing up until her ruined ankle hit the bed frame. "Xander?"

"My name is not Xander," he said, meeting her eyes. "My real name is Alejandro. My birth name is Alejandro Suárez Vega, Prince of Alegría."

Lenora was sure her lungs stopped working, that her heart stopped pumping. "I don't understand."

"My brother..." He trailed off, turning away so Lenora could only see the back of his head.

"That's why Pedro said you're going back home." Her thoughts ran a million miles away, going over everything she'd seen and heard in the last day. "That's why they're worried. They don't want you to go back. Were you exiled?"

He blew out a breath, and when he looked at her, her heart nearly broke. Xander's mask completely disappeared, replaced by teary eyes and a frown. "I wish it were as simple as that."

Lenora moved closer, her feet carrying her forward. She wanted to reach out to him, but the bareness of her skin kept her hands at her side. "What happened?"

"I have an older brother, Augustín," he began again. "Five years ago, he went on a rampage. He killed our parents and our middle brother, Luís. He ... tried to kill me, but I survived. Barely. He broke my legs and beat me unconscious. When I awoke, it was to the sight of my family lying on top of each other, dead. I stayed that way for two days until my uncle Ernesto found us. He told me what Augustín did, then he carried me to a safe house. He charged some of the townspeople with my recovery and paid them to stay quiet while he went back to Alegría. Then he returned a few months later to whisk me away to Newton. To the cabin you found in the Dark Forest. He told me to hide out and that he would come back for me."

He paused, his eyes locked on hers. "But as I waited, I grew angrier. My brother took everything from me. My parents, Luís, my home, my people. I started plotting my revenge, working out how I could avenge my family and make Augustín pay for what he did. When Tío Ernesto returned a year later, I had already made my plan. He agreed, and he's been helping me ever since. So that's why I'm willing to risk this journey. Why I'm willing to return to Alegría. I want to make sure you get home safely, yes. But also because it's finally my time."

Lenora couldn't take her eyes off of Xander.

No. Alejandro.

"Our stories," Lenora whispered. "They're similar. Well, it's not my brother who is trying to kill me, but a relative. And he killed his entire family."

"I know," Alejandro said, shaking his head. "That's why I want to make sure you're safe. If something happened to you..." He stepped closer, his chest rising and falling as he breathed deeply.

Lenora's entire body thrummed with an invisible energy. She had said those words to him. She felt the same way.

What in the Fates' names is going on?

Thirteen

D awn's light greeted Lenora's face in a warm caress through the crack in the curtain. She rubbed her blurry eyes, ignoring the small gashes on her hands and arms. Sitting up in bed, she parted her loose hair down the middle, braided it into two thick strands, and tucked them into each other behind her head. Last night, after Alejandro left for his own room, she took a Fates' blessed bath in hot water and washed away all the blood and dirt from her hair and body.

That was when she got a good look at her wounds. Most were bruises or scratches, but there were several deep slices—likely from the wolves' claws and teeth—and her ankle looked much worse once she cleaned away all the grime. She had applied more of Alejandro's healing ointment before dressing it in a proper medical wrap. With the healing magic woven directly into the salve, she knew her ankle would heal quickly.

Then she'd eyed the clothes Alejandro had bought for her. Obviously the man was perceptive—he had picked out a simple black tunic with black leggings. Her favorite color combination.

A swift knock at the door had her throwing the blankets off her body. When she opened it, she found Alejandro already dressed in a black shirt and loose-fitting black trousers, his bag thrown over his shoulder.

"Ready?" he asked, leaning his arm on the frame.

Lenora raised a finger. "Just let me grab my bag." She hurried to the corner of the room and picked it up, grateful for the weight. It meant he had packed enough for their journey and didn't assume she couldn't carry a heavy load, even with her injuries. The last thing she needed was to be reminded—yet again—how everyone underestimated her abilities.

The inn was quiet this early, so they passed through the main lobby and straight into the kitchen, where María hovered over a boiling pot. Next to her, Pedro leaned against the counter.

Pedro straightened when they entered, then extended his arm for Alejandro. "It's time, then?"

"It is." Alejandro embraced him the same way he did yesterday—each of their hands clasped around the other's forearm. Lenora observed the way Alejandro held on a little too long, and how Pedro didn't make a move out of the hold. She even noted how María placed her hands over her mouth, on the verge of tears.

The woman let them fall, though, when Alejandro turned to her and pulled her into a hug. "Don't cry, María. We knew this day would come."

She batted him away, then used the corner of her apron to wipe her cheeks. "I'm just worried." She side-eyed Lenora. "Be safe, please."

Alejandro sighed. "You know what's coming. But if everything goes according to plan, I'll send for you. You'll be able to come home. After everything you've done for me, I'll make sure you're taken care of."

Pedro patted Alejandro's shoulder. "We didn't help you all these years to get anything out of it in the end. We've all suffered. You maybe more than anyone. As long as you fix Alegría, we'll be happy."

With a nod, Alejandro turned to Lenora, and suddenly all eyes were on her. She had been so caught up watching their exchange, she wasn't prepared for their teary eyes to greet her.

She had never been good at handling emotions—hers or anyone else's.

Lenora put on a grateful smile. These people didn't have to feed her or give her a place to stay, especially after the palace guards had burst into their establishment. "Thank you for your assistance last night. And for your amazing food. I'll always remember the first time I had mole."

Saying the word brought a watery smile to María's face. She grabbed two sealed metal containers from the counter and passed one to her and the other to Alejandro. "I packed you some of last night's leftovers."

"I already grabbed some dried meats and nuts," Alejandro said, but he took the offered package of food.

"*No seas tonto*," María said, cringing at him. "Don't be silly. You don't want to start a four-day journey on an empty stomach."

Lenora almost dropped her box. "Four days?" Norraine was looking smaller and smaller at every turn. It only took two days to travel from one end of her little island to the other.

Alejandro smiled, but it looked more like a grimace to Lenora's incredulous eyes. "Did I not mention that?"

"No," she said, but sighed, resigned to the fact that her journey would take four full days. Going to Alegría was the only option, since it was Newton's only bordering kingdom. "But we'll be all right."

"*After* you eat your breakfast," María added, motioning to the food.

Once they polished off their meal, they thanked María and Pedro one more time before they sneaked out the back door. Lenora's ankle already throbbed in her boot as they made their way through Port Arcadia's side streets and into the Dark Forest.

The thick tree cover cooled the land, but she welcomed the chilly air and the distraction it provided, even as a shudder ran through her.

Alejandro raised an eyebrow. "Should I have grabbed you a sweater?"

"I'm glad you didn't," she said, her eyes trailing up to admire the trees. "This kind of reminds me of home."

"You live in the woods?"

Lenora's lips pulled into an infinitesimal curve, and she met his grinning face. "I meant my father's estate. Before he married my mother and became king consort, he was the lord of Talin, which is famous for its apple orchards. We would go to Talin every fall for the apple festival. The trees... They remind me of Talin and apple picking with my family."

And I hope I'll see them again.

She didn't voice that last thought, but the way Alejandro looked down at his boots let her know she didn't need to.

"In Alegría," Alejandro said, looking at her again, "there are trees everywhere. My parents..." He paused, turning his gaze forward. "They used to let us climb the tallest ones around the castle. As high as we could go. Luís and I would always make it a competition. Who could make it to the top the fastest? I was three years younger, so I always lost. I thought I would never beat him. But one year, papá took me out every day for a month to practice. He taught me how to dig my claws into the bark and how to haul myself up. Then, one day, I challenged Luís again. And I finally beat him to the top of the tallest tree."

Lenora pursed her lips. "You did this in your bear form?"

He gave her a smirk. "You didn't think I climbed trees with my nails, did you?"

Ignoring his sarcasm, she rolled her eyes. "It's a serious question."

"That's right. I guess you don't really know." He rubbed a hand down his face. "Okay, where do I start? My people... We can change from human to bear—and back, of course. Most of us can control it, but there are rare circumstances that can cause a person to lose control over their shift. Children have to be taught when it's an appropriate time to be human or bear. But for the most part, both forms are acceptable. We're encouraged to be comfortable in both forms and to shift at any given time. So, climbing trees would be done while in bear form. Using utensils at the dinner table in human form. Holding court could be done in either, depending on the message that needed to be shared. And the kind of mood my father was in."

She thought back to her lessons under Miss Tabitha's tutelage and her mother's teachings growing up. Elice had always told her Norraine knew very little about the world outside of its tiny island. Is this what her mother meant? Did Elice know there were people who could change into bears?

"The wolves..." She paused, wondering how to phrase her question. "When they attacked me, there was a moment when I thought they could understand me—both my actions and my words."

Alejandro nodded, waiting for her to continue. "Go ahead. Ask me."

"Can they shift too?" she blurted, then immediately regretted her words.

Of course they can't, Lenny! They were just wolves!

Though crazier things had happened—Alejandro was living proof that people who transformed into animals existed.

He sighed. "They can. The ones who hunted you in the forest are part of the palace's special guard. They're shifters, just like me, only they can change into wolves."

Lenora narrowly avoided an exposed root, and she limped around it. "How many other creatures are there?"

"Oh, lots," he answered, then frowned. "Alegría used to be a land of shifters. But once Augustín took over, he banished every type other than bears. He wanted Alegría to be a land of only bear shifters."

"Why?"

Alejandro shrugged. "Tío Ernesto thinks he just wanted to control everything with an iron fist. He made illogical moves only because he could. So he could feel like he had more power."

"But you don't think so?"

With his hands stuffed in his pockets, he stopped walking. "I think my brother was cursed."

A chill ran down Lenora's arms. She halted, turning on her good leg to look back at Alejandro. "What do you mean?"

"What else would drive someone to murder their entire family? He was only eighteen."

She blinked, taken aback. "He was just a kid." Looking away, she focused on the sound of her breathing. It came it short bursts as she tried not to show how the word "cursed" affected her.

Alejandro placed a hand on her shoulder, and the touch shocked her out of her own mind.

"Hey," he said, removing his hand, "I'm sorry. I didn't mean to scare you."

She shook her head, taking a step backward. "I didn't... I'm not..."

"We don't have to talk about Augustín. Or what he did. Sometimes I forget not many people had to go through what I went through. I must be ... desensitized or something."

"It's not that." She shook her head, then wrapped her arms around her middle.

Alejandro stepped into her view, lowering his head so it was level with hers. "What's wrong?"

She turned her head, but he caught her chin and brought it back. When she finally met his eyes, they held so much warmth, she almost melted. His honey eyes reflected the thin rays of sunlight that peeked through the leaves overhead.

"Please, tell me, Lenora," he whispered. "I want to know what I said that made you react this way."

"Cursed," she said, hugging herself tighter. By the Fates, she wished she could control herself around him. She had spent years bottling everything up, but just one look into his hazel eyes and all her hard work was gone. She'd only known the man for one day. "You said 'cursed.'"

Alejandro pulled back, lowering his hand. "I did."

Lenora closed her eyes. When she opened them again, the space between Alejandro's eyes had knitted close together. "Everyone back home called me cursed, too."

His eyebrows shot up. "*Diosa*. I didn't mean—"

She shook her head as she interrupted him. "I know. I know I overreacted. It's been ... a long couple of days."

Alejandro remained quiet, watching her with his knowing eyes. "This has something to do with your fear of touch. The reason you avoid touching people."

"How did you even notice that?" She remembered him saying that within a day of meeting her.

He shrugged. "I watched you closely. Noticed how you brandished your dagger, waving it like you were trying to keep me away."

"You were an eight-foot bear at the time." She raised an eyebrow, then blew out a heavy sigh.

He eyed her from head to toe. "You still don't get too close, and you keep your hands behind your back or tight to your body. Then that whole thing with the broken bowl If I'm wrong, tell me. But I don't think I am."

Lenora used the toe of her boot to dig a small hole in the dirt, her eyes following the motion as she spoke. "You're not wrong, but it's more complicated than a simple fear of touch."

Alejandro angled closer, but he kept a comfortable distance between them as he waited for her to continue.

She met his eyes, surprised to find them so open and inviting. He didn't say a word. The softness in his posture and the slight tilt of his head let her know she was free to continue or stop if she chose. The option lay with her, and her heart called out, reaching for some outlet for all the pain and grief she felt because of her powers.

"I'm cursed," she began, watching as his eyes widened a bit. "I was born like this. Every day of my life has been in a constant state of worry. I'm a mage—a seer—but my type of power is rare. Like most other seers, my visions are triggered by touching someone. Others see happier moments in a person's life, like births or marriages. But not me. My visions are of the person's death. That's it. I don't get to see anything else. Only death."

Lenora scoffed, throwing her offending hands into the air. "And to make it impossibly worse, I also share the vision with the person I touch. Isn't it bad enough I can't even touch my own parents because I'll see the moment they die? My little brother and sister? No, if I ever touch them, I have to show them their death as well."

She turned around, crossing her arms over her chest. "So you can imagine what life was like for me. No one wanted to play tag with the girl who had the cursed sight, even if she was a princess. The servants avoided walking down the same hallway as me in case we bumped into each other. I've lost so many maids over the years because they couldn't stand to be in the same room as me. And when I finally made a friend, I…"

Samantha.

She forced away the memory of that day. Sucking in a choked breath, she desperately held back the sob that begged to release from her throat. "I accidentally touched her. I started wearing gloves after that. All day, every day, until two days ago when Prince Tyree ripped them off while trying to kill me." Lenora unfurled her arms, then looked down at her hands. "I used my powers to show him his death. We both saw Remy use his earth powers to stab a branch through Tyree's back. That's why I was able to escape—Tyree let me go. He knew he was going to die anyway."

A bird chirped into the otherwise silent forest. Lenora's words hung like thick branches in the air, waiting to fall. She closed her eyes, half expecting Alejandro to run now that he knew she was cursed with such a horrible power.

When his warm palm landed on her shoulder, she spun around, wanting to face him, to see if he held the same fear in his eyes that everyone else had.

Yet there was only kindness. Warmth. Understanding. No anger, terror, or even pity hid within in his gaze.

His finger went to her cheek, wiping away a traitorous tear. She hadn't realized she'd shed one.

"There's no reason to fear death," he said, his voice full and strong. "Only the weak fear the things they don't understand."

She shook her head, her heart skipping a beat. "You don't mean that."

"I do. I'm not afraid of death, only of dying without fulfilling my purpose. I have to avenge my family. I have to face Augustín. And I have to kill him. If I die with him, then so be it. But knowing when or how I die—that doesn't scare me."

Lenora almost laughed—or cried, she wasn't sure which. No one had ever said anything like that before. In fact, she had always gotten the exact opposite. She dug into her bag and pulled out the crystal charm necklace her mother had given her, letting the gemstone dangle in front of her face. "I've always used this to keep my powers under control. It's a protection charm, made by a powerful healer. The chain's broken, which means I can't wear it, so it won't work like it's supposed to."

Alejandro eyed the necklace, then slowly reached a hand out to tap a finger against the glistening gem hanging at the end of the chain. "It's beautiful." He raised his eyes, the specks of honey sparkling brighter than the stone.

Her heart panged, and she forced herself to look away. She lowered her hand, tucking the necklace back into her bag.

Alejandro opened his mouth, but whatever he wanted to say was interrupted by a howl deep within the forest.

Fourteen

W e should keep moving," Alejandro said, his hand shooting out to her elbow.

She nodded, her breath suddenly escaping her.

He ushered her along, his grip light but steady on her arm. "It sounds far away, but we're traveling slow. At this rate, we'll get to the Great Gorge by midday."

"I can pick up my pace." Lenora stepped with less force on her injured foot, making her quick hobble look ridiculous.

Alejandro slowed down, causing her to match his speed. "No need. You'll only hurt yourself more. The wolves can smell me from at least a mile away. My scent is a greater deterrent than the whiff they can pick up from you."

"I don't get it," she admitted. "Aren't they after me? Direct orders and such? Wouldn't they do whatever it takes to capture me?"

He gave her a sidelong glance. "They wouldn't risk it."

"Are you saying they're too afraid of you?" When he didn't answer, she smirked. "What did you do to them?"

He released her elbow to scratch at his head. "Wolf and bear shifters kind of have a ... history."

Lenora sidestepped a rock, not wanting to risk tripping on it. "I'm listening."

Alejandro chuckled. "I guess it *is* my turn to share."

"I never agreed to any formal rules, but if it helps pass the time, I suppose we could take turns sharing."

He huffed out a laugh. "One question each, then?"

"Deal."

"I'd say let's shake on it, but…"

Lenora scoffed, placing a hand over her heart. "Your Highness, that was quite rude."

His grin nearly broke her heart, causing her to lose her footing. She snapped her eyes forward, staring intently at the ground as she walked.

"Okay," he said, "what's your question?"

"Just what I asked. Are the wolves … no, wait." She caught herself before she asked him a basic yes or no question. Knowing Alejandro for all of two days, he would wiggle his way out of fully answering. All while wearing a heart-stopping smile. "*Why* are the wolves so afraid of bears?"

"Good question," he muttered. Rubbing his chin, he pursed his lips. "That's a more recent development. We used to have good relations with all shifters. My father's right-hand man, Juan Lopez, was a wolf and colonel in his army, *el Cambiante Militar*. But once my brother took power, he exiled every shifter that wasn't a bear. Tío Ernesto told me how difficult those first few months of Augustín's reign were for the other shifters. If his soldiers found anyone who wasn't a bear shifter, they were killed on sight. Naturally, the other types fled, and many bear shifters left with them—like Pedro and María. Alegría has been in a state of deterioration ever since, yet my brother refuses to do anything to fix it.

"Anyway, the wolves are wary of my scent because I'm a bear shifter. They tend to stay far away from my territory and never get close too me whenever I'm hunting. Pedro said the wolves went through a rough period of transition when they sought refuge in Newton before they got hired on by King Jerome. And ... well, you saw how big I am in my bear form. Wolves don't stand a chance against a fully grown bear."

At the end, he winked, then pushed away a low-lying branch. He held it aloft while she passed under it.

Her mind reeled with the new information, dozens of questions forming on her tongue. She blurted the first one that came out. "How many other shifters are there?"

Alejandro settled the branch back in place. "I believe it's my turn, *princesa*."

Hiding her smile, she ducked her head and continued walking. "Fine. What's your question?"

He walked right beside her. "When we first met, you said you came to Newton as Norraine's ambassador." At her nod, he continued. "What were you supposed to do? You know, before Remy murdered his entire family."

"You have such a way with words, Xander." Lenora rolled her eyes.

Alejandro sighed, then scrubbed a hand down his face. "I'm too blunt for my own good. María blamed it on my seclusion. I... I don't spend a lot of time with other people."

She nodded, her chest aching at his words. She knew exactly how it felt to be alone.

He bumped her shoulder, causing her to look up at his weak smile. "You're trying to distract me. It's your turn to share, not mine."

"Right. I was supposed to learn as much as I could about Newton to bring back home. We're in a peaceful time right now, but it wasn't always like this. We went through a series of civil wars that weakened us. Our people fought each other, and many of our kings were killed, leaving their young children to take their place. It was a time of constant instability until my mother officially ended the war. It took a few years to reopen our borders, then a few more to allow better communication with Newton, where Norraine's founders originally hailed from. Where my ancestors were from. When King Jerome finally agreed to host an ambassador, the council chose me."

She shrugged, remembering the day like it was yesterday, though it had been a couple of weeks since she'd received the news. "I've always wanted to come to Newton. My parents always talked about their days fighting the fire mages and how they learned there was so much beyond our small island. I blame them for my obsession with travel. I could never sit still, even as a child—even with my curse. So, when the council wanted to send someone to Newton to represent them, I applied. Mother was against it, and Father didn't seem too excited about me leaving, but they supported my choice, anyway."

Alejandro nodded along with her. "It sounds like you have good parents. You speak so highly of them."

"My whole family is amazing." A genuine smile broke onto her face as she thought of them. "Mother is so ... so *powerful*. She can control three elements—air, earth, and water."

Alejandro's eyes flew open. "Even I know that's unheard of."

Lenora nodded. "She's also a dream walker. She can pass into the spirit and mind realms and talk with people's spirits. And my father, James, taught me everything I know about fighting. He was the youngest captain in Norraine's history."

"So I can blame him for the nick on my neck?" He chuckled, running a finger along the faint scab.

Lenora gave him an apologetic look. "Then there's my younger brother, James the Second," she continued, "who's the splitting image of our father. Except he's an earth mage, whereas my father doesn't have any magic. And my sister, Patricia. She's only fourteen, but she has amazing control of her air powers. Well, when she's focused. But I'm not worried about her. I know she'll grow into her own formidable force one day."

Silence settled in after her words, and she awkwardly tugged at the hem of her tunic.

Alejandro brushed his shoulder against hers again. "And what about you?"

Lenora frowned at her boots. "What about me?"

"You're part of your family, too. You listed what made everyone else special. What about you?"

She lifted her gaze to his and threw his words back at him. "You're trying to distract me. It's your turn. How many other types of shifters are there?"

He sighed, but she noted the slight quirk on his lips at her avoidance of the question. "A few. Besides bears and wolves, there are large birds, big cats like jaguars and cougars, and some people can shift into reptiles and sea creatures. Alegría used to be very diverse, but now the shifters have scattered south to other lands. My uncle believes they're doing okay, but there's no way to know for sure without direct communication with them." She opened her mouth to ask another question, but he beat her to it. "Now, back to you. What makes you special?"

Lenora blew out a breath. "Nothing."

He stopped, and she had to pivot on her good ankle to meet his stare. "That's not true. I've only known you for two days and I already know you're extraordinary."

She crossed her arms. "You hardly know me, Xander."

He raised his hand and counted off each finger. "You're brave, smart, strong, loyal, fierce when you have a dagger in your hand—"

"Xander—" She cut him off, but he continued, raising his other hand and lifting more fingers, one at a time.

"You're fearsome even without a weapon. Your magic is so rare, you're literally one of a kind. Your hair..." He swallowed, his eyes taking in her hair braided at the back of her neck, the golden strands peaking through the top of her head. "It marks you as special on the outside to match how unique you are on the inside. You're ... beautiful, Lenora. But what makes you so special is your determination. I've never met anyone so stubborn. You're hobbling around the Dark Forest, being chased by wolf shifters who will bring you straight to Stonehold if they catch you, and you show no sign of defeat. That's... That's remarkable."

Lenora released her breath. How did she not realize she had been holding it? She sucked in the cool air, using it to calm her thoughts. No one outside her family had ever spoken to her—or about her—like that before. Not even Lawrence.

A strangled breath caught in her throat. She thought about Lawrence and the other guards who swore to protect her. Where were they now? They were likely dead, all because of her. If she had gone back for them, fought harder for them, maybe she could have saved at least one. If she hadn't come to Newton in the first place...

Alejandro stepped forward and placed a hand on her elbow. "I keep making you sad. What did I say this time?"

She shut her eyes, but an incredulous laugh left her mouth. "It's not you, Xander. I just ... remembered someone."

He stepped back, and her eyes snapped open at his sudden jolt.

"Oh?" He scratched the side of his head. "Is that a good or bad thing?"

Uncrossing her arms, she swung them behind her back in her usual comfortable stance. "You said I was loyal, but I'm not. I came to Newton with several guards, and I left them all behind. One of them, Lawrence—he was my only friend. He was with me when I overheard Remy and Tyree's plot. He wanted to help me escape, but I sent him back for the rest of my guards. And then I left him. He's probably dead now. I could have gone back for him. I could have saved him. Tell me, Xander, does that sound like loyalty to you?"

"What would have happened if you had gone back for him?" He waited for her to answer, but all she did was stare at the ground. "You would have died, Lenora. Remy would have killed you if he found you. I know it hurts, but trust me, holding onto the past will only make it harder to move forward."

She bit the inside of her cheek, the pain making her forget about the tears that wanted to slip out of her eyes. "I don't know how to let go of the past."

He shuffled from one foot to the other, the leaves under his boots crunching and echoing in the forest. "I don't either. Maybe we could learn together."

When she looked at him, his eyes had clouded over, like he was remembering his own dark history.

"Maybe," she answered, and a shimmer, something that looked vaguely like hope, passed across his face.

Another howl met their ears, and Alejandro looked over his shoulder. "It's trailing us. I think it's picked up your scent." His eyebrows drew closer together. "He sounds ... agitated."

That made Lenora's eyes shoot open, her heart thumping inside its cage. "That's not a good thing, right?"

Alejandro shook his head. "Not at all. It either means he's signaling to the rest of his pack that he's found something important, or he's in distress."

"Like he's hurt?"

He looked away, then motioned forward so they could continue walking. Only when he fell in step with her limp did he answer. "Like he's desperate."

Fifteen

J ust after midday, with the sun blazing overhead, Lenora spotted the
first mountain. They had left the cover of the trees and had been
walking completely exposed in the valley between the mountains and the
Dark Forest. Now Mount Ravis stood before them in all its daunting
glory. They would need to hike across a winding path to get to the other
side.

Then they would be in the Great Gorge—the dry, rocky canyon that
housed horrifying creatures straight from her nightmares.

"But it's not so bad," Alejandro said, pulling Lenora from her
thoughts. He was telling her about his first journey across the Great
Gorge, which he called *El Abismo* in his language, when his uncle
brought him to Newton five years ago. "Once you make it past the
fifteen-foot-long venomous snakes. They're the worst."

Lenora raised an eyebrow. "You mean worse than the giant,
blood-sucking spiders?"

Alejandro laughed. "I guess my point of view is biased. The Ravis
winding snake is long, which makes it hard to get away when you're on
the run. Those things are fast and ridiculously powerful when they grab
hold of you. But I'm taller and stronger than the horned spider, so it's
no match for me."

She shook her head. "You mean you fought one of them before?"

"Both, actually. Tío Ernesto got bit by a spider when we slept in its cave during our first night. I had to shift fast to rip it apart before it drank all his blood."

The way Lenora's eyes widened made Alejandro laugh again.

"How tall were you as a bear at fifteen?" she asked.

He twisted his lips to the side. "Hmm. Probably a little shorter than my current height. Maybe seven feet. I don't remember exactly. But that's my point. I can take on a horned spider in my shifted form. The winding snake ... not so much."

"So, avoid the terrifying snakes. Got it."

"Avoid everything, if we can help it. We'll have to inspect every cave we rest in to make sure it's not a spider den, and we look out for any snake skins or tracks in the dirt so we don't happen upon one. Then there are the flesh-eating millipedes, the long-legged scorpion, the thorned bats—"

Lenora stopped at the foot of the mountain and rested her hands on her hips. "Xander, please don't make me turn around and walk back to Stonehold."

Alejandro spun toward her. At first, his eyes were wide, but when he saw the mischievous quirk of her lips, he broke out into a grin. "Don't worry, *princesa*, I'll protect you from the horrible canyon monsters."

She rolled her eyes, but a quiet laugh worked its way past her lips. "You're so goofy."

He took a step closer, his smile still on his lips. "Goofy, or insanely handsome?"

"Let's go," she mumbled, forcing herself to look away from his warm eyes as she walked past him.

"*Sí, princesa,*" she heard him mutter behind her back.

She ignored the way her heart tugged, how it seemed to lurch forward whenever he smiled at her. Yes, he was goofy, and he was also handsome. He was both, and so much more, but she couldn't gather her words properly to tell him. What good would it do, anyway? She was on her way back to Norraine, where she was fated to rule whenever her mother passed. He was on his own journey to Alegría, where he would face off against his cruel brother. They might as well have lived on opposite ends of the world, separated by duty and vengeance and fate.

After several minutes of trekking up the dirt path, Alejandro finally broke the silence. "I did it again, didn't I? I said something weird."

Lenora glanced at him before she returned her eyes to the sharply inclining mountain pass. Though the bleeding had stopped, her ankle still throbbed against the strips of cloth wrapped tightly around it. "What makes you assume that?"

"You got really quiet."

"I'm just..." She hated to use that word again, but it really did fit her best. "Contemplative. People say that about me all the time."

"I guess I'm just reading too much into your silence and your body language."

"You try to read me too much, Xander."

"You express yourself so well without having to say anything. I'm sorry for picking up on the little things. Like how you close your eyes to shut yourself away, or bite your lip to stop yourself from crying."

She halted, swallowing down her surprise. "I don't—"

"Maybe you don't notice it, but I do." He paused beside her, but another howl made him continue walking ahead.

Lenora looked down the mountain in the direction of the howl. They had climbed several feet, but they still had a long trip ahead. "How come we can hear it but not see it?"

His shoulders lifted in a shrug, but he didn't turn her way. "Maybe he's too far." Then he stopped, looking down at where she was looking.

"Although, we should see anything walking through the valley below us. Strange."

"Is it still just one wolf?" She walked to his side, and they both stared at the open expanse behind them.

"Seems like it. Maybe the pack hasn't caught up to him yet. That could be why he's keeping his distance. He won't engage until the rest of the pack has joined him."

"Do you understand their howls?"

He shook his head. "Nah. I can only feel the general intentions behind their noises."

"Is it the same for all shifters?"

Smirking, he shook his head again. "You're taking all my turns."

Lenora huffed, turning around and continuing her hike. "Go ahead."

"I was wondering about your hair," he said as he caught up to her. "Does everyone in your family have those gold streaks?"

"No, just me," she answered. She was used to physical activity, but her body was tired from walking all day and her ankle begged for a break. Breathing in a large gulp of air, she tried to focus on all the meditative tactics her mother had taught her, even though that had never been her specialty. They would rest once they reached the canyon. She just had to make it there in one piece. "What about you? The ends of your hair are yellow, like mine."

He grabbed a lock, staring at the tip. "This is common among my people. Sometimes the color gradients are different, but our hair tends to match the way our fur looks when shifted. That's why I was so interested in your hair. I didn't think it was common for mages, or even non-mages."

"It's not. It's why I got a lot of bothersome comments growing up. I never fit in with anyone back home."

"Well, you'd fit in well with the bear shifters." He smiled, then adjusted his bag over his shoulder. Blowing out a breath, he eyed the mountain pass. "Just a few more hours, then we can rest."

A soft sigh fell from her lips. "Good." She pumped her legs quicker, forgetting the twist her ankle gave with each step.

Just a few more hours.

The last step off the mountain pass felt like bliss. Lenora's entire body shook with anticipation and aching pain as they walked off the craggy path and onto dry dirt. The Great Gorge stretched out before her eyes, soaking up the sun as it angled across the sky. Light glistened off the red rock, and she could see all the cliffs and gaps that posed a hazardous threat if she drew too close. She followed the canyon's sight line until she met the horizon. The Great Gorge encompassed so much land that she couldn't even see the end where it crossed into Alegría.

A flat boulder sat off to the side, and she stumbled to it on one foot. Alejandro ran behind her, his arms around her waist and nearly carrying her to the seat.

"We made it," he mumbled, then shook off his pack to dig around for a canteen. "We can eat and drink here for a moment, but we should find somewhere to rest properly before the sun goes down. I don't want to explain why, just know that we should."

Lenora grabbed the water from his outstretched hand and chugged a large gulp. "I can figure out why, don't worry."

Alejandro broke a piece of dried meat in half, passing one to Lenora while he scarfed his down. "How's your foot? Do you need more time?"

She chewed quickly, thankful Miss Tabitha wasn't around to remind her of her lousy princess etiquette. "I'm good." Pushing herself up, she held back her groan. She tested the weight on her ankle, and though it was better after a few minutes of rest, she knew it needed more for it to fully heal. As soon as they found a cave, she would add extra healing salve. "Are there any healers in Alegría?"

"Unfortunately, no," he answered, frowning as he walked beside her. "My people don't use magic like mages do. Ours goes into transformation, which causes us to shift. But we have nurses who can create ointments and salves for you once we arrive. They might not be magical, but they are helpful."

"Where are we going, anyway? María and Pedro were so worried you would be killed as soon as we got to Alegría. Are we going to walk to a random town?" She realized how insane that would be and hoped he had a good plan to keep them away from his brother's soldiers.

The way the corner of his lips rose let her know he did have one. "I'll ignore the fact that it's my turn"—he raised an eyebrow at her eye roll—"because it's a good question. I should have told you sooner."

He led the way into the canyon, down a sloping trail that hugged close to the rocky wall. "Remember when I told you I came up with a plan? That my uncle agreed to help me with it?" He glanced over his shoulder, catching her nod before he faced forward. "Well, this is part of the plan. I've been designing this strategy for months, getting ready to return to Alegría. The timing has moved up a little, but in a way, that's helpful. It adds to the element of surprise I need. My uncle is supposed to meet me in Monte Paseo, which is a small town right by the border. This pass we're on will let out near the outskirts of the village. It's the same route we took when he saved me. In fact, Monte Paseo is the town he hid me in while I recovered from Augustín's attack."

"So," Lenora began, "your uncle's been waiting for you this whole time?"

Alejandro nodded. "I sent him a note while we were in Port Arcadia. That's what took me so long last night. I didn't just get supplies for our trip. I had to let him know to prepare for the next phase."

The footpath opened up to a wide plateau. Alejandro walked to the edge and whistled as he looked across. Lenora hurried as carefully as she could. The view of the gorge took her breath away. At the bottom, a river gleamed from the sun's rays as it rolled over the bedrock hundreds of feet below.

No, it must be thousands of feet below.

Lenora suddenly felt very unsure about standing so close to the ledge of the canyon, so she took a step back and looked around at the jagged rock formations. Some reached high into the sky, and she angled her neck to take in the sight.

After Alejandro finished inspecting the river, he walked toward her, his face serious and his shoulders set. "My uncle has been working for me for the past few years. Behind Augustín's back, he's gathered a growing force that understands how important it is to take down my brother. There are people who are sympathetic to my family, to the plight of the shifters who were forced from their homes. They think they're following Tío Ernesto, hoping to follow another member of the Suárez family out of the shambles Alegría currently sits in. But who they really follow is me. They just don't know it yet. Not until I show up in Monte Paseo to claim them as my army. When we arrive, they'll be waiting for us. And we'll use them to first get you a ship home and second to destroy Augustín's forces."

Lenora stared at the man before her with wonder in her eyes. He spoke so calmly, even though he talked of war. Whenever her parents brought up their war days, their voices held a hint of sadness, sometimes regret. She wondered if Alejandro would one day look back on these conversations with her. Would grief grip his thoughts, suffocating the old confidence he once felt? Or would he always be this proud, this strong, this sure of himself?

"How do you know the army will be there? That your uncle won't betray you?"

He tilted his head, considering her question as if he'd never thought about it before. "I don't, *princesa*. But I have faith. The goddess didn't have me survive what should have been a sure death, trek across this forsaken canyon, and live alone for five years, with nothing but the trees to keep me company, for no reason. I trust my uncle. If he wanted to betray me, he would have left me for dead. He would have abandoned me in Monte Paseo, or in *El Abismo*. He wouldn't have returned to Newton once a year with news of Alegría or prepare a full battle strategy. The army will be there waiting for me—for us."

"And this ship," she said. "You're sure you can secure one to take me all the way back to Norraine?"

He nodded as he reached out to tuck a stray curl behind her ear. "As soon as we arrive in Monte Paseo, I'll request a ship for you. There are a couple of weeks between this step and the next in my plan, so I'll take you myself to Puerto Nuevo, the closest port town. I want to make sure you board safely."

She looked away, but the ghost of his touch lingered near her face. "Thank you, Xander. I know we're not there yet, but it already feels like we made it to safety."

The downturn of his lips made it look like a wave of sorrow passed over him. "I only wish we had more time together before you had to leave."

The same swell washed over her, drowning her in the knowledge that soon she would have to say goodbye. "When I get home, I'll tell my mother everything. She'll be furious. We're going to have to come to Newton. Once I do, once I see that Remy is dealt with, I'll find you again."

Alejandro stepped into her space, his tall frame towering over her. "I won't be in that same cottage. If all goes according to plan, I'll be in Miravista Castle. I'll be the Alpha King of Alegría." He smirked, dragging his fingers down her cheek. "Just in case you need to know where to find me."

Lenora closed her eyes against his touch. "Then I promise to visit you one day, Alpha King."

"I'll hold you to that, *princesa*."

Warm breath caressed her forehead as his lips lightly pressed against her skin. She shivered, her eyes blinking open as she looked up into his light brown eyes. "Xander—"

Her words were cut off by a long howl. The sound bounced off the canyon walls and down into the deep ravine, where it echoed hundreds of feet away.

The wolf was close.

Sixteen

Another howl resounded throughout the gorge, raising the hairs on Lenora's arms.

Alejandro turned, putting his body directly in front of hers. "He's close. I can smell him now."

She wondered how good his sense of smell was. "Can you tell how close?"

He tilted his head sideways, his nose twitching as he scented the air. "About a mile, maybe two." Then he spun, wrapping his hands around her upper arms. "Listen to me, Lenora. I'm going to have to confront him, otherwise he'll continue to lead the pack straight to us. Scouts are always the fastest, so I'll have to transform if I want to best him."

She nodded, understanding falling on her. "What should I do?"

"You must hide."

Shaking her head furiously, she pulled out of his embrace. "No, I can fight. I still have my dagger."

"And a wounded ankle that will get worse if it's injured again."

She opened her mouth to retort, but he continued.

"I need you to run." He squeezed his eyes shut for a moment. "I ... might not be able to control myself once I shift. And if I do something to you, I'll never forgive myself."

Her mind went back to their first encounter. He had screamed in her face, spraying spit everywhere. It had taken him a couple of minutes to recognize she wasn't a threat. Was that what he meant? Would he harm her while in bear form because he couldn't control himself?

"All right," she conceded.

"When I tell you to run, you run as fast and as far away as you can." He glanced down at her ankle. "Find an empty cave and stay there until I come find you. And keep hold of your dagger. You never know what kind of beast you'll run into."

Lenora gave a single nod and retrieved the blade from her bag. She was ready. Bracing for the pain that would surely race up her leg, she gritted her teeth and clasped her hand around the dagger.

Alejandro lowered his bag to the ground, placed a hasty kiss on her cheek, and bent close to her ear. "Run," he whispered, his breath tickling her sensitive skin and making her shudder.

She twisted on her good foot and pushed off. Just a few steps later, a roar blasted behind her, and curiosity begged her to turn around. She looked over her shoulder as she continued down the sloping trail, her hand tracing the wall for stability.

Her eyes took in the beginning of Alejandro's shift from human to bear, and she stopped dead in her tracks. His black shirt transformed, melting into his body and then disappearing altogether. In place of his bronze skin, spiky brown fur popped up, covering his entire form.

His legs and arms filled out, and his torso elongated until his six-foot frame became eight feet tall. The sharp, square chin on his face elongated, becoming a large snout that opened wide to showcase his pointy canines. Lenora blinked as those same honey-brown eyes stared right at her.

Then Alejandro growled, standing on his hind legs and lifting his paws into the air. When he slammed down, he took one step toward her, and she backed up against the jagged canyon wall. The sharp edges jammed into her spine as a chill ran through her. Just as she thought he would charge, he raised his pointed snout and sniffed.

A low growl broke through the silence, and an unnerving dread rose inside of her. She couldn't move. Fear struck her, completely immobilizing her. Then, just as she finally got her foot to move sideways so she could escape, he turned to face up the hill and ran back the way they came.

Lenora cried out, the fear of having to face off against a bear—against Alejandro *as* a bear—subsiding. She covered her mouth and shut her eyes. The last time she had seen him this way, she was still running off the adrenaline from Tyree's and the wolf pack's attacks.

Right now, she had nothing.

She forced her eyes open. On the next inhale, she dashed down the slope and farther away from Alejandro.

He'll find me. He's got an incredible sense of smell.

With that thought on her mind, she forced down the pain from her wounded ankle and counted her paces. She knew not to choose a cave too close, but she also didn't think she could make it very far injured the way she was. After a few minutes and what she hoped would be over a mile of distance, she began her search for a cave.

The first hole she found was too tiny to fit through, so she hurried past it, scaling as carefully as she could between the open ravine and the coarse rock at her side.

She passed a few more entrances—some too small and others too big—until she found one that was just right.

The opening hung a couple of inches above her head. She could stand upright, but anyone taller would have to duck. There were no ominous spider webs or snake tracks leading into it, so she assumed it wasn't a creature's den.

Lenora peeked her head inside first, remembering Alejandro's tale of his uncle's brush with the horned spider that wanted to drink all the blood from his body. She prayed the Fates would watch over her as she stepped into the space.

She hobbled all the way to the opposite wall, thankful it wasn't too deep so she could watch the opening for ravenous animals. After dropping the bag from her shoulders, she braced her arm on the wall before she slumped her side against it. With the pressure lifted from her leg, she could feel the throbbing and aching that burned deep within her ankle.

By her estimate, she guessed almost fifteen minutes had passed since she ran away from Alejandro. Sliding down the wall, she plopped onto her bottom, sending particles of dirt into the air.

Another few minutes passed, and there was still no sign of Alejandro. Never one to just sit still, she sat straight and rummaged through her bag to search for the healing ointment. She slid the lid off the tin, then frowned. The salve was almost empty.

With a sigh, she put the top back on and threw the can into the bag. She'd have to wait until they arrived in Monte Paseo before she could apply more ointment to her wound. Though it would take them three days to traverse this canyon, she knew it was a sacrifice she needed to make. If Alejandro sustained any wounds, she would need to use the last of the salve on him. If he was injured because of her...

A choked breath forced its way past her parched lips, reminding her to drink some water. They barely had enough for the entire journey, and now they were in the worst of it—the dusty, arid heat clung to her skin and throat. What little water they had needed to last until Monte Paseo.

Once she took a few small sips, she recapped the canteen and put it away. The urge to pace the cave grew, so she leaned against the wall instead, not wanting to aggravate her injury.

Now she estimated thirty minutes had passed since Alejandro's shift. Worry settled deep within her bones. Alejandro should have taken care of a single wolf by now, right?

She took a step toward the entrance, then fell back against the wall again. Alejandro had told her to hide, and she wasn't stupid enough to think she could take on a wolf—especially if it wasn't alone.

Her heart raced, pumping wildly in her chest. What if there was a pack, and Alejandro had run right into a trap?

"No," she whispered, the sound hollow inside the empty cave. "He's going to be all right. He said he would find me. He *will* find me."

As another slow minute passed, fear took root inside her. A shuffling noise outside the cave reached her ears, and she stood ramrod straight. Then a shadow appeared, growing larger as a body hobbled toward the entrance.

"Xander," she cried, her voice a mix of surprise and anguish. "I was so worried." She stepped forward, then paused as the shadow remained silent. "Xander?"

The limping body whined, the sound freezing her in place. She saw the top of the person's head, full of soft brown curls—not Alejandro's locks.

Stepping backward, she brandished her dagger. The person looked up at that moment, and Lenora's arm wobbled until the dagger fell from her hands. "L-Lawrence?"

There he was, standing before her with his back hunched and his arm clutched to his chest. Blood dripped from his arms and legs to the dusty ground.

Lenora covered her mouth, holding in the cry that threatened to escape upon seeing her best friend alive but in such a state. He lost his footing and fell to his knees, so she rushed to his side. She reached out until a flash of her skin caught her attention. Quickly, she threw her hands behind her back.

Lawrence eyed her from head to toe. "You lost your gloves."

A tear ran down Lenora's cheek, but she didn't want to risk bringing her hand forward to wipe it away. Instead, she knelt on the ground beside him and leveled her head with his. "That's really the first thing you say?"

"I'm happy I found you..." His tone trailed off into a question, a smile gracing his lips. Only then did she notice the bruising and cuts on his jaw.

"Fates, Lawrence," she began, "I thought... I thought you were dead. I thought Remy... killed you." A second tear traced the path of the first one, followed by another on the other side.

Lawrence's lips quivered. "I thought Remy had killed *you* when you didn't turn up at the stables. I had gone back to the compound to find our guards when I saw the Newtonian soldiers rounding them all up. It was a slaughter. They just killed them, no hesitation, no warning. Then a soldier came to tell the others that you had escaped, and I knew I had to find you before they did. I tracked you all the way to the Dark Forest, then to Port Arcadia, and now here." He pursed his lips, his eyes shining as he held back his own tears.

She shook her head. "That was so foolish, Lawrence. If they had found you, they would have killed you."

"They would have had to catch me first." He winked.

Winked!

Lenora could have screamed. As if reading her inner thoughts, he grinned, rising to his feet. Then he sucked in a deep breath, his lip twitching, as a roar reverberated, bouncing around the cave.

Lawrence twisted toward the entrance. "Get behind me, Lenny."

She would have been afraid—*should* have been afraid—but she already recognized that sound.

She knew whose roar that was.

"It's all right," she said, then stepped around Lawrence and ran to the entrance.

"Stay back!" he yelled, stretching forward, but she only felt the wind as his hand reached for hers, barely missing her skin.

The giant shape of Alejandro's bear form came into view just beyond the entrance, but he was already shifting back into his human self again. He fell to his knees, wearing only his short pants. His fisted hands landed in the dirt, his knuckles taking the brunt of the fall. When his eyes rose to hers, the sun shone within, making the hazel tones glisten.

Alejandro's biceps flexed as blood trickled from deep gashes that marked the entire length of his arm. Lenora fell to the ground before him, eyeing him for any other wounds. A soft sigh fell from her lips when she found no other marks.

"Lenny, get back!" came Lawrence's shout directly behind her.

She shook her head. "I said it's all right." Peeking over her shoulder, she gave Lawrence an apologetic look. "This is Xander." She knew not to use his real name, but introducing him as anything other than the prince he was felt wrong. Returning her attention to Alejandro, she also gave him a shameful smile. "This is my friend, Lawrence."

Something about introducing the two men to each other made her stomach roil in knots.

The way Alejandro's eyes narrowed at Lawrence didn't help.

Lenora cut the silence with her voice. "Xander, what happened? How did you get hurt? And what happened to the wolf?"

Without ever removing his eyes from Lawrence, Alejandro stood, and she did the same until she stood in the middle of both men.

Alejandro's upper lip lifted as he bared his teeth. "Why don't you ask him?"

Lenora's eyes remained fixed on Alejandro's stiff body. The tension hung thickly in the hot air, and she forced her head to swivel around.

That was when she saw the look of torment on Lawrence's face.

Seventeen

A strangled sound escaped Lawrence's mouth as he opened and shut it several times. He shook his head, then ran his fingers through his hair. "It's not what you think," he finally said, though the words strained against his throat.

Alejandro took a step forward. "You mean you haven't told her?"

Lenora snapped her head toward Alejandro to catch the venom in his stare. The way her heart clenched in her chest hurt worse than the pain in her ankle. She wrenched her eyes from Alejandro, catching Lawrence's expression as it morphed into a look of regret, his eyes squinting and his lips moving soundlessly as he fought for words.

Lenora squared her body until she fully faced Lawrence. "What's he talking about, Lawrence?" When he didn't answer, she sought Alejandro's gaze. "Xander, what are you talking about?"

Alejandro gave a derisive laugh. "Remember when we first met? Want to know why I was so angry when I returned to my cottage? It's because I smelled a wolf inside my territory."

Lenora swallowed the thick dread building in her throat. "But I was attacked... The wolf pack had attacked me, and I wandered into your boundary."

Alejandro finally removed his gaze from Lawrence, his eyes softening when he found hers. "I could smell six different wolf scents on you. Five were faint, as if their scent barely grazed you. The other was strong. It clung to you and your clothes." He pointed his chin in Lawrence's direction. "I recognize the scent. It smells exactly like him. He's been following us this whole time."

"He's been searching for me," Lenora argued, desperate to make sense of what Alejandro was saying. "He's always been a skilled tracker. Right, Lawrence? Tell him." She twisted toward him, her voice reaching a higher octave.

Lawrence set his jaw, and Lenora's anger rose as her best friend stood silent.

Alejandro scoffed. "If you're not going to tell her, then I will."

Lenora swiveled her head to him again, about to scream for someone to say *something*.

"The reason he's a good tracker, and why I've smelled wolf on you this entire time, is because *Lawrence* is a wolf shifter." Alejandro narrowed his eyes. "That's not even your real name."

Lenora's eyes closed, but she needed to see Lawrence's face. She needed to see the truth in his eyes. When she looked back at him, his face held all the confirmation she needed.

Lawrence's chest rose and fell quickly, and his mouth parted, but no words came out. His eyes passed back and forth between hers, a pinch between the bridge of his nose. "I can explain—"

Lenora wobbled backward until she bumped into Alejandro's chest, and he held her steady with a strong grip on her shoulders. "It's not true. I would have known. Lawrence, you would have told me, right?"

"I-I..." Lawrence shut his mouth with a snap, then blew out a breath. "I couldn't..."

Something inside her broke, shattering into a thousand pieces. In its place, an angry flame burned, threatening to spit fire as she stepped out of Alejandro's hold. "Why not? How could you keep something like this from me? You were supposed to be my best friend—my only friend..." She couldn't finish her thoughts as her jumbled mind struggled to process everything.

She thought she knew him. She brought him with her to another kingdom to embark on a new adventure together. When she had no one else, no other friends outside of her family, she had Lawrence. At least, that was what she thought...

An icy chill swept over her, freezing her to her spot. "You work for him. Remy sent you to capture me—to kill me."

Both Lawrence and Alejandro moved at once. Lawrence reached forward, his hand extended. Alejandro swept between them, pulling Lenora safely behind him as if he thought Lawrence might attack.

Lenora let loose a shocked gasp at Alejandro's speed, and her hand went to her waistband for her dagger, only to realize she had dropped it in the cave when she saw Lawrence.

"Stay behind me, Lenora," Alejandro said, his tone cool as he crouched low.

Lawrence shook his head, his hands raised with his palms facing forward. "I'm not here to capture *or* kill you, Lenny. I don't work for Remy."

"How am I supposed to believe you?" she spat, her head angled around Alejandro's massive frame to glare at Lawrence.

"If you would just let me explain—" Lawrence tried to sidestep around Alejandro.

"Don't move, *wolf*," Alejandro ground out, lifting his hands and spreading his fingers like they were claws.

Lawrence worked his jaw, but his narrowed eyes flashed in challenge at Alejandro's threat. "I just need to explain my story."

"Xander," Lenora called. "Let him talk."

Alejandro's back straightened as he sucked in a large breath. "He can say what he has to say from where he is."

Lawrence stretched his neck, looking over Alejandro's shoulder to meet Lenora's eyes. "He's right. Lawrence isn't my real name."

The weight of his words made her shoulders feel like stone, too heavy to lift, and she nearly collapsed under their pressure.

"I was born in Alegría as Lorenzo Lopez," he continued. "My parents' names aren't Isabelle and John—they're Isabela and Juan. They both worked for Alegría's previous king and queen, Fernando and Yasmin. My dad was a colonel in *el Cambiante Militar* under his dad." Lawrence's eyes cut to Alejandro before returning to Lenora. "When Augustín killed his family and banished all other shifters, my parents fled before we were captured. My dad was close with Alpha King Fernando, so he likely would've been killed instead of allowed to leave. We stayed in Newton for a while before my father secured us passage on a ship to Norraine, where they became soldiers and quickly moved up the ranks."

Lenora processed his words, noting the timeline. "Augustín killed his parents five years ago. You moved to Highmore five years ago."

Lawrence nodded.

"Does Queen Elice know?" she asked.

"No one does," Lawrence answered, his tone quiet. "My parents changed our names so we could assimilate with the Norrainians. They made me promise not to say anything about our heritage or where we came from. They worried we'd be sent back if someone found out who we really are. Norrainians had only recently opened their borders to the outside world after years of fearing mages—imagine if they found out about shifters."

Lenora shook her head, appalled at his meaning. "You thought my mother would turn your family in?"

"We couldn't risk it, Lenny. You have no idea what Augustín is capable of."

Her eyes strayed to Alejandro's back, and Lawrence followed her line of sight.

"Speaking of..." Lawrence began, narrowing his eyes at Alejandro. "Do you really know who *he* is?"

Alejandro snickered, crossing his arms over his chest. "Don't you worry about me, wolf. I'm not the one she's angry with."

Lenora finally moved around Alejandro, and he didn't stop her as she stood before Lawrence with a piercing gaze. "He told me everything. About how he survived Augustín's attack and had to go into hiding in Newton. Your stories are awfully similar, except for one thing. *Xander* didn't lie to me for five years."

"I had to, Lenny," Lawrence said, his tone pleading. "You have to believe me."

She held up her hand when he tried to advance. "Oh, I believe you. I believe you thought you had to lie and keep secrets from me. Even after I told you everything about me and my powers, after Samantha, after everything we've been through..."

Lawrence's eyes watered, and he lifted his hand. He halted, just short of touching her arm, causing Lenora's heart to twist at the realization that he had never touched her bare skin. She could see the unease behind his eyes, and she wondered if it had been there the entire time and she had just ignored it.

Or had she never noticed the fear because it was the same look everyone else gave her?

Everyone except Alejandro.

Alejandro looked at her as if she were the moon, the stars, the entire night sky. No one had ever stared at her that way. He dared to get close, closer than anyone, because he wasn't afraid of her or her powers. And she had just met him.

Lenora fisted her hands. "I'll never be able to trust you the same way I used to, Lawrence—*Lorenzo.*"

Lawrence grimaced, jolting backward as if she had brandished her blade at him. "Then I'll have to earn your trust again."

She pursed her lips, and instead of commenting, she turned toward Alejandro. "We should continue moving. We've stayed in one spot for too long."

Alejandro nodded, but his eyes strayed to Lawrence's frowning face. "What should we do with him?" He raised his voice as if Lawrence wasn't standing right there.

"We'll bring him with us."

Alejandro's lips twitched, an eyebrow rising high on his forehead. "Are you sure that's wise? He could be working for Remy."

Lenora's eyes turned to Lawrence. "I don't think he is. Besides, I abandoned my other soldiers. I won't lose another. I need to make sure he returns to his parents." With that, she walked toward the cave to retrieve her bag and dagger.

"Don't think I won't have my eyes on you," she heard Alejandro warn Lawrence, his tone menacing.

"I would never hurt her," came Lawrence's sure voice. Lenora pulled out a piece of cloth from her bag and ripped it into two pieces, then threw the bag over her shoulder and bent to pick up her dagger.

"If you take *one* wrong step—"

"I heard you, *príncipe,*" Lawrence interrupted, his tone now taking on an accent she'd never heard from him before. "But I'm not going anywhere. I'm gonna make sure she's safe. That's *my* job."

When she walked out of the cave, she found both men standing almost chest-to-chest, staring each other down.

Alejandro's lips curled, and his arms flexed by his side. "*Por ahora.*"

"All right," she drawled, moving forward to pass them each a portion of the rag. "Clean yourselves off." She looked at Alejandro's shoulder as he turned toward her. "Wait, Xander—"

"*Xander*," Lawrence grunted under his breath as he began wiping off the blood from his arms.

She ignored the interruption. "Where's your bag?"

Alejandro cleaned himself as well, though he narrowed his eyes at Lawrence. "I lost it when I was chasing this guy."

She shook her head. "What about all the stuff? The food, the supplies?"

Alejandro's jaw clenched. "Gone. *He* knocked it into the canyon."

The blood drained from her face.

Lawrence cleared his throat. "It was an accident. But—about how long will it take to cross the Great Gorge?"

Lenora wanted to cry. Forget the fight with Tyree, the wolves biting at her skin, the pain in her ankle, or Lawrence's betrayal. *This* would break her.

Alejandro cut his hazel eyes—now simmering with a darkness Lenora had yet to see until now—to Lawrence. "Three days."

Lawrence gulped. "Do ... we have enough supplies?"

"*We* did"—Alejandro pointed between Lenora and himself—"when it was just the two of us with *two* full bags. But now we've lost half and gained an extra person. So no, *Lorenzo*, we do *not* have enough."

Lenora rubbed a hand down her face and took a calming breath. "We'll figure it out. Ration the food and water. Take turns sleeping and keeping watch so we can travel as long as we can. That should cut down some of our time."

Alejandro blew out a sharp breath. "Fine." When he turned to her, he had already steadied his anger and softened his eyes. "That's a good strategy. Thank you, Lenora, for keeping a cool head. I wasn't thinking clearly enough to find a solution."

JENNIFER ROACHFORD

He reached for her cheek, then rubbed the backs of his fingers against her skin. Her eyes fluttered, and a fiery blush spread throughout her face. "I'll carry your bag," Alejandro said, and Lenora nodded faintly as she removed it from her shoulders.

When he stepped out of her space, her eyes fought to focus on her surroundings. Eventually, they did—narrowing in on Lawrence's wide eyes.

She straightened her back, awareness flowing down her spine. Lawrence had just witnessed someone touch her—something that would have had people fainting back home. During the last few days, she had gotten so used to Xander's closeness, to his touch, that she had forgotten how things used to be.

The fantasy playing out in her mind ruptured in an instant, bringing her back to exactly what she was.

Cursed.

Eighteen

T his looks like a good cave," Alejandro said, bending down to inspect the dirt. He swiped a hand across the ground, then brought his palm to his nose. After a deep inhale, he nodded. "No other animal scents, no snakeskin. Plus, it's too small to be a den. We can rest here for a few hours and leave before dawn."

Lenora exhaled, then dropped to the ground and stretched her legs out before her. "Sounds great to me."

Alejandro lowered the bag and knelt beside her. "How's your ankle?"

She eyed it as she bent her knee to carefully remove her boot. After unraveling the dirt- and blood-stained cloth, she winced at the swelling. "It could be worse. The healing ointment is working."

Sifting through the bag, Alejandro pulled out the tin can. "You should use the rest of it. Once you wake up, it will look better."

She shook her head, pushing the container away with the tip of her finger so as not to brush his skin. "I'll be fine. We should keep it in case of an emergency."

"She's too stubborn to listen," Lawrence said from where he leaned against the opposite wall of the cave.

Alejandro didn't so much as flinch in Lawrence's direction. "I've noticed." He threw the tin inside the bag, then stood and wiped his hands on his shirt—which shocked Lenora to see him don from out of nowhere. She reminded herself to ask him how his magic worked when they had a moment alone.

"Wolf," Alejandro called, finally looking back at Lawrence. "Guard the entrance. I'm going to hunt for something to eat. You know, since we don't have enough food, thanks to you."

Lawrence pushed off the wall. "That *is* my job. Protecting the princess."

Alejandro opened his mouth to retort, but he snapped it shut. His hands clenched, lifting slightly, and it looked as if it hurt just to keep them at his side. "I won't be far. If she screams, I promise you won't make it out of this canyon alive."

Lenora rolled her eyes. "He's not going to hurt me, Xander."

Lawrence smirked, the gleam in his eyes egging Alejandro on. "See, she trusts me."

"It's not that I trust you," she said. "It's that I'll stab you before you have a chance to hurt me."

He turned wide eyes on her, and she returned the look with a shrug. Lawrence had known her for far too long to call her bluff.

Alejandro's laugh cut through the air. He shook his head, still laughing as he exited the cave.

Lenora ran a hand along the rocky wall behind her, trying to wipe away as much of the dirt as possible before she rested her head against it. Her eyes shut, but she placed a hand on the hilt of her dagger at the waistband of her leggings. If Lawrence tried anything, she wouldn't hesitate to jab the cold steel into his chest. She didn't really think he would try to kill her, but he had lied to her the entire time she knew him. Her hurt feelings raised her guard, making her wonder if there were other things he would hide from her.

"You know," Lawrence began, his voice sounding far away to her exhausted brain, "I never meant to hurt you."

She popped one eyelid open, finding him hovering by the entrance. She sighed before closing her eye again. "I know, Lawrence."

"And I promise, once we return to Norraine, I'll earn your trust back."

Both of her eyes snapped open. Lawrence held her gaze, his eyes begging with her to forgive him. He took a step toward her, but halted. A touch of sadness tinged his face, a frown forming on his lips. "You're my best friend, Lenny. I thought we could... I *hoped* we would, one day, become something more..."

Lenora froze, her mind working to catch up to his meaning. "Lawrence..." She didn't know what to say. He had never verbalized his intentions before, though somewhere in the far recesses of her mind, she had thought that one day in the future, she would marry him. He really was the only person who engaged in real conversations with her. She didn't think she'd have much of a choice about who she would marry—about who would want to marry her.

Lawrence groaned. "I know it will take a lot to get back to where we were, but I won't stop. I won't give up."

She lifted her head, sitting straight against the wall. "I don't know how we can come back from this."

"So that's it, then? I don't get a second chance to prove myself."

"How can I ever trust you won't lie to me or keep something important from me?"

He ran his hands through his hair, his fingers fisting the curls. "I can only give you my word. And I'll show you, from now on, that you can trust me."

She shook her head, her lips trembling as she strained against the tears, trying to keep them buried deep inside. "And your parents. Will they tell my mother and father who they really are? Will you?"

"What do you want me to say?" He moved closer, holding his hands against his chest. "That I'll spread my secret to the entire kingdom? Out my parents just to prove my loyalty to you? Is that what it will take?"

Lenora turned away. "Of course not. That's not what I want. I just want the truth. My mother deserves to know the truth, too. She's not a monster, Lawrence."

His knees hit the ground as he knelt before her. "I'm sorry, Lenny. I couldn't..." He closed his eyes as a tear spilled free. "I thought I couldn't tell you."

She sucked in a shuddering breath. "That's the sad part. We'll never know what would have happened if you had told me. If you had trusted me."

Lawrence reeled back, falling to his haunches. His throat bobbed as he worked to swallow, but he never got a chance to respond.

Footsteps outside the entrance echoed into the tiny space, and he jumped up, halting when he faced the opening.

Alejandro stood there with a dead rabbit in one hand and a few thin twigs cradled in his other arm. He lifted the rabbit in the air. "I suspect you know how to skin this, wolf?"

Lawrence relaxed his shoulders. "The name's Lawrence. And yes, I do."

Alejandro nodded once. "I'll start a fire, then." His eyes trailed back to Lenora, narrowing as she hastily wiped at her wet eyes. Not a single tear had fallen, but she had come dangerously close to losing herself to her emotions.

Lenora jolted awake, pulled from her sleep by a sudden touch on her shoulder.

"It's just me," Alejandro whispered. "I didn't mean to startle you. I tried calling your name, but you didn't wake."

She found his eyes in the dark, and she pushed herself to a sitting position. "Sorry. I think I was in the middle of a dream." Her mind grasped at the tendrils of her sleep, but it slipped away, now long forgotten.

He nodded his understanding. "It's time to go."

Rubbing her eyes, she gave herself a mental push before she lifted herself from the hard ground. They had switched watch duty throughout the night, taking roughly two-hour shifts so the rest of the group could sleep. It wasn't enough, but it would have to do.

There were now two days left of traversing this Fates' forsaken canyon. She was thankful she traveled with people who could shift into animals with great hunting instincts, otherwise she was sure they would've had a more difficult time with the small amount of food they had.

The only issue they faced now—besides the ravenous beasts that made the Great Gorge their home—was their dwindling water supply. Lenora only had two more canteens, and Lawrence had about half of a bottle. With the only water source being the river flowing several thousand feet below the lip of the canyon, they would have to distribute the miniscule amount in a completely unsatisfying way.

After stretching, she adjusted the wrap on her ankle and followed Alejandro out of the cave. Lawrence had the last watch, so he stood outside the entrance. He turned when they stepped out, then tilted his head toward the downward-sloping trail. "Shall we?"

They traveled for a couple of hours before the sun rose, and Lenora swore she heard slithering and crunching on the ground as they hiked. The shadows played tricks on her tired mind, making her see things that likely weren't there.

She jumped when she thought she saw something crawling along the ground by her feet. The motion made her ankle twinge, and she let out a sharp shriek at the pain.

Alejandro looked at her from over his shoulder, and she felt Lawrence move closer from his place behind her.

"I'm all right," she said. "I thought I saw something."

Alejandro faced forward as he spoke. "There are plenty of things creeping along right now. Most of these creatures are nocturnal."

She shivered, wondering what kind of critter had passed by her. "You two can see them, can't you?"

"Yeah," Alejandro answered.

Lawrence hummed in affirmation.

She blew out a frustrated breath, envious of their stronger powers. Alejandro and Lawrence could see better than she could in the dark and shift into powerful predators. What good was her magic when she couldn't even use it?

"Don't worry, *princesa*," Alejandro said. "I'm leading the way, so I'll warn you if there's anything too worrisome in our path."

Lawrence muttered something under his breath, but Lenora couldn't make out the words even if she wanted to.

After the sun brought its stinging rays and intense heat, the trip somehow became both easier and more difficult. Now Lenora could see the crawling animals in her path, but the warmth made them all sweaty.

And thirsty.

By midday, they forced themselves to stop and take a few sips from their canteens. A cluster of rounded boulders made for the perfect place to hide from the sun for a few minutes while they rationed out the rest of the rabbit. They each sat underneath the shadow of a rock, quietly eating.

Lenora threw a piece in her mouth, then wiped her slick forehead with the back of her hand. "Is it hotter today than it was yesterday?"

Alejandro chewed, his face looking toward the sky. "We're heading farther south, and we're in the middle of the gorge now. It's drier here. But we're halfway done with this desolate place. Soon, we'll be in Alegría." He sighed softly, his tone wistful. "I can't wait to see it again."

"What's your plan when we get there?" Lawrence asked from his spot in front of a boulder.

Alejandro snorted. "Like I'd tell you, wolf."

"I told you," Lawrence ground out, "to call me by my name."

"And which name is that? Lawrence? Lorenzo? Is there a third you're also keeping secret?"

Lawrence huffed out a laugh. "You're one to talk, *Xander*. Does Lenny even know your real name?"

"Lenora knows exactly who I am."

Lawrence looked at her for confirmation. Lenora took a tiny sip of water to avoid getting dragged into their argument. She'd been around the barracks long enough to realize when two men were having an unnecessary competition with each other.

"You know he's a prince?" Lawrence asked after her silence, his eyes squinted.

She sighed. "Like I said, he told me everything."

Lawrence sat back against the rock, tearing off a piece of his rabbit with his teeth. "You're still an annoying brat, Alejandro."

Alejandro chuckled, then stood and stretched an arm over his head. "You think you know me, Lorenzo?"

"I used to. You're still as obnoxious as ever."

Alejandro turned away, and Lenora watched with interest. How well did they know each other before Augustín rearranged their entire lives?

"You don't know me," Alejandro muttered. "That foolish fifteen-year-old boy I used to be is long gone. He was murdered by his older brother."

Lawrence swallowed the last bit of his food. "Who are you now, then? Because I still see a spoiled prince vying for every bit of attention he can catch."

Alejandro turned a glare on him. "Like I said. You don't know me. Not anymore."

Sensing Alejandro's rising irritation, Lenora closed her pack and stood. "We should get going."

Lawrence pushed off the ground, his own scowl fighting against Alejandro's. "You plan to take him on, don't you? Are you insane? He'll rip you to shreds."

Alejandro marched forward. "You should stop talking about things you don't know, wolf."

Lawrence laughed in his face. "By the Fates. You really are going after him."

Lenora shouldered the bag, ready to end this ridiculous fight. "Boys, we need to leave."

"So what if I am?" Alejandro asked, his eyes still trained on Lawrence. "What's it to you? This is between me and Augustín."

Lawrence shook his head, his eyes wide. "You've lost your mind, *príncipe*. He'll kill you."

"Not if I kill him first."

"You didn't see what I saw." Lawrence lowered his voice. "When we left Miravista, the entire palace was wrecked. Augustín went on a rampage. So many people died. The bodies... They were unrecognizable."

Lenora stood beside the corner-most boulder, her heart clenching as Lawrence's words struck her. She studied Alejandro's face, watching as his chest rose.

He took a step away from Lawrence. "I sat in my blood—in my parents' and Luís's blood—for two days, thinking I was going to die. I knew my family's bodies were still there because I'd seen them die right next to me. So I know what Augustín is capable of. I know what facing him means."

Lawrence shuddered a breath. "I didn't know... We all thought you'd died."

"No one knows." Alejandro glanced back at Lenora. "Except you two and my Tío Ernesto. He's the one who found me."

"General Ernesto is still alive?" Lawrence's mouth hung open.

"Only because he swore false loyalty to Augustín. He thinks Ernesto is on his side."

"But he's not?"

Alejandro shook his head. "But that's all you're getting from me. Lenora may think you're trustworthy, but I don't."

Lawrence crossed his arms. "You and I have known each other since we were children, *príncipe*."

"And you abandoned your kingdom." Alejandro raised an eyebrow. "*And* you lied to Lenora."

"I've been in hiding, same as you." Lawrence rolled his eyes. "And don't act like you know her well enough to be affronted *for* her."

Alejandro smirked, closing in on Lawrence. "I bet I already know her better than you do."

Lenora, having had enough of the way this conversation was going, spun away. "I'm leaving!" she hollered, waving a hand behind her.

They can catch up if they want to.

She took a step on her injured ankle before a sharp sting ran through it. She didn't have time to look down at her foot before it slipped from under her, and she was dragged across the craggy ground.

Nineteen

B its of rock scraped along Lenora's back, legs, and arms, cutting through her black trousers and tunic. A fresh wave of pain ran through her ankle, and she forced herself to look down at her feet to see what was dragging her across the canyon.

A giant eye stared back at her, blinking several times against the sunlight.

Wait. Not one eye. Eight.

Her face paled as realization dawned on her. A giant horned spider.

Lenora lifted her gaze to the vicious-looking horns on either side of its head. The sharp points oozed a clear, sticky liquid. The same substance leaked from its two spiky fangs as the creature opened its mouth and released a shrill screech. She covered her face as spittle flew everywhere, the venom landing on her arms.

She screamed at the burning sensation where the venom scorched her skin. When she lowered her arms, she dared a look at the spider again, hoping to find a way to free herself from its clutches.

That was when she noticed two of its eight legs digging into her already injured ankle, tearing into her foot. Its limbs ripped through her skin on both sides, and her ankle felt like it was being ripped in two.

A roar greeted her ears, and she looked back, searching for Alejandro.

She already knew the sound of his bear's roar. He was coming for her.

Quickly, she thought of a way to trip up the spider, to make it loosen its hold or release her completely. Her eyes scanned the ground for a large enough rock or stick, but she found nothing. The giant creature was moving down the trail at a speed she didn't think it was capable of.

Must be all the legs.

She cringed, thinking of the hairy things jammed into her ankle.

A jagged rock protruded in front of her, and she latched on as the spider pulled her past it. Her fingers caught the corner, its sharp edge ripping open her skin. Wincing through the pain, she held on tight.

The spider screeched again, its venom burning through her shirt and scalding her stomach. It yanked, but she gripped the rock with all her strength. It was her only lifeline.

With her free foot, she kicked out at the creature. She connected with one of its legs, but without the proper leverage, all she did was anger it.

The spider tugged once, twice, then a third time until Lenora's fingers slipped from the embedded rock. A high-pitched cry burst from her throat. The skin on her ankle ripped to shreds, the spider's limbs digging straight through the muscles and breaking her bones. Her back once again scraped along the ground as it continued to drag her away.

The creature made a sharp turn, entering a dark cave. With a heave, it swung her across the opening and into its web-covered den.

Lenora landed with an *oof*, but she was finally free of its hold. She felt for her dagger, slipping it from her waistband and holding it in front of her body. She rolled onto her burning stomach, then pushed up to her one good leg, letting her broken foot rest on the tips of her toes. Still, that bit of pressure sent a horrifying jolt through her leg, and she bit her lip to keep her scream inside.

The spider stood on all eight legs, its massive body hovering a foot over her and threatening to drip venom onto her head. Lenora took a step back, finding herself against the wall, webs clinging to her ripped shirt. It opened its maw, the sticky venom glistening with the tiny amount of light that slipped through the entrance. She braced herself, her dagger ready. If the creature injected her with its venom, she would stab through its mouth and kill it along with her.

Another roar sounded, this time just outside the cave, and the spider hesitated, its mouth wide open, ready to crunch down on her.

Then it flew backward, hitting the opposite wall.

Lenora blinked, her body trembling and her mind reeling to catch up.

Alejandro, in his bear form, held the spider by two of its legs. He bellowed in its face, and the spider screeched back. It snapped one of its legs toward Alejandro, but he ducked away.

Lenora watched as Alejandro's massive frame moved with agility, awed by how he evaded each swipe or drop of venom. He raised a huge paw and smacked the spider's head, sending the creature flying sideways.

She thought that would slow it down, but it came back with a new vengeance. It lowered its head and rammed its horns toward Alejandro's belly. He dodged in time to avoid getting nicked, but she heard the sizzle of the venom meeting his gold-tipped fur.

Alejandro growled, his round eyes narrowed. He stood on his hind legs, raising his paws toward the cave's ceiling, then slammed them down on the ground. Dust swirled, the webs hanging from the ceiling swayed, and Lenora covered her mouth and nose as she coughed.

The spider responded in kind, scraping its two front legs across the dirt. Lenora's heart raced, sensing the charged air as Alejandro and the spider sped toward each other.

One of the spider's long legs reached forward first, but Alejandro ducked underneath, then grabbed the creature by its middle. Lenora's eyes opened wide as venom shot out of the spider's mouth.

Alejandro didn't react as the toxin dripped onto his fur. He pulled his arms apart, ripping the spider in two.

Lenora covered her mouth as the spider's screech went silent. Alejandro huffed and threw the two pieces toward the back of the cave, knocking down most of the webs. His huge chest swelled with his inhalations, and he wiped a paw across his face where the venom left a stream of smoke on his brown fur.

She lowered her hand and hesitantly stepped toward him, but her leg gave out, and she screamed from the pain. Alejandro's eyes shot to her, and his nose twitched.

"X-Xander," she said, her voice trembling from the diminishing adrenaline and the agony in her foot.

His ears flattened against his head, and he pawed the ground before he came closer. She pushed herself against the wall, then scooted along its surface, inching toward the opening. Movement caught her eyes, and she saw a gray wolf standing just outside. She turned back to the massive bear, afraid to keep her eyes off Alejandro for too long, but she heard the wolf's yelp morph into a human-like grunt.

Lawrence heaved in a few breaths. "Lenny," he said between breaths, "get out of there."

She shook her head. Alejandro advanced another foot, then stood on his back legs. With a *thud*, he dropped his paws against the wall above her, then lowered his head until he stood level with her face.

"Xander," she whispered. "Shift back now. You're scaring me."

His ears twitched, and he snapped his mouth with a low growl, making Lenora yelp. Leaning forward, he sniffed her hair, which had come loose from its braid during the attack.

"Yes, it's me," she said, pleading with him to recognize her. She didn't know if it would help, but she couldn't think of anything else to say or do to make him shift. Maybe if she kept talking, he would see her as a friend and not a threat. "It's Lenora. Remember me?"

He pulled his face away, but his eyes remained glassy, as if he couldn't focus. He let out another rumble from deep within his chest, raising his paw, and Lenora closed her eyes. She didn't want to watch if he attacked. She had seen how strong his paw was.

"Lenny!" Lawrence yelled, but she couldn't look at him.

Instead, her eyes flitted open, and her hands flew forward. She gripped the thick, wiry fur along Alejandro's neck. "Alejandro, it's Lenora! Please, look at me!"

He froze, his arm behind his head. Blinking, he leaned forward again, his maw parting, and a soft sound reminiscent of a purr escaped it.

A single tear slid down her cheek when Alejandro's height lowered, as bear legs turned human, and his muzzle was replaced by the strong jaw she'd grown to admire. Fur changed into hair, his signature locks with honey tips forming on his head.

Then Alejandro's hazel eyes stared into hers. His smooth skin beneath her fingers where she had gripped his fur sent a chill down her arms.

Wait. His skin?

She gasped, but it was too late.

Alejandro threw his head back, his mouth dropping open as he struggled to breathe. Lenora wanted to pull her hands away, but the vision gripped her.

The edges of the cave darkened until her sight blurred. The spider's den disappeared, and in its place, a warmly lit bedroom came into focus. Lenora stared at an open door, a crisp breeze blowing through a high balcony, making the white curtains sway into the room. A massive four-poster bed with delicate swirls carved into the wood rested against a wall.

On the bed lay Alejandro. She hurried over, wanting to get up close to this vision, but she stopped just shy of the footboard when she saw herself already there.

I'm here. In the future.

Gray hair flowed down to the center of her back, her curls now limp with age. A gold crown with soft arches sat on top of her head. Future Lenora sat on the edge of the bed, her hands gripping Alejandro's.

Lenora hesitantly walked closer until she stood before her future self. Tears leaked down her wrinkled cheeks, and though she looked sad, her eyes had a fondness in them as she looked down at Alejandro.

Lenora finally glanced at him. His once hazel eyes were gray with old age, and he stared directly at future Lenora. A soft smile touched his lips as he breathed his last breath, and she heard future Lenora suck in a choked sob.

As the vision blurred, pulling her back to the present, she glimpsed Alejandro's crown. She twisted her head back to her future self, then returned her gaze to Alejandro.

They matched. The gold arches, the thin bands reminiscent of spiraled tree branches. The crowns Lenora and Alejandro wore in the future were identical.

Her lungs filled with air as she jumped back to the present. She squeezed her hands against the shock of pain now shooting through her body.

Her fingers closed against something stiff, and her eyes opened with a jolt.

She still had her hands against Alejandro's neck, the thick cords of muscle taut against her palm.

Alejandro hovered over her, panting, and Lenora realized how out of breath she was too. Neither of them moved, but she felt faint and didn't think she could hold herself up any longer.

She dropped her head forward, her forehead resting against Alejandro's bare chest. "I..." She trailed off, trying to form words. "I'm sorry."

It was what she was used to. Apologizing for her powers—for the one thing she couldn't control—whether she used them or not.

But she *had* used them, and she showed Alejandro the exact moment of his death. He would hate her now. He'd never forgive her for tormenting him with such a vision. Would he change his mind about helping her return home? Would he abandon her in Alegría and refuse to get her a ship? Her heart clenched at the thought of losing another friend.

That was what Alejandro had become—a friend. He was the first person to make her feel normal, accepted, *wanted* for who she was. He had told her his deepest secrets, saved her over and over again. He had shown her the power of touch with the slightest brush of his fingers against her cheek.

She didn't know how she would feel if he snatched it all away from her.

Lifting her head, she removed her hands from his neck, but he reached for them. The surprise move made her eyes widen. They were holding hands. She waited, her breath stuck in her throat.

But nothing happened. She didn't get pulled into another vision.

In her nineteen years of life, she had only touched a handful of people, and she had never touched that same person twice. Looking at her bare hands as they rested against Alejandro's, she let go of her breath. She didn't have a second vision. She could... She could touch him again and *not* have another vision of his death.

Slowly, a smile spread across her lips. Alejandro mirrored it as he rubbed his thumb along her knuckles.

"Please, my Nora," Alejandro said, his voice raspy and deep. "Never apologize for the gift you've given me."

Her throat seized on her, refusing to work. All she could do was stare.

Alejandro brought her fingers to his lips, the press of them on her skin making her shudder.

Then her body finally gave out, and she crumbled to the ground.

Twenty

Alejandro's sturdy arms wrapped around Lenora's worn-out frame, one slipping behind her back and the other underneath her legs. "I got you," he whispered, his face inches from hers.

He hurried out of the cave, passing by Lawrence, who stood frozen to his spot by the entrance.

"What..." Lawrence hesitated. "What happened?"

Lenora couldn't speak. She couldn't even open her mouth to make a single noise.

Alejandro brushed past Lawrence and into the sunlight. "Don't worry about it. It doesn't concern you."

Tremors racked Lenora's body as fatigue and blood loss set in. Alejandro sat her on a fragmented portion of the mountain that jutted onto the trail. He bent low and swept his eyes over her body, passing over the bleeding slashes on her exposed skin. "Did it bite you?"

Lenora leaned her temple against the mountain, shaking her head since she was too weak to reply with words.

His eyebrows pinched. "Did it pierce you with its horns?"

Another shake, and his frown deepened.

"It didn't inject you with its venom?" he asked.

Lawrence shuffled closer beside them, leaning in to inspect her wounds as well.

She worked her mouth open to force her words out. "Just on my arms. My stomach."

His eyes roamed to the burn holes in her clothing, and he exhaled a relieved sigh. His shoulders sagged until he caught sight of her foot. "Nora, your leg."

She angled her head, then winced when she saw the gashes where the spider's legs had dug in. "Just its claws. That's how it dragged me."

Alejandro's eyes flashed with violence, and his body tensed. "You won't be able to walk like this. Your previous wound reopened, and it looks like your ankle is broken. There are two holes... I... I can see the bone."

Lenora finally scanned her body. Burns littered her skin where the venom had singed through her clothes. Blood oozed out of the puncture marks on her ankles. Other deep cuts bled through rips and tears on her tattered shirt and leggings. She could only imagine what her back looked like. Rocks had cut all along her body when the horned spider dragged her through the ravine. No wonder she felt so weak—she lost a lot of blood.

"Wolf—" Alejandro began, then amended himself. "I mean, Lorenzo. Get Lenora's bag."

Lawrence ran up the trail, likely to where the bag had slipped off when the horned spider grabbed her, while Alejandro removed Lenora's torn-up boot. He ripped some of the fabric at the bottom of her pants and used it to apply pressure to her wounds.

When Lawrence returned, Alejandro took the bag and opened it. "Thank the goddess you saved the last bit of healing ointment." He held the tin can aloft and threw off the cap in his hurry. Then his frown deepened. "There's not enough."

"It'll have to be," she mumbled, her body trembling against the ledge she sat upon. "Besides... We'll be in Alegría ... tomorrow night."

Alejandro's worried gaze deepened as she fell slack against the wall. "I'll wrap it tight. But we'll have to move slower now, which means we probably won't get to Monte Paseo until the next morning."

Two more days. Lenora's racing heart sank into her heavy chest, weighed down by her mistake. "I'm sorry I let ... that thing catch me." Shame brought her down even further. Her parents would be so disappointed. After all the training and words of wisdom, she did the one thing they warned her not to do—let her guard down.

Alejandro clenched his fist around the can, glancing over his shoulder at Lawrence. "It's my fault. I should have heard the spider approach. Should have smelled it. I let myself become distracted, and because of that, you could have died."

"It's my fault too," Lawrence muttered from behind Alejandro's shoulder. "I'm sorry, Lenny."

Lenora lifted a wobbly hand to wipe at her sweaty forehead. "If I could just get some rest, I'll be fine."

Alejandro shook his head, then reached into his bag for a water canteen. "We should get as far away from this den as possible. I smelled other spiders. The one I killed likely had a family, and they'll be angry." With the canteen hovered over her leg, he winced apologetically. "I have to wash it. Brace yourself." At her nod, he poured a small stream over her ankle, washing away the blood.

Lenora bit her lip as the water brushed over her wounds, but sighed once Alejandro applied the last of the ointment. The cooling effect from the herbs and the remnants of healing magic sent a shiver throughout her body.

Too bad they didn't have any more.

After wrapping her ankle tightly with the remaining cloth, Alejandro pushed himself up. He sucked in a breath, then bent over to scoop her into his arms. Lenora opened her mouth to protest, but Alejandro cut her off before she could make a sound. "I'm carrying you until we can find a safe place to rest."

"But—" she began.

Alejandro spun around, the movement making her dizzy. "Lorenzo, carry the bag." Then he maneuvered around the boulder and marched down the path. "Just rest, Nora," he whispered, his low voice near her ear. "I'll take care of you."

Hesitantly, she placed her free hand against Alejandro's chest. A shirt had emerged, appearing out of nowhere, so she wasn't touching his bare skin.

But she could have. She would have been able to brush her fingers against his broad shoulders and not spark a vision.

Her lips split into a grin. It must have been the blood loss that made her feel so loopy, but a giggle slipped from her, causing Alejandro to lift an eyebrow.

"You okay?" he asked, but there was a hint of humor in his tone.

She nodded, then rested her head against his shoulder. "I'm all right."

For the first time in a long time, she actually meant those words. That made her giggle again, a high-pitched sound echoing down the ravine. Given the circumstances, she had no business being fine, yet there she was, being carried by a gorgeous, protective, powerful man whose deathbed she would weep over.

And all she wanted to do was laugh.

Fates help me.

It took an hour until Alejandro found a spot he deemed safe enough to stop for lunch. He had carried Lenora the entire time, and he showed no signs of fatigue even after his battle with the horned spider. His own wounds still dripped blood, but scabs were already forming where the creature's venom had burned him.

He set his jaw as he gently lowered her onto another lip in the canyon. Then he fussed with her ankle, removing the boot again to recheck her injury. Fresh scarlet blood soaked the shredded portion of her pants that he had used as a makeshift medical wrap, and he grimaced. "We have nothing else to wrap it with. And we don't have enough water to continue washing it. I'm afraid it'll get infected."

Lawrence set the bag beside her, his own face a mask of concern. "And you can't keep carrying her, otherwise you'll wear yourself out."

Alejandro cut his eyes at Lawrence. "Don't tell me what I can and can't do."

"Don't start," Lenora grunted, glaring at both men. "I mean it. I will start walking to Monte Paseo right now."

That made them shut their mouths, but Lenora saw the way Alejandro's mouth twitched and Lawrence's lips pursed. It took them a great deal of effort not to say anything else.

They spent a few minutes picking at the nuts Alejandro had packed, drinking it down with a few sips of water. They were quickly running out, and the dry desert air had rubbed their throats raw.

Lenora closed her eyes after she ate, getting a much-needed nap with her side resting against the rock wall.

Alejandro tapped her arm a while later, jolting her awake. The sun had lowered some, so she estimated she had slept for about an hour.

"Are you ready?" he asked, his gaze traveling down to her foot.

She nodded, though when she went to stand, her leg buckled.

Alejandro was there in an instant, as if sensing her collapse. He hoisted her up again, adjusting her in his arms. "Let's go, Lorenzo," he called as he walked south down the path.

Lenora knew better than to protest. It was either slow the group down because she had to walk on one foot or be carried by the huge bear shifter who didn't seem to break. At the rate Alejandro was going, they could make it to Alegría tomorrow night—or at least by dawn the next day.

Once the sun hid behind the western mountains, Alejandro and Lawrence looked ready to drop. They had to take a few extra breaks since their lack of water clearly affected them, and the men looked exhausted. She knew sleep, even for just a few hours, would help.

As they traveled further south, the trails became more expansive. The route smoothed out, and great plateaus—or *mesas*, as Alejandro called them—stretched before them.

Alejandro led them away from the canyon and out onto a plateau where several trees grew on the sparse land. He sat Lenora under the canopy of a wide tree, and she leaned against the trunk.

"This is the first tree we've seen since the Dark Forest," Lenora noted, her eyes drawn up toward the vibrant green and yellow leaves. Upon closer inspection, the yellow was thanks to small flowers that bloomed on the branches.

Alejandro lowered himself to his haunches in front of her. "It's a Palo Verde tree. They grow all over Alegría, but a few have sprung up this far north. They're very drought resistant." He picked up a fallen flower, twirled it in between his fingers, then leaned forward to stick it behind her ear.

She knew her hair looked a Fates' forsaken mess, but at that moment, with Alejandro's bright eyes never straying from hers, she felt beautiful. Her heart leaped, and a hot blush spread throughout her face.

"I'll go find some food," he said, his eyes already scanning the wide path they just left.

"I could hunt this time," Lawrence suggested from where he stood a few feet away.

Alejandro stood, turning toward Lawrence as he said, "You watch the camp. It's my job to make sure she's fed."

For a reason unknown to her, this made her blush darken. Even a minute after he had left, her stomach continued to flutter.

Lawrence gathered a few dry branches from the edge of the path, then started a small fire. After he got it going, he stood guard, facing north—the way they came—for a few minutes. Then he changed his position to the path ahead. After that, he faced east, and finally west. Lenora eyed him all the while, wondering when he would work up the courage to look at her.

For her part, she remained silent. She knew they would eventually need to discuss *everything*—especially the vision she shared with Alejandro. Fates knew she needed to talk to *Alejandro* about it first.

But she had known Lawrence for five years. They were best friends. Now...

Now, their relationship seemed destroyed—whether by Lawrence's secrets or her anger, she didn't know.

She resolved to speak with him once they were back in Norraine. There, they could have the space to talk freely without Alejandro nearby. They could discuss what Lawrence said in the canyon when she first learned he was a wolf shifter, and she could tell him that if it hadn't been for this trip to Newton, they might have had a chance for something more.

Lawrence turned abruptly, and Lenora braced herself. He had that look on his face—the one he gave when he was determined. His lips pursed, his hands went to his hips, and he took in a deep breath. "Lenny—" He stopped, his eyes narrowing.

The sound of feet crunching over pebbles met her ears as Alejandro approached from the distance. Lawrence huffed and faced him. "More rabbit?" he asked with a cringe.

"What kind of wolf doesn't like rabbit?" Alejandro lifted the dead animal into the air. "You don't have to eat if it's not good enough for you."

Lawrence wiped the look of disgust from his face as he took the rabbit from Alejandro to skin. Lenora eyed their exchange, wondering why her spitfire friend often relented to Alejandro, even after originally pushing back. Did it have to do with Alejandro being a prince—a prince from Lawrence's home kingdom—or was there something else going on? Some baser instinct Lenora knew nothing about?

After the men roasted the animal and they filled their bellies, Lawrence took up first watch. Both men decided Lenora could not perform adequate guard duties—to which she reluctantly agreed, though she glowered at them as they suggested it. She would rest and pray to the Fates that she would be well enough by the time they took off again.

As Lawrence shifted into his wolf form and walked the perimeter, leaving his scent to ward off other animals, Alejandro settled beside Lenora underneath the tree. She watched Lawrence stride around, still amazed at his transformation. Feeling eyes on the side of her face, she turned to find Alejandro staring at her with a curious expression.

She raised an eyebrow. "What?"

He leaned back and crossed one ankle over the other. "I was just thinking about the vision."

Oh. I guess we're having this conversation now.

Lenora allowed him time to continue, but he kept his eyes on her, his mouth quirked into a half-smile.

"What do you think it means?" she finally asked.

"I think it means a lot of things." He raised his gaze to the stars, their glow visible between the leaves in the tree. "One, I think it means I'll be successful. I'll defeat my brother."

She nodded. That was one of her first thoughts. Seeing him with that gold crown meant he would be king.

Alejandro's smile grew. "It also means I'll live a long life. I think I looked around eighty, maybe ninety years old."

The way he turned toward her, so quickly, with so much purpose, made her gasp.

He reached for her hand, and she couldn't help the urge to twitch. The reflex to pull away, to avoid contact, persisted. In reality, she could only touch Alejandro because she'd already had a vision of his death. If her hand landed on anyone else...

"You were there too, Nora." His eyes twinkled, as bright as the stars above. "I think I know what that means, but ... I'm afraid to say it aloud."

She sucked in a sharp breath. "It could mean anything, Xander."

"I don't think so. In fact, I hope not."

Lenora pulled her hand away. It was too much. She'd only known him for a week. She was running for her life, still unsure if Remy had his wolves searching for her this very minute or why he would even continue looking. He had what he wanted. Remy was the king of Newton now. Surely he wouldn't want to kill her anymore, right? But she couldn't risk that chance, so here she was, escaping by the skin of her teeth. Yet her heart ... her very soul was distracted by the man sitting next to her.

Alejandro leaned away, giving her much needed space. "I know you're not ready to talk about this. That's okay with me. I won't rush you. I just..." He looked away, and Lenora followed his line to where Lawrence sat back on his haunches, his nose scenting the air. "I want you to know that for shifters, something like this is ... important. Marking someone as a mate is sacred. And when I first inhaled your scent, I could smell him on you."

Lenora removed her gaze from Lawrence to turn her frown on Alejandro. "You already told me that. That was why you were so angry. You thought a wolf was in your house."

He shook his head slowly, looking down at his fingers. "That's not what I mean. The wolf—Lorenzo—marked you as his. It confused me the entire time we've known each other. At least until he showed up. Now it makes sense."

A deep ache drummed in the center of her belly. "What do you mean?"

Alejandro's lips curved upward, though the expression didn't look like a smile. If anything, it looked like a pained grimace. "You two are together. It's why he followed you all the way to *El Abismo*. Why he risked fighting a bear just to get to you."

"No, we're... We're not. We never..." She groaned, throwing her hands up. "He was my only friend. My best friend. Maybe, if we hadn't embarked on this trip, we would have discussed marriage, but that was before. Things are ... different now." She bit her lip. Her head still felt fuzzy and her body ached all over. Now would not be the right time to go there. To talk about the stirrings in her heart that developed the moment she met Alejandro.

Alejandro nodded, his full lips protruding into a frown. "That's what I feared. That you two were ... something more."

She waited, hoping he'd fill the silence with one of his silly jokes or a brush of his fingers on hers. Now that she'd felt his hands, she didn't think she could ever let go.

He relaxed against the tree again with a soft sigh. "But not to worry. I have faith in your vision. In the meantime, I'll just have to make it clear to the wolf that you're mine now."

Somehow, the protectiveness in his words made her feel safe, cared for.

She knew the Fates worked mysteriously, but she didn't know they worked quickly, too.

Twenty-One

B y the time night fell on the second day, Lenora had to drag herself out of Alejandro's hold. He had carried her most of the day, only letting her stretch her legs a few minutes at a time before he hauled her into his arms again.

The toll on his body finally showed once the sun had set, but they were already scouting for a spot to set up camp. Lenora hopped onto her good foot and pranced away before he could grab her again.

"Just go find some food, Xander," she grunted, then plopped against a Palo Verde tree. There were more clusters now, providing glorious shade throughout their trek.

Alejandro held his hands up. "Okay, I got it." He nodded at Lawrence as if the two of them now shared a silent language. Lawrence took that as his cue to mark their perimeter.

Lenora knew she should be thankful they weren't arguing, at the very least.

Sleep came easily, but once Alejandro shook her awake before sunup, she rolled away, not ready to open her eyes. Her body felt heavy, and her eyelids refused to open.

He tapped her shoulder once more. "We'll be there in just a few hours. Shortly after sunrise, I'd guess."

A shiver racked her body. Every part of her ached to her bones. Lifting a heavy hand, she rubbed at her forehead, coming back with sweat on her palm.

Alejandro grasped her hand and pulled it close to his nose. He gave it a sniff, then blew out an angry huff. "You have a fever."

Lawrence appeared in front of her, his eyes large. "You must have an infection."

"Get the water," Alejandro ordered, and Lawrence rushed away.

"No," she mumbled, her lips barely moving. "We must save it... Still a few hours ... left."

Lawrence returned, then handed the canteen to Alejandro. The bear of a man whirled to her other side in one motion, then held the bottle to her lips as he used his free hand to hold her head up.

"Drink," he ordered, his voice both gentle and firm.

She opened her mouth, letting the water slide down her parched throat. The last two days were grueling, but she had essentially trained for this scenario with her father. She almost choked as she remembered King James's idea of preparing her for the worst—when he stranded them in the middle of the barren Lowlands for two days with only one water bottle.

This heat, this illness, was *nothing* like that. Though, she'd heard the story about how her father had survived a fire mage attack, and how her mother worried he'd die from his injuries as they trekked for three days through the desert. If he could survive, so could she.

She pushed herself up, grasping Alejandro's outstretched hand. "I'm fine. I'll be all right. We just have to get to Monte Paseo."

"The sooner the better," Lawrence said, looking right at Alejandro.

Alejandro lifted the corner of his lip. "You don't have to remind me, Lorenzo." Then he turned and swept Lenora into his arms.

She rested her hand on his shoulder, but her arm felt like a block of stone. She was sure the limb would slip off and fall to the ground.

Sweat grew on her brow as they walked. The weight of her arm prevented her from lifting it to wipe the sweat away, so it gathered on her forehead and dripped down the side of her face. Alejandro's gaze continued to meet hers, and his breathing became harsh as the journey wore on him.

At first, Lenora watched him with equal worry. She didn't want him fainting before they made it to Monte Paseo. What would they do then? As the sun rose, her fever became worse. Her vision slipped in and out of focus until the onerous effort to keep her eyes open faltered.

"Just sleep, Nora," Alejandro muttered, his breath coming out in pants. "We'll be there soon."

As if that was all she needed, she allowed her eyes to close.

Opening her eyes was a mistake. Pain enveloped her body immediately, wrapping her in aches and heat that threatened to burn her to the core.

Lenora threw her forearm over her head, hoping to block her suffering and force herself back to sleep, if only for a few more minutes.

Rough cloth rubbed against her forehead. She inspected her arm, eyeing the fresh bandage and the herbal scent of healing balm.

Lenora twisted her head to the side, sending pangs down her spine. To her right, Lawrence's head lolled as he slept uncomfortably in a wooden chair. Awareness crashed through her—the soft mattress beneath her, the thin blanket around her, the stiff bandages encasing most of her body, including what felt like a wooden splint around her ankle. The pain in her foot persisted, though it was significantly less now than it had been in the Great Gorge. The overwhelming smell of herbs permeated the air, calming her even as the soreness in her body remained.

She worked her mouth, trying to revive her hoarse throat. "L-Lawrence," she breathed, choking on her words.

Lawrence sprang up, rushing to kneel at her side. "You're awake."

Nodding, she opened her mouth again, but Lawrence shushed her.

He reached to the side and came back with a metal cup. "Drink some water. You barely broke your fever."

She sat up and drank, slurping the water in a most undignified way.

After wetting her throat, she fell back onto the bed. "Where are we? Where's Xander?"

Lawrence's frown didn't go unmissed as he placed the cup down. "We're in Monte Paseo. We made it shortly after sunrise, almost two days ago now. As soon as we got here, Alejandro brought you into town. A nurse cleaned your wounds and force-fed you something for the pain since you were still unconscious. She also gave you something to keep you asleep while she reset the bones in your ankle and wrapped your foot in a splint, but you'll most likely need to see a healer when we return to Norraine. As for Alejandro... He's with General Suárez—his uncle. They've been in conference for several hours."

Lenora's stomach growled. She couldn't remember the last time she ate. She pushed herself up, immediately regretting the movement. "I need to find some food."

Lawrence stood and held his hands out. He kept his distance as he waved her back down. "You need rest. I'll send for some food, and for the nurse. Besides..." He ran a hand through his messy hair. "I... I'd like to talk first. Alone."

Lenora remained sitting on the bed. Her eyes roamed the tiny room. Only the small cot she currently sat on, the chair, and a bedside table filled the space. A bright lantern and the metal cup she had just drunk from occupied the surface of the table. When she returned her gaze to Lawrence, she fought the urge to look away.

She had a feeling she knew what he wanted to talk about. She had hoped to have more time, to build up enough courage. The determined look on Lawrence's face let her know she couldn't put it off any longer. Sick or not.

Nodding, she scooted over on the bed and patted the wide space beside her. From experience, she knew he wouldn't get too close. Her necklace was still broken, so she couldn't wear her warding crystal, and she didn't have any gloves to protect him from her touch.

Lawrence sat on the edge of the cot, his fingers intertwined on his lap. "I know things are ... different now. I can feel the change. I know I hurt you, and that you have a right to be upset. Fates, I'd be upset too, so I understand where you're coming from. But Lenny, you're my best friend. You'll always be my best friend, and best friends fight. I... I don't want to let go of everything we've been through. You mean so much to me. You're worth fighting for. And I will, if I have to. I'll do whatever it takes to earn your trust back."

Lenora felt tears leak from her eyes. For the first time in years, she didn't bother holding them back. She'd never felt such heartbreak, such pain in her chest. Lawrence meant every word. She knew that in her soul. That knowledge hurt her because she didn't want to break his heart, not after what he had been through with his home kingdom being in such turmoil.

"Lawrence," she began, wiping a tear away with the back of her hand. "I know why you kept your past a secret. But I'm still upset—still hurt. Though, I don't blame you for what you went through, or why you didn't tell me. It was something you couldn't control. Your parents took you to Norraine for a new life, and you were so young. You never expected this to happen. For your secret to come out this way."

"I was going to tell you," he said, angling his body toward her. "I promised myself that one day, I would tell you everything. I guess I just waited too long."

She smiled as more tears ran down her cheeks. "I believe that. And one day, I will be able to forgive you—forgive this situation we're in."

He pursed his lips. "But not today."

Lenora sighed, looking toward the door. "There's so much going on right now, Lawrence. We're in a foreign land that's on the brink of a civil war. We won't be safe until we're back in Norraine."

Lawrence nodded. "And there's the whole matter of Prince Alejandro."

She bit her lip. "Yes, there's that."

"What did you see? In the cave, when you had that vision. He seemed different after that. Much more annoying."

Lenora willed herself to look at him as she explained exactly what she saw. Lawrence's eyebrows seemed stuck in a perpetual furrow as he listened.

"I still don't know what it means," she said, finally looking away. "Xander thinks it means that we're ... supposed to be together. But it could just mean we're both rulers of our own kingdoms and I visit him on his deathbed." She shrugged. "I don't know."

Lawrence blew out a breath. "That's why he's trying to claim you, then."

Lenora, remembering her conversation with Alejandro, snapped her gaze to Lawrence. "What does that mean, exactly? And how does that work?"

"Well, shifters leave their scent mark on their mates. It's basically just a really potent scent that warns others that the person is taken or in a committed relationship."

"Does that require consent?" She lifted an eyebrow.

Lawrence shifted in his seat, looking uncomfortable. "Usually."

"So why did you mark me? Xander told me you left your scent all over me, like I was your... Does that mean we're..." She didn't know which word to use. Mated? Married? Her world was blending with this new one she'd happened upon, and she didn't know if there were any similarities between them.

Lawrence shook his head fervently. "No, we're not married or anything. I might have accidentally left my mark on you. I didn't mean to. I promise."

She furrowed her eyebrows, wanting him to elaborate some more. All of this was new, and so very confusing.

Lawrence perked up, his spine going straight. Lenora turned to the door, her body still on guard.

Alejandro opened it a moment later, his face dropping as his eyes shifted from Lenora to Lawrence. With narrowed eyes, Alejandro growled at Lawrence. "Give us a minute?" he asked, though his tone made it known it was a demand. "And send for the nurse."

Lawrence simply nodded, giving Lenora a look before he disappeared out the door.

She shook her head. "You can't keep doing that, you know. Ordering him around. Glaring at him every two seconds."

Alejandro sauntered closer, then brushed her messy curls from her forehead. "He's one of my subjects. Of course I can."

"Technically, he's *my* subject." She batted his hand away, but he grasped her fingers and intertwined them with his. The action made her blush as flutters filled her empty stomach.

He chuckled, then sat beside her on the bed. "Technicalities aside, there's something I need to talk to you about."

She froze at his sudden change in tone. "What's wrong?"

"You can read me that well already, huh?" Alejandro chuckled, then shook his head. "I met with my uncle and several other leaders. They were ... shocked to see me alive, to say the least."

At his pause, she clenched his hand, thinking the worst.

They won't follow him. After all his planning, they refuse to help him.

He squeezed her fingers, a smile growing on his lips. "Everyone's on board. They welcomed me, and they're ready to throw themselves behind me and my mission."

Blowing out a breath, Lenora relaxed. "That's great, Xander."

His smile faltered, not quite reaching his eyes. "Here's the bad news. Augustín's forces are on the move. Essentially, he's not where he's supposed to be, which means we're reworking the plan. I haven't been privy to all the updates since I've been in Newton, so our spies have had to catch me up. Augustín's actions are convoluted. He's all over the place, moving his troops to various, unpredictable locations at his whim. He was supposed to be at Miravista Castle during the spring and summer months, but now he's all the way in Cima on the east coast. That changes everything. Instead of being a short two-day march, it'll take us a week to head him off. We can't lose the element of surprise we have. Once word gets out that I'm alive, he'll come for me."

Alejandro tucked some of her hair behind her ear. "I'm sorry, Nora. I have to break my promise to see you off safely. I won't be able to accompany you to Puerto Nuevo."

"It's all right, Xander," she said, pulling his hand to place it on her cheek. "I'll find a way."

"I already made the arrangements this afternoon. Tío Ernesto secured your passage on a ship heading to Norraine. He also has a carriage that will take you to Puerto Nuevo."

"Really?" Lenora's hand gripped his tighter.

Smiling, Alejandro gave her a slow nod. "Plus, I'm sending you with two of my people. Tío Ernesto hand-selected them for me, but I knew them when I was a child. They're trustworthy. Two of his best fighters. They'll protect you in my stead." He placed both hands on her cheeks, framing her face. "I wish I could be the one to protect you. To make sure you get on that ship. I won't sleep until I know you're back home, safe and away from all this fighting."

"I'll be fine, Xander. I've trained my whole life for situations like this. And you have protected me. Without you, Remy would have found me a week ago."

"Will you write to me as soon as you arrive? Give me peace of mind?"

She nodded. "Where should I send the letter?"

"I'll give you the address of someone here in Monte Paseo. They'll find a way to get it to me."

Her hands squeezed his where he held her face in a gentle embrace. "I'll take care of your guards when we make it to Norraine. I'll treat them as if they're my own citizens."

A smile graced his full lips. "There's one good thing to come of this. You'll have to return my guards to me, so I'm certain we'll see each other again soon."

That notion brought a furious heat to her cheeks.

She would find a way to see him again. She had to.

Twenty-Two

Aknock on the door interrupted Lenora's thoughts before a woman entered, carrying a tray of supplies. Lenora spied a tin can that surely held salve, a few strips of clean gauze, and metal medical instruments. The nurse's silver hair was tied in a bun at the top of her head. Years of laughter and love crinkled her skin in soft pleats. She wore a gray dress that stopped at her ankles and dark brown sandals cinched closed with string.

Spotting Alejandro, the nurse lowered her head, muttering a few words Lenora couldn't quite catch.

"*Está bien*, Irma," Alejandro said, removing his hands from Lenora's face and standing. "Please see to your patient."

Irma spluttered, her tone one of apology. Lenora tilted her head to the side, trying to understand anything the woman said, but her words flew out much faster than Alejandro's, María's, or Pedro's. Even though she couldn't understand what any of them said, either, at least she had heard syllables and letter sounds she could try to make sense of. The nurse, however, spoke so quickly, every letter blended together until Lenora's head spun.

She raised a hand to her forehead, suddenly dizzy.

Irma rushed to her side, setting the tray on the side table and grabbing a cold, wet cloth from it to place on Lenora's brow. "Lay down."

Nodding only made her head throb more, so Lenora did as she was told. As soon as her head hit the soft pillow, her eyes drifted shut.

Alejandro's presence hovered beside her, and his fingers slipped through her hair, tangling in the knots. "I'll send someone with food. If there's anything you need, just call out. I have two guards stationed outside your door. But please do as Irma says and try to rest. You'll feel better in the morning."

Lenora cracked her eyes open to catch his worried expression. "Will you stay? For a bit?"

Alejandro's shoulders rose as he drew in a breath. "Trust me. I'd rather be right here next to you. But I have to get back to General Ernesto. There's so much to do and not as much time as we'd hoped." He leaned forward and kissed her cheek, making her head spin twice as fast. "Besides, you need your sleep. I'll only distract you."

Lenora laughed at his grin. "You're right. Go take care of your people."

He looked over his shoulder. Irma gawked at them as she absentmindedly mixed freshly ground herbs into a container with a metal spoon. When he looked back at Lenora, his expression had hardened into a face she recognized as the one she often wore in front of her citizens when they needed to see their leader. "I'll see you later."

Alejandro hesitated a moment longer before he finally stood and exited, leaving Lenora with Irma. The nurse pursed her lips, still stirring the salve. Then she pointed to Lenora's ankle. *"Infectado."*

Since the woman enunciated slowly, Lenora grasped what she was trying to tell her. "My ankle is infected?" That much she could have guessed on her own.

Irma gave a single nod, then began unwrapping the gauze from Lenora's various wounds and the removing the wooden splint that held her ankle together. Lenora winced at every touch, but once Irma freed her foot from the brace, pain shot through every nerve in her body.

Irma gave her a look of apology as she applied fresh ointment on the various wounds, adding an extra potent salve to her ankle, and reapplied clean bandages around her waist and arms. A few of the worst injuries had neat rows of stitches, and her back had thick pieces of gauze over the many cuts she'd received on the rocky floor. The woman worked with practiced precision, only uttering short, curt commands.

As soon as Irma reattached the splint, a knock on the door signaled the arrival of a new guest.

Irma called out, and the door opened to an older man with salted hair. He carried a tray of food that made Lenora's mouth water even though she couldn't see the contents. She just knew her stomach had begun to eat itself at that point, so she'd take whatever anyone gave her.

The man placed a tender hand on the middle of Irma's back, then gave her a quick kiss on the cheek. "*Esta comida es para la niña.*"

Irma bobbed her head, motioning for him to step closer.

Lenora sat up and eyed the platter as he angled it toward her.

"For you," he said, his accent as thick as Irma's.

"Thank you," Lenora said, grabbing the tray. She instantly recognized the tortillas and shredded chicken, but the rest of the food was new to her. The smell of roasted herbs and spicy flavors had her scarfing down as much as she could without overfilling her empty stomach. After going so many days without proper nutrition, she knew better than to eat too much all at once, no matter how good the food tasted.

The man chuckled and murmured something to Irma before kissing her and leaving. At the door, he waved at Lenora before ducking through the opening.

She caught a glimpse of the night sky and two massive bodies right by the door. A man with a bald head looked over his shoulder, seeing the door still cracked open. He leaned forward to grab the handle, his eyes landing on hers. With a wink, he dragged it shut, closing her inside.

Irma came into view as she placed the back of her hand on Lenora's forehead. She realized how close the woman was, not showing a hint of fear of being so near. Lenora jerked back, her body still accustomed to that old reflex.

When Irma frowned, Lenora swallowed her bite of food. "Thank you for taking care of me, Irma."

That brought a smile to Irma's face. "Welcome. Now eat, then sleep. You can leave tomorrow, *si te sientes mejor.*"

Even though Lenora nodded, she only vaguely understood the last part of her sentence. After finishing her meal, she took the proffered vial Irma handed to her.

"For pain," the nurse said, nodding toward the glass container.

Lenora downed the clear liquid, then washed it away with the water Irma had passed her. Almost immediately, exhaustion rippled through her body in soothing waves. Allowing the warm meal and the medicine to work, she was lulled into a gentle sleep.

Hours later, a soft touch brought her back, and she blinked her groggy eyes open to find Alejandro's smiling face.

"I didn't mean to wake you," he whispered, running the backs of his fingers down her cheek. "I just wanted to check on you. Then I saw how peaceful you looked while you were sleeping."

"So you had to wake me," she said, raising an eyebrow.

"I did." He grinned, melting her heart at the sight.

She couldn't be mad at that smile. She covered her mouth as she yawned, then rolled onto her back. "What time is it?"

"A few hours after dawn." Alejandro reached for the metal cup beside her bed and helped her sit up.

She drank the water, happy to find the liquid had remained cool all night. "Irma said I could leave the room today if I was feeling up to it. At

179

least, I think that's what she said."

Alejandro chuckled. "Yes, she briefed me. She said you're healing quicker than she'd originally thought."

"She's not a healer, though, right? You said your people don't have that kind of magic."

He shook his head. "She's not a healer, but she's an excellent nurse. She was the one who helped me when my uncle brought me to Monte Paseo."

Lenora held onto the cup, taking tiny sips until it was empty. "And the man who brought my dinner—was he her husband?"

Alejandro tilted his head sideways. "Possibly. Old, gray, soft voice?"

She nodded. "And he kissed her, but I didn't want to assume they were married since I don't know anything about your culture."

Chuckling, Alejandro leaned forward to press his lips to her forehead. "Maybe that's one thing that's universal."

Fates, be gentle.

He seemed to enjoy making her blush, and she fought hard to push it down. The heat didn't subside, not while his face was so close to hers.

"Xander," she mumbled, looking up into his eyes.

He pulled back an inch, giving her the space she needed to breathe. "I'll send for a walking stick. Do you think you can manage with it?"

Glad for the change of subject, she lifted her head and peered at her wrapped ankle. "I think so."

"Good. I'll have someone come to help you change. Then, if you're up for it, I can show you around the town."

Something blossomed inside her, bringing a sense of joy and excitement. That feeling she longed for, the one that sent her to Newton in the first place, sprang up from within her hardened heart. The past week had put a damper on her need for travel and adventure, but the thought of exploring this new town opened it up again.

She envisioned walking arm-in-arm with Alejandro as he pointed things out and introduced her to his people. Would she get to try new foods, maybe pick up some of his language? The thought made her giddy, even if she needed a cane and wore ghastly bandages all around her body.

Alejandro laughed. "I'll take that grin as a yes. I'll be back soon." He brushed her arm, then stood and spun toward the door.

Hobbling on one foot, she busied herself in the tiny, attached bathroom of the one-room lodge. She didn't have time for a bath, and she was sure Irma would stew herself into a fit if Lenora wet her bandages, so she resigned to clean herself up with a rag and the fresh water from the basin.

When she was done, she used the rest of the water to wet her hair so she could run her fingers through the coils. Her first instinct was to braid it and wrap it behind her head. Of course, she didn't have any oils to tame her curls, but she felt like she was on the cusp of a new adventure.

So why not be adventurous? The thought set her nerves ablaze.

A smile broke out on her face, creasing her cheeks in an unfamiliar way. Leaning her weak body against the wall, she rummaged through the cabinet beside the basin and found a bottle of oil that smelled a lot like rosemary with a hint of something else she couldn't identify. She dropped some onto her palm and ran it through her hair.

A tiny mirror above the bowl allowed her to glimpse her wild curls. Her golden strands peaked through, waving in greeting as they billowed down to her shoulders. Though she had never likened herself to her mother, she couldn't help but picture Queen Elice reflected in the mirror. Her mother preferred to let her dark curls loose whenever she could, which seemed to be always.

Lenora's chest clenched at how much she missed her family. This was the first time in days that she had a calm moment to think about them.

She only had one more day in Alegría before she had to board the ship heading back home.

Then she hurt in a different way. Once she left Alejandro, she didn't know when she would see him again. She knew what he was getting himself into. There was a very real possibility he wouldn't survive this coup on his brother, no matter what her vision showed her. She might never see him again, and that made her throat choke up as tears rushed to her eyes. It had only been a week since she walked into Alejandro's life, but the thought of never seeing him again hurt more than the horned spider's venom on her flesh.

A knock at the door brought her back, and she cleared her throat before she called for the person to enter as she hopped to the bed.

A teenage girl appeared with a handful of dresses and shoes. Her tanned skin and brown curls with red streaks shined with the glistening sun behind her before she shut the door. "*¡Buenos días, princesa!*" the girl shouted, then curtsied. "*Me llamo Rosa.*"

"Good morning, Rosa," Lenora said, hoping that was the right response.

The girl grinned, then held out her arms. "*Para ti.*"

Thanking the girl, she grabbed the garments and spread them beside her on the cot. Lenora motioned toward the options. "Which do you suggest?"

Rosa tapped a finger against her lips, then pointed to a bright pink dress. "*Al príncipe le encantaría este vestido.*"

Not understanding what she said, but absolutely not wanting to choose the pink dress, Lenora tapped the dark blue—since it was the closest to black out of all the options. "I think I'll choose this instead."

Nodding, the girl grabbed the garment and helped her into it with delicate movements, careful of all the bandages. It was a simple design, with sleeves that flowed to her wrists, a scalloped neckline, and a few hard pleats that ended above her ankles. It was a little tighter around the waist thanks to the wrap feature that tied into a dainty bow on her left side. She hadn't worn anything so feminine in years. But the overall loose fit allowed her bandages to breathe while covering up most of the cloth.

She slipped on a pair of hard-soled slippers with thick straps that wove around her ankle—thankfully mitigating the eyesore that wrapped around her injury. Turning to Rosa, she splayed her arms to the side, lifting an eyebrow. The girl pursed her lips, walking around Lenora as she balanced on one leg.

Stepping forward to adjust Lenora's hair, the girl fluffed and finger twirled some of the peskier curls until she gave a satisfied grin. "*Estas lista, princesa.*"

Lenora figured she meant she was ready, so she thanked Rosa and watched as she opened the door. Her nerves twisted into a ball, eager to see the town but anxious to see Alejandro.

Twenty-Three

Rosa spoke to the two guards, then grabbed something from the bald one's outstretched hand. The girl returned, a shiny black cane in her grasp. Rosa presented it to her, lowering her head, and Lenora took a moment to test the device in the room before she followed Rosa outside.

Lenora eyed the two guards right away, their gigantic frames as they guarded the door hard to miss. They bowed as she passed, and she gave them each a firm nod. They wore crisp, all-black uniforms. Their buttoned shirts and slim pants looked freshly pressed, and Lenora noticed a few badges pinned to their lapels.

Then her eyes found Alejandro. He had changed from his earlier laid-back outfit. Now, he wore a uniform that matched the guards, though his collar had a vibrant sea-green emblem shaped like the triangular top of an evergreen tree above three wavy lines. He watched her move closer, his gaze devouring her. He lingered on her hair, making her smile at the stunned expression on his face.

"*Mi princesa,*" he muttered, reaching his hand out to her.

Lenora slipped her fingers into his, intertwining them until she didn't know where hers ended and his began. "My prince."

That phrase bolstered him, causing his chest to swell and his lips to twitch into a smile. He cleared his throat and turned to the guards. "Allow me to introduce you to your guards. Manuel, Carlos." The two men stepped forward, then bowed again. "This is Princess Lenora Moore-Taylor of Norraine. General Ernesto may have already apprised you of the situation, but I want to make myself clear. You are to make sure she returns to Norraine safely. Under no circumstances will you stop, change directions, or become distracted until she gets home. You will not allow her to get hurt, and no one—I mean *no one*—will lay a single finger on her. Do I make myself clear?"

Lenora listened in awe at Xander's commanding tone, watching as his gaze hardened. She would be lying if she said her heart didn't respond by beating itself out of her chest.

Manuel and Carlos lowered their heads.

"Of course, Alpha King," the taller of the two said, lifting his head only slightly. He had thick hair, so dark it was almost black.

The other kept his eyes on the ground as he muttered his own response, the brown skin on his head shimmering in the sunlight. He was the bald one she saw last night closing her door.

Placated, Alejandro nodded and turned his attention to Lenora. "Shall we?"

"Where are you taking me?" she asked, her eyes roaming her surroundings.

The dirt road led into the town, a few hundred yards away. Her small lodge sat close to a few others, with only about a foot between them. They all seemed to be similar in size and style—one room, with only one window in front and one on the side, likely for the bathroom.

Alejandro shrugged. "I just thought you'd like to see the town, meet a few people."

He offered his arm, and she slipped her free hand through, the other using the cane to alleviate the pressure on her broken leg. The thrill of being able to walk like this with someone lifted her spirit. She had never held anyone's arm this way, and it seemed to rest perfectly atop Alejandro's.

As they walked, Manuel and Carlos kept pace behind them like silent sentinels.

She watched as the buildings ahead drew closer. "Whose house was I staying in?"

"It's part of the visitor's complex. They're usually empty outside of holidays. I have the one next to yours, and Lorenzo took the one beside me."

Guilt washed a bit of her enthusiasm away. She hadn't thought of Lawrence since she saw him last night. "Where is Lawrence? Is he all right?"

Alejandro turned a sideways glance her way. "He asked permission to go into town to gather supplies for your trip."

She could tell he didn't want to talk about Lawrence, so she changed the subject. "I'd like to send a letter to my mother to let her know I'm on the way. I don't want to tell her what happened, just that something's come up and I need to return. That way she'll be expecting me."

"Of course. Whatever you need." Alejandro looked behind at the guards, and the one with curly hair strode away. "I wish we could have done that in Port Arcadia, but with the ports shut down, it likely wouldn't have left Newton anyway. Maybe I could have sent it here with my letter. I'm sorry I didn't think of it earlier."

"It's fine, Xander." Biting her lip, she peered behind, catching the bald guard's observant eye. "Actually, should I not call you Xander anymore?"

He laughed, placing his hand on top of hers where it rested on their joined arms. "You can call me whatever you like."

"It's just... The guard called you 'Alpha King.' Is that your title now?"

Halting, he turned so they fully faced each other. "Not yet. If for some reason the crown doesn't pass from parent to child upon the ruler's natural death, our laws dictate that only the person who defeats the previous ruler can be the Alpha King. Augustín killed my father, which made him the Alpha King. Until I defeat him, I'm just a prince. My uncle thinks it's good for morale, though, so he's having everyone address me as the king." He frowned, scratching behind his ear. "I don't know how I feel about it. I've not earned the title yet. So please, call me anything but 'Alpha King.'"

Lenora smirked. "Sure thing, my prince."

He matched her smile, though his eyes lowered as he stepped into her space. "If you keep calling me that—"

"My King!"

Alejandro's jaw snapped shut, and Lenora pressed her lips together to hold back her laugh at the irritated look on his face.

The curly-haired guard who had stepped away returned, waving a paper in his hands. In his other, he had a folded sheet with an envelope tucked against his side. "*¡Hay un informe!*"

Alejandro wiped the annoyance from his face. He grabbed the letter from the guard—Lenora still didn't know which was Manuel and which was Carlos—and began reading. He turned to her, his eyes squinted in apology. "I'm sorry, *princesa*, but I have to take this to General Ernesto right away. It's news from one of our operatives."

"Go!" she urged, giving his arm a slight push.

He furrowed his brow, then turned to the guards. "Stay with her. Don't let her out of your sight." When Alejandro looked at her, he sighed. "I wanted to show you the town."

"This is more important. I'll see you later."

He gave a single nod, then bent to kiss her forehead. She closed her eyes, wishing to feel his lips on her skin a little longer, but he pulled away and hurried toward the edge of the town where a few red brick buildings formed a line.

Lenora blew out a breath before turning her head to her new guards. She had to learn their names so she could tell them apart. "Those introductions earlier were a little more formal than I'm used to." She gave a tiny wave. "I'm Princess Lenora."

They both eyed each other until the bald one elbowed the other. Stepping forward, the curly-haired guard bowed. "I'm Manuel, but everyone calls me Manny." He pointed his thumb over his shoulder. "That's Carlos."

"*Encantada de conocerte, princesa,*" Carlos said, reaching his hand out. "Nice to meet you."

Lenora eyed his outstretched hand, subconsciously throwing her arm not holding the cane behind her back. "It's nice to meet you, too."

Manny and Carlos eyed her carefully. All she could do was offer a polite smile.

Shaking his head, Manny extended the envelope and paper. "For you, Princess."

Grabbing the proffered items, she thanked them. "Is there somewhere I can sit to write?"

Carlos pointed to the town behind her. "The postal office. And we can get breakfast at the cafe next door."

Lenora motioned forward. "Please, lead the way."

Hobbling in between the guards felt like passing between two stone towers. Manny was maybe half an inch taller than Carlos, but they both stood at almost six feet. They seemed only a couple of years older than her, possibly in their early twenties. Both had rich brown skin stretched taut over thick muscles. She could only imagine how huge their bear forms were.

The dirt path led them to the beautiful, two-story red brick buildings in the center of Monte Paseo. Some of the buildings were homes, and she could hear the families inside talking through the open windows. As they walked deeper into town, the homes turned into markets, offices, and businesses. In the middle of the street, a few stalls were erected, and several merchants sat on stools selling their wares. She paused in front of a food cart, the glorious smell of roasted meat entrapping her senses.

The man behind the cart wiped the bead of sweat from his brow with the back of his hand. "*¿Qué te gustaría?*" He held a metal spatula in his other hand as he hovered over a flat grill. Several tortillas sat steaming on a flat slab of black iron, making her mouth water.

Lenora looked back at Manny and Carlos, not knowing how to respond. Manny stepped forward and pointed to a metal pot that held a red liquid. "Do you like birria, *princesa*?"

At Manny's words, the vendor's eyes snapped to Lenora, widening in shock.

"I don't think I've had it before." Lenora looked into the container, spying a few pieces of meat floating in the sauce. "I'd love to try it, but I don't have any money." She didn't even know if they had the same currency.

Manny pulled three silver coins from his pockets and dropped them onto the cart. "*Tres tacos, por favor.*"

"Yes! I'm starving," Carlos exclaimed, reaching for a paper plate from the vendor's hand. He scooped the crispy tortilla, stuffed with saucy meat and topped with green herbs and onions, then dipped it into a tiny cup filled with the red sauce on the corner of his plate. He bit into it, and the sauce dribble down his chin.

Lenora couldn't wait to eat hers. Carefully, she reached for her own plate.

"Cheers," Manny said, lifting his plate in the air. "*Salud!*"

She copied his movement. "*Salud!*" she tried, her tongue tripping over the word. The men laughed heartily as they ate. It warmed her to share this meal with two of Alejandro's citizens, though she wished he were the one beside her.

Instead of wallowing in her disappointment—she knew what it was like to put her duties first—she grabbed her taco and dipped it into the sauce. It was the color of a deep burgundy wine, and as soon as the first drop touched her tongue, her mouth exploded with a blend of earthy, slightly spicy flavors.

"Oh my Fates, this is good." She moaned, then took another bite.

"I guess she likes *birria*," Carlos said, licking his fingers clean. He threw his empty plate in a nearby trash bin, then wiped his hands on his black trousers.

"I'm going to miss this food," she said, then threw the last bit of taco into her mouth.

Manny tossed his plate away and gave Carlos a knowing look. Both men raised an eyebrow at each other.

"I don't mean to pry—" Manny began, only to be interrupted by Carlos.

"But we really want to know what happened." Nonchalance was obviously not Carlos's thing.

Lenora watched as Manny threw an elbow into Carlos's side.

"What we want to ask," Manny drawled, "is how did you come to meet our Alpha King? We get that you're from Norraine, and you were in Newton, where he was hiding. All General Ernesto told us was that you had to escape a dangerous situation and needed an immediate ship to Norraine."

"And that we were to escort you," Carlos added.

"It's a long story," Lenora said, sighing. "We have a long trip ahead of us, so there's plenty of time to talk." She didn't want to share the entire tale here where anyone could hear them.

Nodding, Manny turned around, then pointed behind her. "There's

190

the postal office."

She followed him as Carlos fell in step with her. "Did you two know each other long?" he asked.

Lenora shook her head, blushing. "I've only known him a week. Xander—Alejandro saved me from Newton's wolves."

Manny looked over his shoulder with wide eyes. "The Wolf Brigade is after you?"

Carlos whistled, stuffing his hands into his pockets. "Wow, you must've pissed off someone very important."

Her eyebrows scrunched. "The Wolf Brigade?"

Manny slowed his pace to flank her other side. "Newton's wolf guard. They're led by Captain Acosta, who used to be a captain here under Alpha King Fernando."

"Alpha King Alejandro's father," Carlos threw in.

"I've only heard stories about Acosta," Manny continued, as if Carlos hadn't interrupted. "He's one of the most ferocious wolf shifters out there. That's why King Jerome put him in charge of his Wolf Brigade when the other shifter types were banished from Alegría."

Carlos lowered his voice and leaned in close. "They say Acosta rips his victims' hearts out of their chests while they're alive and eats them whole."

Lenora's lips thinned. "You're just trying to scare me."

"He's being dramatic," Manny said, glaring at Carlos.

Carlos shrugged, as if they were speaking of the weather. "I'm being real. Those are the rumors we hear."

Lenora turned to Manny, who bit his lip.

"Well..." Manny hesitated, tilting his head one way and then the other. "I guess, technically, that's one story. But I doubt it's true."

"It's probably true," Carlos said, throwing Manny a look.

"Unlikely," Manny countered.

"Maybe."

Twenty-Four

M anny held the door open for Lenora, and she walked inside the expansive lower level of the brick building. Several boxes and dozens of stacks of parchment lined the walls. A short man with thick, blond curls—the ends a dark brown—draped across his copper face leaned against a desk at the far end of the room.

The man looked up as soon as they entered, sniffing the air with a quizzical look on his face. "You're back again, Manny?"

Manny nodded as they walked up to the counter. "Just helping our guest send a letter."

The man tilted his head. "She smells like the Alpha King."

Lenora's eyes widened. Having learned about shifters and their sense of smell, she understood the implication of his words.

Carlos chuckled, leaning his elbows on the desk and reaching for a pen lying by the man's arm. "That means you'll make sure this letter gets sent right away. High priority. Right, Daniel?"

Daniel nodded. "Yes, of course. Anything for the Alpha King and his mate."

Lenora waved a hand in the air. "No, no. You have it all wrong. I'm—"

"They're not mated *yet*," Manny interrupted, reaching for Lenora's flapping hand.

She gasped, jumping away from his touch and nearly tripping on her cane. Her heart raced, and she clutched her fingers to her chest.

Three sets of eyes gawked at her. Manny's eyes nearly popped out of his head. Daniel looked at her as if she had attacked him with fire magic. Carlos mainly looked amused, with a slight crinkle by his eyes and lips.

Lenora cleared her throat, willing herself to calm down. "What I mean is, we're not mated *yet*. Like Manny said. It's still new." She motioned for the pen, and Carlos brandished it toward her with a little bow. "I'm just going to write this letter."

She slunk off to the far side of the desk, angling herself and the paper away from their prying eyes. Even though the three men made small talk in their language, she could feel their occasional gazes on her back as she penned her letter.

It took a few seconds to gather her thoughts. She knew she had to keep it short and to the point. She would tell her parents she had arrived in Newton as planned, but something went amiss, and she had to return home. Since all the ports in Newton were closed, she had to seek help from another kingdom. A ship was set to sail from Alegría, and she would arrive in Norraine soon.

Lenora bit her lip. In case this letter got intercepted, she didn't want to leave any actual names, precise locations, or dates. With a prayer to the Fates that her mother and father would receive her missive, she tucked the parchment into the envelope and handed it back to Daniel.

"How soon will it get there?" she asked, eyeing him as he looked over the envelope.

He squinted as he read the address. "Highmore Castle? All the way in Norraine? Hmm. Might take a few days."

Carlos, still leaning against the desk, shook his head. "Even for the Alpha King's mate?"

Manny crossed his arms. "Surely you can do better than that for our new Alpha King?"

Lenora's cheeks heated, wanting to set them straight but wondering if this would actually work.

Daniel grabbed a sheet beside him. "I suppose I can send it with this evening's delivery carriage. It will get to Puerto Nuevo by tomorrow morning."

Lenora peered over, reading the paper. It was a log of all outgoing carriages and ships. A list of several kingdoms she hadn't heard of immediately caught her attention, and she wanted to ask a dozen questions. Instead, she focused on the matter at hand. "Are there any ships going to Norraine tomorrow?" From what Xander had said, her ship would leave in two days. Hopefully there was one that would arrive in Norraine before she did.

Daniel tapped the paper. "Yes. Tomorrow morning. It'll make port in Norraine in three days."

"That's perfect!" she exclaimed. She turned to Manny, who looked at her with a smile, then at Carlos. He nodded, a wide grin stretching his lips and forming dimples on both cheeks.

Daniel sighed, eyeing both men. "Okay. I'll make it happen. But put in a good word for me with the Alpha King. I met him yesterday, and he seems like an okay guy. Hope he turns out better than the last one."

Lenora felt her mouth drop open in surprise at Daniel's bluntness. Manny shook his head, stepping away from the counter. Carlos just chuckled, grabbing the pen from her hands and making her jolt before he tossed it onto the counter.

"Don't worry," Carlos said, turning away from the postal worker. "We'll tell him."

"I mean it, Carlos!" Daniel yelled as Manny opened the door to leave. Carlos threw a wave behind his back as he led Lenora out.

She leaned against the closed door, blowing out a breath. Both guards turned to her, questions brimming and threatening to spill over. She merely shook her head. "Not now."

Carlos raised his hands. "Hey, I didn't say anything."

Manny threw his elbow at him. "Relax, man. Before you *do* say something."

Lenora eyed the two men, noting how comfortable they were around each other. "Are you two brothers?"

"Twins," Carlos answered with a grin.

At the same time, Manny said, "Unfortunately."

"Wow," Lenora said. "My mother's a twin. Sometimes they are so in sync it's scary, but most times they're complete opposites."

Manny nodded. "That sums it up perfectly."

"So tell me," Carlos said, changing the subject with a light tone in his voice. "What's with the..." He motioned with his hands, throwing them behind his back in an exaggerated attempt at copying her.

She shook her head. "I'm not talking about that out here." She knew the trip to Norraine was definitely going to be long.

"Then what about the whole mate thing?"

"Not. Now." Lenora narrowed her eyes.

Carlos smirked. "Because if you're *not* taken—"

"Bro, shut up," Manny grunted.

"Then maybe—" Carlos stopped short, dropping his smile as he spun around. Manny did the same, blocking Lenora with his body.

"Wolf," Manny bit out. "You're supposed to be in your cabin."

Carlos growled, the sound rumbling deep in his chest. "Alpha's orders."

"I was given permission to stock up on supplies," said a voice Lenora instantly recognized.

She maneuvered around Manny, finding Lawrence carrying a large basket full of bags and a couple of canteens in his arms.

"Lawrence!" She said his name like she hadn't seen him in weeks. Something gripped her heart, reminding her of his recent betrayal. Though she knew why he lied to her, it still didn't lessen the pain.

One side of Lawrence's mouth lifted. "Hey, Lenny." He eyed the two bear guards. "I see you have new protection."

"It was Xan—I mean, Alejandro's idea. They're accompanying us to Norraine."

He nodded as Manny and Carlos exchanged glances. Manny stepped forward between Lawrence and Lenora. "Hurry and gather the supplies. You know it's dangerous for you to be here. If word gets out of Monte Paseo that there's a wolf in Alegría... Well, I'm sure I don't have to tell you what that would mean."

Lawrence backed away, allowing space for them to leave. "I guess I'll see you tomorrow, Lenny."

She waved, then followed between the two bear shifters.

They spent the next hour inside a small eatery, where they ordered a full breakfast. The entire table was stacked with plates, and she tried a little of everything, enjoying flavors she never knew existed.

"What's this again?" she asked, lifting a crispy tortilla shaped like a triangle. It was covered in a spicy red sauce and had bits of cheese and eggs. Throwing it into her mouth, she closed her eyes and savored the unique texture and flavor caressing her tongue.

"Chilaquiles," Manny answered, scarfing down a spoonful of smashed beans.

"Fates. So good." Lenora wanted to take the recipe back home with her. She had to introduce this to her people.

Carlos hummed in agreement beside Manny on the opposite side of the table.

It took a few more minutes to finish their meal, then another few to find the energy to get up. With a full belly after days with so little food,

Lenora felt ready to tackle the day—and there was still so much daylight left.

Manny and Carlos were great guides. They took her inside every shop and let her try different food from multiple stalls. Their witty sibling banter reminded her of her own relationship with her siblings, and the familiarity eased her homesickness. By late afternoon, though, a throbbing in her ankle reminded her that she needed to rest.

She sat on a brick fence, resting her cane against her leg. The guards flanked her side, but Manny—the more astute of the two—looked down at her splint. "Should we take you back to your room?"

"Are you kidding, Manny?" Carlos asked, his tone incredulous. "She's only here for a day. There's still so much to see. Besides, are you forgetting what tonight is?"

"I thought the nurse said she needed to rest." Manny looked at Lenora. "We can come back for you after you take a nap or something."

"What's happening tonight?" she asked. She looked around the square, but nothing seemed off. She likely wouldn't be able to tell, anyway, since this was her first time here.

Carlos grinned. "A celebration for the return of our Alpha King. We're marking a change in leadership and hopefully a new way of life. There's going to be music, and dancing, and food..." He let that last word hang in the air, already knowing Lenora wouldn't pass up the chance to try new food.

Manny rolled his eyes, sighing. "Yeah, it'll be fun. I'm sure the Alpha King will want you there."

She bit her lip. It did sound like something she would want to attend. "Maybe I should go back and rest. What time will it start?"

Manny eyed the sky. "Right at sundown. You'll be able to get plenty of rest."

"We'll wake you before it starts," Carlos promised.

Nodding, she pushed off the fence and allowed them to guide her back to the cabin. As soon as she took off her shoes, she lowered her aching body onto the bed. Her eyes snapped shut, and she fell fast asleep.

When her lids opened again, she felt his presence before she heard his voice.

"Darn. I tried not to wake you this time."

Lenora winced as the light poured in from the open door. Alejandro stood in the opening, and she could see both Manny and Carlos leaning against the exterior wall. They peered inside, Manny giving her a nod as Carlos winked, before Alejandro shut the door behind him.

"Alejandro," she muttered, still groggy from sleep.

He walked to her side, then kneeled on the floor and enveloped her hands in his. He placed a kiss on each knuckle, his eyes never leaving hers. Her heart flipped. She didn't think she would ever get used to his touch.

"Never thought I'd like hearing the sound of my name so much." He bent down to kiss her fingers. "Or maybe I just like the way you say it."

"Fates," she breathed, yanking her hand away. This man was doing crazy things to her mind. She needed some space before she lost it completely.

Chuckling, he helped pull her up so she could sit, then sat beside her. "Manny and Carlos let me know you want to go to the celebration tonight. I was going to tell you about it earlier, I just didn't have time before I was pulled away."

Lenora understood the obligations he faced. She prepared her entire life for the same ones. "Is it almost time?"

Alejandro nodded, but he wore a frown. "There are a couple of things I'd like to talk to you about first." He held his hand out, and she couldn't help the pull she felt as she laced their fingers and rested them together on her lap. "We have a few spies with Augustín's forces. The letter I received earlier was from one of them. He said Augustín left Cima and is heading back to Miravista. That was two days ago. We have an opportunity to cut him off, but only if we march right away."

Lenora's heart sank. "When are you leaving?"

"At dawn. We should cross paths in a day, maybe two."

"So, you'll leave before I do." She stared at their hands before meeting his gaze.

"That's the other thing. Tío Ernesto received a note from the captain of the ship you were supposed to leave on. It's leaving earlier than scheduled. The captain wanted to make sure Tío knew so he could make sure his 'shipment' arrived on time. You'll have to leave tomorrow morning as well to get to Puerto Nuevo before it leaves."

"Oh," Lenora said, blinking. "Yes, I'll be ready."

"I want to see you off before I go." He ran his fingers through her wild curls. "If that's okay with you."

"Of course," she said, her tone one of pleading. "Please don't leave before saying goodbye." Her voice wavered on the last word.

Alejandro breathed deep. "I have something for you." He dug into the pocket of his black trousers and pulled out a silver necklace.

Her eyes lit up as recognition hit her. "My protection charm!"

He held it in the air, letting the clear crystal at the end dangle in front of her eyes. "I took it from your bag when we arrived. Had someone in town fix it for you. May I?"

Lenora turned away, then grabbed her thick curls and held them to the side. Alejandro looped it around her neck and clasped it into place. His fingers lingered on the back of her neck, trailing the line of her dress and sending shivers down her spine.

Spinning, she found herself encircled in his arms as he slipped them around her waist. "Thank you," she whispered, then lowered her head to his shoulder. A sense of peace settled over her. She could stop fearing touch so much now that she had her necklace.

Alejandro pulled her close, then placed a kiss on top of her head. "Just promise me you won't go touching other guys."

She lifted her head, catching the twinkle of humor in his eyes. "I promise."

Twenty-Five

T hick clouds of smoke rose into the air from massive fire pits. Several bonfires spread across the center of town, lighting up the night. As soon as Lenora saw the fumes and heard the laughter, she was transported to nights along the southern coast of Norraine with the Nomads. Nostalgia took over, and a sense of longing made her hobble with her cane as quickly as she could. Alejandro and her new guards matched her pace, never once making her feel out of place as they walked to the square.

During the Last Mage War, the Nomads had remained neutral, though their close ties with mages meant they would have sided against the crown if they'd been forced to choose. So, when her mother finally ended the war after fifty long years of fighting, they embraced her and her family with open arms. Sophia, one of the Nomad's leaders and a powerful healer, became like family. Lenora always felt like she belonged whenever she visited the southern territory.

Celebrations with the Nomads left fonder memories in Lenora's mind than any social gathering at Highmore Castle. Whenever she was in Nomad territory, she never had to worry about uncomfortable stares or people jerking away from her touch. She always wore her double protection—her warding charm and her gloves—but the Nomads never treated her as abysmally as the lords and ladies of her mother's court. Balls and court appearances were torture. Fates, even the servants at the castle made her feel worse than vermin.

Despite that, she kept her head up as she wore her dark gowns and thick gloves. She knew that one day she would be worthy of the crown destined to sit upon her head. She would earn it through hard work and determination. If she returned home with valuable information on how to improve her people's lives and actually made changes that benefited them, they would finally see her for who she was behind the layers of protection she wore around her body. Also, if she found a way to somehow better manage her powers, she could return as more than just a cursed princess.

In the quiet recesses of her mind, she admitted how much she enjoyed balls and dancing. No one ever asked her to join them on the dance floor, but she liked to tap her feet and hum to the melody played by Highmore's royal violin trio. Her sister Patty loved to make fun of her for singing quietly on the raised dais, but it calmed Lenora's turbulent soul.

As she drew closer to the town square, music reached her ears, making her wish she could run along the gravelly path.

"Excited?" Alejandro asked with a grin.

Lenora nodded, not bothering to hide her smile. "I already love the music from here."

This would be the first party she attended where no one knew her. The Alegrías didn't know about her past, what mistakes she'd made, or of her Fates' cursed powers. Tonight, she could dance with Alejandro—and actually hold his hands without gloves, which was something she could never do with the few dance partners forced upon her.

The musical notes differed from she was used to. The closer she got, the more she realized she didn't recognize the instruments. A booming sound, one that banged a rhythmic beat, accompanied a higher tone underneath a repetitive strum. Then she finally turned the corner, and the entire central plaza came into view. A stage was set up in the middle of the town, where a band played in front of the crowd.

She stood transfixed to her spot, her eyes drinking everything in. Carts with food and drinks lined the outskirts, and people in colorful skirts of purple, red, and orange placed their orders. Before the stage, a makeshift dance floor of thick wooden planks absorbed the sound of thumping boots as men and women twirled and spun and clicked their heels in time to the musicians' beat. The most amazing assortment of people spread out around the area—people with various shades of brown skin and different colored highlights throughout their hair. She felt as if she found a great sense of belonging, greater even than when she was with the Nomads.

Lenora's blood pumped with the beat, begging to tap her feet in time with the unknown song.

Then, one of the musicians belted out a high-pitched cry. It rang across the plaza, and the sound echoed as others joined in. Soon, the musician twisted his stringed instrument to the side, away from his face, as he began singing. More people joined in, their collective voices weaving together with the rich melody.

Lenora wished she could understand the words. Instead, all she could grasp was the emotion behind the song. A deep longing and sadness wafted through the air, riding the waves of sound as nearly every man, woman, and child sang and swayed along.

A warm arm slung around her waist, pulling her closer. She leaned into Alejandro's side, lifting her aching foot to ease the throbbing, completely entranced by the music and the atmosphere. The smell of the spices and cooking meat further lulled her senses until he spun, standing in front of her, pulling her to his chest.

He held her there, both of his arms secured around her back. Her cane fell with a *thunk* when she raised her arms around his neck, allowing him to sway their bodies from side to side.

"What's the song about?" Even though she whispered, she was so close now that she knew he heard her above the noise.

"A lost love," Alejandro answered, his tone just as quiet and so near her face. "It's about a man whose love was taken from him, sent to the underworld because her beauty made Itzela, the moon goddess, jealous. He goes mad and begs Itzela to return his lost love to him. The goddess asks why he loves the woman so much when she's a mere mortal. His answer is that he's not asking for the moon, only for love. Outraged by his answer, the goddess continues to keep his love locked away. By the end of the song, he's so struck by his heartache, he begs the goddess to send him to the underworld to be with her. Tired of his mania, she obliges, and the man is finally reunited with his true love in the other realm."

Lenora leaned back, catching Alejandro's eye. "That's such a tragic story."

He shrugged a shoulder. "Adults sing that song all the time, even to their children. It's like an anthem—almost like a warning."

"Like a fable?"

Alejandro looked away, his eyes wandering the crowd. "You could say that."

Lenora turned her head toward the stage, where the singer crooned the last notes. As the song wrapped up, the crowd clapped and whistled before a fast-beat strumming began, signaling a new song.

"What kinds of instruments are those?" she asked.

Starting from the left of the stage, he pointed to a man with two drums connected by a wooden center. Then he pointed to the woman holding two identical devices with a narrow handle that she shook in time with the drummer. "Those are bongos. And the woman on the right has maracas." Lastly, he motioned to the man in the center. "The singer in the middle has a guitar."

Lenora noticed the similar structure between guitars and violins. However, the guitar was much larger and didn't require a bow to glide over its strings. "The music is magical. I've never heard anything like it."

Alejandro lifted her up, spinning her around. Now, she could stare at the stage without having to crane her neck. He rested her on the ground again, then continued to sway, leading her in a careful shuffle that she quickly picked up on. She watched her feet, wary of her injury and the pain she felt whenever she stepped on her healing foot. Alejandro was a good dancer, though, and he guided her in a gentle rock, his body in full control of hers.

Behind Alejandro's shoulder, a man with a thick beard appeared, his black uniform matching the guards except for the blue collar and the decoration of gold pins along the lapel. He cleared his throat, and Alejandro threw his head over his shoulder. "Tío Ernesto!" he exclaimed, earning him a slight smirk from the older man.

"*Sobrino*," Ernesto replied, his smile quickly disappearing. He covered his cough with his fist. "I mean, *Rey Alfa*. How are you enjoying your night, my king?" He turned a pointed stare at Lenora.

Alejandro released an arm from her hips to wave a hand in her direction, though his other remained locked around her. "General Ernesto, please meet Princess Lenora. Princess, this is my uncle."

Lenora didn't think Alejandro could wipe the smile off his face no matter how hard he tried.

Ernesto bowed low, and she copied the movement, grateful for Alejandro's other arm holding her steady against his side. Similar to what she did in Newton when she met the royal family, she placed one palm against her chest. The customary habit of her people came to her even now.

"Ah," Ernesto uttered, his tone light as his eyes crinkled, and little wrinkles appeared near the corners because of his smile. "I haven't seen this Norrainian gesture before, but I have heard of this custom while traveling in Newton."

Reminded of Remy's crude snicker, Lenora dropped her hand to her side. "My apologies, General. I hope that isn't offensive in Alegría."

Ernesto waved his hands around. "Please don't misunderstand me. I've heard some Newtonians speak lowly of the gesture, but I think it's admirable for a people to show their respect for one another in such a beautiful way. It's heart-warming to see."

Alejandro passed his eyes back and forth between Lenora and his uncle, his grin still plastered to his lips.

Lenora gave Ernesto a smile, amazed by how naturally it came. "We thank the Fates for allowing us to greet our loved ones and neighbors every day. So we place our hands over our hearts whenever we see someone we care about or meet someone new."

Ernesto nodded slowly, his eyes shifting to Alejandro. "The Fates, huh? Is that similar to our goddess?"

Alejandro looked down at his feet and scratched behind his ear. "Princess Lenora doesn't know much about our belief system, Uncle."

"Of course," Ernesto said, though his tone held a bit of curiosity. "You're right. I'm sure you haven't had the chance to talk about it yet."

"Not while being chased by wolves and attacked by horned spiders." Alejandro raised an eyebrow.

Ernesto turned to Lenora, pointing at her ankle. "I heard about what happened to you. You must be very strong to have survived all that you did."

Lenora blushed, not used to such praise.

"You should see her with a dagger," Alejandro added, his lips slanting as he smirked.

Lenora's cheeks burned hotter as Ernesto chuckled.

"I'm sure it's a sight," Ernesto said, "given what I've heard of your parents. But I won't keep you two any longer. Though the night is still young, we all have an early day tomorrow." He raised both brows at Alejandro, ensuring his meaning was clear.

They would have to turn in early.

As he walked away, Ernesto nodded at Manny and Carlos. Lenora registered their statuesque presence, and instant regret settled in. "Why don't you two go enjoy the party?"

Carlos jumped at the suggestion, but Manny turned a questioning glance at Alejandro.

Alejandro shook his head, though his mouth quirked up. "Go. I can watch the princess on my own."

"Thank you, Alpha King," Manny said, bowing.

"We never doubted your defense skills for one second, my king," Carlos said, already jogging off toward the dance floor.

Lenora laughed. Alejandro watched as Manny muttered an apology on his twin's behalf before he stalked off in the opposite direction. As soon as he was gone, Alejandro sighed and pulled her back into his arms.

"Now, where were we?" Alejandro asked.

Lenora melted into him. The light from the bonfires glinted off his honeyed eyes, and she became mesmerized as she stared directly into them.

"Hmm?" she mumbled, lost in his embrace.

He leaned his forehead against hers, and she forgot where they were. They were no longer in the middle of Monte Paseo, but floating on a cloud high in the starry expanse of black velvet. Her eyes closed on their own, and she indulged in the feel of Alejandro's head against hers and his arms around her middle.

"Nothing," Alejandro mumbled. "Let's just enjoyed out last night together."

Lenora shut down the ache that came with those words. She was good at blocking uncomfortable emotions. That little voice in the back of her mind reminded her what she was, and that she still wasn't worthy of anything good.

Yet.

She promised herself that one day, she would get everything she wanted. No matter what she had to sacrifice to get it.

Twenty-Six

Lenora rubbed her groggy eyes, forcing herself to wake up. Against their better judgment, Alejandro didn't walk her back to her room until after midnight, and she only got a few hours of sleep before she had to get up again.

Today was the day.

So much was happening. She couldn't wrap her mind around a single thing. Alejandro and his troops were mobilizing, preparing to attack Augustín and his army before they reached Miravista. Lenora was setting off at an earlier time than originally planned, with Lawrence and her designated guards, Manny and Carlos, so Alejandro could see her off. It would be a half-day's ride to Puerto Nuevo, where they would board a merchant ship heading to Norraine. The vessel would make port in the Fishing Villages along Norraine's eastern coast in two days.

Soon, she would be home.

A fresh wave of excitement passed through her nerves, giving her the energy she needed to hop out of bed. Rosa must have visited her room while she was out at the celebration because a new leather traveling case with her name engraved on the handle sat by the foot of the bed. A wardrobe consisting of black tunics, leggings, and boots were neatly folded within.

Apparently, Alejandro had told Rosa exactly what to pack.

Lenora washed up and changed by the light of the single lantern in her room, then braided her hair back—two strands wrapped tightly, connecting at the back of her head, hiding most of her illustrious golden strands. The last thing she wanted was for her messy curls to become tangled during the trip without the proper tools needed to tame them.

More importantly, she wanted to avoid standing out when she needed to hide until she was safely within Norraine's borders.

As she re-adjusted her splint and tied the laces on her boots, she wondered when her mother would receive her letter. If Daniel from the postal office did as he said, he mailed it off yesterday and it would be on a speedy ship to Norraine right now. She hoped it would arrive later today or tomorrow, while she was already at sea. The nearest fort to the Fishing Villages was Fort Brant, which would welcome her as soon as she arrived. The current commander of Fort Brant was Queen Elice's personal friend, Commander Harlem Fletcher, an air mage whose magic manifested in the form of lightning. Lenora knew that if Elice told him, Harlem would have his entire garrison meet her at the port to escort her to Fort Brant.

If she made it to Norraine, however, she wouldn't need an army to greet her. She'd be safe. What she needed was the army to prepare to travel to Newton, if she could convince the Council of Ten to attack Remy for trying to have her killed.

Thinking about her revenge emboldened her. She still couldn't believe Remy killed his family just to take the throne and that he was trying to capture and kill her, too. She didn't know what propelled him outside of her hearing about his plan. It was all moot now, since he was finally the king of Newton. Once she had left Stonehold, he should have given up the chase. Instead, he sent a Fates' forsaken wolf pack to hunt her down.

As soon as she made it home, she would tell her mother exactly what

211

happened. If she knew her mother, Elice wouldn't let Remy's actions go unpunished.

Elice was quite scary that way.

Evidently, Lenora was too.

She paused in the middle of throwing on a loose black coat, the silver buttons still undone, allowing the fabric to drape over her bandaged limbs. Never before had she likened herself to her mother. A wry smile worked itself onto her face. People had told her all her life that she was just like her mother, but Lenora hadn't seen it until now.

She knew there were some differences between them, and she relished the idea that she was her own person while still being similar to the woman she admired most.

A knock on her door made her look up. She called for the person to enter as she finished the last button and tucked her necklace beneath the collar of her tunic.

Her smile only grew as she caught sight of Alejandro. His crisp black uniform and brimmed cap made him look polished, but the wrinkle between his brows let her know how he truly felt.

The sight sent a flare of panic pumping through her veins. Would this be the last time she saw him? She hopped toward him on one foot, and he opened his arms to lift her up. Her hands immediately went for the skin on his neck—right where she touched him for the first time—to remind herself of her vision.

This couldn't be their last meeting. The Fates had shown her the future. She was there with him on that fateful day, and that had to mean something.

Alejandro sucked in a deep breath through his nose, and Lenora understood what that meant by now. He was inhaling her scent, probably memorizing it. She used to wish she were a different kind of mage, but now, for the first time, she wished she could shift into another creature altogether. Then she could have a truly special power, one that gave her the ability to transform into a ferocious beast and have incredible senses like this.

Alejandro leaned forward, pressing a kiss to her forehead and lowering her to her healthy foot. "Are you ready?"

"I am," she answered. "Although I wish I had more sleep."

"I'm sure you can rest in the carriage." Alejandro ran a finger down her cheek, and she leaned into his touch until he cupped her face with both hands. "I trust you'll have a safe journey. The path to Puerto Nuevo is open space, so no one will bother you. Once the ship is in open waters, though, you'll need to be on the lookout. The captain knows to keep watch. I just want to make sure you know, too."

Lenora nodded, her cheeks squished within his hold. "I'll be fine, Alejandro. I'll have Lawrence, Manny, and Carlos with me."

He blew out a breath, but nodded along with her. Taking her hand in his, he led her as she used her cane to walk out of the hut, and they headed toward the perimeter of town. Only a few lampposts lit the way, and she glimpsed the true size of the rebel army.

Lenora's eyes widened. Alejandro's troops arranged themselves into neat rows, grouped in several straight lines. By her estimate, there were two hundred soldiers ready to march. She didn't know if that would be enough, since she had no clue how many Augustín had with him.

Several captains stood to the side, barking orders at their groups. She spotted Ernesto at the head of the entire brigade, watching with focused eyes, his hands folded behind his back.

Alejandro helped her along the edge of the visitor buildings, where Lawrence, Manny, and Carlos stood waiting beside a horse-drawn carriage. Thick metal wheels held up the small frame, and the whole thing looked like it could handle a quick speed over a long distance.

Lawrence bowed first, and Manny lowered his head, elbowing his brother so he would do the same.

Alejandro pointed a thumb behind his back. "The princess's luggage is still in her room." He was looking at Lawrence, but Manny raised his head.

"I'll get it, Alpha King." Manny took off toward Lenora's room.

She rolled her eyes, but she knew what Alejandro was doing. He had to assert himself as their leader by commanding respect. By the looks of it, he didn't need to try that hard to gain Manny's deference. Carlos was a different animal altogether, and Lawrence—he simply narrowed his eyes at Alejandro, no doubt wanting to gnash his teeth at the bear shifter but not wishing to cause a scene in front of everyone.

Alejandro surveyed the carriage, checking the wheels, making sure the horses were fed and watered, and pulling on the reins and other straps to ensure they were tight. Once Manny returned, both twins secured her luggage to the back of the carriage with the rest of their belongings. Lenora noticed a fourth case, one she assumed belonged to Lawrence.

With everything packed, Alejandro returned to her side and grasped her hand. He brought it to his lips, kissing her knuckles. "Don't forget that letter."

The corner of Lenora's mouth quirked up. "Never."

Alejandro's eyes furrowed, and the sight brought an intense ache to her chest. She didn't want to say goodbye, and he looked like he didn't either.

Instead, he gave a curt nod and turned to her guards, eyeing all three. "I don't need to tell you how important Princess Lenora is to me. I trust you'll keep her safe, otherwise you wouldn't be going with her. But I will stress this one time, and one time only. Please take care of her. Make sure she gets home. And when I see the three of you again, you'll receive a handsome reward as my gratitude."

Carlos bowed. "It's our honor to serve you and your mate, Alpha

King."

For Fates' sake, Carlos.

Lenora turned her head to catch the flustered look on Alejandro's face. He wiped it away when he looked at her, forcing a smile to replace the nervous tremble of his lips.

Quickly, he turned to the men again. "You know which route to take?"

Manny nodded. "We'll stay off the main path. It'll take us an hour longer, but we'll get to Puerto Nuevo just after sunrise, before the ship sets sail."

"Good." Alejandro looked at Lawrence, his lips pursed. "Lorenzo," was all he said to him with a tip of his chin.

"The next time I see you," Lawrence began, "hopefully you'll be the rightful king of Alegría."

This brought a grin to Alejandro's face. He nodded again, then his attention fully returned to Lenora. Manny and Carlos took that as their cue, and they climbed onto the driver's bench, promptly fighting over who would control the reins. Lawrence backed away, then disappeared inside the carriage.

With their prying eyes gone, Lenora dropped her cane, wrapped her arms around Alejandro's neck, and buried her face against his chest. "Thank you for everything, Alejandro. You didn't have to help me, and you've gone out of your way to make sure I get home safely. I owe you so much."

Alejandro lifted her chin with his finger, gazing into her eyes. "You owe me nothing, my Nora. I selfishly wish we had more time together. Maybe my desire to bring you to Alegría was rooted in that selfishness because I got to spend more time with you, but I'm thankful to have met you." He tucked away a curl that had already come loose from her braid, then trailed his finger along the shell of her ear, making her spine shiver. "I'm thankful for the time we had and hopeful for the time we'll get in the future. Which is why I'm not saying goodbye. This is more like ... see you later."

Lenora chuckled. "See you later, my prince."

He closed his eyes briefly, hiding his hazel orbs from her view for a moment. "See you, *mi princesa.*"

Alejandro stooped to retrieve her cane, then backed toward the carriage. He pulled it open with one hand, then intertwined his fingers with hers. She followed him, then allowed him to help her inside. Gulping, she sat on the edge of the seat, still not ready to let go.

This was the first hand she'd held in over nine years. The last hand she'd gripped was Samantha's as they swam in the pond on her father's estate. She had held onto her friend's hand as they both sank beneath the water, consumed by the vision. Lenora nearly drowned that day.

Samantha did.

She had promised to never touch anyone ever again. The grief, the pain, the fear of causing that kind of devastation again had debilitated her for years.

Now, she had at least one hand to hold.

Lenora ran the tips of her fingers across his palm, relishing in the feel of his warm, rough skin. She memorized it like he memorized her scent.

Once she studied each line, wrinkle, and crease, she looked up into his eyes. A crinkle knitted his eyebrows together, and his jaw was set like a slab of stone.

Quietly, without uttering a word, they pulled away, their fingers sliding apart until their tips slipped away from each other. With his eyes locked on hers, Alejandro shut the carriage door, effectively cutting off all contact with her.

Lenora realized leaving Alejandro was akin to heartbreak. It was like ripping out your heart with slow, agonizing slices. Her mind replayed that heart-wrenching song the band played last night.

She could envision herself going mad with this grief, and she didn't need to use her powers to see the pain flash before her eyes.

Twenty-Seven

Rolling hills and beautiful Palo Verde trees encompassed the hard-packed trail. Lenora stared out the window, though her tired eyes begged for some rest. Lawrence sat quietly the entire time, and she was too busy wallowing in her nerves and sorrow to make small talk.

She didn't think Lawrence would want to talk about Alejandro, anyway, and he was all she had on her mind.

Instead, she soaked in as much of the scenery as she could through a tiny crack in the curtain until the foothills gave way to flat ground, the smell of brine and fish seeping through the carriage walls. After a few hours, Manny and Carlos steered them off the quiet back road to enter Puerto Nuevo's busy streets. The sun had roused the land and people, sending them bustling from building to building.

Lenora peeled back the thick curtain an inch. The town reminded her of Monte Paseo with its colorful atmosphere. She wished she could bottle this up and bring it back home with her.

Her guards led the carriage directly to the port, coming to a stop beside the docks. The door opened a crack, and Manny peeked his head inside. "We're going to check in with the first mate. Wait here until we come back." His eyes flashed to Lawrence, and they nodded wordlessly at each other before Manny closed them back inside.

Lenora sat back against the wooden bench. She knew better than to make a noise. Remy might be looking for her still, and she didn't know how far his reach extended. Besides, Lawrence was *definitely* not welcome in Alegría. If the wrong person caught his scent, they would be in trouble.

A few minutes later, a patterned knock on the door caused Lenora to sit upright. Lawrence threw himself in front of her, still careful not to get too close. She remembered belatedly that Lawrence didn't know she was wearing her protection charm.

The door creaked open to Carlos's grinning face. "Sorry, guys. Didn't mean to scare you." He beckoned with his arm.

Lenora pursed her lips as Lawrence huffed an annoyed sound. She climbed out of the carriage with her walking stick, and her eyes flitted across the town as quickly as they could. The docks were on one side, while the hustle and bustle of the townspeople were on the other. Manny grabbed two trunks from the carriage and passed them to Lawrence, then returned for the remaining two.

Carlos angled his head to the port. "Follow me. We should hurry, unless you want someone to scent ol' wolfy boy here, if they haven't already."

Lawrence gave a whining groan, and Lenora bit back her laugh. She never realized until this moment how much of a *wolf* her friend was, but now that she thought about it, he growled and whined and yipped just like a dog. The realization made her smile.

Carlos led the way down the wooden wharf. Several boats swayed on the water, tied to the pier by a thick, corded rope, but only one ship large enough to carry cargo lolled on the rocky waves. The salty foam from the ocean smashed against the wooden stern, rolling around the tip and passing underneath the dock. She inhaled the Enchanted Ocean's scent and lavished in the crashing swells that reached her ears.

They walked past a few sailors carrying barrels and bins, some working together to lift the heavier cargo. Carlos stepped onto a gangway that led to the ship, and they all filed on after him. As she passed, she caught the name *La Marinera* engraved in a beautiful script on the side.

A tall bear of a man with rich brown skin greeted them as soon as they walked onto the deck. His grizzled beard and long hair twisted in thick strands made him appear rough, but his smile seemed warm and genuine. He wore a thick leather coat with gold buttons, and a long sword was tucked into the sheath at his hip.

He raised his wide arms, motioning around at the chaos as another man with a thick accent yelled at the sailors from the quarterdeck. "Welcome, Your Highness. My name is Capitán Torres, and I own this beautiful ship. It was a gift from our previous Alpha King Fernando. I hope to repay the favor he gave me so many years ago by ferrying you safely across *el Océano Encantado.* May our new Alpha King Alejandro have a long, prosperous reign."

Lenora stared at the man before her with wonder. General Ernesto must have had strong, respectful connections if people were already calling Alejandro their king. Hope and pride flowered within her.

Captain Torres whistled, waving toward the quarterdeck, and the shouting man snapped his head their way. With a grin that showcased his gold tooth, the captain returned his attention to Lenora. "I'll introduce you to my first mate, Señor Ortega. He'll get you squared away. I know General Ernesto said to keep a low profile, but it's not every day we have a princess on our ship. Please make yourself at home. My ship is your ship." His eyes passed over her shoulder, narrowing as his nose twitched. "But perhaps exercise caution. The waters are heavily guarded right now, especially in Newton territory. I'm sure you know what I mean." He winked, and Lenora nodded just as the man from the quarterdeck appeared at his side.

"You must be Princess Lenora," the man said, his voice gruff. He had a thick, braided beard that stretched past his chin. "I'm Señor Ortega."

Lenora placed a hand on her chest, lowering her head in a curt bow as she balanced herself on the rocking ship with her cane. "It's great to meet you, Señor Ortega."

The first mate tilted his head at the gesture, catching his captain's eye. Captain Torres clasped Señor Ortega's shoulder before he excused himself to the helm, where he stood watch, his eyes roaming over the entire ship.

Señor Ortega smiled, then greeted Lenora's guards. "If you'll follow me, I'll show you to your room." They walked down the deck toward a rickety staircase leading to the lower level. "Unfortunately, since this is a cargo ship, there aren't many spare rooms not filled to the brim with barrels or boxes. The only space we have available is a storage room we had fitted with a few beds. That does mean you'll have to share. My apologies, my lady."

Lenora shook her head. "I understand, Señor Ortega. My guards and I will be just fine with what you have. And you have my gratitude for helping us."

He beamed at her over his shoulder as he fished out a key ring from his pocket. He stopped by a door, unlocked it, and let her inside the small room. Two bunk beds were attached by several huge bolts on opposite walls, and a small, round table and two stools sat in the middle. Only one circular window in the back of the room allowed natural light to seep in, but it was perfect. That was all they needed.

She gave her thanks to Señor Ortega once more as Lawrence and Manny stacked the luggage in the corner.

The first mate dipped his head. "We'll set sail soon. Once we're out in open water, I'll return to show you to the dining room for your meal. The tour will have to be quick and quiet. I understand there was a need to keep this secret."

She nodded, thankful for the secrecy Ernesto imparted to this crew. "Yes, as much privacy as we can afford."

With a final wave, he closed them inside the storage room. Lenora leaned against the wall, exhaustion taking over. She needed to rest her foot. A collective sigh escaped each of her companions.

Carlos was the first to speak up. "I call a top bunk!" Then he hopped up onto the nearest bed, climbing the three steps built into the furniture to claim his spot.

Manny shook his head. "You didn't have to announce it, bro. You could have just sat yourself down quietly and fallen asleep." He walked the short distance to the cot below his brother and plopped down.

"Where's the fun in that?"

Lenora chuckled to herself. She missed the bickering between her own siblings. In just two days, she would be back home again. The first thing she would do when she saw her brother and sister again would be to hug them, then she would throw a quip in there to make up for the number of taunts she missed from them over the last week.

Then she'd hug them again and tell them how much she loved and missed them.

Maybe, if she were feeling bold, she would hold their hands.

Lawrence remained quiet throughout the trip. He followed behind Lenora, Manny, and Carlos through the halls when Señor Ortega guided them to the dining room. Then, back in their quarters, he sat on his top bunk, not uttering a single sound.

Lenora assumed he wanted to draw as little attention to himself as possible. A wolf on a bear's ship during a banishment would likely not go over too well if there happened to be someone loyal to Augustín on board. However, with the way Captain Torres spoke about King Fernando and Alejandro, she thought it highly unlikely he would allow anyone who supported Augustín into his crew.

She sat on a stool, her foot elevated on her nearby cot and her elbows on the round table, next to Manny as Carlos hovered beside them. It was the middle of the afternoon, their second and last full day at sea. The twins were teaching her a game they usually played when they were bored, and she had quickly grasped the rules.

Carlos bit the corner of his lip as he shook a cube marked with dots ranging from one to six. With a bit too much bravado, he tossed the dice onto the table. It rolled around for several seconds until it toppled off the table. Quickly, all three of their heads flew underneath, watching to see what number it landed on.

"Ha!" Carlos yelled as the cube landed on "six."

Manny rolled his eyes as Lenora folded her arms with a huff. Lifting a pouch filled with leftover pinto beans from the kitchen, Manny held it open for Carlos to dig inside. "I still think you're cheating."

"Don't be a sore loser, bro," Carlos said as he counted out six beans. "Okay, your turn, Alpha Mate."

Lenora grabbed the cube after Carlos tossed it onto the table for her. "I thought I told you not to call me that."

Carlos shrugged. "What else should I call you? Are you not the Alpha King's mate?"

"You ask too many questions," Manny grumbled under his breath.

Lawrence rolled over, facing the wall. "*Way* too many."

"Hey," Carlos shouted at Lawrence. "Mind your business, wolf. Unless you finally want to stop your brooding and come join us. I wouldn't mind beating you at this game, too."

Ignoring them, Lenora shook the cube, then released it. It rolled and rolled until it stopped on "one." "Come on!" She blew out a breath and grabbed a single bean from the bag Manny held toward her. She added her bean to the small collection beside her on the tabletop. With only twelve beans, she was in last place. Manny had around thirty, and Carlos must have had over fifty by now.

"We can't all be winners," Carlos said, his smug grin calling for Lenora to wipe it off with her fist. For the most part, she enjoyed Carlos's company. Sometimes, though, he spoke a little *too* much.

Just as Manny reached for the cube, the ship jolted to a stop, as if the anchor snagged on something sturdy on the ocean floor.

The three of them froze, and Lawrence sat up in bed before he jumped down to stand beside Carlos. "Did we stop?" he mumbled, his voice low.

Manny stood from his stool and walked to the window. "We can't be there already."

Sweat grew on Lenora's palm. Nothing good could come from them stopping in the middle of the ocean, a whole day before they were due to arrive in Norraine.

Quickly, she estimated just how far out to sea they were. Dread welled up as all three men stood before her, blocking her from the door.

They looked around at each other, understanding falling on them at the same time.

The ship was still in Newton's waters.

Twenty-Eight

Footsteps pounded on the wood above their heads. Lenora lowered her broken foot from the cot as her heart picked up speed.

When a loud banging knocked on their door, she almost jumped out of her skin. Her hand flew to her boot, where she'd tucked her dagger this morning.

Señor Ortega threw the door open, his eyes frantic. "We must hurry. Newtonian soldiers are attempting to board the ship."

Her eyes grew wide, though she had already guessed.

"Why did you stop the ship?" Lawrence asked, stepping forward.

The first mate shook his head. "We're in Newtonian territory. Facing mages, might I add. If we fail to stop when we see their ship waving us down, they could sink us with their fireballs."

"It's all right," Lenora said, and they all turned to her. "I understand."

Señor Ortega waved to the hallway. "We can hide you in the cargo hold. *El capitán* will try to get them off quickly so we can be on our way."

Lenora nodded, then hurried behind the first mate's quick steps. Over her shoulder, she caught Lawrence's worried expression. Manny and Carlos clung close to her as they wound down another short staircase and through a narrow hall, where Señor Ortega unlocked the only door.

The cargo hold was one massive room, stretching from bow to stern.

It was stuffed with round wooden barrels, large rectangular metals boxes, and a few cases of glass bottles full of what seemed to be red wine.

Señor Ortega led them to the back of the hold, where the four of them squeezed behind the largest box.

"Stay here until I come for you," the first mate said before he scurried away, locking the door behind him.

A chill settled over her as she sat against the metal container, her heavy splint squeezed against the wall of the ship. Even though it was much colder down here, sweat gathered on her brow. Her thoughts spiraled for what felt like hours as she imagined what was happening on the top deck. Were the Newtonian soldiers looking for her on this ship? Would they pressure or even threaten Captain Torres until he told them she was on board? What would she do if they found her?

Lawrence, sitting in the outer corner, looked over at her, his eyebrows furrowed. "It'll be all right, Lenny."

"Yeah," Carlos said from his corner by the wall. "We won't let them take you."

"They probably won't even come down here," Manny, sitting beside her, said.

She could only nod, too afraid to voice her fears. The knife in her boot rubbed against her uninjured ankle, the cool metal reminding her to never give up. She would fight her way out if she had to.

But then what? She had no idea how many soldiers there were. Señor Ortega said there was an entire ship of Newtonian mages, all working for Remy. She couldn't take them on by herself with a single knife, especially in her sorry state. And what of the crew of *La Marinera*? The last thing she wanted was to put them in danger.

After about a half hour, the echo of boots stomping down the tiny hall met her ears. Lenora's shoulders rose, and she looked at her guards. They sat stiffly, likely having heard the sound before she did.

A jangling of keys and then the door creaking open assaulted the otherwise silent hold. Then, shuffled footsteps filed into the room, making it seem as if dozens of people had entered.

Captain Torres's voice boomed in the large space. "Have a look if you want, but everything I have listed on the inventory is accounted for. Only grains, spices, and some sangría. You could have a bottle if you want. I'm told Newtonians love wine just as much as Alegrians."

A lone person sauntered the hold, and Lenora could tell they were taking their time as if they had more than enough. After a pause, a voice she instantly recognized filled her ears. "Hmm. It looks like you have a lot of good stuff in here."

She held her breath before rage burned through her. She knew that voice. The smug, prideful tones wafted off of him like smoke from a wildfire blazing through an entire village. She'd heard him speak only once before, but she had committed his voice to memory. Remembering the rude, arrogant way he spoke to María and Pedro enraged her all over again.

"Sí, Capitán Acosta," Captain Torres said. "We're on our way to Port Francis, where we usually set up for a week to trade with the locals of the small Newtonian village. Then we'll make our return trip to unload in Puerto Nuevo and—" The sea captain's lie was cut off by the Newtonian captain's angry shout.

"Enough! Start the inspection. Make sure you check *everything*."

"We've never had to succumb to a rigorous search before, Capitán." Torres's angry tone peeked through his carefully guarded words. "Surely, based on our friendly history with Newton, you could make this quick so we can get this cargo where it needs to be. I wouldn't want to be late for our delivery. That would spread an unfavorable message about me and my crew."

"You don't have anything perishable," Captain Acosta drawled. "Unless, of course, there's another reason why you're in such a hurry."

Silence filled the air, and then Captain Acosta chuckled, the sound mocking and drawn out.

At the snap of a finger, dozens of boots shuffled throughout the hold. Lenora took slow, measured breaths. The minutes passed at an agonizingly slow pace as soldiers opened and closed several containers.

Lawrence, sitting at the edge between their box and another, fisted his hands. His back hunched over as a boot came into view. Beside her, Manny leaned closer, sniffing the air. Lenora slowly slid her hand inside her boot as Carlos pushed himself into a low crouch.

Lenora withdrew her knife as she waited for the soldier to spot them. The foot turned, and she followed the line of the soldier's leg before it disappeared behind another box. A slow breath escaped her mouth, and she allowed her shoulders to relax. The soldier cracked open a container, and the sound of glasses clinking together resounded near their heads. She didn't know if the soldier had opened the box next to them or the one they hid behind, but she didn't dare move.

Curiously, she heard some gulping, and her guards looked at each other as the smell of rich berries met her nose.

Ah. He's helping himself to some of the wine.

She wanted to laugh, but a shout from the other side of the room sent her senses flying back to her.

"Madero! Did you find anything?" Captain Acosta sounded both annoyed and angry.

The soldier near them gasped, nearly choking on the wine. "N-No, sir."

"Then hurry up."

"Coming, sir." The soldier slammed the lid, and Lenora heard him place the bottle on the floor. It must have toppled over, because the glass clanked against the boards and rolled away. Her eyes widened as it rolled around the corner, landing right by Lawrence's boot.

No one moved as a hand dipped low, grabbing for the bottle. Instead of glass, the soldier grasped Lawrence's leather boot.

Lawrence wasted little time. He jumped up and pinned the soldier to the floor, but Madero had already shrieked, causing a flurry of commotion to head their way. Manny cursed beneath his breath as he stood, his hands splayed in front of him. Lenora pushed to her healthy foot at the same time that Carlos jumped up.

Now that she could see over the container, she realized what they were up against. Over a dozen men and women wearing the dark gray uniform of Newton's army ran toward them, moving around the various barrels and boxes in their way. Captain Torres stood by the door, his eyes glistening with apology.

Lenora shook her head at him. She didn't want him to feel any guilt. He had tried to get the soldiers out quickly. None of this was his fault.

Soon, the soldiers crowded the back of the hold, their eyes narrowed and their hands held in front of their bodies in attack positions. Lawrence remained where he was, his hand pressed against Madero's neck, the soldier clawing and gasping for air.

A cough made the soldiers part, and a man around his mid-thirties with light brown curls and a mischievous grin walked between them. He chuckled, shaking his head as he brought his hands behind his back. "Looks like we meet again, Your Highness."

Lenora set her jaw firmly in place. "I've never met you before," she ground out.

The man's eyebrows rose as he touched his cheek. "You don't remember me? You gave me a swift kick to the jaw a week ago somewhere in the Dark Forest."

Racking her memory, she tried but failed to place his face.

He continued walking until he stood directly before the metal container, the corner of his lip tilted up in a smirk. "No? Perhaps you remember my teeth almost severing your foot from your leg?"

Lenora jumped back at the smack of his words. "You're the wolf that attacked me." Her eyes flitted down to her ankle before returning to his face. She had *him* to thank for her first injury, the one that made her escape even more difficult.

"My name is Josue Acosta, captain of the Wolf Brigade." He flashed her a grin. "I've been looking for you. If you come with me now, I'll let your friends live." Then he looked at each of her guards, his smile turning to a grimace.

She narrowed her eyes at him. "You're saying if I go with you, you won't hurt my friends."

Lawrence stood, bringing a blubbering Madero with him before throwing him toward the other soldiers. "Don't trust him, Lenny."

Carlos lifted his chin, not taking his eyes off Captain Acosta. "You know he's lying. Look at that wolfish grin."

Captain Acosta laughed, lifting a hand to wipe a fake tear from under his eye. "You bear shifters are always so ... haughty. Come, princess, surely you understand it's only you we're after. We couldn't care less about these ... people."

Manny's chest rose and fell heavily as he lowered his voice to a whisper. "Don't do it, Princess. We can shift."

"We can take them," Carlos added, crouching as if he was prepared to shift right then.

Lenora reached behind Manny and touched Carlos's shoulder, and he lowered his wide eyes to her hand. "Stand down." She gave him a nod before glaring at Captain Acosta. "Promise me you'll let my friends go, Acosta. If you give me your word that won't hurt them or anyone else on this ship, I'll go with you."

Acosta did something Lenora didn't expect. He placed both palms, one on top of the other, over his chest, right above his heart. "I promise, by your Fates, that no harm will come to your friends or anyone else on this ship."

Lenora blinked. To pray to the Fates was something Norrainians took to heart, just like the gesture they made to respect those they loved. The Newtonian goddess was known to her people as one half of the divine Fates they prayed to. To Lenora's knowledge, Frieda, the all-powerful goddess of mages, had shown herself to only two people: her mother, and Lenore, her namesake. Yet, she remembered Alejandro talking about the moon goddess his people seemed to worship—the one their anthem warned their children about, who was jealous of a mere mortal.

Acosta could have mentioned Itzela, his people's goddess, or even Frieda, the goddess of the people who took him and his wolf shifters in. Instead, he chose to promise in the name of the Fates. He chose to pull on her heartstrings, to make sure she understood he meant what he said.

After picking her jaw off the floor at Acosta's use of her customs, she nodded. "All right, I'll come."

"I'm coming with you," Lawrence said, already stepping forward.

"Us too," Manny and Carlos said simultaneously.

She nodded at Lawrence, then turned to the twins. "No, please return home. Xander will need you. Tell him..." She paused, suddenly drowning in the weight of her actions. There would be no escape. She was truly captured, about to be handed directly over to Remy. She didn't know what he'd do to her now that he had her.

Her throat choked up, and a heavy ache pounded in her chest. "Tell him—" she croaked out, her voice hoarse.

Manny nodded, and Carlos's usually grinning face transformed into a frown.

As she shuffled around the container toward Acosta, she expected him to shy away from her closeness. Surely the soldiers knew about her

231

powers—at least, they would if Tyree had a chance to tell them before he died. Instead, Acosta watched her carefully, eyeing her hands as she placed them before her body, her wrists touching as she surrendered herself.

Acosta huffed. "There's no need for handcuffs, Your Highness. I've not only brought my entire brigade, but several mages. You won't risk running or attacking when you're this badly outnumbered and out-matched. Now come. King Remy is waiting."

Without another word, Acosta turned and waltzed out of the hold, passing a subdued Captain Torres. Lawrence drew in close to her side, his breathing ragged as he tried to contain his anger. The soldiers encircled her as best as they could in the space, ensuring she followed.

Lenora chanced a glance behind her, catching the twins' eyes. Manny stared on, his lips pursed. Carlos looked like he was still thinking about shifting, his eyes dark and his arms spread out.

With as much emotion as she could muster, she called out to them. "Tell him I said 'goodbye.'"

Twenty-Nine

Lenora stared at the wooden planks beneath her feet as she walked across *La Marinera's* deck, wishing she had her black walking stick. Tears fought for freedom, wanting to run down her cheeks and splash against the ship, forever leaving their imprint.

She was so close. Norraine was only a day away, just across the great expanse of the Enchanted Ocean. Lifting her blurry eyes, she took in the beautiful cascade of blue. The way the sun glinted off the waves promised hope.

Instead of joy, despair rocked against her as she walked across the gangway connecting *La Marinera* and the massive Newton ship that teemed with Newtonian soldiers.

There was no hope. Not anymore.

When she limped onto the other ship, the soldiers who had accompanied her and Lawrence formed a circle around them. Through a gap, she saw Acosta staring at *La Marinera's* crew, a triumphant smile decorating his lips.

"Let's be off," he muttered, and the man to his right ordered the soldiers to remove the plank and set a course for Port Francis, the closest town.

Port Francis. Lenora's heart sank to her feet. It was a town located at the very tip of Newton's eastern coast. They were indeed so close to Norraine.

As the ship sailed away, heading west instead of north toward her home, she turned to Lawrence. His eyes carried the same weight she felt. He kept his lips pursed, but she knew by the way they twitched how badly he wanted to say something.

"You're all dismissed," Acosta said, and the circle dispersed.

Lenora sucked in her emotions, schooling her features as the wolf captain approached. Would he send her to the brig? She doubted he saved a room for her, or even a soft cot. She'd likely sleep on the cold, wet floor and be given scraps to fill her belly until they docked. After that, she probably wouldn't get a full meal at all. From Port Francis, it would probably take a few days on horseback to get to Stonehold Castle, and even longer if Acosta planned on making her walk on her injured foot.

Judging by the smirk he wore, he was going to make her walk.

"You know," Acosta began, "I should thank you, Princess Lenora. Because of this ordeal you've put me through, chasing you all around Newton and even out to sea, I've become a better tracker. You concealed yourself somehow, masking your scent with another, one more over-powering than yours. It took us days to figure out you ran into the Great Gorge, so I figured there were only two options. One, you went there to die. Or two, you escaped to Alegría. Following that logic, I set out to sea, the only way you could get home."

Her eyes narrowed at his chuckle. Acosta stepped closer, and Lawrence growled, drawing himself between them.

Finally forced to break her eye contact, he glared at Lawrence, sniffing his scent. "You're a traitor to your kind, boy. You have no business in Norraine's affairs, yet you place yourself in the middle of it." Acosta's expression changed, softening as he tilted his head. "But it's not too late. I picked up your scent throughout this journey. You were tracking her, too, and you found her before me. I could offer you a place in my pack, among your kind. Join my Wolf Brigade. I could use a good tracker like you."

Lawrence growled again, his chest rising and his shoulders straightening. "I'm a Norrainian citizen now. Protecting the crown princess *is* my business. My parents taught me it's not a place that makes a home, but a people. Norraine welcomed us when Alegría banished us, so I'll never turn my back on them. I'll never join your pack."

Acosta stepped into Lawrence's space, his nose twitching. "Who are your parents?"

"I'm the son of Isabela and Juan López," Lawrence said, his tone reverent. "A former captain and a former general under Alpha King Fernando."

With a nod, Acosta looked away. "So that's what happened to *los Lópezes*. I thought Augustín got you guys."

A whistle blew from somewhere near the stern, and Acosta's eyes widened with excitement. Lenora only had a moment to process what that look meant before Acosta yelled, "On my signal!"

Several soldiers ran toward the back of the ship, lining up in a neat row. She turned, placing her hand on the starboard-side rail, trying to see what the soldiers were looking at. Were they being attacked? Was *La Marinera* coming back for her?

That small spark of optimism fell like an anchor when she saw *La Marinera* off in the distance, still not moving from its spot. She wondered if they were waiting for the Newton ship to get farther away before they set off again. They still had a delivery to make.

The soldiers at the stern raised their arms, and in an instant, fireballs lit up their palms.

"Fates," Lawrence muttered beside her.

"Oh no," Lenora breathed.

Acosta hollered, "Fire!" as he lifted a hand straight in the air.

All at once, a dozen fireballs blasted across the sky. They pummeled *La Marinera*, setting the ship ablaze. The port side crackled, and the sails burned to a crisp within seconds. Even from this distance, Lenora could hear the screams and a few bear roars as the crew scrambled about.

"Again!" Acosta screamed, and the fire mages lifted their arms. "Fire!"

Another round of fireballs flew, and the ship, already burning, took on more flames. The fire grew, fueling itself as it raged into an inferno. Lenora looked back at the deck, and that was when she noticed another line of air mages, their arms outstretched and moving in a circular motion. They were fanning the flames, containing the smoke and fire around the ship, making sure *La Marinera* was destroyed.

Enraged, Lenora turned to Acosta, her eyes holding as much heat as the fire burning the ship of the people who aided her. The people she put in this position. Their screams burned her ears, generating more anger within her.

Acosta must have felt her gaze, because he snapped his eyes to her. His mouth fell open for a moment before he closed it.

Then the Fate's forsaken fool *smirked*.

Lenora almost lost her mind, but instead, she directed some of her pain and anger into her words. "You lied. You told me the crew would be safe. You promised not to harm them."

Acosta inclined his head. "Did I? Hmm, I must have forgotten."

The soldiers had confiscated her knife before they boarded the ship, so she had nothing to stab him with. Instead, she used the only power she had.

She dug her hand into the collar of her shirt, and Acosta's eyes followed. Grasping her necklace, she yanked, breaking the chain. It fell to the wooden deck with a clank. Forgotten, just like his promise.

Just like her promise to Alejandro that she wouldn't touch anyone else.

She hobbled closer to Acosta, who still eyed her warily. "You've made a mistake, Acosta. You should have tied me up."

He laughed in her face. "Don't be foolish, Princess. You have no weapons, and you're surrounded. What are you going to do? Slap me?"

A few of the soldiers looked on, some joining Acosta's laughter.

Lenora smirked, raising a hand. "I don't have to." Then she pressed a single finger on Acosta's arm.

He opened his mouth to laugh again, but his eyes went wide and his mouth fell agape as Lenora's vision took over.

She planted her good foot as her sight blurred, like it always did. Transported into the future, she found herself surrounded by mountains. Instantly, she recognized where they were.

All around, chaos reigned. Hundreds of people clashed together, with shouts and cries of pain reaching her ears. Fireballs littered the sky above her head, gusts of wind blew with overwhelming force, waterspouts spiraled across the dirt, and rocks and branches flew in every direction. Swords and shields, metal versus metal.

This was a battle. And it was right outside of Stonehold Castle.

Before her stood Acosta, his body scrunched in pain as blood dripped from a gaping wound in his back. A sword plunged through the hole, the tip sticking out of his body. Then it withdrew, and his body slumped to the ground as the battle continued to rage. In front of the spot where he had stood, she saw herself in the future, holding the bloody sword.

Lenora's mouth fell open as her future self turned and ran in the opposite direction, jumping back into the fray.

She looked around for only a second, trying to catch as much of this battle as she could. She looked for clues that could tell her when this would take place, who would be fighting, and where Remy was, but the vision ended, sucking her back to the present.

Once she drew in a real breath, Lenora stepped away from Acosta, her eyes hungrily taking in his shocked, horrified face.

"What..." he muttered, his voice tight. "What did you do?"

"I showed you your death, Acosta," she spit out, her legs wobbly.

He sputtered, looking directly at her. "You... You goddess-cursed witch! You have the cursed sight!"

She placed a hand on her hip to steady herself. "So you see why I don't need to hurt you right now. I'll do it later."

Acosta fell back, his steps scrambling for purchase as he put as much space between himself and Lenora. The soldiers looked back and forth between them, confusion marring their expressions as they took in their captain's frightened actions.

"Put her in the brig!" Acosta yelled, pointing at her from the starboard side of the ship. "But don't touch her!"

No one moved, afraid to get too close. Lenora heard the mutters, reminding her of her days in Highmore as she navigated the castle. People had whispered behind her back, not even caring that she could hear them. These soldiers did the same.

"She's cursed."

"The cursed sight? What's that?"

"By the goddess, I'm not going anywhere near her."

"Should we throw her overboard?"

Lenora threw her eyes in the direction of that last voice, glaring at the person who threatened her. The soldier's eyes grew wide, terror taking over as she stepped closer. The soldiers all backed away, and that did something to her. It emboldened her, made her lift her chin in spite of the anger and anguish she felt.

She had magic. After nineteen years of living with it, she finally realized her magic was powerful.

She was powerful.

Her eyes found Acosta hiding behind a group of his soldiers. She shook her head.

The coward.

"I'll show myself to the brig," she announced, already turning toward the stairs. "Send someone to lock the door."

Footsteps behind her made her look over her shoulder. Lawrence followed her, his eyebrows pinched and his hands working themselves into a knot.

She wanted to feel bad for scaring him—for scaring everyone—but she couldn't find it within to feel remorse. Not when a whole ship had just burned, the ashes now floating away on the gorgeous blue ocean. Not when an entire crew likely suffered so much pain from an unsuspecting attack. And *definitely* not when Manny and Carlos, two unlikely friends who attempted to protect her when they didn't even know her, died on that ship.

Her fury surged again as she slammed her hand against the metal door to the cell, pushing it open. Lawrence walked into the one next to her, shutting the door behind him. He leaned his forehead against the frame and sucked in a deep breath.

"So, you wanna talk about it?" he asked, his tone indicating he didn't really want to, but he was trying to be a good friend.

Lenora leaned against the wooden wall, lowering herself until she plopped onto the wet floor. "No."

Lawrence sighed, then lifted himself from the metal door. He walked to the bars separating them, extending his hand through the gap. "Here. Thought you'd want this back."

Lenora lowered her gaze to his hand, finding her necklace dangling from his fingers. The chain was broken, but the clear crystal at the bottom shined as bright as the day she got it over nineteen years ago.

Her mother had told her about the day she was born. According to

Newtonian tradition, every newborn of the Newton line was given a protection charm, just like the one she wore. Elice missed out on that tradition because of the unusual circumstances of her birth, but both she and Auntie Alice needed a protection charm at one point in their lives. Her aunt still wore hers, otherwise her dream sight would overpower her every waking moment with visions of doom, much like the cursed sight. Her mother, on the other hand, didn't need to wear one anymore, thanks to her incredible meditative control. Elice had turned her curse into dream walking, and she could pass in and out of the mind and spirit realms, which was how she was able to communicate with Frieda, the goddess who gave mages their powers.

When Lenora was born, Elice gifted her with the charm Sophia had made years ago. The very charm Lenora carried around with her was so powerful, Elice had used it to lock Orser inside the Tomb of Souls. Elice made her promise to always wear it to keep her visions at bay, and even though the chain had broken twice now, rendering it useless for warding, she still craved its nearness. She needed it, and she was thankful for Lawrence's foresight.

Lenora reached out for it, then slid it into her boot. "Thanks, Lawrence."

He nodded, then paced the tiny cell, his eyes downcast and glued to the drenched floor.

Lenora watched him walk for a few seconds before she turned, looking out the small window.

Tendrils of smoke rose in the distance, marking the last place her friends had been. Finally, she allowed a tear to slip from her eye as she thought about Manny, Carlos, Captain Torres, Señor Ortega, and the rest of the crew.

They all died because of her. What would Alejandro think when he found out that not only was she captured, but his people had died trying to save her? What would he do?

Lenora blew out a rueful huff. By the time he found out, she'd be at Stonehold. There would be a battle, that much she knew, but would she be dead before he even knew she was there?

Thirty

A few hours later, Lenora found herself walking off the ship between two soldiers. They gave her a wide berth, too afraid to even make eye contact, let alone get too close. Lawrence had his own set of guards, but they held tight to his arms as they forced him down the plank and toward a waiting carriage.

Lenora focused her eyes on the back of Acosta's head as he led the way. He must have felt the daggers that flew from her pupils, because he looked over his shoulder every two seconds. Each time he caught her staring, he would snap his head around or yell an order at one of his soldiers.

She enjoyed her newfound power. Watching Acosta and the Newtonian soldiers squirm as she climbed into the carriage sent ripples of satisfaction along her body. She scooted across the bench to make room for Lawrence as a soldier threw him inside. The door slammed shut, and she heard the click of a lock snapping into place.

Now that all eyes were off of her, she slumped against the bench, resting her back against the seat and exhaling deeply. Lawrence rubbed his wrist. A pair of cuffs connected to a chain held them together in front of his body.

"At least we get to sit," he muttered, eyeing the tight metal digging into his skin.

"Sorry they were rough with you," Lenora said, wanting to reach out and touch him. She kept her hands firmly in her lap. The last thing she wanted was to scare away her only friend.

Lawrence shrugged, lowered his hands, and then dropped the back of his head against the bench. "I'm kind of glad they were too afraid to cuff you. One less thing I have to worry about."

She snorted before falling into silence. Lawrence closed his eyes, and she watched as his breathing evened out. The sound of hooves hitting dirt and soldiers shouting commands signaled it was time for them to leave. Soon, the carriage rolled down the path she didn't have time to survey as she was led inside.

The horses moved at a fast pace. Lenora figured Acosta wanted to get to Stonehold as soon as possible so he could rid himself of her. That thought brought a smile to her lips. She didn't know when, but she would get her revenge on Acosta for throwing her from her horse, biting her ankle, chasing her out of Newton, and killing Manny and Carlos—not to mention the crew of *La Marinera*. The comfort of her vision gave her something to look forward to.

She rested her head against the windowless interior wall and drifted off, only waking hours later when the carriage stopped. She heard the telltale signs of horses being exchanged and the soldiers making conversation not too far away.

Lawrence, now awake, eyed the door, waiting for someone to open it to give them food. Lenora waited anxiously, since her stomach growled, reminding her she hadn't eaten since breakfast and it was now well past dinnertime.

Yet, when the carriage moved again and no one checked on them, she realized the soldiers had no plans to feed their prisoners.

Lawrence turned his worried gaze to her. They both likely thought the same thing.

They would go the whole four-day trip without food or water.

Acosta planned to starve and dehydrate her.

A nervous sweat built on her forehead and her palms. Her breathing quickened, and the carriage suddenly felt too small. Just when she realized her true potential—her true power—she would lose it. If she arrived at Stonehold too weak to fight, she would lose any battle that might begin. Remy would waste no time in ending her life.

She thought of the ways he could kill her. With a thick, sharp branch like the one he used to end Tyree. Or would he use a sword, taking off her head with one swing? He could also make it a spectacle and hang her in front of a crowd. The possibilities were endless, and she thought of them all as she hyperventilated in her seat.

Lawrence's face came into view as he moved in front of her. "Hey, Lenny, look at me."

She averted her gaze, staring at his bound wrists, his skin red and rubbed raw. The sight only made it worse as tears caught in her eyes.

He lowered his head, forcing her to look at him. "Look right at me. Just breathe."

Lenora shook her head. If she passed out, maybe that would make the trip easier.

He squeezed his eyes, blowing out a breath before he looked at her again. "Remember that time we got lost in Explorer's Pass?"

Nodding was the only thing she could do. She couldn't even draw a deep enough breath to fill her lungs.

Lawrence continued as if she wasn't having a breakdown. "We thought we could handle the Emori Mountains on our own, so we broke away from our parents' group and tried to forge a new path. Too bad a freak storm appeared, otherwise I think we might have succeeded. They would have named the pass after me, since it was kind of my idea to begin with."

Her lip twitched, and she sucked in air. "Wasn't your idea."

"Oh, it was. Don't you remember? I said, 'we should go this way,' and you said, 'all right.'"

This time, Lenora laughed. "That's not how it went."

Lawrence sat back on the bench. "That's how I remember it."

She allowed herself a real breath, distracted by correcting Lawrence. "Well, it was already raining, for one. We trailed behind because we were trying to see if we could get away with it, testing our parents' boundaries. Then you slipped, dragging me with you. We fell halfway down the mountain, and our parents didn't even realize. By the time we climbed back up, they were long gone, and we had no idea how to get back to Fort Emori."

Lawrence snorted. "That's *not* how I remember it *at all*."

The quirk on his lips made her roll her eyes. "You limped all the way back to the fort."

"But we did find a new path. Too bad it was full of snakes."

Lenora waved a hand. "They weren't even venomous and were more afraid of us. Remember how loud you screamed?"

Lawrence laughed, his eyes closing. "No way. That didn't happen."

"Why are you lying to me? I was there!"

Their laughter continued for a few moments until it died down. Lenora gave one last chuckle, eyeing her best friend. "Thanks. For calming me down. For ... everything."

Lawrence shrugged. "Don't mention it."

"What are we going to do?"

His smile faded until his lips turned downward. "I don't know. Just save your energy. They'll have to give us water, unless they want us to die before we even make it to Stonehold. Food... Not so much."

An average person could survive about three days without water, and roughly three weeks without food. She understood Lawrence's argument, but even going two days without water, and only being given enough to last one more day, frightened her.

Her eyes met Lawrence's. He had said 'us,' but her mind wandered back to Acosta's earlier words.

Acosta said they only cared about her.

If he meant it, they would let Lawrence die of thirst, then throw his lifeless body in a ravine.

Lenora would have to watch her best friend slowly die of dehydration, unable to save him.

Tears came, and she sank lower on the bench. She was tired. Tired of hiding herself. Her powers. Her past. Her *hair*. She didn't want to fight to prove her worth anymore. If this was where trying hard got her—a prisoner to a deranged murderer—then she would give up the battle.

The war was lost, anyway. There was no more fight left within her.

Lenora smacked her dry lips. Lawrence leaned lopsidedly on his bench, his legs sprawled out and his arms hanging awkwardly across his chest.

The soldiers had stopped a handful of times to change horses, eat, and drink. Each time, Lenora held her breath, waiting for the door to open. After several minutes, the lock would pop, the door would open, and a soldier would toss in a moldy loaf of bread, a near-empty canteen, and a dirty bucket.

The bottle had a few sips of water to share between her and Lawrence, and the bucket was so they could relieve themselves. Before the carriage rolled away again, another soldier would return for the bucket and canteen, then the door would lock again.

This carried on for almost two days. By nightfall on the second day, Lenora was ready to throw herself at the soldier who opened the door. Lawrence's wrists bled, forming crusty scabs that would scrape off if he moved his arms barely an inch.

She was determined to change their circumstances. Surely the Fates wouldn't let her die this way. Her clothes reeked and her hair was a matted mess. The lack of food and water left her exhausted, weak, and delirious enough to think she could take on an entire troop of mages and wolf shifters.

The carriage halted, and several horses whinnied. Shouts rang off, but it sounded too far away to be from the soldiers surrounding her carriage. Lawrence hauled himself up, his eyes wide. Lenora's heart raced as she tried to comprehend what she was hearing.

The sound of scraping metal against metal and the distinct yell of Acosta commanding his men reached her ears. But to do what, she couldn't quite make out. The smell of fire burned, perhaps from the fire mages. She could tell the other elements were being used because gusts of wind rocked the carriage, water rushed loudly in the background, and bits of rock banged against the exterior.

Suddenly, a sharp cry had her sitting forward in her seat, straining her ears. Lawrence, with the little energy he had, sprang up to block her as the lock jangled.

"Someone's breaking in," Lenora mumbled, her voice low.

Lawrence nodded as a sword slashed through the wooden door. Lenora let loose a scream. The sword pierced the door again and again until a hand shot through the opening. It gripped the splintered wood, ripping it apart. Then a head popped through the hole.

"Oh," the woman said, a curious smile on her face. "Hello."

Lenora swallowed as the woman removed her head. Lawrence looked at her from over his shoulder, shaking his head in disbelief.

"It's not him!" someone shouted, and Lenora thought that voice belonged to the woman. "Just a couple of prisoners! What should we do with them?"

The door creaked, then blew into bits, sending pieces of sharp stakes in every direction. Some cut into Lenora's skin, and Lawrence grunted as he took on the worst of the blast.

When the wood stopped flying, Lenora peered over Lawrence. Her eyes landed on a man, his arms and legs spread wide in a deep stance. Once he finished breaking down the door with his earth powers, he stood at attention.

Another man with platinum strands mixed in with his brown curls stepped in front of the opening. "Good job, Trevor," he said to the earth mage behind him. "We didn't need the key after all."

The woman came to his side. "Acosta ran away like a coward. Should we give chase?"

The older man shook his head, but his eyes remained on Lenora. "We'll run into him again, Salina. We must remember to be patient."

Lawrence jerked as the man stepped forward. His eyes shot to Lawrence, assessing him. "Be calm. I won't hurt you. I see you two were Captain Acosta's prisoners. That means you're not Remy's lackeys."

The way he spat out Remy's name made Lawrence relax a pinch, but Lenora remained where she was, her back pressed against the wall.

"Please," the older man said, extending his hand. "Come out of the carriage. We'll set you free. We can even help you get home."

Lawrence moved forward and climbed out. Lenora hung back until Lawrence's eyes turned to her. "Let's go, Lenny. It's okay."

At those words, she released her breath. It was over. It was actually all right.

With weak legs, she hobbled out into the starlit night, and a gasp escaped her. Dozens of men and women gathered around, armed with swords or with their hands raised as if ready to call upon their magic. A few were bleeding, but each one wore a triumphant smile and a curious gaze.

The man's eyes trailed across Lenora and Lawrence, and he shook his head with a frown. She imagined what they looked like. Hair unkempt, clothes soiled, Lawrence handcuffed and bleeding, and Lenora still wearing a splint around her ankle and bandages around most of her body. "You poor kids. Acosta really did a number on you two. Listen, my home is not far from here. How about I take you in for the night, and we can sort you out tomorrow?"

Lawrence angled his head toward her, leaving the choice up to her. Really, though, they had no other option. It was either go with this stranger or somehow find a way back to Alegría for Alejandro's help. Even then, there was no guarantee they would make it to the border in the state they were in.

Making the smartest decision she had available, she nodded. "Yes, please. And thank you." She cringed at the rough tone in her voice, and it ached to even speak.

The man smiled, his straight teeth shining against his brown skin. Deep dimples in his cheeks made him appear youthful, even though he was likely around forty or fifty years old. "My name is Bryan Drake, by the way. And these are my Brentwood Warriors. We're... Ha." He threw his arms to the side, his grin growing. "We're trying to start a rebellion."

Thirty-One

When Bryan Drake said his home was nearby, he didn't mention it was miles away, beyond the hill where the carriage had stopped. He also didn't mention his house was a mansion.

As they crested the hill, an expanse of trees blanketed the valley, encircling a large estate. Lenora stared wide-eyed, trying to keep her frail body upright. She had turned down help, not wanting to touch anyone, and even Lawrence, chain dangling between his arms, stubbornly declined a shoulder to lean on.

Bryan turned a devilish grin at her as the rebels sprinted down the hill. "Welcome to Brentwood."

Lenora narrowed her eyes as she limped down the hill with Lawrence and Bryan on either side. "Who are you?"

"I've already introduced myself," he said, an eyebrow raised. "I'm Bryan. Perhaps we should get you inside and fed so you can sleep. How long has it been since they last fed you properly?"

She ignored his question. "How did you come upon this estate? Did you and your rebels seize it?"

Bryan laughed. "Oh. I see. It was handed down to me over many generations. When I die, it'll go to my son."

"You're the lord of this estate?" Lawrence asked skeptically, eyeing the garish man.

Bryan smiled at Lawrence. "Of this province. I'm the lord of Brentwood. It stretches from the edge of Port Francis and borders the Great Gorge and Stonehold. It's the largest province in Newton."

Lenora's mind scrambled for clarity. Only those with familial ties could become lords and ladies in Newton—at least, that was what she thought. She had planned on meeting the nobles during her ambassadorship, but then everything had turned upside down. "How are you related to the Newtons if your last name is Drake?"

Bryan sucked his teeth, obviously perturbed by the question. "You two aren't from Newton, are you?"

She shook her head as Lawrence cleared his throat. "We came from a small village near Port Francis," she answered. Technically, it was partly true. They did just come from Port Francis, after all.

Bryan hummed, his eyes passing back and forth between them. "Forgive me, but what are your names?"

"I'm... Lenny. This is Lawrence." She wasn't sure if she should tell him exactly who she was.

The older man nodded. "Well, at any rate, this is my family's estate. We're from the lesser Newton line, one that branched off centuries ago. The land continued to pass down my ancestor's line until it came to me. I guess you could say I'm part of the weaker Newton branch—a far distant cousin of Remy's."

Lenora covered her shock by discreetly meeting Lawrence's eyes. If Bryan was a distant relative—centuries removed—of Remy's, then he was related to her. Even if that connection was so long ago. After all, her Moore ancestors had split from the main branch centuries ago as well. Would he have stronger ties with Remy rather than Lenora?

It made her even more sure of holding her tongue about sharing exactly who she was until she learned more about this man.

Bryan noticed their shared glance, so he let out a chuckle and shook his head. "Don't worry. I have no love for the person who currently occupies the Newtonian throne. I've known Remy all my life, and, of course, Tyree and Matilda. What Remy did to his family..." He trailed off, and Lenora noticed the way his lips pressed together.

"When Salina found us..." Lenora searched for the right words, her brain still fuzzy from lack of food and water. "Were you looking for someone?"

"I had a scout report about seeing a carriage bearing the Stonehold crest, so I sent a few of my people to investigate. When they saw Acosta, we figured it was as good a time as any to strike. We didn't know who or what would be inside the carriage, but if we could take out the leader of the wolves, that would certainly help our cause, am I right?" Bryan grinned, obviously proud of having attacked Acosta's convoy.

Lawrence cleared his hoarse throat. "And what, exactly, is your cause?"

"Like I said, dear boy," Bryan said as they reached the bottom of the hill. "We're staging a rebellion! In the short week that Remy has reigned, we've already seen where he plans to lead this kingdom. He's threatening more random wolf searches and attacks on helpless townspeople, breaching his citizen's privacy looking for some foreign ambassador—probably to kill her or something. Besides, look what he did to his family. Slaughtered. All of them. We stand on the cusp of ruin, like our neighbors to the south. If we don't want to end up like Alegría, we need to put an end to Remy now."

A shiver ran down Lenora's spine as Bryan turned his head toward the mansion. The front door burst open, and a young man ran outside, his frantic eyes trained on Bryan.

"Father," the newcomer shouted. "Salina just told me there was an attack and that you found some prisoners."

Bryan raised his hand to stop his son from continuing. As soon as they were close enough, Lenora got a good look at him. His curls hung the same as his father's, but they were thicker and a darker shade of brown. His chestnut skin and full lips also matched Bryan's, but his eyes were bigger and brighter, bursting with youth and hope.

"It's all right, Mattias," Bryan said, patting his son on the shoulder. "These are the prisoners we saved from Captain Acosta. Why don't you have a servant ready some rooms for them?"

Mattias looked from his father to Lenora and Lawrence. "Of course, my lord."

She watched Mattias's retreating form as Bryan waved for them to continue walking. "Let's get you kids inside," he said. "I'll send a healer to your rooms, and then I'll have someone bring you food."

"Thank you, Lord Brentwood," Lenora said, her chest lightening at the prospect of a healer. She'd been in pain every day for over a week. "That's very kind of you."

Lawrence voiced his own thanks as they climbed the front steps into the manor. Lenora immediately understood how much wealth Bryan's family had. Beautiful white stones lined the exterior of the mansion, which had three floors and several balconies jutting from the front. As they passed through the door, held open by a servant dressed in a custom-fitted black suit, Lenora's eyes went straight to a glass mosaic painted above the opening. The scene depicted the rich woodland encompassing the estate, with an immense detail of the trees and rolling hills in the background.

In the foyer, tall, willowy plants billowed into the hallway, making it a tight fit as Lenora limped into the house. She heard whispers coming from down the hall. As they entered the main sitting room, Mattias bounded toward them from the left.

"Ah, good," Bryan said. "Show these two to their rooms, Mattias."

Mattias, still eyeing Lenora's and Lawrence's injuries, nodded, then motioned toward the stairs. "Right this way, please."

Lenora looked Bryan in his eyes, trying to convey as much sincerity as possible. "Thank you once again, Lord Brentwood."

Bryan smiled, and he inclined his head. "It's my pleasure to assist all those who have suffered under Remy's cruel hands."

Turning, Lenora and Lawrence followed quietly behind Mattias. He led them down a vestibule connecting the main room to a grand hall with dozens of potted plants, some vining high into the vaulted ceiling and hanging onto a curved staircase. Of course, even the lesser Newton branch showcased their earth magic—the entire line was full of earth mages, though there were the odd few that had other powers.

Mattias occasionally passed a glance over his shoulder, but he kept his mouth pressed into a line. The winding halls of the first level opened up to a rotunda with a high glass dome. Lenora bit back the pain and exhaustion seeping through her bones, knowing she would soon have a real bed to sleep in.

At the end of the hall, Mattias opened a door, then continued walking in his stewing silence. There were a few doors in this section, and Mattias stopped in front of one of them, pulling out a key ring. It jangled as he searched, looking at the numbers etched into the metal.

Finding the right one, he unlocked the first door, then hurried to another across the hall. Without a word, he motioned to one door, then the other. "You're free to choose which one you want. Might I suggest ladies first?" He gave Lawrence a pointed stare, then nodded at Lenora.

"Oh," Lawrence said, smirking. "Of course, my lady. You choose first."

Lenora wanted to throw an elbow into his gut. "Thanks. Such a gentleman." Though she rolled her eyes, she had to admit she was happy to return to her usual banter with Lawrence. The last two weeks had been rough on their friendship, but she wanted to believe they would always remain friends. And he had certainly proved his loyalty by staying beside her this entire time. Even though he'd kept his secret past from her, she knew she could fully forgive him if they ever made it out of Newton.

Mattias raised an eyebrow at their exchange, stepping away toward the exit. "I'll make sure the healer sees to you both soon." With a short bow, he turned on his heel and scampered down the hall.

Lawrence turned his expression on her, then burst out laughing once Mattias was out of sight. Lenora covered her mouth, not wanting to appear rude even though their host was no longer present. "Lawrence! Stop it!"

It was no use. He bent over, leaning his hand against the wall to support himself as he laughed. "You should have seen the looks he was giving you. Alejandro would have ripped his head off if he were here."

A furious blush crept up her cheeks. "I don't know what you're talking about." With a huff, she turned to the closest door and staggered into the room, wishing she hadn't left her cane behind on the ship in her scurry to hide in the cargo hold. "Go get some rest, Lawrence. You're delusional."

With his lips tilted up into a smirk, he entered his own room. "Whatever."

Lenora closed the door, taking a moment to lean her head against the hard wood. Lawrence had surely lost his mind if he thought Mattias was looking at her with anything other than disgust. She'd been in a carriage for two days without proper food or water, no bathroom, no hairbrush, and no change of clothes. She didn't need a nose to smell or a mirror to see to know she looked an outright mess.

Although, Alejandro had spent days with her in a similar state during their journey through the Dark Forest and the Great Gorge. He hadn't seemed to mind, and his nose was surely sharper than Mattias's.

Turning, she eyed the tiny space Lord Brentwood offered her. While small, it had everything she needed. A bed, a side table for the items she would have carried with her if she had any, a bowl of fresh water on a vanity, and a stool.

Sighing, she hopped on one foot until she reached the bed frame, then she fell flat on her face. Sleep grabbed her as soon as her eyes closed, and she slipped into a familiar dream.

She saw herself in her old room, the dark furnishings welcoming her back home. Her mother sat on her settee, her lips pursed and her glorious curls flowing down to her hips. Elice wore a simple pink gown, fitting her form perfectly. Lenora looked down at herself, running her hands across the bodice of a beautiful black dress with lace overlay all around her chest and sleeves. It was her favorite. She'd worn it on many occasions when she wanted to feel and look special while still wearing her signature color.

That was how Elice always saw her in this dream. Whenever Lenora was here, both women looked exactly the same.

Lenora burst into a sob and rushed into her mother's arms.

This was the only place Lenora would allow herself to touch Elice.

Because this was no ordinary dream. Her mother may be able to control air, earth, and water, and she may be the queen of a kingdom, able to bring grown men to their knees before her, but her strongest, most powerful skill was her ability to dream walk.

Thirty-Two

"Mother!" Lenora yelled as she buried her face against Elice's shoulder, hiding in the long spirally curls.

"My dear daughter," Elice mumbled, her lips moving against Lenora's gold-streaked hair. In this space, Elice always envisioned Lenora with her hair down, the curls falling just below her shoulder.

Elice pulled back, gripping Lenora's face in her hands. "I received your letter a few days ago. Harlem had his battalion ready to greet you at Fort Brant, but you never showed. He was expecting you two days ago, but I didn't find out until yesterday. I've been trying to find you in your dreams. You know how hard it is to spirit walk without knowing where the other person is, so I've been worried sick. Your father was about to board a ship headed for Newton. I had to talk him out of it and give you another day in case you were somehow delayed."

Lenora allowed her mother to take a deep breath. Elice did that when she was nervous—she spoke fast, blurring her words and sentences together, often pacing like she wanted to wear the fabric out of the rug beneath her feet. The pause Lenora took also let her enjoy her mother's presence, the rising pitch in her voice, the gleam of love in her eyes. She blew out a breath, steeling herself for her story.

"Something happened in Newton," Lenora began, cutting straight to it. She started with Remy and how he murdered his family. Elice let out an audible gasp, her mouth dropping open. As Lenora recounted her escape with Tyree's help, Elice stood from the settee and paced.

"Where are you now?" Elice interrupted, and Lenora could see the thoughts flowing through her mother's head as she determined the best course of action.

"I'm still in Newton. All the ports are closed. I had to flee to Alegría, which is how I got on the ship, but the Newtonian soldiers found me."

Elice continued pacing. "Alegría? They must have been searching every ship to look for you if they stopped an Alegrían vessel. They're not the most open people, believe me."

Lenora squirmed in her seat, realizing her mother must have been referring to Augustín. She wondered if her mother had tried reaching out to him in the last few years. Had she known Alpha King Fernando?

"Either way," Lenora said, "the Newtonian soldiers stopped the ship, and I turned myself over so they could leave the ship in peace. Turns out, they lied, and their fire mages blew up the ship with everyone in it. It was all for nothing. They died for nothing." She sucked in her sob, her mind picturing Carlos's silly smile and Manny's serious expression. They didn't need to die for her.

"Fates," Elice muttered, coming to a stop in front of Lenora. "I'm so sorry, Lenny. You've been through quite an ordeal. Do the soldiers still have you? Your father and I can get there on the next ship. Just tell me where you are."

"I'm not with them anymore." Lenora explained how Lord Brentwood attacked Acosta's caravan, which caused him to abandon her carriage in his escape, and how he let her and Lawrence stay in his estate. Then she hesitated, knowing she left out some important details but not knowing how to share them with her mother.

Elice, still eyeing her, furrowed her eyebrows. "What is it? Do you not trust Lord Brentwood?"

"It's not that." Lenora turned away, thinking of a set of hazel eyes.

"Listen to me, little one," Elice said, drawing Lenora's attention by using the nickname all mentors call their young mage trainees. Her mother had always called her that, but now that Lenora had used her power and gained some respect for it, the words hit her differently.

She finally felt worthy of the term. Like she really had a power capable of training up into something strong.

Like *she* was worthy of being strong.

Her eyes fell on Elice, taking in every word her mother said. "Go to Lord Brentwood and tell him who you are. If I know anything about nobles, it's that they'll do anything to win your good graces. And if he's as wealthy as you say he is, he'll be greedy. Tell him I'll pay whatever he asks if he'll help you get home. Fates, tell him to send an envoy to the nearest port town to meet *me*—and your father, because he'll never let me leave without him. I'll get on the next ship and pick you up myself. Just have him get you to the nearest port."

Lenora held her mother's outstretched hand and squeezed. "I will. I'll tell him the next time I see him."

With her free hand, Elice touched Lenora's cheek, where a tear slid down and fell to her lap. "I haven't seen you cry in years."

That brought another sob, and Elice pulled Lenora to her chest. Lenora wallowed in the comfort of her mother's arms. Though she knew the dream walk wasn't real, it felt so amazing in her mind. Almost as good as when Alejandro pressed his lips against her forehead.

Pulling back, Lenora met her mother's watery eyes. "There's something else—"

Before she could tell Elice about Alejandro, a loud knock sucked her out of sleep, ending the dream.

Blinking back to reality, she rubbed her weary eyes as someone pounded on the door again. She wished to see her mother once more. Lenora had never been skilled at dream walking, so she'd have to wait for Elice to reach out to her.

Groaning, she lifted her heavy head and called for the person to enter.

The door pushed open a crack, revealing an elderly woman. "Hello, sorry to bother you. I'm Healer Misha. Lord Brentwood sent me to see to you."

Thanking the Fates, Lenora hauled herself to a sitting position, ready to be healed by the woman. With a single hand, the woman touched every aching part of her body, removing old, stinking bandages as she went and chucking them into a bin. Lenora kept her hands fisted to avoid touching the healer. Her charm remained tucked into her boot, proving itself useless even after she removed her shoe to allow the woman to heal her legs.

Healer Misha eyed the wooden splint wrapped around her ankle. She tsked, lifting the foot with steady hands. "How long has this been broken?"

Lenora winced at the movement. "I injured it almost two weeks ago, then the bones broke a few days after that."

The healer tsked again, then closed her eyes in concentration. "Hmm. This one needs a little more work. Hold still, please."

Lenora rested her eyes, focusing on the remaining injury. Soon, a tingle started in her ankle, deep within the bones. It spread outward, igniting a crackle as the bones snapped together. She opened her eyes, watching in awe as her brown skin knitted itself anew, glowing as if it had never been sullied.

Standing on healed feet, Lenora rolled her previously broken ankle.

Stepping back to inspect her patient, Misha nodded and pursed her lips. "How do you feel, little one? Any spots I missed?"

Lenora blinked. "'Little one'?"

Smiling, the woman poked Lenora's ribs, searching for another injury. "I can tell another spirit mage when I see one. Plus, you had that charm necklace in your boot. I take it you're a healer, or someone made you a very strong protection charm."

"I'm not a healer," Lenora said, knowing how fast gossip would spread if she told this woman the truth. She had to talk to Bryan first.

But her mind lingered on the term 'spirit mage.' Was that what they called healers in Newton? What about seers like her? She supposed the two would be lumped together, just as the other four powers were labeled together as elemental magic.

"If that's all," Misha said, an exhaustion behind her eyes, "then I'll check on your friend. If you need anything else, you can find my room at the end of the hall."

Lenora nodded, noting that this must be the servants' quarters.

As Misha opened the door, Lenora called out to her. "One last thing. Where can I find a change of clothes and a bathroom?"

Misha pointed out the door toward the end of the corridor. "A couple doors down is the washroom. I'll ask someone to send some clothes up for you and your friend."

A few minutes after the healer left, another knock sounded at her door. Lenora opened it, relieved to see someone carrying a tray with stew and a pitcher of water, a bundle tucked beneath her arm.

Lenora forced herself to sip the water and stew, knowing how long ago it had been since she'd last filled her stomach. After draining half of the pitcher, she grabbed the towel and a plain cotton dress and hurried to the washroom. A few stalls with curtains lined one wall of the rectangular space. Another wall had toilets with metal doors for privacy, and a third had sinks with a few spigots.

She worried the showers would only have cold water, but the knob turned all the way to the left, and steaming hot water poured down from the overhead valve. She eyed the communal shampoo and hopped into a stall, closing the curtain behind her. She took her time washing off days' worth of grime from her hair, relishing in the peppermint scent permeating from the suds.

A matching cream sat next to the shampoo, and she used her fingers to work out the worst of the knots. Finally, she scrubbed the dried blood and dirt and horrible stench from her body with a bar of lavender soap.

After drying off with the scratchy towel, she slipped on the cream dress. She sneaked a few dollops of cream into her hair, hoping it would help tame her curls. She wanted to look her best for when she next saw Bryan.

If she wanted his help, she would need to act the part of a princess. How could she convince him of who she was? With Alejandro, it was so easy. She told him she was a princess, and he believed her—then helped her. Of course, he was a prince in hiding himself, so he knew firsthand what that scenario looked like. Lord Brentwood, however, might not believe her. And if he did, there was no guarantee he'd help.

When she returned to her room, she braided her hair back and tucked herself in. Tomorrow, she would speak with Bryan.

Lenora awoke with a start at the sound of a knock. There were no windows in this interior room, so she couldn't tell what time it was. Looking around, she stretched her arms over her head. Another knock came from the door, this time more urgent.

Standing, she opened the door to find a grinning Lawrence.

"Good morning," he said. "I figured you'd be all healed and ready to talk about how we're going to get back home. We have to come up with a plan."

"About that..." She widened the door for him, and he stepped through. Then she told him about her mother visiting her in her dream, something that always fascinated Lawrence. Now she knew why—he was from Alegría, where mages like Elice were legends from stories told to children about those from other lands.

"So, you're telling Lord Brentwood?" Lawrence asked, his head skewed to the side.

Lenora nodded as she slipped on her hard boots. The messy shoes clashed with her cream dress, but she had no other alternative. "As soon as I find him. I'd like to do it early so I can let my mother know the next time she visits me."

Lawrence scratched his scraggly chin. "If you're sure..."

Lenora stood still, eyeing her best friend. "You don't trust him?"

"There's something about him. I don't know how to describe it."

"Perhaps we're being paranoid." She thought back to the trying weeks she'd had.

"Maybe."

With one look, Lawrence conveyed everything he was thinking. Lenora could read him like a book.

He didn't trust Lord Brentwood.

Truthfully, Lenora didn't either. Too bad she had no other choice.

She moved down the halls, through the domed rotunda, and past the winding corridors until she made it to the main hall. It felt amazing to walk again, to not feel a single ache on her body.

Lawrence stayed close behind, never letting her out of his sight. Only a few servants bustled about, and judging by the low angle of the sun, she guessed it was only a couple of hours after dawn.

A figure on the opposite side of the foyer caught her eye. Mattias froze upon seeing her.

"Excuse me, Mattias," Lenora said, lifting her head and portraying as much confidence as she could muster. "Please send for your father. I have an urgent matter to discuss with him."

Mattias blinked. "Sure... I'll go tell him." He pointed the way he came, through a set of double doors with gold filigree wrapped around the frame like thin branches.

Lenora eyed the door. "Is he in that room?"

Mattias gave a nod. "He is."

"And it's private?"

He nodded again, his eyes cutting to Lawrence briefly.

"Perfect." She pushed past him, opening the door without waiting for him to give her permission to enter.

Inside was a study with a few shelves lining the walls. A massive desk and two padded chairs on opposite ends perched in front of the open window, allowing a gentle breeze to float in. Bryan sat facing the door, and he lowered his reading glasses as Lenora waltzed in.

"What is the meaning of this?" Bryan asked, setting his spectacles on the desk.

"My apologies, Lord Brentwood," she began.

"I'm sorry, Father," Mattias said, coming up beside her. "She just walked right in."

Bryan narrowed his eyes briefly before he wiped the disdain from his expression. "Is something the matter, Lenny?"

Raising her shoulders, she put on her invisible crown, the one she wore in Highmore Castle as she stood before nobles and soldiers as their crown princess. "I have an important matter to discuss. In private."

Bryan's eyebrows rose. He scrutinized her for a moment before turning his attention to Mattias. "Watch the door, son."

Lenora looked over her shoulder, giving Lawrence a command with her eyes.

Watch the door, Lawrence.

He nodded, letting her know he understood.

Mattias passed a nervous glance at Lenora, then Lawrence, and finally landed on Bryan. Lord Brentwood nodded, and Mattias frowned, but he stepped outside and closed the door behind Lawrence.

Without an audience, Lenora realized she had no witnesses to her proposed arrangement with Bryan. If she could get him to help her, she would need to get it in writing so she could have proof. Her parents taught her that nobles were only after one thing—what was best for them.

As Bryan smiled a cheeky grin, she knew she would need to hold steadfastly to her invisible crown and handle his bustling ego.

Just like her mother taught her.

Thirty-Three

Bryan motioned to the armchair across from him, and Lenora strode toward it. Rather than sitting, she clasped her hands together and stood behind the high back. With her chin lifted so her eyes narrowed down at Bryan, she held his eye contact in silence for several seconds.

"I come to you this morning," she began, her voice steady, "with a proposal."

Lord Brentwood leaned forward in his chair, one elbow resting on the arched support arm so his fingers could cup his chin, while his other hand extended across the wooden desk. "Go on."

"Last night, I didn't tell you the full truth about who I am."

"Oh?" He raised an eyebrow, his lips quirking up. "And who are you, exactly?"

Lenora clenched her fingers tighter. "I'm Lenora Moore-Taylor, the crown princess of Norraine."

Bryan held his expression together for a few seconds until he blew out a breathy laugh. "I thought you were going to say you were one of Remy's followers."

She pursed her lips. "You don't believe me."

"Well," Bryan said, standing and walking over to his open window to gaze outside. "I've heard stranger things. But tell me, why should I believe you? And what kind of proposal do you have in mind?"

Her eyes drifted to the trees just beyond the window. She knew it would be hard to convince Bryan of her identity. What could she say or do to make him believe her? When she met his eyes again, he was staring at her curiously. "You said you heard he was looking for the missing ambassador. I'm her—the ambassador from Norraine, and its crown princess. Why else would Acosta go to such great lengths to capture me and secure me in a carriage? He'd been tracking me for days on Remy's order because I heard him planning to kill his family. I'm sure he plans to kill me for that, and for outrunning his soldiers for so long."

Bryan tilted his head. "You being Acosta's prisoner could mean anything, honestly. For all I know, perhaps you were just an escaped prisoner, maybe an enraged citizen they meant to lock up."

He had her there. Her words would not be enough proof. "There's nothing I can say to make you believe me, except maybe to tell you about my family. Something only a royal member of the Moore line would know."

Bryan shrugged and walked back to his desk, plopping dramatically into his chair. "I know little about the Moores. What you have to say could very well be lies to me. I wouldn't be able to tell the difference."

Lenora turned, facing the door. Her ankle twisted, unused to being healed and able to move freely without a thick bandage. That was when she realized what was in her boot. She bent down and retrieved her charm, then held it out for Bryan to see. "You may not know the Moores, but you know the Newtons."

Bryan squinted at the gem. "It's a crystal. What does that have to do with the Newtons?"

Smiling, Lenora turned the stone over, letting the rays of light reflect through the prism and cast a rainbow on the floor. "It's not just a crystal.

It's a protection stone, made by a powerful healer to keep my visions at bay. My mother, Queen Elice, gave it to me the day I was born. Her mother, Queen Julice, was given a similar charm when she was born, as well. I'm a daughter of Newton. When I was born, there was a risk of me having the cursed sight, like all children in the Newton line."

"I remember Princess Julice, before she married King Edgar of Norraine. I was just a boy." At Bryan's wide eyes, Lenora lowered the charm. He knew exactly what she meant. "But you're not wearing the charm," Bryan muttered, eyeing her hands. "Or do you not have the curse?"

Lenora dropped the gem back inside her boot. "I ripped the clasp off on Acosta's ship after he captured me. Like I said, Remy wants me dead, so I was trying to escape."

Bryan gulped, his eyes never straying from her fingers. "And... Do you have...?"

Lenora smirked. "I do."

Shaking his head, Bryan pushed himself to his feet. "Mattias!"

The door opened immediately, and Mattias jumped into the room. Lenora noticed his battle stance, as if he planned to attack her if Bryan ordered it.

"What is it?" Mattias asked, his eyes darting from her to his father and back several times. "What's the matter?"

Behind him, Lawrence peeked into the room. Lenora shook her head, and Lawrence turned around, still playing guard.

"Shut the door!" Bryan yelled at his son. When Mattias slammed it, Bryan pointed at Lenora. "Prove it!"

Lenora jolted, not sure what to do about Bryan raising his voice at her. "Excuse me?"

Catching himself, Bryan adjusted his white button-up shirt and cleared his throat. "You say you have it. Prove it. Touch Mattias."

Mattias gaped at his father. "What?"

Lenora rolled her eyes but lifted her hand, pointing a finger out. "You do realize what you're subjecting your son to, Lord Brentwood?"

Bryan paused, then looked at Mattias's confused face. Mattias still had his jaw open, his eyebrows raised.

"Never mind," Bryan whispered, falling back into his seat. "Let's say I believe you. What now?"

She rubbed her hands down the front of her crunchy dress. "As I said, I have a proposal."

"And how do you know I don't plan on turning you in to Remy?"

Mattias turned toward Bryan. "Father! You wouldn't."

Bryan glared at him. "Oh, shut up!"

Lenora smiled. "There's my proof that you have no plans to work with Remy regarding my capture. Besides, I can offer you more than he ever could."

This seemed to enthrall Bryan. A tiny smirk lifted his lips, and he sat straight against the back of his seat as she continued. "I've been in contact with Queen Elice. She will give you whatever you ask for if you help me get to Port Francis."

Bryan sat in quiet contemplation, his mind obviously working over the many things he could ask for in return for aiding a crown princess to escape sure death at Remy's hands.

"I seem to be missing something," Mattias mumbled aloud, his statement not aimed directly at anyone. "How do you know the queen of Norraine, and why are you so important to her?"

Bryan sighed. "Haven't I taught you to stay quiet when people are negotiating?"

Mattias snapped his mouth shut, but his eyes focused on Lenora, eyeing her up and down as if trying to see what made her so special.

Lenora waited for Bryan to say something to her. She realized he would make her sweat, worry about whether he would accept her offer.

After a few more seconds, Bryan shook his head. "I'm afraid I can't think of anything I want from Queen Elice."

Lenora's stomach dropped to her toes. What kind of lord would turn down this type of proposition? An offer to receive any amount of money, or a plot of Norrainian land, or even a thousand gold pocket watches—he could have asked for all of it.

Just as Lenora planned a rebuke, Bryan stood, clapping his hands together. "I think I have an idea!"

She smiled and nodded. "Yes, let me hear it and I'll bring it up with the queen."

Bryan matched her grin. "This would be a great way for all of us to get what we want. It would help my rebellion and help you get home."

She couldn't wait to hear his suggestion. If he seemed this thrilled, surely it would be great indeed. And if it helped depose that rotten Remy, she would be all for it.

Bryan walked around his desk and gripped Mattias's shoulder, still beaming. "What if you marry my son, Mattias?"

Lenora blinked, not sure she heard him right.

He continued, oblivious to Lenora's and Mattias's shared bewilderment. "You can claim the throne as a daughter of Newton, and you'll be wedded to a son of Newton. That would solidify your right to the crown. With my rebels, we can storm Stonehold, destroy Remy, and take the throne for ourselves. The people would rejoice not having Remy as their king, and they'd welcome you with open arms. You don't have to be married long—just long enough to establish Mattias as a good, fit king, and then you can return home."

She stared at Bryan as if he spewed fire from his eyeballs. "I..." What could she say? If she turned him down outright, would that anger him? Would he turn her away, refusing to offer any kind of aid? The man just offered her his rebel group. Didn't she want revenge on Remy?

It was Remy's fault her ambassadorship was ruined before it truly started. She blamed him for nearly dying at the hands of the wolves that dragged her through the forest and that horned spider that nearly ripped her leg off. The crew of *La Marinera* died because of Remy's relentless pursuit of her. Manny and Carlos died, and because of what? Remy's ego? Because he couldn't stand the fact that he ordered Tyree to kill her, and instead Tyree saved her?

The burning sensation she had come to know as rage bounced around in her heart, taking up residence where her goodwill usually lived. She turned her gaze to Mattias, shocked by what she saw. He was staring at her with heated eyes, as if he, too, were thinking of the possibility of marrying her. Was Lawrence right when he said Mattias was giving her looks that would make Alejandro jealous?

She returned her attention to Bryan. "I'll have to discuss it with the queen."

Bryan lowered his head in a bow. "Of course, Your Highness. It's a big decision. It must not be taken lightly. In the meantime, now that I know you're a princess, I'll have someone ready a proper room for you and see to your wardrobe."

She nodded. "Thank you, Lord Brentwood. I'll alert you once I have made my decision."

"Would you do my family the honor of having dinner with us tonight? It is only me, my son, and my daughter, and we would enjoy your company."

"I would love that," she answered, thankful for the change in conversation.

Bryan turned to Mattias. "Have Almira ready a guest suite for Princess Lenora. Then show her to the dining room for breakfast." He grinned at Lenora. "I'm sure you're famished after the ordeal you've had. Please help yourself to any meal you like as you recover. And your friend outside is welcome to eat as well."

Once Mattias opened the door, Lawrence spun toward her with questioning eyes. She would fill him in later, but right now, she shook her head at him. He gave an imperceptible nod and followed as Mattias stopped the nearest servant to pass along Bryan's message for Almira.

Mattias glanced over his shoulder. "Follow me, please."

Lawrence gave Lenora a look that she ignored. Her mind had to focus on one thing at a time. Right now, it was on breakfast.

After eating a full breakfast of eggs, toast, and roasted sausages in the private dining room with Lawrence, Mattias appeared with a maid he introduced as Almira. He quickly made an excuse to leave, and Almira, who looked around thirty years old, offered to get Lenora situated in her new suite.

Almira walked silently, her soft slippers making little noise on the carpet as she led them through more curving hallways. Lenora could tell they were on the opposite side of the estate because there were fewer servants, more artwork on the walls, and plants in huge pots lining the corridors.

The maid opened the door at the end of a hall to reveal a large anteroom. Several doors adjoined the space, and Almira pointed at each one in turn. "This suite has two bedrooms. One for you, and one for your friend. The larger one is on the left, my lady. I've already hung up some dresses in the wardrobe and placed a few nightgowns in the cabinet. Your companion will also find a few selections to choose from in his room. There are connecting bathrooms for each of you and a balcony in the back of the sitting room for your enjoyment. Should you need anything, please use the bell, and I will be right up."

Lenora's strained shoulders relaxed once Almira left the room.

Lawrence turned a raised eyebrow at her. "Now can you tell me what happened? I take it he believed you are a princess? Will he help us get to Port Francis?"

She blew out a breath and fell back on the chaise in the middle of the antechamber. "You might want to sit down for this one."

After he sat on a matching wing-backed chair next to her, she told him about Bryan's literal proposal. Lawrence's face molded into a hostile glare, his nose flared and his lips scrunched up.

"The nerve of that guy," he finally muttered once Lenora finished. "I knew I didn't like him."

She wrung her hands together. "He might not have such a bad idea after all."

Lawrence bared his teeth. "You can't be serious! Marrying that *kid*?"

"He's literally the same age as us."

"What about Alejandro? Or have you not thought about him since we left Monte Paseo?"

Lenora narrowed her eyes. "That's not fair, Lawrence. You know it's not that easy. And of course I have. With what happened to Manny and Carlos, not to mention *La Marinera* and its crew... Xander is all I think about. I feel so guilty. That's why I have to do this. I have to make Remy pay for what he did. If Bryan will help me do that, then I'll use his rebels any way I can. Besides... I think... Well, I saw this happen. There's going to be a battle."

Lawrence's jaw clenched. "Is this about the vision you had when you touched Acosta?"

Nodding, she replayed the vision in her head. "I was standing in Stonehold's inner field. There was a battle going on all around me. I held a sword in my hand, stabbing right through Acosta. He dies, and then I run off to join the fight. I didn't look any different than I do now. I'm sure this is going to happen. Bryan will lend me his rebels, and we'll fight against Remy."

Lawrence blew out a breath, his shoulders slumping. "I know how stubborn you are, so I'm not even going to argue with you. But if you're going to do this, at least talk with your mother about it. Maybe she'll have some advice for you. Being married to a weakling like Mattias will not be easy. I'd pick Alejandro over Mattias."

"Wow," Lenora breathed, huffing a laugh. "Remind me to tell Xander that the next time I see him."

He pursed his lips. "Not a chance."

She leaned back against the cushion, closing her eyes.

Lawrence shifted, and she popped her eyes open when he cleared his throat. "Since we're talking about this subject," he said, "where does that leave us?"

She shook her head. "I'm not sure. I know you're my best friend. I love you, but maybe not in the same way I think you love me."

Sighing, Lawrence lifted his head, staring at the ceiling. Then he met her eyes, turning serious. "Just know I'll always be here for you. I'll always..." He swallowed his words and looked away.

He didn't need to finish. Lenora nodded, allowing the tears to flow from her eyes. She knew he'd always love her, no matter what.

Thirty-Four

Almira held out a shiny yellow dress, and Lenora squinted across the room at the silk material, trying not to let it burn through her retinas.

Lenora shook her head, rushing toward the wardrobe and pushing aside all the bright-colored choices. "Don't you have something less ... bright?"

Almira appeared by her side, looking over Lenora's shoulder. "There's that lavender gown. Ooh, or the red one!"

Lenora held in the words she wished to use regarding the two colors. Finally, just when she thought she was out of options and would have to wear the purple, her eyes landed on a silver dress. She grabbed the hanger and pulled it out. Bright sequins lined the hem, shining like diamonds in the gray fabric. It was showier than she was used to, but it would have to do.

The maid smiled, running her hands down the length of the long skirt. "This is perfect! Lord Mattias loves gray."

Lenora's eyes widened. "I'm not sure what you're implying." Though she was sure gossip had already spread throughout the mansion.

Almira stuttered, stepping away. "My apologies, my lady. I didn't mean to—I'm only saying..."

Lenora turned toward the connected bathroom, already wishing she could avoid this dinner and get past the pleasantries. However, if she planned to accept Bryan's offer of help, she'd be spending a lot more time with the Drakes—Mattias, especially. "Please, just help me get ready. I don't want to be late."

Half an hour later, Lenora stood outside the dining room. A guard pulled on the double doors, then stepped aside. With a deep breath, she walked in.

Warm, low-light candles adorned the walls, hanging on intricate sconces. Several more candles lined the center of the table on tall sticks, with a six-pronged candelabra directly in the middle. The eight-person table had been set for four—two head chairs and two in the middle on either side of the rectangle. Both male Drakes—Bryan and Mattias—sat at each head, and a young girl around fifteen with thick curls and rich brown skin sat facing Lenora. All three stood upon her entrance, giving dramatic bows.

Lenora tipped her chin, acknowledging them. "Good evening, Lord Brentwood, Lord Mattias. And you must be Miss Drake."

The girl smiled, her cheeks darkening with a blush.

Bryan waved a footman over, and he pulled out a chair for Lenora. "This is my daughter, Annette. Please, have a seat, Your Highness, and we can all get better acquainted."

The first few minutes were silent as servants brought out plates and poured water into tall glasses. Bryan sat patiently, his eyes swinging to Lenora every so often. She sat back and watched the family's dynamic. Mattias and Annette were so reserved, their eyes fixated on their plates as they lifted their forks to their mouths. This contrasted Bryan's robust demeanor and active personality. For a man who had his own militia and attacked trained Newtonian soldiers on the regular—from what he said—he had raised two very demure children.

Bryan took a sip of water, then lowered his glass with a soft *thunk*. "I trust you're finding your new accommodations to your liking, Your Highness."

Lenora swallowed her bite of food and patted her lips with her napkin. "I am, Lord Brentwood."

He hummed, chewing quietly. "And have you had a chance to think about what we discussed?"

"Father," Mattias pressed, his eyes staring pointedly at Bryan.

"Have you had a chance to explore the estate?" Bryan shifted the conversation as if he had meant to ask this question instead. "Spring is a wonderful time to walk around the gardens. The earth mages in residence love sprucing up as soon as the frost has melted, and everything is in full bloom right about now. Isn't that right, Mattias?"

Mattias looked up at the mention of his name. "Yes, that's right."

Lenora gave Mattias her attention. "Are you an earth mage?"

A hint of a smile grew on his lips as he nodded. "I'm the first earth mage in the Drake line in over a century. Annette is the second."

"But my magic isn't as strong as Mattias's," Annette added, excitement in her voice. "He grows all the plants within the house. He took over after mother died."

Silence took hold after Annette's words. Lenora watched as each of the Drakes' lips turned down, grief suddenly gripping their expressions.

She didn't know if she should remain quiet as well, but the awkwardness made her uncomfortable. Mustering up a smile from somewhere within, she turned to Mattias. "Would you show me the gardens? My mother also has earth magic, so seeing you use your powers would remind me a bit of home."

The grin on Mattias's lips made his dark skin shine bright. "I'd love that, Your Highness."

Bryan clapped his hands together, the sound drawing Lenora's eyes toward him. "Excellent idea! Perhaps tomorrow after breakfast?"

She caught on to Bryan's scheming, but she had to admit, she would need to spend some time with Mattias since she would likely go along with Bryan's plan.

Her heart lurched, and she looked down at the vegetables on her plate. Did she want to marry Mattias? Even if it were only for a few years?

She brought her gaze to the earth mage, catching his dark eyes. Lenora's insides twisted again. Those weren't the eyes she wanted to stare at. She wanted to get lost in the caramel eyes she had become so fond of, the ones she saw when she closed her eyes and thought of her future. The future where she remained beside those bits of honey until they closed for the last time.

Lenora bit into her food, swallowing down her disappointment. Her anger. Her grief. Her pain.

She really needed to talk to her mother.

Elice's pacing slowed, and she came to a halt behind Lenora's chair. Lenora strained to look behind her, even in this spirit form.

"Tell me again how many rebels you saw?" Elice asked before she paced the bedroom again.

Lenora followed her mother's moving form. "Around three, maybe four dozen."

The queen groaned. "That's not nearly enough to take on Newton's soldiers. Remy would squash that attack quickly."

"Lord Brentwood made it seem as if he had enough soldiers to win. Perhaps he has more than what I saw that day they rescued me from

Acosta's carriage. Brentwood is a large province."

Elice nodded, still walking around the room as she muttered, "Perhaps."

As soon as Lenora had fallen asleep, her mother was waiting in her dreams. Her spirit form floated effortlessly into Elice's waiting arms, melting into a hug. Nothing was better than being embraced by her mother, no matter how old Lenora was or how corporeal her spirit form felt.

As she explained her conversation with Bryan, and his actual proposal for his son, Elice took on a stern look. She hadn't sat down since.

"Should I accept?" Lenora asked, her voice suddenly small in front of her mother. When she spoke to Lawrence, she was confident. She needed Bryan's help. She needed revenge. Then she could return home, and perhaps she could see Alejandro again one day.

But now, with her mother's worry hanging over them, Lenora felt less sure. If she had Elice's approval, it would make the next step easier.

Elice paused, turning around to look at her daughter. "I don't know, Lenny. I'm with Lawrence on this one. Something about Lord Brentwood rubs me wrong, and I haven't even met him. But I must admit, having his help would be useful. And aiding him with his rebellion would be worthwhile. Remy should be deposed by those from Newton, and if we can help Bryan get rid of him, that could bode well for trade relations. Maybe this could be a form of your ambassadorship. As long as you get to make the rules, of course. I won't have you enter a bad situation."

Lenora nodded. "I'd want to have some sort of contract written up detailing everything. And the exact date the marriage will be absolved."

Elice stepped forward and grabbed Lenora's hands. "Your father and I have a ship ready to go. We'll leave tomorrow morning now that I know you'll be at Port Francis. I'm going to bring soldiers with me, and together, if you accept Brentwood's offer, we'll march on Stonehold. But only if this is what you want to do."

Gripping her mother's fingers, Lenora took a moment to think about the plan. What did she want? She had wanted to spend the next four years in Newton, learning about its people and customs. That was what she had set out to do. With the prospect of marriage, her plans looked vastly different. Then there was Alejandro and the feelings that had grown shockingly fast.

But if she could still explore the kingdom and go back home with innovative ways to help her people, would that be worth a few years married to a stranger? Worth the bit of heartbreak she'd feel every time she sat beside Mattias, wishing he were someone else? Could she rule a kingdom other than her own, knowing her obligations led her one way and her heart led her somewhere else?

And she couldn't forget her plans to investigate her powers. She had yet to learn a single thing other than the fact that Newtonians feared her curse more than Norrainians. If she lived in Stonehold for four years, she'd have access to every book, ledger, article, and report within the castle.

Lenora set her jaw, her eyes intent on her mother. "I'll take care of the contract. We'll meet you at Port Francis."

Elice lifted her hand to Lenora's cheek. "You're sure?"

With a nod, Lenora gave an overly confident, "Yes," hoping that one word would convince her mother she had no reservations about the choice.

The way Elice's eyebrow lifted let Lenora know she couldn't lie to her mother, but Elice nodded regardless. "Then I'll see you in three days."

The next morning, Lenora walked with a brooding Lawrence to Bryan's office. Along the way, Lawrence asked her several times whether she was sure, and she had to resort to ignoring him by the fifth time. The paper in her hand was now crumpled, and she hoped she hadn't ruined it.

"I just want to make sure you're sure," Lawrence added as they stepped into the main foyer. "Because if you're not sure, and you tell Lord Brentwood you accept his help, then you're stuck. So, just make sure you're—"

"Sure," she interrupted as she came to a stop outside Bryan's study. "I know. And I am."

She knocked before she could talk herself out of it. From within, Bryan's voice called for her to enter, and she pushed the door open as Lawrence plastered himself against the wall.

"Ah, Your Highness," Bryan said, waving a hand forward. "Please come in. To what do I owe the pleasure?"

Lenora swallowed down all of her fears, drowning them with thoughts of Remy, Manny, Carlos, Captain Torres, that Fates' forsaken horned spider, and her fully healed ankle. She needed to do this.

Think of all the good that could come of this. I could learn so much while I'm here. I don't have to go home just yet if I do this. I can complete my mission and return worthy of the crown I'll wear because I'll already have experience as a queen. And I'll have the chance to find out more about my cursed powers.

Never before had she felt the weight of her crown more than in this moment. She could be a queen. Of course, she always knew she would be a queen one day—she'd trained her whole life to become Norraine's next ruler. Now, a different crown stood before her, offered up on a silver platter with a side of vengeance. It only occurred to her now that she might be a little too obsessed with getting back at Remy, but it was too late. She had made a decision, and she would stick to it.

Xander and I must be perfect for each other. All we care about is revenge.

She shut that thought down immediately. For one, it was clear they both cared about other things besides their need to kill the person who had betrayed them. Second, it made her chest hurt thinking about him. Right now, she had to focus, and Bryan was staring at her with a comical expression on his face as he waited for her to say something.

"I've come to tell you," Lenora began, adjusting her shoulders, "that I will accept your offer."

Bryan stood from his chair, the indentations from his dimples on full display as he smiled. "That's excellent news, Your Highness!"

"But I have a few stipulations," she said before the man could continue. She unfolded the rumpled parchment and held it up for him to see.

Bryan nodded as he eyed her paper. "I see. That's perfectly understandable. Should I bring in my solicitor?"

"Not yet. We should discuss the terms between us first, and then we can draft an official contract."

Bryan sat again and nodded. "Please, sit down. We can go over anything you'd like."

Lenora turned toward the door. "Should we send for Mattias?"

"There's no need. I've already gotten his full approval to accept whatever agreement we set up."

Lenora sat, then read from her sheet. "First, this marriage will be a mutually beneficial agreement only. Meaning the only expectations we have are those laid out in our contract. Anything outside of that will be null."

The corners of Bryan's lips lifted. "You mean there's to be no love between you and Mattias?"

"This will not be a *traditional* marriage," she clarified. "I'm offering to help Mattias claim the Newtonian throne, and you're keeping me safe."

Brentwood leaned back, his fingers steepled under his chin. "How long do you propose this contract last?"

"Four years. That should be more than enough time to establish Mattias's reign. I can also accomplish what I originally came to Newton for."

"Yes, you were supposed to be Norraine's ambassador. I'm shocked they sent their crown princess, but it turns out they chose the right person for the job."

Lenora stared at Bryan, gauging his words. "You mean a weak girl who had to go on the run from a murderous traitor?"

Bryan leaned his elbows on the desk. "A young woman who knows what she wants and will stop at nothing to get it. That sounds like the perfect representative of the Norrainian people. Unless your people are weak, you portray them well."

Clearing her throat, she continued past his compliment, not knowing what to do with it. "I will be able to travel the kingdom at my leisure, meeting the people and learning all I can about how things work in Newton. After four years, the marriage will be absolved with no hard feelings, and I will return to Norraine—or go wherever I wish—with all the knowledge I've gained."

"What about Mattias?"

"He will remain king if he wants to continue leading Newton. I will have no hold over him."

Bryan pursed his lips in thought. "And me?"

Lenora bristled at the question. "What do you want, Lord Brentwood? Do you want more than seeing your son on the throne?"

His lips twitched. "I just want to make sure I still have my estate and everything I started this negotiation with."

"Your estate will remain yours. I make no claim on anything that belongs to you, Mattias, and the Drake line. Just as you and Mattias make no claims over anything belonging to the Moore, Taylor, and Moore-Taylor lines."

"Mattias will not try to take your kingdom from you. I can assure you of that."

Lenora narrowed her eyes and threw his words back at him. "And you?"

Bryan chortled and then slapped the top of the desk. "I like the way you think, Your Highness. I promise I will not try to steal your kingdom from you."

"Forgive me, Lord Brentwood, if I don't take people's promises as a guarantee anymore. You understand. We'll get everything in writing."

Still smiling, he relaxed in his chair. "Which is why we should call for the solicitor to finalize the contract."

She lifted her parchment. "I still have a few things to go over with you. Queen Elice will arrive in three days with more soldiers to aid our attack. We need to come up with a battle strategy. And I need to meet her at Port Francis."

Bryan waved a hand. "Yes, yes, anything you want. I'll also call in Salina and Trevor. They're my masterminds. They'll come up with a plan and guide you safely to the port. For now, let's celebrate our pact. We'll throw a party in honor of your engagement to Mattias tomorrow night!"

Dread settled in the pit of Lenora's stomach.

She was now engaged to a man she didn't know, and all she could think about was another man who had stolen her breath with one growl.

Thirty-Five

After breakfast the next day, Lenora found herself strolling beside Mattias as he pointed out the various trees and flowers he grew using his powers. Lawrence walked behind them, ever her dutiful guard.

"And this is a vine maple," Mattias continued, touching the trunk of a tree. "I love these because they grow luscious and green during the spring and summer months, but when they lose their leaves in the fall, their bark is a vibrant red. They only reach a height of about twenty-six feet—"

"Only?" Lenora interrupted with a smirk.

Mattias chuckled, looking down at his feet. "They also need a lot of water, so we employ water mages to keep them properly fed."

She stretched up to pluck a leaf from a low-lying branch. She twirled it between two fingers, admiring the thick foliage. When she looked up, Mattias's eyes were on her, an expression she couldn't name passing behind his eyes. "You pay your servants well?"

Snapped out of his stare, Mattias continued walking through the garden. They were surrounded by tall trees on all sides, the thick canopy draping over their heads and casting a glorious shadow to block out the intense sun. "Yes, I believe we do. Since we have such a large estate, and Brentwood is the largest province in Newton, we have the means to provide a healthy wage to our employees."

"You call them 'employees.' That's so different from what we call our workers."

Mattias stopped next to a large fruit-bearing tree, admiring the orange spheres that dangled from its limbs. "What do you call them in Norraine if they're not employees?"

Lenora shrugged. "Servants, mainly. Especially if they work within the castle."

"Perhaps that's one thing you can change when you return. People like to know their work is appreciated, and calling them servants goes against everything you are as a princess and future queen."

Her eyebrows knitted together. "What do you mean?"

"Well, don't you work for your people?" He reached up and plucked a fresh orange. "Aren't you supposed to provide for their basic needs, ensure their safety? Seems to me like a king and queen are servants of the people, not the other way around."

Lenora gaped as Mattias passed the orange to her. She snapped her mouth shut and grasped it, careful to avoid his fingers. "Thank you, Mattias." She felt Lawrence shift closer, but she kept her eyes on the earth mage.

He smiled, and Lenora got to see the dimples in his cheeks up close—two fully formed indents that reminded her of his father's. He continued down the path farther into the sprawling orange grove. "Oranges are my favorite. They were my mother's, too."

Lenora passed the orange back and forth between her hands. "You miss her."

Though it wasn't a question, Mattias nodded in answer. "She died several years ago. She got really sick, so Father hired Healer Misha and gave her a room in the employee wing of the house. Misha couldn't rid her of the disease in time before it spread throughout her body."

"I'm sorry." It felt like the worst words for such a sad story, but she couldn't stop them as they flowed out of her mouth.

Mattias ripped a twig from a thick tree, carrying two oranges with it. "It seems like so long ago now. You'd think we'd get over her passing, but the grief never fades."

"I don't think you can ever get over losing a loved one, especially a parent. My mother lost her father over twenty years ago, and she's still hit with sadness from time to time. I can see the way her eyes tear up whenever she talks about him. Those we love will always have a place in our hearts. I don't believe we're meant to forget them. They shape who we are, who we will be."

Mattias turned watery eyes on her, but the muscles in his jaw were clenched tight. "Thank you for your kind words, Your Highness."

"Please, call me Lenora."

He frowned momentarily, then cleared his throat. "Of course. Lenora."

The way he said her name made her think of a certain someone. Her name had rolled off *his* lips in a different way, hitting her eardrums and bouncing all the way to her heart.

"I swear by the Fates, I will send that man on a no-return trip to the spirit realm myself if he does anything to hurt you."

Lenora stared at her mother wide-eyed, finally seeing where she got her attitude from.

"Relax, Mother," Lenora coaxed, trying to calm Elice down. "We wrote the contract this afternoon and I have my own copy. Lawrence was there as a witness, and we looked over every single detail I could possibly think of."

"Well," Elice huffed, her spirit form seeming much more translucent now that she was flustered. "You tell this Lord Brentwood if he even *thinks* about betraying you, he will face every ounce of my wrath—not to mention your father's sword. Which would go right through his gut. Twice."

"Noted."

"And that boy—"

"Your future son-in-law," Lenora supplied, smiling at her mother's glare.

"If he puts his hands on you without your permission—even *with* your permission—I will slice it off. He'll wish he had never been born."

"You sound like Father."

"Yes, well, he told me to say that last part." Elice threw herself on the lounge chair. "Forgive me. I had to get that off my chest. I'm so exhausted. Your father and I have been planning nonstop. I barely slept last night. You know how I get when I'm worried. Plus, the cots on this ship are so uncomfortable. But we'll be there in two days. I'll get to see you with my own eyes. Make sure you're all right."

Lenora knelt before Elice, holding her hands. "I am all right. They're treating me well here. You should've seen the accommodations my last captors gave me."

"That's not funny, Lenny." Elice sighed, running her fingers through Lenora's curls. "Have I ever told you how much I love your golden hair?"

Lenora jerked backward. "No. Never."

Elice's smile was soft. "I remember the day you were born. I took one look at you and your beautiful golden peach fuzz, and I knew you were going to be special."

A tear sprang free, leaking down Lenora's cheek, and another followed on the other side. "What happened, then? Why am I not special?"

Elice gasped, sitting up. "What do you mean you're not special? Lenora, you're the most unique, strong-willed, *amazing* person I know."

Lenora sent a few tears flying as she shook her head. "I'm not as special as you. I'll never be."

Gripping her daughter's head in her hands, Elice looked deep into her eyes. "You're better than I could ever wish to be. Apparently, I didn't do my job as your mother if you can't see that. Maybe I didn't tell you enough how much I love you, or how important you are. But that changes today, Lenora. You matter. You're special. And even *that boy* will see it."

Lenora sniffled and rubbed at her nose. "You can call him Mattias."

Elice harrumphed. "We'll see." She looked around, her eyes glazing over as if she weren't really there. "I think someone's trying to wake me. I better go."

Lenora opened her mouth. There was still more she had to tell her mother. She hadn't even told her about *him* yet. What would Elice think about Alejandro, or about Lenora's vision of him? She was already so worked up about Mattias, and she didn't even know about Alejandro or how Lenora's heart fluttered just thinking about him.

Her mother furrowed her eyebrows. "Is something wrong? You can still call off this marriage. I'll be there soon to help you leave—"

"No," Lenora blurted. "No, it's nothing. I'm just tired. I think I need my normal dreams back."

At Lenora's sarcastic smile, Elice shook her head. "All right, I'll limit my visits. I'll reach out the night before we're due to dock. If anything changes—"

"I can't walk the spirit realm like you can. I'll save any vital information until you visit my dreams again."

With a final touch to Lenora's cheek, Elice blinked out of her dream, and Lenora's eyes snapped open. She was back in her Brentwood suite, covered in a thick quilt. Sleep long forgotten, she threw it off.

Grabbing a robe from the foot of the bed, she walked to the desk at the back of the room. With a piece of parchment and pen in her hands, she wrote, "To X," on the top left corner.

Alejandro had made her promise to write him a letter as soon as she arrived in Norraine. Since that didn't go according to plan, and her last two days had been a whirlwind, she just now had the chance to write to him.

Now that she had the opportunity, her mind went blank. She stared at the paper, unsure of where to start.

At the beginning, then.

To X,

I hope this letter finds you wherever you are. If my wish has come true, you're sitting in your castle, now the Alpha King of Alegría. I hope this is true. I pray to the Fates you are safe.

I apologize for just now sending you this letter. Unfortunately, a lot has happened since I left Monte Paseo. The ship your uncle secured for me was waiting right where it was supposed to be, and everything was going fine. Until it didn't.

A Newton ship stopped us and demanded to board. They were looking for me. The ship's captain tried to hide us in the cargo hold, but the Newtonian soldiers found us. I gave myself up, thinking the Newtonian captain would let the crew, along with Manny and Carlos, go free.

But the captain lied to me. He ordered his fire mages to blow up the ship. Everyone on board died. I'm so sorry, X. Manny and Carlos died because of me. That poor crew...

No, they died because of Remy. I have to remind myself of that. But it's hard separating what damage I inflicted and what was

---

caused by Remy's absurd obsession with capturing me. Sometimes I think I'm in a losing battle trying not to blame myself.

After the ship blew up, the Newtonian soldiers took me and Lawrence (Lorenzo, I know) to shore. I was locked in a carriage for two days with little food and water. I thought they were going to starve me to death.

Then, someone attacked the envoy. All of the Newtonian soldiers fled, leaving me with a small rebel group. The leader is a man named Bryan Drake, Lord of Brentwood.

Here is where things get... Well, things have gotten complicated, and I don't know how to explain it to you.

Bryan has offered to help me get revenge on Remy. He's willing to use his rebel group to attack Stonehold. Once we get rid of Remy, I can claim the throne. My mother is even coming to help. (I told you this before, but she has the power to enter the spirit and mind realms. She calls it "dream walking," and it's really awesome.

Anyway, she visited me in my dreams, which is how I explained the situation to her.) She arrives in Port Francis in two days. I'm going to meet her. From there, we'll march to Stonehold and launch an attack. We still have a lot to work out in two days, but...

Well, I had another vision.

I know, I know. I promised I wouldn't touch anyone else, but I had a good reason to. Captain Acosta, the man who captured me and lied to me about letting the crew go, had it coming. I touched him and saw that I would kill him in battle. I stab him right through his gut.

Gruesome, I know. But he was the one who attacked me in his wolf form and tore up my ankle. He'd been following me ever since, trying to take me back to Remy.

He's the one who came to María and Pedro's inn. I'm getting off topic. I'm sorry.

Oh, my Fates, I'm so sorry.

The future I saw of us together on your dying day... I think I might have changed it. I didn't mean to. I've been trying so hard to just survive that I might have made a drastic choice.

You see, in exchange for Bryan's help, I had to promise him something in return.

He has a son. Mattias is nineteen. He...

We have a contract in place. An agreement. It's not real... What I mean is...

When I claim the Newtonian throne, Mattias will be king alongside me. We have a pact for four years. After the four years are up, I'll be able to leave Newton.

It's almost as if I still get to be an ambassador. Only...

I hope you understand why I did what I did. I might have made a selfish decision. I'm still assessing my motives.

I don't know what else to say to you. I wish I could see your face, to know what you're thinking as you read this. Are you mad at me? Disappointed? Is your nose twitching like it does when you want to say something but you're too upset to talk?

If you never want to see me or talk to me again after this, I understand. Honestly. I know what we had was brief, and though we never established what we were—are—it's still important to me.

You're important to me.

What I'm trying to say is I'm sorry. I don't know how many times I can say that before you forgive me. Will you forgive me?

Please continue to stay safe.

Yours truly and forever,
Nora.

Thirty-Six

Lenora stood in her anteroom, waiting for Almira to grab the envelope from her outstretched hand.

"This is going where?" Almira asked, finally taking the proffered paper.

"Monte Paseo. That's in Alegría. The full address is on the envelope." Lenora's eyes caught Lawrence hovering near his doorway. "Please send it as discreetly as you can."

"Yes, Your Highness." With a bow, Almira excused herself and hurried from the room.

"Monte Paseo," Lawrence said, walking toward her with his arms crossed. "Does this have anything to do with a certain bear?"

Lenora sat on a velvet-covered chair, one of four identical seats in the anteroom. "I had to let him know about ... things."

Lawrence hummed. "Well, hopefully he understands. Knowing him, he might just show up one day and threaten to battle Mattias for you."

Lenora looked away. "You're being ridiculous."

"Am I? Tell me you don't see Alejandro running straight here, ready to swipe Mattias—and Bryan, for that matter—across their pretty, dimpled faces."

"We don't have time for this." She stood, walking toward the door.

"We're meeting with Salina and Trevor in a few minutes, and I want to make sure we're there before them."

Lawrence followed her. "True. We can't have them making any plans without us."

Lenora caught his eye before she opened the door. "Exactly."

Upon entering the study, she blew out a relieved breath. They were the first ones there. She took the seat across from the desk—Bryan's seat, she noted with a quirk of her lips—and laced her fingers together on top of the wood. Lawrence took up the space beside the window, his arms crossed once again.

A couple of minutes later, the door opened. Mattias popped his head in, smiling when he saw her. "Good morning," he said, nodding to both her and Lawrence.

Lawrence grunted. That was about all he did these days when he wasn't speaking to Lenora.

She gave a little wave. "You're early, Mattias."

"As are you. I just wanted to beat my father. He likes his tea in here before he arrives."

Lenora looked down at his hands, only now seeing the steaming mug he held. "You're such a good son."

His cheeks darkened as he set the cup down.

The door opened again before he could respond, and in walked Bryan, Salina, and Trevor. Bryan wore a burgundy vest over a cream long-sleeved shirt, the collar popping out to rest on the vest. Salina and Trevor wore full-black attire, with leather vests and thick boots. Now that Lenora was of a clear mind, she could take in their features. Salina had short-cropped curls that hung just below her ears. Trevor wore his cut almost to his scalp, with just a small amount of growth. They each had scars and hard eyes, though a curious smile touched their lips as they took in Lenora's cleaned-up demeanor.

"You're here, thank the goddess." Bryan went straight for his mug, then did a double take at Lenora sitting in his chair. He chuckled awkwardly, then lifted the cup to his mouth for a quick sip. "Let us begin. Salina, Trevor, the last time you met Princess Lenora, you didn't know she was a princess. Your Highness, please allow me to introduce you to Salina and Trevor."

Lenora eyed the long, thin sheath attached to Salina's slim waist. "Longsword?"

Salina patted the hilt. "A Malinite longsword. The weapon of choice of my line, the Malins."

"My father's line preferred a broadsword, but I favor a short sword."

A curious smile spread across Salina's lips. "Close-combat fighter? Nice."

Lenora matched her conspiratorial smile.

Bryan cleared his throat. "Ladies, if we're done talking about sword measurements, we have a lot to plan in a short amount of time."

"Which is why we shouldn't throw a ball tonight," Mattias muttered.

"I agree," Lenora said, catching Bryan off guard.

He sputtered, then sighed. "Fine." He raised his hands. "I just thought it would be good for morale—"

"No ball," Salina interrupted, cocking her hip to the side and leaning into her sword. Though she was short, her confidence made her appear larger than life. "Glad we got that cleared up. Next on the agenda."

Trevor lifted a finger into the air. "That's where I come in." He pulled a rolled-up parchment from his back pocket and splayed it across the desk.

Lenora stared at the upside-down drawing. "It's a map."

Trevor retrieved a stick of charcoal from his breast pocket and drew an X on the map. "This is where we are." He drew a short line toward Port Francis, then circled the town. "This is where we need to be by tomorrow night to meet Queen Elice and King James." Then, he drew a long, winding path to Stonehold, all the way on the other side of the paper. "And this is where we'll end up. I reckon it'll take a total of five days before we breach Stonehold proper."

Salina leaned over the map. "I'd say you're right, provided we don't come across any mishaps."

"We should account for six when estimating how much food, water, and other supplies we'll need, considering we're adding Norraine's soldiers," Lenora added.

Salina laughed. "I like this one. Quick on her feet. You picked a good one this time, Mattias."

This time?

Lenora's eyes shot to Mattias, who stared pointedly at the map. She turned to Bryan, taking in his shining eyes and too-bright smile. What was he telling everyone? She figured he wouldn't outright say he secured his son a bride through a bit of scheming, but how far would he go when telling people about their engagement?

Trevor pulled another roll from his other pocket and laid it out on top of the map. "Here's what I suggest. With our two-hundred-strong militia—"

Both Lenora and Lawrence shared a look. That was more than either of them had anticipated.

"And Norraine's..." Trevor paused, looking at her. "Say ... two-hundred plus?"

"I don't know how many Queen Elice and King James brought on the ship with them," Lenora supplied. She held back her grimace, wishing she'd had time last night to ask her mother more questions.

Bryan placed both hands on the desk, leaning over the numbers Trevor had listed. "If Queen Elice cares even the slightest bit about her daughter—and I'd wager she cares a whole lot—she packed that ship tight.

There should be over five hundred on board. That's capacity for standard ocean liners."

Trevor pulled the sheet closer and wrote the new number down. "Five-hundred plus. All right, that gives us seven hundred. What's Remy got behind him?"

Salina tilted her head side-to-side. "A thousand, give or take. That's just what he has in residence, unless he recalled others from the outer camps. Not to mention the wolves. Surely they count as double."

Lawrence shifted on his feet. They still hadn't told anyone he was a wolf shifter. Now would *not* be the right time to open that bag.

"Can't forget about the wolves," Trevor muttered, rolling his wrist in between a pause in his writing. "Right, that makes fifteen hundred enemy soldiers against our seven hundred."

Lenora's hope shattered as it fell to the floor.

"We're outnumbered and outmatched," Lawrence mumbled from the back of the room.

"But not out-planned," Salina said. "Trevor's the brains of our operation. He'll come up with a solid strategy."

Trevor hovered over his notes. "There's no need to fret, Your Highness. Give me a day. By this time tomorrow, I'll have a plan." Then he began muttering to himself, jotting random words and crossing out others, only to do it all over again.

Bryan looked over his shoulder at Lenora. "Why don't you have breakfast? We'll send for you once Trevor is ready."

Lenora hesitated, her eyes catching Lawrence's.

Mattias stepped close, his hand stretching forward before it fell to his side. "I'll go with you, if that's all right."

With her lips pursed, she nodded, even though her gut told her she should stay here to watch over Bryan.

She didn't fully trust him, but her growling stomach reminded her to eat, otherwise she wouldn't be able to focus.

Besides, it gave her some time to talk with Mattias without his father's spying ears and eyes.

Lawrence took his meal in his room while Mattias and Lenora sat in the dining room. Annette, having eaten an early breakfast so she could meet with her governess, had already left.

That left the two of them alone, sitting next to each other.

Lenora eyed him over the rim of her glass of freshly squeezed orange juice. He chewed his food slowly, thoughtfully, as if he had all the time in the world and they weren't currently planning on overthrowing the tyrant king of Newton.

He looked her way, holding her eyes. It was only then that Lenora noticed he did that often. Most of the time, he seemed shy, but he had strong eye contact and spoke with a clear, deep voice. She wondered if he was more like Bryan than he let on.

"I know what you're thinking," he said, setting his fork down.

Lenora blinked. "Do you?"

"You're wondering how you got stuck in this mess with me."

A breath escaped her mouth. "I was wondering how *you* got stuck in this mess with *me.*"

He chuckled. "I can assure you, I'm not upset with you, nor do I place any blame on you. I know this was my father's idea. I'm sorry he somehow tricked you into this ... arrangement."

Lenora swallowed some juice, suddenly parched. Now would be as good a time as any to set clear boundaries with her future husband. "We should talk about this..."

"Arrangement?"

She shook her head at his smile. "Yes, sure, arrangement."

"Lenora, I don't want anything you don't want. If this is to be strictly business like it says on the contract we signed, then that's all it is. But I'm sure we can become friends over the course of the next four years. That is, if you want to be."

"That would be nice," she said, nodding. "The truth is, I've always wanted to visit Newton. I'll probably spend most of my time traveling the kingdom."

He took a small bite of eggs, chewing slowly. "That would give me an opportunity to learn how to be a king when you leave."

She smirked. "And perhaps find a good wife *next time*."

Mattias froze, his fork hovering midair. "You caught that, then?" He lowered his fork and sighed. "I'll just come out and say it. There was ... someone. But obviously it won't work out now. I tried to remind Father of my feelings for her, but once he gets an idea in his head..."

Lenora frowned, feeling bad for making Mattias out himself this way when she was no better. "To be honest, you're not the only one. I also had someone... Looks like that won't work out for us, either."

Mattias remained quiet while Lenora pushed around the eggs and sausages on her plate.

"You know," he said, his voice low, "once our contract is up, we'll be free to be with whomever we wish."

Meeting his eyes, she swore she saw them shimmer like bits of hope hanging from twinkling stars, just within reach, rather than millions of miles away. Whoever this girl was, he loved her.

She thought of Alejandro. What was he doing right now? Had he already met his brother? If so, what was the outcome of their battle?

Mattias returned to his food, and they sat in companionable silence.

This was what the next four years would look like when she wasn't on the road. Quiet. Somewhat bleak. Periods of intermittent conversation. But overall, loveless. Maybe one day she would grow to care for Mattias, but would she love him?

The pressure in her chest told her no. She wouldn't.

A soft breeze flew by overhead as she crouched low on the dock, with Lawrence on one side and Salina on the other. All two hundred of the Brentwood Warriors were deep in the woods, hiding in the tree line behind them.

Last night, Lenora spoke with Elice in her dreams and told her of the plan.

Lenora still couldn't believe they had worked something out, but Trevor truly had a gifted mind. In the end, it all came down to her. The entire plan hinged on Lenora.

As soon as she had walked into the study after dinner, Bryan appraised her with a sly grin. "You're the key to our success, Princess Lenora," he had said. "You're going to be the one to take out Remy."

Of course, that was what she wanted. She wanted to drive a sword straight through him. Whisper Manny's and Carlos's names in his ear before she withdrew her blade. Watch his confused expression as he fell to the floor, dying before she could tell him who they were. Remy didn't deserve to know, though. He would die without knowing the names of his victims. They were too good for him.

Yet, as a thick fog rolled in, her nerves ran amok. Where were her parents? They had waited beside the dock for almost an hour. Had they run into a Newtonian ship? What would Lenora do if Remy had her parents and five hundred of their soldiers killed? The thought of losing her mother and father threatened to rock her to her core.

Lawrence bumped his shoulder against hers. "I can see you're worried."

Salina shushed him, a reminder that they didn't want to get caught.

As if a big ship isn't going to dock here at any moment.

At least, that was what she hoped for. Her parents had to be all right. She prayed to the Fates that they were.

Salina pointed across the water, and Lenora strained her eyes.

A dark outline floated atop the water, barely visible due to the fog. That had to be the ship.

As it broke through the clouds, Lenora registered the possibility that it could be a merchant ship, or even a ship loaded with Newtonian soldiers.

The three of them waited as the ship slowly docked. A gangplank lowered, and they held their breaths, not making a move. They had to be sure this was a Norrainian ship, but it was too dark and foggy to see the Norrainian crest—her mother's six-pronged crown—on the bow.

The first person to step off the ship wore thick boots that thudded against the wooden dock. Lenora stood as another figure walked beside the first. Then she ran.

She heard Salina's voice whispering after her, but she didn't stop.

Especially once the two figures started off toward her.

"Lenora," Elice called, her voice carrying on the wind and landing gently in Lenora's ears.

"Sweetheart, is that you?" James's firm voice asked, making Lenora lose her footing. She hadn't heard her father's voice in weeks, and she didn't realize how much she had missed it.

Lenora quickly caught herself and finished her run until she stood in front of her parents. She wanted to throw herself into their arms, to be swallowed up in their warm embrace. Elice was already shedding tears, and James's arms were outstretched. They wanted to hold her, too.

But she couldn't touch them. Lenora hadn't had time to fix her necklace, and she didn't care to wear gloves anymore. All she could do was show her parents how far she'd come in three weeks.

So she wiped away the wetness on her cheeks and held her head high, grinning at them for the first time in years.

Thirty-Seven

"You made it," Lenora exclaimed, her tone lighter than it had been in nearly two weeks.

Elice lifted her hand and hovered it near Lenora's cheek. "With the help of the other water and air mages, we created this fog to keep us covered the entire time. The captain was a little angry, but yes, we made it."

"My dear," James said, his tone terse as he stepped closer. "I need to hear it directly from you. Are you well? Are you safe?"

"I'm safer now that you're here," she answered, then realized that probably wouldn't sound too good to an overprotective father. "I'm all right. There were some ... moments, but I handled it."

"I know you can handle anything." James finally touched her shoulder, giving it a light squeeze. That tiny act of love, coupled with his praise, made her smile. When was the last time she smiled so freely around her parents?

Elice looked up the gangplank at the waiting bodies lining the rails. "We should have the soldiers disembark. Is your camp nearby?"

"We're just beyond the trees." Lenora threw a glance behind her, catching Salina and Lawrence where they stood a few feet away. She waved them over, and Lawrence came bounding down the dock.

"Your Majesties," he said, bowing.

Elice smiled at him. "Lawrence. It's good to see you. Thank you for taking care of Princess Lenora."

Salina walked a little more hesitantly, then lowered her eyes to the ground as she bowed low. "It's an honor, Queen Elice, King James."

"This is Salina Malin," Lenora said.

"It's a pleasure to meet you," Elice said.

James eyed Salina's sword. "You carry a longsword?"

Elice rolled her eyes. "Not now, honey. Let's get our camp set up before you dive into sword-talk."

Lenora held back her laughter as she caught Salina's eyes.

"This is where you get your love of swords from?" Salina whispered, leaning close to Lenora.

"You have no idea," she responded.

It took over an hour for the Norrainian soldiers to disembark, unloading their supplies as they went. The town remained quiet, though a few late-night passersby eyed them warily.

Salina and Lawrence led the soldiers two-by-two through the town until they disappeared into the forest. Lenora stayed behind with her parents to oversee the debarkation. Her shoulders were almost weightless now as she overheard her father giving their soldiers direction while Elice and a few air and water mages controlled the fog over their people. Her parents spoke in sure, strong voices that commanded respect.

Lenora hoped to have the same effect on her people one day.

Soon, she would have to step into that role. Admittedly, it was happening a lot sooner than she thought. She always assumed she would have to wait almost an entire lifetime before her mother died and she could take the crown passed down to her.

Now, she was forcibly taking someone else's. She didn't think she deserved to rule Newton. She wasn't born here, and even if her grandmother was, did that give her the right to stake a claim?

What Bryan said repeated in her mind. Remy was a tyrant after just a couple weeks of rule. He would only get worse. Mattias, as a distant relative and Newtonian citizen, had more right to rule Newton than she did. Helping him gain the crown would be worth it if they could rid Newton of Remy.

The way Mattias spoke so eloquently and reverently of the people who worked for him made Lenora believe he would make a good king. He was thoughtful, reserved, and through his ties to Brentwood, he had the experience of making important decisions for the good of those under him.

She had to believe she was doing the right thing.

And once this was all over, perhaps she could seek her own happiness. She could see herself free to be where she truly belonged—and with whom she truly belonged.

A hand on her shoulder pulled her from her thoughts. Her instinct to jump back from the touch was slow, and she realized she didn't fear touch quite as much as before. However, she did keep her hands close to her side, just in case.

"You seem lost in thought," Elice said, her hand still on Lenora's arm.

"Aren't I always?" She huffed, the sound blowing the dense fog away from her face. "It's been a long few weeks."

"It's only going to get longer. You know that, right?"

She understood what her mother meant, so she nodded.

Elice sighed, her eyes heavily lidded. "That's the last of the supplies. Let's make our way to camp so I can meet this Lord Brentwood and that boy."

"You won't call him that, will you?" Lenora walked beside Elice as James came up behind them.

"Not to his face," James added.

Lenora held back her grimace, hoping her parents wouldn't embarrass her.

The street remained quiet, even after an entire fleet had strolled through. Stealth would be their friend throughout this journey, and her mother's soldiers knew how to manage that.

Just beyond the trees, the first few tents were being set up. The plan was to spend the night here and start their trek at dawn. Brentwood's scouts would go ahead of the group to signal for any trouble. At night, several parties would stay awake as well.

As Trevor had warned, it was best not to face any wolves head-on. Since their senses made them excellent trackers, it was very possible the wolves would smell, hear, and see them before they even approached Stonehold.

In the center of the camp, an enormous, bright orange tent with the Brentwood orange tree crest on the flap stared down at her. Lenora blew out a breath, looking over her shoulder at her mother, then her father. "Brentwood can be a bit … flashy."

James narrowed his eyes. "Doesn't he understand our need for stealth?"

Lenora shrugged, but if she knew the lord as well as she thought she did—which wasn't much—she figured he wouldn't understand modesty.

As they approached the entrance, Bryan's guards stepped aside and held open the fabric, their heads lowered.

Upon walking inside, all talking ceased. Bryan stood in the middle of a circle while Trevor held out the map and his charcoal. Lawrence, Mattias, Salina, and two others from Bryan's team looked over at Lenora and her parents before everyone bowed.

"Your Majesties!" Bryan said once he stood straight. He extended his arms and moved away from the circle. "Welcome to Newton. I wish it were under different circumstances that we meet. However, there will be good news on the horizon. Please allow me to introduce myself. I am Bryan Drake, Lord of Brentwood." He swiveled his head around, motioning for Mattias to step forward. "This is my only son, Mattias Drake. Your future son-in-law."

"Let's make ourselves clear," Elice said, eyeing both Drakes. "We both know the *circumstances* of my and my husband's presence here. Is it safe to assume everyone in this tent knows the truth?"

Bryan's lips trembled as he fought to maintain his false smile. "Right! Well, let's move past the pleasantries. There is much to discuss."

Salina caught Lenora's eyes and raised an eyebrow, but Lenora ignored it and dove into the mission. Bryan was right about one thing—they had a lot to do.

Over the course of their journey, their combined troops began their hike through the forest as the sun rose. It turned out that Elice and James had stuffed the ship past capacity. The king and queen brought over seven hundred and fifty mages and non-mage soldiers, making their total close to one thousand.

Yet they were still severely outnumbered.

Hopefully, the strategies they designed would prove to be the difference maker in this battle.

At night, the camp would set up again, and small, controlled fires would be erected to roast wild rabbits or deer, then be put out so they didn't draw too much attention.

Then, at dawn, they would set out again.

By the third day, Lenora was thankful they had healers among them. Her feet were sore, and blisters developed on her toes that needed to be seen to. She wasn't the only one. The healers ran around the camp, gently touching people's injuries or aches and pains, removing them as if they were never there. They worked in shifts, some healing while others rested, so there were always a few healers available at a moment's notice.

How she wished she could have had a healer when she and Alejandro were escaping Newton.

The thought of his light brown eyes, rich skin, and thick dreads with golden tips send a shiver down her spine, reminding her of the first time he touched her cheek. She placed a hand there, a phantom memory of his touch making her blush.

Her father plopped down beside her on the ground near a roasting deer. He had a bundle in his hands, and Lenora wiped the ridiculous, wistful smile from her face.

"I have something for you," he said, unwrapping the cloth. A black leather sheath rested on his lap, a T engraved in fancy script directly in the center of the casing.

Lenora knew what it was before she even laid eyes on it. That didn't stop the tingle of excitement from rushing through her.

"I heard you lost your dagger." He narrowed his eyes. "The one I gave you for your eighteenth birthday. And that you left your sword—the one I gave you for your nineteenth birthday—at Stonehold when you escaped. So, I thought you'd need something."

Lenora practically buzzed as James held the sheath in one hand, then grabbed the hilt in the other. With a *zing*, he pulled the blade free from its case.

"Grandfather's sword," she muttered, eying the short sword in her father's hand.

James nodded. "I know I never let you touch it before, but I figured now would be as good a time as any for you to use it." He turned the blade over, grasping it with precise fingers, and presented the hilt to her.

Lenora stared at the glinting silver as she grabbed it. This sword was a gift from one grandfather to the other. King Edgar, Elice's father, was close friends with Lord Jair, James's father, and the king had presented this as a wedding gift when Jair married James's mother, Cherise. Jair was a master swordsman who kept a varied collection of blades. This short sword was his prized possession, though it never saw action in battle.

She brought the sword closer, her eyes taking in every detail—like she did when she was a child, staring at it from its place in the Taylor display case in Talin. A single diamond the size of her thumb rested in the center, glittering even in the darkness. The smooth, sharp blade cut a domineering presence even though its length was less than grand.

That was why she loved using a short sword, even though she couldn't stand being close to others. People underestimated its size, thinking the wielder would be at a disadvantage by having to fight in close combat. But with the right blade, and with years of practice, a skilled person could disarm—or kill—their opponent just as well as with any other weapon.

This sword was perfect in her hands. The balance between the hilt and blade was evenly distributed, making it more comfortable to hold. James must have had it sharpened recently because the tip and edges were smooth and sharp.

Lenora looked up at him, taking in his watery eyes. Hers were bursting with tears too, and she allowed them to fall. "Thank you, Father."

James choked back a sob, his emotions always at the forefront, and wiped her cheeks with the pad of his thumb. "You're welcome, my dear."

After everyone had gone to their tents, Lenora stood in hers, her new sword in her hand. She went through the motions General Vic had taught her. She bent her legs, angled her arms, and took slow, measured breaths as she worked through her stances. Middle, high, low. Thrusting forward, she followed through and swung to the side, swiping through the air at an invisible foe.

On and on she moved, slashing and piercing and pretending to parry. She imagined fireballs flying over her head, funnels of air blasting at her face, bits of earth clawing at her skin, and strong forces of water beating down her back. She envisioned Remy's face as she struck him down, making him pay for all the damage he had done.

She practiced until the sounds of the camp waking made her stop, attach her sheath across her waist, and store her sword at her hip.

The next day, they crested the last hill outside of Stonehold. All one-thousand soldiers filed into a neat line behind her. The next part of their plan was clear. They needed to be covert if they wanted any kind of element of surprise on their side. So far, they hadn't encountered any issues, which Bryan indicated was odd.

Lenora knew it too. From the knowledge she had gained about Remy and his soldiers—especially the wolves—they didn't miss a thing. The wolves could pick up scents from a mile away. Their hearing and sight were impeccable. And Lenora was traveling with a huge force.

Remy wouldn't let that slide off his purview. Would he?

Lenora walked near the front of the line, her father and mother in front of her, and Lawrence, Salina, and Mattias behind. Lawrence pressed a hand on her back, making her look over her shoulder.

He shook his head just as a howl went off in the distance. Several more sounded, but those were farther away.

Ahead of her, her parents stopped, and the mix of Norrainian soldiers and Brentwood Warriors halted, holding their breaths. They all knew what a howl would signify. They waited for an attack, for wolves to jump out at them at any moment.

"It's a signal," Lawrence muttered, and several heads turned his way. "We've breached their barrier. They've just alerted the castle that we're here."

"There goes our element of surprise," Salina said, putting all her weight on one hip. "Time for plan B."

James nodded. "Let's get to the bottom of the hill and regroup. We need to make sure everyone is in position in case Remy decides to meet us head on."

They continued down the small hill, and once everyone had gathered, Elice paced in front of them.

Lenora stood beside James, Mattias, and Bryan, all facing the crowd. She braced herself, holding a brave face in front of everyone. They needed to know she was strong and ready to fight. Otherwise, if they picked up on her fear, they would surely tuck their tails, too.

She looked at her mother, who always seemed to emulate calm and poise, even when faced with danger or hardship. Lenora always looked up to Elice. She wanted to be like her so badly. It hurt when she thought she could never live up to her legacy.

Now, as she held her chin high, she realized she would *never* be Elice. She could only be *Lenny*. And that was good. Being Lenny was amazing. She had faced a pack of wolves, a treacherous canyon with little food and water, fought off a venomous horned spider (with a little help, of course), survived a ship attack, and was locked in a carriage for two days. If she could handle that, she could handle anything.

Elice eyed the soldiers with her hands on her hips. "We know what we're here for. We know who we're fighting against. Some of you have faced enemies worse than Remy. You may think he's tough, and he certainly is, but he's weak compared to us."

A few loud cheers erupted as the soldiers hollered and lifted their fists.

Continuing, Elice raised her voice. "We will show Remy what happens when you attack one of our own. His actions will not go unpunished. We will capture him and make sure he faces trial for all the wrongs that he's committed."

Lenora's eyes met Mattias. He stared impassively, reminding her that she shouldn't show a reaction to her mother's statement.

She still hadn't told her parents that part of the plan. Now that she thought about it, only a select few knew what they discussed that day in Bryan's office. They hadn't brought it up since.

A prickly sensation rose in her throat. She would have to kill Remy. Mattias and Lawrence knew it. Bryan, Salina, and Trevor knew, too.

Her parents, their soldiers, and the rebels did not.

Over the past three weeks, she thought about making Remy pay. She craved—no, she *ached* for revenge.

Now, she was on the cusp of it. It would soon be before her, waiting for her to grab it and take it and make it hers.

It was all she wanted, the reason she chose to stay in Newton and marry someone she didn't know.

So why did her chest hurt and regret blossom in her mind?

Shaking it off, she jumped back into her mother's speech, only to find that it was over and the troops were lining up again. She found Lawrence eyeing her, his knowing stare reading her body language.

Before he could ask if she was all right, she turned and walked alongside the group.

She could do this.

For all those Remy had hurt, she needed to.

Thirty-Eight

The setting sun's rays hovered over the edge of the horizon, just above the farthest hilltops and treetops. Lenora strode down the hill beside Lawrence, Mattias just behind her. She could tell Lawrence wanted to talk to her, but with so many people around, he wouldn't dare say it aloud.

Lenora gasped as the outer walls of Stonehold's bulwark came into view, the tall iron gates wide open. Remy stood in the middle of his forces, his arms spread wide with thick vines curling around them toward his torso. Slowly, the vines wrapped around his body like armor, sticking their jagged ends out in protection.

All around him, his soldiers were armed just as heavily. Mages held their powers at the ready, their elements hovering near their hands. A few non-mage soldiers wielded swords, some with shields. A large pack of wolves gathered near the front lines, their teeth bared and saliva dripping down their open jaws.

Remy's face angled toward the setting sun, as if absorbing the last of the light. He almost looked at peace. His father's silver crown tipped crookedly on his salt-and-pepper curls, and his smile was just as skewed.

He looked as if he had already won the battle before it began.

Elice stepped forward, blocking her daughter from Remy's view.

"Prince Remy Newton, son of King Jerome Newton," she began, ignoring the way the Newtonian soldiers gasped at her improper greeting. They had expected her to call him "King." Lenora smiled. Her mother wouldn't deign to call Remy a king when her daughter came here to depose him. "My name is Queen Elice of house Moore. I've come to rid this land of your despicable reign and ensure you receive punishment for your act of treason against King Jerome, the murder of your entire family, and the attempted murder and kidnapping of the crown princess of Norraine. *My daughter.*"

James leaped forward, unsheathing his broadsword and brandishing it. His chest heaved as he leveled a glare across the open field at Remy.

Lenora looked around, taking in the faces of her troops. Lawrence growled, hunched over like he was ready to shift into his wolf form. Even Mattias wore a stern scowl, his eyebrows furrowed close together as he splayed his fingers at his side, ready to call upon the earth.

When her eyes landed on Bryan, his impassive expression shocked her. She hadn't expected him to feel angry on her behalf, but the Newtons were also his family—no matter how distant and removed the Drake line was. Surely he felt *something* at their deaths.

Then he looked at her, and a sense of urgency passed through his eyes and into her. His words echoed in her mind.

You're going to be the one to take out Remy.

That was their secret plan, the hidden key to their success. It was all she thought about. What she strove for ever since Tyree helped her escape the first time.

She had to be the one to kill Remy. That would solidify her claim and let the citizens know she was their new leader.

Lenora nodded once, and Bryan matched it with a tip of his head. Then she took a step past Elice, releasing her grandfather's short sword from its sheath and holding it before her.

As she readied to take another step, her eyes trained on Remy, an arm shot out, impeding her movement. Lenora followed the limb to her mother's tight face.

"I'll handle Remy," Elice muttered, her voice strained. Lenora had never seen her mother so angry. "We're both mages, and I can counter his earth magic with my own. I'll also have my air and water magic to aid me."

Lenora opened her mouth to protest, to tell her mother that she needed to be the one to do this, when a loud roar echoed down onto the field.

She knew that sound.

Her body snapped around, looking for the source, when her eyes landed on the hill southwest of her troops.

A brown bear stood on its hind legs, its mouth wide open as it let loose another deafening roar. Behind it, hundreds of bears pounced onto the hilltop, all of them growling or snarling down at them.

But Lenora's eyes remained on the first bear. The one she could recognize even with her eyes closed. The way his honeyed eyes found hers from such a distance, the twitch of his nose, the deep sound of his roar, the thick, coarse fur with gold at the tips—that was her bear. And she was his.

That was Alejandro.

The entire field—mages, non-mages, and wolves—froze, their faces a mix of horror and shock.

Everyone except Lawrence, at least.

"Great," James whispered, his eyes wide. "Do we have to fight bears, too?"

Lenora realized she hadn't told a single person about the bear shifters. With all the battle preparations and trying to convince her parents not to slice Bryan's head off in his sleep, she didn't think to tell anyone about her new friends from the neighboring kingdom. The last she knew, they were busy fighting their own civil war. Alejandro was supposed to be deposing Augustín, and she didn't expect their battle to be over so quickly.

Her heart leaped in her chest. His battle was over. Since he was standing there before her, that must have meant he won. He defeated Augustín. She should have known better than to question the Fates and the vision they gave her.

But how did he know to come here?

She remembered the letter she wrote to him explaining what had happened to her and how she would march on Stonehold. She had even told Alejandro when they would be leaving. He must have read her letter—must have come straight away to help her.

Elice and James angled sideways, prepared to take on both Remy and the bears. Lenora had to act fast, because at that moment, Alejandro gave another screech and took off down the hill with his bears in tow.

"Wait," she yelled as her troops raised their hands, magic and swords primed. "They're... They're friendly bears."

Elice looked scandalized. "Bears are friendly?"

"These are! Just trust me, Mother. They're allies."

"You'll have to explain that to me after we win this battle." With that, Elice faced Remy again and threw a brutal gust of wind toward him.

That was the signal her soldiers were waiting for.

Both troops charged at each other, rocks and wind and fire and water all hurtling at fierce speed across the field. The wolves snapped their jaws, biting down on anything within reach. Swords clanked against swords, and screams and cries soon rent the air. The bear shifters reached the bottom of the hill and ran through the field on the opposite side of Lenora's troops.

She held her breath as she ducked under a Newtonian air mage's wind attack, swung her sword, then pushed him off her weapon. She took a moment to survey the field. With her forces coming in from the east and Alejandro's forces from the south, Remy's were pushed up against the gate. They had nowhere to go besides back into the castle, but fighting in such close quarters would prove difficult and would essentially trap them inside.

Remy was effectively cornered.

The battle continued as she fought off several soldiers in silver uniforms. A wolf even squared off against her, clamping down on her boot hard enough to sink its sharp canines into her foot. The pain reminded her of her injury, and she sliced down on the wolf's backside.

With a grimace, she turned away, disgust pulling her out of the moment. All around her, Newtonian soldiers in gray uniforms and wolves in silver and brown fur fought against Norrainian soldiers in green uniforms and Brentwood Warriors in a mix of black and brown leather vests. There were also large brown bears roaring as they swiped their massive paws, knocking entire bodies to the ground. Lenora wheezed as she grappled with the death growing around her. With the death still to come.

Lenora held in her frown, but a smile formed instead when her eyes landed on Acosta.

Her vision sprang to the forefront of her memory. He scowled in her direction, and even though he was in human form, he looked very much like an angry wolf.

She stalked toward him like he was her prey. "Funny seeing you here," she said, not bothering to hide her delight.

"Let's end this," Acosta yelled, lifting a sword. "I don't care about that stupid vision. I make my own destiny. I won't let some cursed witch tell me when I'm going to die."

She spun her sword in an arch, letting his words roll off her skin. She swiped first, aiming high and making Acosta lean backward. With his body off balance, she plunged her blade toward his chest.

He turned, spinning around until he landed on his feet. "I won't let you get too close. I know how your cursed vision ended, and I'm going to make sure you don't get the chance to make it come true."

She let him talk, taking measured steps closer to him. He mimicked her, stepping back whenever she moved forward. With a jump, he stabbed with his long blade, trying to keep her away. It was as if he were solely on defense, trying to protect himself.

The vision is haunting him.

She saw the dark bags under his eyes, the way he blinked a little too long. He likely wasn't sleeping well, which would make him sloppy.

Lenora could make that work in her favor.

She changed her tactic, lowering her sword to waist level and freeing up her chest and head. It was a mistake she was taught never to make. General Vic would likely scream her ear off if this were practice.

However, it was a real battle, and Lenora knew what she was doing.

Seeing the opening, Acosta grinned and thrust himself forward. Lenora threw her free hand onto his wrist, lifting and twisting his sword into the air. She wasn't afraid to make contact with his skin—she'd learned, thanks to Alejandro, that she couldn't trigger another vision by touching the same person a second time.

But Acosta didn't know that. His arm jutted upward with her thrust, sending his sword flying away. He let out a gasp, looking down at where her hand held his wrist. He scrunched his face, his features contorted. Then he blinked, slowly lowering his eyes to her.

He laughed, the sound loud in her ears despite the raging battle. "You... You can't have a second vision of me." He sputtered, his laughter dying out. His eyes widened as he coughed. "What... What have you done?"

Lenora stepped back, withdrawing her sword from where she had plunged it into his ribs. Blood oozed from the wound, puddling on the floor. He had been so distracted by his attack and her hand on his that he didn't watch where he was going. He ran straight into her sword.

"You ... witch..." he muttered, then he collapsed to the ground.

Lenora stared at the spot where he had been standing, trying not to think about the squelch she heard when she pulled her sword from his body. She had to shake it off. She had to find Remy.

Turning, she jumped back into the battle, raising her sword to block a blade flying toward her head. She pushed her new opponent back, knocking them right into a fireball.

A rock pelted her forehead, sending sparks of light through her vision. She faced the direction it came as a burst of water flew over her shoulder to take out the earth mage that had hit her.

All around, chaos reigned. She could barely tell who was fighting with her and who was fighting against her. Roars and snarls mixed in with yells and screams.

A warm trickle ran down her forehead, and she wiped at it. When she brought her hand to her face, blood coated her fingers.

That rock must have hit me pretty hard.

She wiped her hand on her black pants, but when she went to lift it again, something held her back.

Looking down, vines wound their way up her legs and were snaking up her arms, holding her in place. She tried to step out of their hold, but the vines held firm.

One thin yet sturdy branch worked its way up until it reached her hand, then wrapped around her sword. With a flick, it tossed the weapon away.

Lenora expected it to land on the drenched ground, but it landed in Remy's waiting hand instead.

He flung his hand forward, and dirt flew up into her eyes. They burned from the debris, and she couldn't use her hands to wipe them.

Remy's laughter taunted her, and she fought the pain in her eyes to glare at him. His grin showcased all of his teeth, and he looked downright giddy. The sight churned her stomach.

"I finally have you," he said. He stood a few feet away, his spiky armor protruding from his body. "I must say, it took a while to capture you, but oh, has the chase been worth it."

"What do you want with me?" Lenora bit out, struggling to pull her arms away.

"I don't *want* for anything," he said, turning her grandfather's sword around in his hand. "Now that I think about it, I suppose it wouldn't have mattered if I let you get away. I got what I wanted—the crown, the throne, the castle, the army. Maybe I just wanted to finish what I started. I told my worthless brother to end you when I should have done it myself. You heard what I was plotting, and I feared you would have warned my father. But you couldn't have, anyway. By the time Tyree set you free, I had already killed my mother, father, and sister. Then, when I found out what Tyree had done, I killed him too. I probably would have done that regardless—less people to vie for the throne. You understand."

Lenora's mouth curled up in disgust. "You talk about killing your family like it means nothing—like *they* mean nothing. You hunted me down for no reason. Innocent people *died* because of you. Yet you stand there acting like it was no big deal. What in the Fates' names is wrong with you?"

Remy sneered and clenched his fist, and the vines tightened around her, squeezing her legs and cutting into her skin. She fell to her knees, the compression on her body too much to handle. Tears sprang in her eyes, and she sucked in a shallow breath. The vines worked their way up her chest, tightening around her neck.

Lenora couldn't take in a proper breath. She tried again, but the crushing pressure on her throat prevented air from entering. She fought to lift her arms, but the vines held strong.

Remy laughed, his head thrown back. The sound of a roar hit Lenora's ears, and then a flurry of brown fur entered her hazy vision. A bear stepped between her and Remy, lifted its massive paw, then swung hard at Remy's face.

Thirty-Nine

Remy flew sideways and landed on the ground as spittle and blood sprayed from his mouth. The vines fell off Lenora's body right away, and she desperately sucked in air. Dry tears made her eyes blurry, but she knew who had come to her rescue.

Alejandro roared, stomping his forelegs on the ground in front of Remy's body. Remy scrambled backward, finally aware of his surroundings. It was too late, though, as Alejandro used his paws to grasp one of Remy's legs and pull him closer.

Spit peppered Remy's face as Alejandro let out a blaring sound, the pitch lower than his normal roar. Remy struggled to stand, his eyes wide and frantic.

Alejandro stood on his back legs again, growling as he lifted his paw. Lenora watched in horror as he smacked Remy's shoulder, slamming him back into the dirt several paces away.

Remy lay still, his shoulder hanging at an unnatural angle. Clearly, Alejandro wasn't done. He stood and padded toward Remy, his nostrils flaring and his enormous chest heaving.

If Alejandro didn't stop now, he would kill Remy. What would that do to her plan? It hinged on Lenora deposing Remy to secure the throne. Alejandro needed to shift back, and fast.

Lenora pushed herself up, standing on bleeding and wobbling legs. She took one shaky step, then two, picking up her pace until she threw herself before Alejandro.

With her hands stretched out, she grabbed onto Alejandro's furry chest, twining her fingers into his fur. She was vaguely aware of the faces turned her way. Alejandro's attack on Remy had garnered the attention of the soldiers in the immediate vicinity. Soon, the sounds of battle ebbed out until all was quiet. Hundreds of eyes were on her as she grasped onto the huge, angry bear, while Remy lay motionless behind her.

"Stop!" she yelled, lifting her head, her voice pleading with Alejandro to see and hear her.

He didn't, not the way she wanted him to.

Alejandro screeched in her face, and she closed her eyes against the force of his breath. Slowly, she trailed her fingers up his chest, standing on her toes until she reached his neck.

"Alejandro," she whispered, "it's me. It's Lenora."

He took a deep breath, and his nose twitched as he picked up her scent. She was breaking past his rage, passing through the bear to the man within.

Her mother screamed her name from across the field, but she kept her attention on Alejandro. His caramel eyes skittered about, staring at the carnage around them. She had to get him to focus on her.

"It's your Nora," she said, her voice soft. "Come back to me, my prince. I need you, but not like this. Not when you're angry and can hurt me. You promised... You promised we'd see each other again. I held up my end of the bargain. I'm here, and now I need you."

His eyes snapped to her, and his maw opened, baring his teeth. Just when she thought he would bite down on her, his snout morphed into the jaw she had grown to love running her fingers across.

Alejandro shifted slowly, and Lenora felt the change from fur to skin beneath her hands. A hiccupped sob flew out of her mouth, but she covered it by burrowing against his broad, shirtless chest.

Fates, I hope he remembered to shift into some pants.

Muscled arms wrapped around her waist, pulling her closer.

"*Princesa,*" Alejandro whispered above her head, the puff of his breath blowing her wild curls.

She pulled her head away from his chest to look up into the eyes she'd missed so much. It had only been two weeks, but she craved the way his arms held her tight, longed to see the way the corners of his eyes crinkled when he smiled at her. A stubbly beard was growing on his chin, and she lifted a hand to cup his rough cheek. She traced the line of a new scar, one that wasn't there the last time she saw him.

"You brought me back again," he said, nuzzling into her hand. "All I could think about was finding you. Protecting you. Doing whatever I could to make sure you were safe. I'm sorry if I scared you."

"You could never scare me," she said, lost in his words and the feel of him under her fingers. "I know you'd never hurt me."

Alejandro brushed her cheek where a trail of blood ran from the wound on her head. His eyes turned dark, the color of burned caramel, and he turned his glare on Remy.

Remy, who was now moving, scurrying away on his knees and his uninjured arm, his back to her.

She jerked out of Alejandro's hold, ignoring the many stunned faces staring at her, and picked up her discarded sword. She walked toward Remy, then pointed the tip of her blade into his back, right on his spine. He stilled, his back arching away from the sword.

"Stand!" Lenora yelled, digging her sword in further and making him yelp.

Remy rolled onto his haunches, then rose. His shoulder hung limply at his side. Tears left dirt-streaked marks down his cheeks, and his crown lay completely lopsided, barely holding on. His shirt was torn in several places, and mud and blood caked his pants where he had crawled along the ground.

He looked pathetic.

She raised her sword, and Remy's eyes widened like saucers. Hesitating, her arm hovered in the air.

I can do it. I can strike him down.

Another inch higher. Then another, until her arms strained.

And then she dropped them.

She couldn't do it. She couldn't.

But there was something else she could do.

Lenora held her sword in front of her, protecting her body in case Remy attacked. "I won't kill you," she said, loud enough for those around her to hear. "But this is over. You've lost. Your army is half destroyed. You're outnumbered. Your family is gone. You have no allies. Accept surrender, hand over your crown, and I will let you live. I will show you the mercy you failed to show your family, the compassion you seem to lack. I will give you this last act of kindness because I am not like you. Even though you tried to kill me, I will forgive you because of *me*. *For* me. If I kill you, I will be a monster just like you. So you'll live in the dungeons until the citizens of Newton decide what to do with you."

Remy didn't move. He didn't even flinch. When he finally blinked, he sucked in a resigned breath and blew out a sigh, then raised his good arm.

Alejandro shifted closer to Lenora, and in her periphery, she saw Mattias, Lawrence, and her parents moving in as well.

Remy eyed his surroundings. Lenora realized the moment he knew he had truly lost. Pain flashed behind his eyes, and his hand went to the crown on his head. He removed it, then held it out for her to take.

She grabbed it before he could change his mind. Cheers erupted all around, and her soldiers pumped their fists in the air to celebrate.

Remy fell to his knees, looking up at her with tired eyes. Mattias jumped in between them, helping him stand.

Lenora caught the gleam of silver shining in his hand, but it was too late. Mattias had already withdrawn a dagger from Remy's chest. Right over his heart.

Slowly, life seeped out of Remy's eyes, and Mattias pulled away, letting him fall face down to the ground.

"No!" Lenora yelled, rushing to Remy's side. Alejandro's strong arms grabbed her, holding her back. The damage was done, though, so she didn't know why she was yelling, why she was trying to run to Remy's side. "What have you done, Mattias? How could you?"

She didn't know why she was crying. She had wanted this, planned this. Remy deserved to die for what he'd done. What he'd tried to do.

So why in the Fates' names was she shedding tears for this madman?

"I did what we planned to do," Mattias answered, his eyes taking on a hardness she hadn't seen before. "I did what I had to so we could rule the right way."

Alejandro, still holding her hips, pulled her tighter against him.

Lenora scrubbed her wet cheeks. It was done. She could do no more.

Elice and James appeared at her side, eyeing her with a mix of curiosity and anger—most of the fury emanated from her father as he stared at Alejandro's hands on her waist. Alejandro continued to hold her, merely clearing his throat.

"Lenora," Elice prodded, her motherly eyes boring into Lenora. Her long curls, now wet and limp, clung to her green tunic, and blood seeped from a wound on her leg. "I believe your father and I are ... missing something."

"Me too," Mattias muttered, wiping his bloody hands on his pants while his eyes lifted to Alejandro briefly.

"Same," Alejandro added, eyeing everyone.

Lawrence hovered nearby, entertaining himself with Lenora's spectacle. He had claw-like rips all along his clothes, and several gashes peeked out from them.

Bryan, somehow completely soaked yet free from dirt and blood, popped up right behind Mattias. "I've asked Salina and Trevor to organize the clean-up. Why don't we all hop inside the castle and ... talk?"

"Good idea," James said, dusting off his green uniform shirt that had taken on a muddy shade of brown. He had a few cuts that bled through his uniform, but he looked no worse than Lenora felt. In fact, between the lot of them, she was sure she actually looked worse.

They all filed into Stonehold Castle, past the grand foyer, and into the large ballroom in the back of the main hall. Though it wasn't secluded, the castle was quiet and empty. Lenora was confident they'd have a few minutes of privacy, and that was all she needed to tell her tale.

She addressed everyone, starting from the beginning, when Tyree gave her the horse and how she survived the initial wolf attack. Now, with all the pieces in place, she had a better picture of the events of the last three weeks. Acosta was the Wolf Brigade leader, and he had broken her ankle trying to take her back to Remy.

She went on to explain how she met Alejandro and how he was a bear shifter, ignoring the shocked looks her mother and father gave him. Once she got to the part where he had helped her escape Newton and set up a ship for her to get home, their eyes had softened. Even Mattias and Bryan nodded appreciatively. At least, until she told them about the vision. Then they stared at him with wide eyes. Alejandro had the decency to look sheepish, which only made her blush worsen.

Then she told them how Acosta found the ship, took her back to his vessel under false pretenses, blew up *La Marinera*, and then nearly starved and dehydrated her in the carriage.

Finally, she told them about the daring rescue from Bryan and his

Brentwood Warriors. Somehow, that was the hardest part. She could barely make eye contact with Alejandro, but she felt his stare on the side of her face as she explained the contract.

With her chest rising and falling heavily and her throat parched, she finished her story with, "And that's how we ended up here."

Elice and James exchanged glances. Alejandro's glare burned holes into Mattias's face, but the earth mage likely didn't notice because he stared pointedly at his shoes. Bryan looked around at all of them, his smile making his eyes gleam with mischief. Lawrence looked the most comfortable out of everyone, which surely said something about his closeness to the situation.

"All right, sweetie," Elice said carefully, adjusting her stance so she fully faced her daughter. "Obviously I have concerns."

Mattias finally lifted his head. "Lenora, you don't have to do this. I won't force you into anything you don't want." He had enough bravery to meet Alejandro's eyes.

Lenora nodded. "I know, Mattias. But I made a promise. I signed a contract that I can't really get out of."

"Well, the contract will only last four years. That's not really a long time, not compared to forever." He smiled, his dimples on full display.

"And the people of Newton will need my help recovering after the damage Remy caused in so short a time."

James leaned closer, capturing her attention. "Honey, are you sure this is what you want? After everything you've been through, I'm certain Lord Brentwood would be an honorable man and let you go from this contract."

"Well," Bryan mumbled, raising a finger. "I mean... You see, the thing is—"

Lenora shook her head. "I'm sure, Father. I owe it to the citizens to do what I can. I feel somewhat responsible for Remy's mad fascination with capturing me and all the people that suffered in some way because of it." She remembered the raids, how María and Pedro were subjected to a hostile search of their inn, the soldiers who died in this battle, Manny and Carlos, the sailors... The list went on and on.

She looked at Alejandro, and suddenly, the room around her vanished until she could only see him. Her eyes traced the scars and dirt on his face, the new beard spreading on his cheeks, the sad look in his eyes. "What do you think, Alejandro?" She realized no one else's opinion mattered on this subject but his and hers. If they could be all right with this, they could handle anything. If she had his support, she could stay in Newton as its queen—as Mattias's wife—if only in name.

Because Alejandro had her heart. She was so sure of it now, even as she stood with her parents, Lawrence, Mattias, and Bryan. The pull she felt to look at him, be near him, hold his hand—he was the most important thing. Not revenge. Not shame. Not guilt, or sadness, or the weight of her powers.

Only him.

When he grabbed her hand and brought her knuckles to his lips, she knew he felt the same way.

"I'll go along with whatever you want, Nora," he mumbled against her fingers.

Forty

O nce they returned outside, Lenora took a moment to survey the
field. The Norrainian soldiers in their green livery had gathered
together, collecting the bodies of their friends and fellow soldiers lost
in battle. Many of the Brentwood Warriors huddled together as well,
tending to their wounded as healers went around, patching up the most
critically injured.

Her eyes landed on the Newtonian soldiers last, donned in silver,
standing near the castle entrance, looking lost and broken. She and
Mattias would need to walk among them, weed out any who would not
accept them as their rulers. It would need to happen before the night was
over lest she wake up with a knife in her belly.

Lenora shivered at the thought.

Then the bear shifters caught her attention. They were loud and
boisterous, already leaning against the outer wall with canteens in their
hands and laughing as if they were merely camping out.

Two familiar faces turned her way, and she nearly lost her breath.

"Manny," she whispered. "Carlos."

Alejandro, who walked by her side, gave her a sly smile as the two
shifters hurried toward her. "I thought it would be a nice surprise."

Lenora gaped at him. "They're alive. You... You read my letter, knew

I thought they were dead, and you didn't *tell me*?"

Now Alejandro grinned, and if Lenora wasn't so tired, she would have been angry.

Instead, she sped toward the approaching guards, meeting them halfway across the courtyard.

"Princess!" Carlos yelled as he came to a stop before her.

"Carlos." Lenora practically sobbed his name, then turned her watery eyes on his twin. "Manny. You're both alive. Thank the Fates."

Manny smiled. "We're happy to see you're alive as well, Your Highness."

"Or should we say 'Your Majesty'?" Carlos grinned, waggling his eyebrows.

Manny elbowed him. "When your letter made its way to our campsite, we were so thankful to know you survived whatever Acosta had in store for you."

"Though we knew you would," Carlos added. "There was never any doubt you could handle a dog like Acosta."

"The Alpha King told us what had happened and what you were planning to do to Remy. We all decided to come and help."

"Good thing, too. Did you know you were so severely outnumbered?" Carlos raised his thick eyebrows in question.

Lenora chuckled. It was so good to hear their voices, to see their faces. "How in the Fates' names did you survive the ship's attack?"

Manny scratched behind his ear. "Well, as soon as you were taken aboard Acosta's ship, we talked to Captain Torres about using a longboat to follow after you. We had just climbed aboard when…"

Carlos frowned, an unusually serious expression on his face. "When it caught fire."

"We had tried to get Captain Torres and Señor Ortega to hop in with us, as well as anyone nearby, but they decided to go down with their ship."

Lenora covered her mouth, holding back her tears. A warm hand touched the middle of her back, and she looked up into Alejandro's molten eyes. His anger at hearing about their deaths was palpable.

"Manny and Carlos found me a couple of days later," Alejandro said, his voice tremulous. "Then I received your letter, but I was already planning on returning to Newton to search for you."

The tears that fell from her eyes turned to steam because of how hot her cheeks became.

Carlos cleared his throat, though his smile had returned twofold. "We should probably leave you two alone. You have a lot to catch up on, I'm sure."

Manny rolled his eyes. "Why do you always have to make things awkward?"

They both bowed, but as they turned to leave, Lenora heard Carlos mutter something about the situation already being awkward, and Manny reminding him that he didn't need to make it worse.

Alejandro laughed, shaking his head. When he turned to her, his grin dissipated, and his expression turned somber. "We do have a lot to talk about."

Nodding, Lenora opened her mouth, but her name being shouted from across the courtyard interrupted her.

She snapped her head around and saw the Newtonian soldiers gathered in an organized group. Mattias and Bryan stood facing them. Elice and James looked right at her, her mother's eyes urgent as she waved her toward them.

Alejandro gave her a little push. "Go to them."

Lenora looked at him, her brows curved toward each other. She didn't want to leave his side now that he was so near. "What will you do?"

He paused, his lips making a thin line. "I have to tend to my people."

She placed her hands on his bare chest. Her mouth opened and closed several times, but no words would come out.

Kissing the top of her head, he inhaled her scent before stepping out of her reach. "I'll find you later."

"Promise?" She already missed him standing so close.

With a soft smile, he nodded. "Promise."

Lenora sucked in a breath, tucked her hair behind her ear, then turned toward the soldiers she was to now lead.

As she approached, all eyes turned toward her. She wished she could have bathed, or at least wiped off the blood and changed her clothes. However, she knew the sight of her bloodied and unkempt after such a battle made her look ferocious. At least, that was the look she hoped to give.

Lenora set her jaw in a firm line. James always taught her that soldiers responded best to tough leaders. She would need to emulate strength, discipline, perseverance.

Mattias's shoulders lowered as she stood beside him, visibly thankful to see her. He angled his body toward her, bringing his mouth closer but out of view of the soldiers. "I don't know what to say to them," he muttered for her ears only.

Neither do I.

She couldn't say that, though. The whole reason Bryan wanted to marry his son to her was because she had 'experience.'

Lenora grew up training for this moment. She would need to step up and handle this and hope Mattias was a quick learner.

She looked at her parents, catching their nods. If they could believe in her, then she could believe in herself, too.

Walking closer to the group, she made eye contact with as many people as she could. "My name is Lenora Moore-Taylor," she began. "I am the daughter of Queen Elice, the Great of house Moore, and granddaughter of Julice Moore of house Newton." She noticed some of the soldiers' eyes widen at the mention of her lineage.

She paced a few feet down the line, catching more expressions as she went. "I am now your queen. Those of you who wish to stay as my soldiers will bow before me. Those who do not are free to leave Stonehold and never return."

Coming to a stop, she looked around the crowd, expecting to see many of them turn and walk away. Movement near the back signaled the first to leave. Her heart clenched, waiting for the numbers to rack up with the departing soldiers. While a few vacated their positions, she was pleased to see so many had stayed.

That was a good sign, and the smiles on her parents' faces bolstered her resolve even more.

"I am a daughter of Newton," she continued, using King Jerome's words. "For those who have remained by my side, I will work with you to rebuild what Remy undid in such a brief span of time. I will rebuild your confidence in the crown and in the throne. We will no longer hunt the innocent but search for truth and justice. We will not use our power to intimidate, but to serve the greater good for all. Even for those who decided to leave, and for those who are not here to make that choice, I will be their servant. I will work *for* them, because that is the true role of a king and queen."

Lenora looked over her shoulder, seeking Mattias. She wanted to let him know she had heard what he said, that his words were being used in such a positive, powerful way.

Instead, her eyes fell on Alejandro. He stood with his shifters behind Mattias, all of them listening to her speech. The look in Alejandro's eyes made her knees go weak. He looked ... proud. The smile he wore was so big, she could see his white teeth from where he stood dozens of feet away.

His eyes bore into her soul, seeing past the dirt and blood and tattered clothes. Past the crown she was born into and the one thrust upon her. Past her magic and the tragic history she kept locked in the back of her mind.

He saw *her*. Only her.

Mattias shifted, and she remembered what she was supposed to be doing, so she turned her head toward him. His eyebrows crinkled, but he gave a subtle nod toward the troops waiting for her to finish what was supposed to be a rousing oration.

With her attention back on the soldiers, she noticed how exhausted they were—their glassy, half-lidded eyes, and not to mention their battered and bruised bodies. They did just have a battle, after all—one in which their side lost. She needed to wrap this up and send them to their quarters.

"Tomorrow, we will start anew. Tonight, let us clean up and then get some much-needed rest."

Lenora eyed the several-hundred soldiers as they dispersed, walking through the courtyard to finish picking up the damage of the fight. Mages used their powers to clear away the debris left behind from their elements. Non-mages retrieved swords and shields. Healers still ran about, seeing to the wounded. She thought she might be the only seer in residence. Did King Jerome employ her kind in the castle? She would seek the answer to that question starting tomorrow.

She knew her night was not done, and she sought those who seemed to be leaders, introducing herself and making plans to officially meet with them tomorrow. Soon, her parents joined her, and then Mattias and Bryan slid in close, listening and watching aptly as she did her job.

Hours later, the field was in much better shape than before, yet she would see it fully patched up in the morning.

For now, she walked with her parents inside, hoping to find a servant—no, an *employee*—to prepare their rooms.

Elice stopped in the middle of the foyer, tapping Lenora's elbow. "You did well tonight, Lenny."

James nodded in agreement. "We're so proud of you."

Her chest constricted. Those were the words she had longed to hear since she was a child. She always wished for their approval—to feel worthy of being a princess.

Now she was a queen, even if it was for a different kingdom. Of course, she would need to have a proper coronation, and then a wedding...

Tomorrow. I will worry about that tomorrow.

"I learned everything I know from you two." Lenora looked down at her mother's hand on her shirt, thinking about how nice it would be to feel her mother's touch, to lay her hand atop hers.

Elice removed her hand. "Let's find someplace to sleep. Tomorrow you can work with the staff to set about making a proper room for yourself and your guests."

They spent the next thirty minutes walking the corridors to the guest wing, where King Jerome had taken Lenora her first day in Newton. Her eyes spotted the portrait of Queen Lizette on the way. She paused, wondering once again what had happened to her.

Another question for another day.

Her parents found a room next to the one Lenora was originally supposed to stay in. They bid her goodnight, and she walked to her suite.

Inside, the signs of her fight with Tyree were still there. Chairs lay toppled over, bits of cloth were strewn about, and even her luggage with her stuff was knocked over, their contents spilled onto the floor as if someone had rummaged through it.

Tomorrow.

She pulled a chair to its feet and plopped into it, but not a second later, someone knocked on the lopsided door, still partially broken from Tyree's burst of air. "Come in," she yelled, thinking it was either Lawrence or Mattias coming to wish her good night.

The door opened, revealing Alejandro—finally with a shirt on.

She pushed herself to her feet. "Alejandro."

He hovered near the threshold, gripping the broken door handle. "May I...?"

She nodded, her fingers flying to her hair in a late attempt to fix the wildness. He'd seen her in a much worse state—several times, in fact.

He stepped inside, closing the door behind him. When he reached her, he grabbed her fiddling hands to still them. "How are you feeling?" His eyes traveled across her body, stopping on the places where Remy's vines had cut into her skin. "You should see one of your healers."

"I'll be fine. I'll get seen tomorrow before I meet with the soldiers and staff." That was another thing to add to the list. "Tell me about the battle with your brother."

Alejandro pursed his lips, making them curve downward. "He got away."

Lenora's eyes went wide. "What happened?"

Sighing, Alejandro ran his fingers through her hair, playing with a golden strand, and entwined his other hand with hers by their sides. "We found his camp two days after we left. We caught them off guard, just like we hoped. It was ... a bloodbath. A lot of them fled, along with Augustín. My people celebrated, and his troops that stayed behind pledged their loyalty to me. Running is a sign of cowardice among shifters. No true alpha would ever run away."

Lenora squeezed his hand. "So, you're the new Alpha King?"

"Not officially. But for now, the army has backed me. I sent Tío Ernesto and half my troops to Miravista to hold down the castle in case Augustín shows up."

"Wait," she blurted. "You came here to help me when you should be at Miravista to claim your throne?"

Alejandro cupped her chin. "My heart will always be pulled wherever you are, Nora."

Shaking her head, she stepped out of his reach. "Alejandro, you have to go. Your people need you."

He frowned. "I thought you needed me."

An ache panged in her chest. "I... I couldn't have won today without you. I'm so thankful you came, but..."

Turning away from her, he let out a low growl. "I don't trust him."

Lenora jerked from the sudden change. "Who?"

He turned his molten honey eyes on her. "Mattias. You weren't going to kill Remy. You said, loudly and clearly, that he would face a trial from the people. Then Mattias stabbed him behind your back. I don't trust him."

Lenora swallowed the rising bile in her throat. She didn't want to think about that moment again. Seeing Remy's eyes flicker out like a snuffed candle, watching the blood pour out of the stab wound in his chest. The fact that Mattias used a dagger when he could have used his earth magic befuddled her. Why didn't he call on one of the many sharp branches that lay by his feet? A blade was a very non-mage way of killing someone—a very *Lenny* way, with her non-elemental powers. Why did he have a dagger? Had that always been his plan—Bryan's backup plan should Lenora fail?

It didn't sit right with her, either.

Alejandro took a step closer to her. "You inspired me tonight. I thought I needed to kill Augustín to avenge my parents and Luís. I thought that was the only way this could end. When Augustín fled, I was angry. Even with the people on my side, I thought I had failed. But you had the option to kill Remy tonight, and you chose not to. And you looked *powerful*. But Mattias took that power from you, soiled it.

Are you sure he won't do anything like that again? Undermine your authority?"

"I'm not going to be Newton's queen forever, Alejandro."

He grabbed her hands, bringing them to his chest. "Then come with me. Come with me to Alegría. You could be my queen. Forget whatever you promised him and be mine." He placed his fingers on her cheek, then threaded them through her curls. "I'm already yours."

Lenora closed her eyes, her mind lost to the possibilities. Alejandro's breath mingled with hers as she felt him move closer, and she leaned in, wanting to forget her obligations. She could have this forever, just like her vision suggested.

His lips crashed onto hers, and she threw her hands over his shoulders. Her thoughts jumbled together as she moved her lips against his until she could only focus on the sensation of Alejandro's mouth, his hands tangled in her hair, the rise and fall of his chest against hers.

He pulled back, took a deep breath, then dove in again. Lenora didn't know kissing could be like this. This kiss with Alejandro consumed her soul. She fell in and out of consciousness like she was bobbing on a wave in the middle of the ocean, only to be swept up again.

Alejandro's arm circled her waist, and he growled, removing his lips again to press them to one cheek and then the other. He was panting, drawing air like he had been deprived of it for ages.

When she finally opened her eyes, she could barely stand the look in his. The heat in them had drained, and he lifted a hand to wipe her cheeks. They were wet. When had she started crying?

"Alejandro," she whispered, her voice cracking.

He only nodded, still drying her face with his fingers.

"I can't." Those words burned her throat on the way out, and she wished she could take them back. "I made a promise to help the people of Newton. They need me. And I'm still Norraine's crown princess. I have... I have so many obligations, and it's so hard to choose between what I need to do and what I want to do. In my heart, I want to go with you."

His eyes snapped shut and his face scrunched up.

Lenora cupped both of his cheeks, drawing his eyes to her. "Give me some time to figure everything out. I can amend the contract if I need to. I just need some time to think, to plan."

Alejandro turned into her hand and placed a kiss on her palm. "I'd wait forever for you, Nora."

Another tear slipped down her face as Alejandro pulled her against him. She rested her cheek on his chest, thinking about forever and what it would mean for them.

If her vision was taken literally, then all it proved was that she'd be there when he died. But did they have a life together in between now and his death?

What if they ended up spending their entire lives apart, only to be reunited at the end? Would go on to become the queen of Norraine while he remained in Alegría, ruling his own kingdom? She didn't want to think about living without him. That thought alone sent a flame through her veins, making her lightheaded.

No. That couldn't happen. She had found the one person she couldn't live without. She would sacrifice a year, even two, and she would definitely give up Newton's crown for him.

Norraine's was a different matter.

She had plenty of planning to do indeed.

Epilogue

Alejandro

The smell of eggs and toast greeted Alejandro's nose as he walked through the hallway, filled with portraits of Newton's past kings and queens. One day, he knew Lenora's picture would be there, painted in gorgeous detail, yet still not quite grasping the beauty and majesty she held within her soul.

Alejandro rubbed his black buttoned shirt above his chest, hoping the ache would vanish. He worried it never would. A similar throb pounded around in his head, creating a cacophony of ruin he could do nothing about. At least, not yet.

The longer he waited, the worse it would get.

Though breakfast was being served in the food hall, his nose followed a different scent. One he had memorized since the first moment he inhaled it—fresh pine after a rain shower and sweet apples, reminiscent of a forest. Or an orchard.

Down in the main hall, a small group had gathered. He stopped mid-step, his foot hovering on the final stair. Lenora stood with several Newtonian soldiers—her new soldiers. Half of her body was angled toward him, her arms rigid by her side, but her eyes were on the men and women around her. She spoke with such grace, an elegant calm that belied her age. Her natural wisdom shone from within, bathing the entire room and everyone in it with her glory as morning light filtered in through the glass windows.

His heart thudded loudly, just like it did every time he looked at her.

Diosa, I'm such a sap.

Alejandro wanted nothing more than to run to her side, to sweep her into his arms and press his lips against hers like he did last night. The urge to show everyone in this room, in this castle, that they belonged to each other clawed through his body.

Resisting the compulsion, he took slow, deliberate steps.

As if sensing his presence, Lenora looked his way. Her eyes widened slightly, shining with delight. The look almost sent him to his knees.

She turned to the soldiers. "We'll continue this discussion later." Dismissed, they filed through the hall, some walking out the front door while others went through another corridor.

Now that they were alone, he went to her, allowing himself to relish in her essence.

If only for a little while.

Last night, he had told Lenora he would leave in the morning. He'd already sent word to his bears that they would have a quick bite to eat and then they would begin the journey home.

Home.

He hadn't been to Miravista Castle since that fateful day.

Now that he was going back, it didn't feel right. It felt like he would be leaving a piece of himself behind.

"It's time?" Lenora asked, the smile on her face small.

Nodding, he stepped closer. He resolved himself to be proper—this was now her castle, and she had to maintain a certain persona in front of the people who thought she was engaged to Mattias.

Though, technically, she was.

The reminder made him growl.

Hearing the noise, Lenora touched his arm. The tiny spark between them broke his resolve. He reached for her and pulled her against him.

Just like that, all propriety was gone. His arms wrapped around her middle, and he splayed his fingers on her back as their mouths collided. Lenora's hands went to his hair, tugging on the ends of his locks. He didn't know how long they stood there or if anyone saw them. Part of him didn't care. The bear inside him wanted to stake its claim, remind everyone that they belonged to each other.

But he couldn't. If he did, it would begin his descent, and he needed to have a clear, healthy mind to lead his people.

Alejandro pulled away, the noise he made in the back of his throat rumbling deep in his chest.

If he didn't stop now, he feared he never would. He might just stay here with her, because what good was having a heart if he couldn't feel it beating?

But he couldn't stay. Everything he had worked for the last five years was within reach. All he had to do was stay strong a little longer. Finish what he set out to do.

Lenora was right. His people needed him.

If she could be brave and sacrifice what she wanted for what she needed to do, Alejandro could, too.

He stared at her red, swollen lips. "I have to go."

The nod she gave was slow, as if her brain was still trying to catch up to the world around her. Then a tear fell from her eye, and he hastily wiped it away.

"Remember," he muttered against her lips, still not wanting to back away, "if you need anything, all you have to do is write to me. I'll come whenever you need me."

Another nod. This time, her eyes closed. The sight made his chest ache again.

Goddess, give me strength.

The sound of thick-soled boots pounded on the marble floors behind them. Manny and Carlos bounded up the entrance, their black uniforms now bearing a new emblem on their lapels. The mark—a single branch protruding from the top of a tree-shaped triangle—signified their change in status. Now, they were officially guards. *Very* important guards.

Lenora moved out of Alejandro's embrace, but not before Carlos gave them a sly wink. One day, Alejandro was sure this man would be the cause of his stress. He was much too exuberant, especially during moments where silence was preferable to loudness.

Alejandro watched as the twins bowed to Lenora, and she greeted them with the ease of a long, caring friendship. He knew, just by this quick interaction, that he was making the right choice.

"Before I go," he said, taking her hand, "I have another surprise."

Lenora's shocked face brought a grin to his lips. "What is it?"

Carlos spread his arms wide. "It's us! Surprise!"

Manny rolled his eyes. "We've been assigned as your guards. Officially."

Lenora turned from Manny, to Carlos, then to Alejandro. "Really?" she shrieked.

Alejandro's shoulders shook as he chuckled. "These two have pledged to guard you while you're here. With your permission, of course. But I'd feel better knowing some of my people were here to protect you. These two have already proven themselves as loyal to both you and me."

As if unable to contain her excitement, Lenora threw herself into Alejandro's arms. He sighed, content with his decision.

"I'll make sure to take better care of them." She pulled out of his embrace, then turned to her guards. "I owe you two so much."

"Don't mention it, Alpha Queen," Carlos said with a smirk.

"*Ay, diosa,*" Manny muttered, pulling on his brother's sleeve as he backed out through the door. "I'll get this one out of your hair, Your Majesties."

"What did I say?" Carlos whispered hoarsely.

With only a few moments left before he had to make his leave, Alejandro returned to Lenora, trying to ignore the throbbing in his heart. "You're sure you'll be okay with them as your guards?"

"I'll be better than okay," she said, grabbing his hand. She looked down at their intertwined fingers. "At least it'll feel like I have some part of you near me."

He bent down, pressing a quick kiss to her forehead. "You'll always have a part of me." With the back of his hand, he brushed her cheek.

Through the main doors, he could hear his soldiers arriving in the field. He squeezed his eyes for a moment, then stepped away.

"See you later, Nora," he whispered, praying to the goddess that would be sooner rather than later.

Lenora blew out a breath. "See you later, Alejandro."

As if his feet had dug themselves into the ground, he pulled with all his strength, forcing them to move and carry him toward his troops.

The feelings he had for her had grown in such a short time. He knew what it was—its name was revered throughout shifter kind—but he was hesitant to use it. Unwilling to open that bag before they could act on it.

Lenora didn't know about shifter lore. And right now, she had too much on her plate. If he added one more thing, he feared he would push her away—scare her from what they shared.

When she's ready, I'll tell her. But not before she can handle it. I can't end up like Augustín. My people need a sane ruler. They need me.

If she ran from this, it would doom them all.

Augustín

Darkness permeated nearly every inch of space. Not a single crack or crevice allowed the sun's rays from above to pass through. The only source of light was from the candles interspersed throughout the cave.

Gloom reigned, and the bear shifters who remained loyal to Augustín grumbled to each other, thinking their Alpha King couldn't hear them.

But he could. He heard every protest and every word of gossip they whispered behind his back.

"*Diosa,* he really has lost his mind," someone said, their voice low yet not quiet enough.

"Maybe he has a plan," someone else suggested.

"Plan? The guy's been without a plan for five years." This one dared raise his voice, but Augustín stayed where he was, sitting in the darkest corner, still licking his wounds.

"Well, he had *one* plan, and look how that turned out. He failed to kill his youngest brother. Now, he's come back with a vengeance. I swear, Alejandro will come for us all. Did you see the look in his eyes?"

Augustín finally raised his head, wanting to see who spoke last. Of course, it wasn't Julio, his most loyal subject.

It's not Julio. Yet. But soon, he'll turn on you, too. They all will.

Augustín shook his head. No. These shifters loved him. He provided so much for them. He gave them better food, better status, a chance to prove themselves. Alegría was better off with him as their Alpha King.

He just had to prove who he was—that he was better, stronger than Alejandro. He would have to kill his youngest brother. Finish the job he started all those years ago. He would destroy Alejandro and retake his crown and kingdom.

Stop this. You love Alejandro. He's your baby brother. You've already lost mamá, papá, and Luís. Don't do this.

Augustín buried his head in his hands, smothering the voice within. Sometimes, when his mind was clear, the inner voice spoke with such clarity, and a smile would shine through his lips. He felt like his old self again, back before it all went to the underworld.

Then the madness would return, and he would shove the goodness down, burying it until all he felt was rage and violence.

Soon, the voice quieted enough that he no longer heard it. Just how he liked it.

He only had room for one voice in his head, and the good one had to go.

Note from the Author

Thank you for reading The Cursed Sight, book one of my new series, Lenora, the Cursed! Lenora's story continues in book two, A Curse Awakened, available June 30, 2026.

Looking for more from this world? Start at the beginning by reading Elice's story, inspired by Rapunzel. The Secret Mage, book one of Elice, the Great, is available now.

If you enjoyed this book, please spread the love by leaving a review to help other readers find out about it!

WANT EXCLUSIVE BONUS CONTENT?

READ EMBERS OF FATE, A PREQUEL NOVELLA ABOUT LENORE AND ORSER, FOR FREE BY SIGNING UP FOR MY NEWSLETTER.

DOWNLOAD YOUR COPY FOR FREE ON MY WEBSITE AT JENNIFERROACHFORD.COM.

To be informed about future release dates or to sign up for my Advanced Reader Copy (ARC) list, join my newsletter at jenniferroachford.com. Are you ready to join my Army of Mages? Join my exclusive street team, where you'll get first access to my books, as well as swag and other fun giveaways. Visit Jennifer's Army of Mages Reader Group on Facebook to be part of the club.

Pronunciation Guide

This book features characters inspired by Hispanic and Afro-Latino cultures. I believe all cultures deserve a place in fantasy books, and it's been an honor bringing part of my Hispanic heritage to life in this book.

To help you as you read through this book, I've created a handy pronunciation for your reference. Happy reading!

<u>Names</u>

- Alejandro (Ah-le-han-dro).

- Vega (Vey-gah): Alejandro's maternal side of the family.

- Suárez (Swar-ez): Alejandro's paternal side of the family.

- Augustín (Ah, goos-theen).

- Luís (Loo-ees).

- Itzela (Eet-zel-ah): Alegrían moon goddess.

- Los Lópezes (Los Loh-peh-zes): the Lopezes.

Places

- Alegría (Ah-leh-gree-ah): a kingdom south of Newton.

- El Abismo E-bees-moh): the Alegrían (Spanish) name for the Great Gorge.

- Monte Paseo (Mon-theh Pa-seh-oh): a border city in Alegría.

- Puerto Nuevo (Pwuer-toh Nweh-voh): a port city in Alegría.

- El Océano Encantado (El Oh-seh-ah-noh En-kan-thah-doh): The Enchanted Ocean.

Words and Phrases

- Espera (es-peh-rah): wait.

- Princesa (preen-sess-ah): princess.

- Príncipe (preen-see-peh): prince.

- No te preocupes (noh theh pre-oh-coo-pes): don't worry.

- Sí (see): yes.

- Diosa (dee-oh-sah): goddess.

- Tío (thi-oh): uncle.

- ¿Cuanto sabe ella de nosotros? (kwan-thoh sah-beh e-ya deh noh-soh-thros): How much does she know about us?

- Nada (Nah-dah): nothing.

- ¿Qué estás haciendo? (keh es-thas ah-see-en-doh): what are you doing?

- Solo estoy comiendo (soh-loh es-thoy coh-mee-en-doh): I'm just eating.

- Eres increíble (eh-res een-kreh-ee-bleh): you're incredible.

- No seas tonto (noh seh-ahs thon-thoh): don't be silly.

- El Cambiante Militar (el Cam-bee-an-theh Mi-lee-thar): The Shifter Military.

- Por ahora (por ah-oh-rah): for now.

- Mesa (meh-sah): plateau.

- Está bien (es-thah bee-en): it's okay.

- Infectado (een-feck-thah-doh): infected.

- Esta comida es para la niña (es-tah coh-mee-dah es pah-rah lah nee-ñah): this food is for the girl.

- Si te sientes mejor (see theh see-en-thes meh-hor): if you feel better.

- Buenos días, princesa! Me llamo Rosa (Bwen-ohs dee-as, preen-sess-ah! Meh yah-moh Ro-sah): good morning, princess! My name is Rosa.

- Para tí (pah-rah thee): for you.

- Al príncipe le encantaría este vestido (al preen-see-peh leh en-khan-thah-ree-ah es-theh ves-thee-doh): the prince would love this dress.

- Estas lista (es-thas lees-thah, preen-sess-ah): you're ready.

- Mi princesa (mee preen-sess-ah): my princess.

- ¡Hay un informe! (eye oon een-for-meh): there's a report!

- Encantada de conocerte (en-khan-thah-dah de coh-noh-ser-the): nice to meet you.

- Qué te gustaría? (keh theh goos-theh-ree-ah): what would you like?

- Birria (bee-ree-ah): a meat (either beef, lamb, or goat) stew originating from Mexico.

- Tres tacos, por favor (thres tha-cohs por fah-vor): three tacos, please.

- Salud (sah-lood): cheers.

- Chilaquiles (chee-lah-kee-les): a saucy tortilla dish with eggs and cheese, often served during breakfast.

- Sobrino (soh-bree-noh): nephew.

- Rey Alfa (ray al-fah): alpha king.

- La Marinera (Lah Mah-ree-neh-rah): The Mariner.

- Capitán (Kah-pee-than): captain.

- Señor (seh-nyor): mister, or sir.

- Sangría (san-gree-ah): traditionally made with red wine and fruit.

Also by Jennifer Roachford

ELICE, THE GREAT

The Secret Mage (Book One)
Tomb of Souls (Book Two)
Army of Mages (Book Three)

LENORA, THE CURSED

The Cursed Sight (Book One)
A Curse Awakened (Book Two)
Coming Soon (Book Three)

Acknowledgements

Here I am, writing a thank you note for my fourth ever published book. I still can't believe I'm doing this, embarking on my second series. So many people have helped and guided me along the way, and I want to take a moment to express my gratitude.

This book is a testament to my ancestry. I spent a lot of time thinking about how I could pay tribute to my heritage. For those that don't know, I am of mixed ancestry. I am Black. I am Hispanic. I am an Afro-Latina. For many years, I didn't understand what or who I was. I didn't feel as if I belonged in any of those categories, that I didn't fit the typical "label."

It took a long time for me to realize how important my mixed heritage is to me. I always knew how beautiful both my Black and Mexican sides are, but I just didn't see it in me. When I finally realized I am my culture, it opened up a newfound love of history. I wanted to share that with the world.

Ancestry plays a vital role in this book as an external background force that drives Lenora. Without her ancestry, she wouldn't have her (cursed, sorry girl) powers. She embarks on a journey to find herself, battling her feelings of inadequacy and sense of belonging.

In this book, and in this entire series, you'll find the beauty of both cultures, of diverse skintones, of curly hair, and, of course, of language. I want to show that Black and brown people belong, especially in fantasy books. Especially in love stories.

So, thank you to all my readers for sticking with me, Lenora, and Alejandro as we tell this tale. I couldn't have written this book without my ancestors and without my readers.

An enormous shoutout goes to my friend and fellow author, D.L. Howard, for saving me on my map quest. You are such an amazing friend, and your help during a difficult time gave me the last push I needed to get this book out there. Thank you once again for your beautiful map design!

Thanks to my beta readers, Ashlee Sheffer and Keshia McEntire. You gave me such great advice and helped me shape up this manuscript!

To my editor, Angela Knotts Morse. This is the third book you've edited for me, and I would be lost without you. You know my characters better than I do at this point. Thank you for all your guidance throughout my author journey.

To Amanda Johnson-Lindsey. Thank you for stepping up to help me during this final stretch. You came into my author world when I needed your help the most. I'll always be grateful for your expertise.

A special thanks to my cover designer Jessica at Esthetica Cover Designs. You captured my vision perfectly, and you are so amazing to work with. I look forward to working with you many times in the future.

Last, but never least, my family. My rock. My reason. Everything I do, I do for you. To my husband, thank you for always supporting me as I walk this path. To my children, thank you for being the guiding light I follow when times get dark.

About the Author

Jennifer Roachford is a wife, mom, and the author behind the **Elice, the Great** and **Lenora, the Cursed** trilogies—diverse fantasy worlds built for readers who have always wanted to see themselves in the pages of a book.

As an Afro-Latina, Jennifer believes representation isn't just important, it's essential. Her passion for storytelling was born from a lifelong love of books, and she channels that love into every character she creates and every world she builds.

When she isn't writing her next novel or editing someone else's manuscript, you can find her in the garden daydreaming about books or hunting down the perfect cup of coffee on snow days. She also bakes—because every great story deserves a good snack.

www.ingramcontent.com/pod-product-compliance
Lightning Source LLC
Chambersburg PA
CBHW021237190726

48289CB00005B/1372

*9 7 8 1 9 5 7 9 8 6 1 2 8 *